FARPOINT AWAKENED

(Farpoint Series, Book 1)

Vincent Bek

To my Parents.
For all their love, support and guidance which
helped me become the person I am.

CHAPTER ONE

Kasey woke slowly to a dull hum reverberating from the inside of his head.

Did I drink last night?

Somewhere far away a steady mechanical knocking could barely be heard—which he promptly ignored, attempting to find his way back to sleep. He didn't want to open his eyes, they felt sore and seemed to be sealed shut. That was ignored as well. It was not until he attempted to stifle a yawn that panic nearly set in.

What the hell?

Bringing a hand up took much longer than he expected. It seemed to be immersed in a thick gel-like substance. The shock was only slightly offset by finding his head to be encased in a helmet of some sort. There were no obvious openings. He knew he should panic, he even tried to panic, but a numbing feeling in his mind wouldn't allow it.

The movement must have set off an alarm. He felt the goopy liquid being sucked away. Jets of warm liquids and air followed in waves across nearly every part of his body.

Oh, stasis.

The flushing went on for some time as slight sparks

of memory started flittering back into consciousness. He slowly remembered being placed in a stasis pod to travel somewhere. Why, where, or how completely escaped him.

Slowly he relaxed as the realization settled in. He was only slightly unnerved when the pressure was lifted off his eyelids, or when a slimy coating slid off his iris leaving him blinking uncontrollably.

Moments later, a seam of blurry light appeared and grew as the helmet was disassembled and removed. The process was automated, he casually noted with pleasure. This was not some hack job; someone had paid for equipment far above what he was used to.

Trying to order jumbled thoughts, he focused on the one word that floated to the top of memories. Farpoint.

What was Farpoint?

As if the question was the key, his recollections flooded back—if still a bit muddled. He recalled that Farpoint was a colonization project funded by the Terrantine Federation. The Federation encompassed the majority of human civilization and, in Kasey's opinion, controlled its populace through fear.

Wait, I would never join the Federation... Oh... But I did. Why?

More questions led to more answers. The Farpoint project was sending massive ships far beyond the Terrantine's frontiers, further than any human had traveled before. Not just distant, but thousands of light-years beyond any human worlds. Some of the largest colony ships ever conceived were being built for the endeavor. It was a huge risk, but the benefits seemed larger still.

Family had been everything to Kasey for decades, until they were taken away from him. His freedom loving parents, along with many others, were killed while trying to rally support for a small, independent world attempting to replicate the singular technology that controlled humanity. The cure for aging, or more correctly, the treatment of aging. The ability to stop the aging process gave the Terrantine Federation a powerhouse currency—time. It became a commodity like water; it wasn't just needed, it was required.

A fairy tale to scare children; once upon a time, people would get old and die. Citizens of the federation took aging treatments for granted. They were a free and expected part of Terrantine life. Not so for societies existing beyond the bounds of the Terrantine controlled space. Not that treatments were withheld from any of humanity. The federation made every effort to seek out and provide access to all of humanity, for a price. Even the newest and most remote settlements were routinely visited every year, without fail, by fleets of medical ships bringing immortality to the masses. The cost was the killer.

Kasey knew this first-hand. The year after losing his parents was one of anger, he had wanted nothing to do with the Terrantines or their treatments. Nineteen months later he was at a medical facility for a simple broken arm when the true price-shock set in. The nurse took one look at his records and called in a specialist. The bone, he had explained in a well-rehearsed bureaucratic tone, would mend fine, but the extra procedures necessary to unnaturally age the standard healing medium would drastically inflate the cost. He went on to explain how this cost would increase over time unless he submitted to a corrective aging treatment soon.

The more Kasey questioned the doctors, the more overwhelming the explanations became. In the end Kasey yielded, allowing the corrective aging treatment alongside the bone healing procedure.

It was complete crap as far as Kasey was concerned.

Whether the medical details were genuine or not, it was now a financial fact that Kasey could not afford to ever miss a treatment again. Kasey spent the next three years juggling shady short-term loans and double shifts to pay off the procedures to bring his aging treatments up to date.

"Enough!" He croaked, using his voice for the first time since waking in the chamber.

His parents had perished defending the right for non-Terrantine people to develop age-free technology. The federation made it clear to all that only they would own this power. A point they made evident when they bombed the colony his parents were trying to help from orbit. A glassy crater was all that now remained—a monument of remembrance for all who attempted to enter the gates of freedom.

As if sensing his frustration, all movement from the stasis chamber suddenly stopped with a hiss of released pressure as the remaining tubes and sensors eased themselves off his skin. Sitting up to rub the glare from his eyes, he noticed a few blurry wall screens winking into existence. One was blinking a warning of some kind. Standing to move closer, he noted the floor was warm and soft. The words "Malfunction Encountered" in large letters could be seen, but he could not make out any other details with his impaired vision. Giving up, he located a chair to wait in while his eyes adjusted, glad that the drugs that kept him calm were still working, if only slightly.

"Show me the Farpoint project," Kasey commanded the nearest wall. Blurry images sprang to life on the wall, each begging for attention as his eyes wandered their way. Shaking his head in frustration, he waved the images away to wait for his vision to clear.

The project confounded his thoughts. It wasn't just that it was a Terrantine based project and that they were funding the bulk of the effort, it was that they controlled who was able to join the expedition. That was the catch, he had to join the thing he hated most. The nation that took away his family.

There was a loophole, or maybe just a chance of a way out from under the strangling dominion. So far from the federation itself, there could be no real power to hold over the people. At least not for very long. Something would go wrong; the control will be broken. There would be no support system for the local government to fall back upon. Someone had once told him there was no power without control. He hoped that whatever small fragment of government was joined to the venture would soon lose any real control once people realized they had none.

It was a huge gamble, and fifteen thousand light-years, about thirty years in stasis, was the price to find out.

There was only one thing that had been holding him back from making the leap years earlier. One person who had kept him grounded. AnnaChi. She had been the outward tempest that calmed his personal turmoil. Without her he was once again lost in the storm.

Kasey's smile disappeared as the remembrance of her death slammed into him anew.

CHAPTER TWO

Closing his eyes, the memories flowed back fresh and painful, taking him back to their time together in the Daveri system.

The tropical moons of Daveri Two called too many who wanted to get away for a while, but Kasey was not among them. He had gone to that luxury system with another purpose in mind.

Piloting shuttles and transports had been a necessary skill across the frontiers beyond Federation control. The planets his family labored for were works in progress, barebone settlements before the actual settlers arrived. To get anywhere beyond a few kilometers you either needed to be a pilot or you waited for someone who was, and most simply stayed put. Kasey had always felt the need to get out and explore and as soon as he was able, he sought out any flight training he could find.

Flying quickly became a passion he could not ignore. The simple two-seater he bought on his twentieth birthday was barely more than a dirt skimmer with wings. Actual wings, as if it was an ancient plane. If it hadn't been a lower gravity world, it wouldn't have flown at all. At the time, it was everything, it was his freedom. Transporting a passenger or fetching gear from other settlement sites on the world payed just enough credits to keep it working and fueled.

Kasey knew he was no ace pilot, but he was above average, and that was good enough for him. He still believed flying to be a freedom on par with his parent's ideals for a free existence for everyone. On Daveri Two this skill was a means to an end. Farpoint would need pilots, good pilots, willing to spend a minimum of seventy years away from the rest of humanity.

To even apply to one of the many companies hiring for Farpoint, he needed a Federation approved system-wide transport license. With few credits to his name, Daveri Two was the perfect steppingstone. The vacation system employed more system-wide pilots than most of the federation. Many of the resort transport companies provided free training and license testing for workers as a basic perk. A few quick years had Kasey licensed and running ships full of passengers between Daveri Two and Daveri One.

If it wasn't for her, he would have been gone from the system and working for a Farpoint destined company. AnnaChi's presence in his life pushed thoughts of Farpoint far away. Weeks flowed into months, when he realized he wanted nothing more than to stay right where he was.

To say he was in love was petty, true though it was. More than that, he felt that he was home with her. He was where he belonged.

AnnaChi was a blustery wind in Kasey's existence. She was the kind of person that appeared both calm and ready to brawl at the same time. He remembered her short, jet-black hair, curling inward at the ends in a way that Kasey could never tell was natural or just due to the years of wearing flight helmets. But it had been her bright green eyes that had pervaded Kasey's being. They showed every ounce of her feelings in an instant. To most, she was a creature you crossed at your own peril, but to him she showed only honest contentment.

Somehow, he had charmed her – the verse knew how. All he knew was, one day she was laughing at him and it was a friendly laugh, uncharacteristic of her usual manner. That was it.

* * *

Over a period of a few months, AnnaChi, and Kasey by extension, had been involved in increasingly risky ventures with a series of shipments. A captain of her own ship, she had known to stay away from such deals, but the credits had been too good to ignore.

Kasey, always trusting her judgment, took a commission to transport some vacationers along the same route and schedule. Recruiting a couple other pilots with similar jobs, they had daisy-chained transports together to save resources. A common practice that also allowed passengers and crew to socialize and exchange news on longer trips.

Near the halfway mark of the journey they woke to the unmistakable sounds of a ship docking with their group. AnnaChi was sharing Kasey's bunk at the time and dashed out toward her craft, the Cintian, in a panic for her passengers. It was obvious to them both that something was entirely wrong; docking never took place without the pilot's acknowledgment, even when in a cluster.

There were no weapons on board Kasey's own chartered craft, so he quickly gathered the passengers he could locate and readied the ship's systems he would need for a quick departure from the cluster if necessary. Then he ran to find AnnaChi.

He saw that the passageway to her transport was blocked by a pair of armed thugs dressed in Federation Police outfits that were noticeably phony. As quickly as he could, he found a vantage point along the causeway that provided a view into the occupied vessel. Thankfully the hull was still in translucent mode, which most passengers enjoyed. Gradually he moved along until he could see the full scene and nearly screamed in frustration. AnnaChi and a handful of others were being roughly handled and questioned. They seemed to be demanding something—most likely the goods she was illegally transporting.

Abruptly three figures, AnnaChi's loading crew by the looks of them, sprang from a nearby room attempting to wrest the weapons away, and she jumped up to help them. A flash lit the room as some weapon was fired and everyone stopped in shock. Both groups had weapons out as they backed away from each other slowly.

Something wasn't quite right. Kasey couldn't seem to get his brain to understand what happened. Then AnnaChi unexpectedly dropped in a lifeless heap as blood pooled around her still form. Someone leaned down to check her and shook their head sadly. Flashes erupted an instant later from both sides.

Kasey screamed in angry frustration and was running toward the chaos before he even knew what he was doing. There was only one guard at the portal now and his attention was on the fight inside. He never knew what hit him when Kasey started bashing his head into the edge of a control box.

Kasey let the unconscious man's body fall and knelt to retrieve the rifle the guard had dropped. Before he was able to reach the weapon, he was forced to leap away as a wave of heat washed over him from fist sized gashes of red-hot slag ripping into the deck. Two men with plasma rifles were running towards him from the secondary docking port, to reinforce their partners. Anguish washed over him as he dove back through the portal. Pausing to enter a quick lock-out command, he sprinted back toward his craft. A great sob overtook him the moment her body was no longer in sight, knowing she was now gone from his vision forever.

Pulling along the few passengers he encountered on the way, he sealed the hatch and input the command to depart. The other friendly ships in their cluster, he noted, had already launched. Once clear, he had a good view of the vessel belonging to the attackers. Taking careful aim, he jettisoned a half-empty fuel tank at their engines and watched as it splintered, spewing the thick fuel in a sticky cloud around it. With luck, he thought, that would delay their ability to ignite their engines long enough for his transport to escape, and possibly allow the system's actual police to track their ship.

Kasey booked passage out of the system within hours after making the nearest port a week later—there was nothing left for him in the Daveri system but pain.

* * *

The memories brought a cold dampness to Kasey's eyes. Rubbing them dry, he found his vision improved as he looked back towards the wall screens. He was drawn to the large text scrolling across the top of each screen.

Farpoint, Expedition Thirteen, Trias system...

Checking the stasis pod's screens again showed the pod's malfunction was caused by a deficiency of some required substances. Per the display, they were only a handful of months from their destination. That was a huge relief. With a journey of nearly thirty years he had no desire to go back into a defective stasis pod so soon after waking.

He stared into the picture of himself on the screen, brown hair, green eyes and a miserable looking forced smile that would not have fooled anyone. He would have to work on that he supposed, people liked other people who at least seemed happy.

Memories of boarding the enormous ship were foggy still. He knew now it was named the Abscond. Several murals of the ship were displayed on the walls, the only real decoration in this drab room. The Abscond looked to be constructed primarily of two immense long columns coiled around each other like a corkscrew, with a multitude of cross sections connecting the two. The ship, in general, resembled the human DNA double helix, although whether by accident or on purpose was another unknown. The ship on a whole was constructed to be broken up in self-sustainable segments as needed by the Farpoint project. Currently three main segments, or stations, were planned, but that could change as the expedition evolved.

The resemblance to the human genome stopped as the mammoth antimatter generator and engines became the focus of his attention.

The generator had been specially developed around a man-made black hole, which both helped to keep the antimatter containment in check and provided a sufficient, if unstable, way to deal with unwanted radiation. One interactive mural showed that the generator itself consisted of a series of nine concentric spheres, layered with powerful magnetic fields guiding the many accelerated particle streams that ran an interlaced gambit between the orbs. Once a particle stream reached the proper speed, they were pushed into head-on collisions with other streams, creating a steady source of antimatter for the engine.

Containing antimatter for any length of time was

difficult at best on this scale, as any interaction with normal matter caused both particles to instantly annihilate each other. Yet with the help of the small black hole residing in the center of the spherical generator, the antimatter was funneled into a high orbit slurry where it could easily be harvested as needed. The Abscond's engine itself generated a significantly large, if classical, bubble of warped space-time, which was then twisted into a corkscrew-shaped vortex. This funneling of space-time, once it reached sufficient speeds, increased the warp bubble's movement by several factors.

Kasey, having always loved ships and their many engine designs, was amazed by all that appeared possible. This powerful propulsion design, however, was far and beyond anything he had ever imagined being possible. Tearing his eyes and thoughts away from the ship's diagrams to survey his accommodations, he found himself feeling a bit impatient.

The room was stocked with basic supplies, along with a food synthesizer unit that would undoubtedly produce an amazing variety of dull, bland foods for as long as required. Well, he thought, this time next year he would be eating freshly grown foods, some of which would be newly discovered from around the Trias system.

Once he was dressed and fed, he selected a ship map and enlarged it to cover the wall. There were several gathering areas not far away, but first he wanted to check on his cargo. Besides, he considered, no one would be awake for quite a few weeks yet.

CHAPTER THREE

Cargo bay 748 was as massive as most others on the Abscond. Stacks of storage crates created a maze of corridors, even if it was a well-organized maze. Still, it wasn't long before Kasey located his own small container. He found it hard to believe that everything he owned was in that one small space. Opening the door did little to help the feeling. Smaller boxes secured along the crate walls left a pathway down the center, leading to a large oddly shaped container in the back.

Kasey had sold nearly everything he owned, all but what still resided in this crate. Most of the credits went toward the contents of that container. He only hoped it would give him an edge in the new world.

Releasing the vacuum seal, the lid tilted back to reveal a small ground-based scouting vehicle commonly known as a Bard. The name was due to the sound it made when using the vehicle's limited jump jets. Primarily a recreational ground vehicle, the jump jets were short-ranged, giving no more than a half kilometer jump on level ground. The thorium core would provide a nearly limitless power source for close to ten years, well longer than he would need. He hoped.

Not a top-of-the-line model, and small compared to

most variations, yet this Bard was highly customized for Kasey's needs. Several non-standard boxes were mounted along the frame, as well as a second bank of controls and screens that were discernibly non-standard. All were part of an expensive scanning system for both above and sub-surface scanning. Mining, he knew, was an advantageous business on any new world; in a completely new system cut off from the rest of civilization, it should be several times as lucrative.

While Kasey didn't plan to mine, he had learned enough to prospect and lay claims to worthwhile land good enough to rent or sell to the mining teams. Having flown for a few mining operations before, he was confident he would be able to make quick connections with enough of the new system's crews. Land claims were one of the benefits of being a settler. Anyone could lay claim beacons on a plot outside of the initial settlements and government use areas. Once the markers were officiated, the property was as good as owned. He already had several marker beacons that would allow him to place a temporary claim if he found a valuable area of land.

As a licensed pilot, he hoped to be able to transport the Bard anywhere on the new planet, exploring areas few others easily could. All he needed was a cheap transport ship to rent between jobs, then he would be able to take the bard exploring anywhere.

Hoping his skills would position him to hear about areas of interest, he planned to search out jobs that might give him an edge. He figured, if he could locate some of the main mining offices and obtain a planet-side shuttle contract nearby, it would provide some decent leads. People always talked on long flights, particularly when something exciting was happening. If that failed, flying new colonists who were looking for homes and opportunities around the planet would provide a wealth of information alone.

Taking a deep breath, he focused his attention back on the machine. A quick diagnostic showed that the Bard had traveled well over the last three decades, even the power levels remained fully charged. After a complete visual check, he resealed the container, it would not be needed for a while yet. Checking a few other small crates, he slowly made his way back to the opening, pausing suddenly as he heard the distinct sound of approaching voices. He was surprised that he was not the only one out of stasis this early—perhaps a maintenance crew? Edging toward the door, he silently pulled it shut, waved off the light panels and listened—knowledge was as good as credits any day.

"No, I just don't think he understands how difficult the processing of this stuff is going to be."

"Sure, okay," another man responded, "but no one really knows. I mean, how could he? We didn't know the damned stuff existed until we were about to set sail."

"True enough, true enough," cut in the first man again, "but the government suits knew, and someone needed to know to bring whatever special equipment they needed. They want to mine the stuff, right? And what do you think is in all those secured bays?"

"Maybe you are right. Certainly, half the crew seemed eager to join the mining crews once this ride is over. Still, I don't understand how dirt can fall upwards to begin with…"

The conversation drifted out of hearing. Kasey stood in the dark for a long time before moving, more out of confusion than any fear of being caught eavesdropping.

What the hell were they talking about? Kasey thought. Having worked for several mining teams over the years, not to mention all the research he had done on materials of value they would be likely to find or need here, nothing came to mind that fit with what the workers had said. He had even compiled a program to automatically estimate the worth of rare materials against the current colony prices as he located them. But what these workers were talking about was beyond anything he knew of—they had said it "didn't exist," what did that mean? And what did he say about "dirt falling upwards?" That was impossible!

Nothing made sense. Maybe he was over thinking it all. Possibly, he thought, he had taken that conversation out of context. He shoved the thought aside—it didn't matter yet, but he now seemed to have the time to work it out if it did.

Activating the lights again, he moved back to the container holding the Bard and set a security lock on it. You could never be too secure when confusion existed. It seemed his investment could well pay off a good bit higher than he ever expected, if only the puzzle could be solved.

CHAPTER FOUR

Kasey spent his free time reviewing his research on the Trias system, his soon-to-be new home, combing through data for something he had apparently missed, but finding nothing. A few data feeds from the probes launched years prior to the Abscond were now available, but nothing revealed anything out of the ordinary as far as he could tell.

A handful of others who had woken early were already releasing reports of their own analysis from the probe data, but still nothing seemed to be out of place. He expected the reports to be scrubbed with all the secrecy surrounding this, but he still hoped for something. Studiously he took note of anything that seemed even slightly inconsistent, but not much filled his logs. He knew he was out of his league, the majority of the data pouring in was at a level far beyond his understanding.

Casually he spent a lot of time around the various common areas around the ship, hoping to pick up more information. There weren't many people about, most were still in stasis, but certainly not all. Quite a few pods had malfunctioned over the last couple years, but suitable replacements had been found for most. Small numbers of crew were revived for short periods during the journey, but in the past year, many had declined to return to stasis while so close to the destination. Not to mention the probe data alone caused either fascination or anticipation far beyond what anyone had prepared themselves for. It took on a nearly addictive quality while waiting for the next data burst to stream into the nearest displays.

Kasey tried to stay on track, but so far, the only related information he had heard was speculation about what was locked away in the private government storage bays. Besides that, most of the revived crew seemed to be afflicted with "gold rush fever" and were betting on what materials would bring the most wealth. The mentality was common on many of the colony worlds Kasey's parents had lived on over his life.

Most Federation controlled worlds generally had access to any materials they needed, but their cost was dramatically different based on where it came from. While some systems had abundances of timber, ores, or even water sources, many others had only meager supplies when starting out and needed to import from other systems at great cost for years while building up infrastructure.

While most scarce but necessary materials caused gold rush levels of excitement, gold itself was not usually considered rare. However, it would be many years before serious space mining would be able to be conducted in the new systems. All mining would be planet-side, or perhaps lunar, until ship plants were built and started churning out system-wide capable ships, and that was ten years out at least. With few exceptions, all materials needed to be found in ground-based operations or brought along on-ship. Still, many wagered that mining gold and other precious metals in the Trias system would once again be as prosperous as in the ancient days of Earth Prime—at least for a while.

Kasey tried to keep it all in perspective and not get caught up as he searched for answers to his mystery material. Many times, he had nearly given up his search, but an odd look or overheard side comment from crew was proof enough for Kasey that he had not misconstrued the comments he heard in the cargo bay. He tried several times to befriend those he deemed in the know, but even when he was invited to join them for a few drinks the talk was kept on other subjects.

Nearly a month passed before he caught a break.

* * *

Joining a prep team for the impending planet-fall was a requirement of all able settlers. Everyone had a minimum number of service hours to fulfill. In Kasey's mind, the sooner he could complete his time the sooner he could start on his own ventures. With so many people out of stasis months early there was no reason to delay the work any longer.

The work group he was assigned to was unpacking the assortment of smaller landing shuttles that would be used primarily for taking people to and from the surface. The craft would be the public transportation of colony centers for the first few years. The shuttles were sealed in a plastic shell that was sprayed on during the vacuum packing process like so many other items that wouldn't fit in the storage containers.

Using a hooked knife, he carefully perforated the first in a line of shuttles and fell back as the hissing intake of air threatened to suck his hand into the vacuum. A boisterous laugh startled him as the foreman ran over to help him up.

"Ya need to make a quick wide opening on these ones!" he shouted above the sucking noise as he scooped up the dropped knife and slashed a wide wound into the material, then backed up to admire his handiwork. The wrapping quickly puffed out like a balloon being filled. "Don't worry about hurting these craft, they all have self-healing hides in this generation."

"Oh," Kasey replied, a bit embarrassed. "My old system-wide had a healing membrane too. Crappy stuff, the reentry panels needed to be resealed every few months or it would start ripping off in sheets."

"Ah, well you will be happy to know most companies are not using membranes on this expedition. The whole outer hull is made of some polymer that reforms itself completely. Not just a patch sealant like the membranes used. Here, watch."

He took the blade again and, pressing hard, scored a long scratch down the exposed hull. Almost before he stopped, the mark disappeared as if it had never been.

Kasey rubbed his fingers over the area. There was no trace to show anything had happened to it.

"See there now, no need to be gentle with these." He gave Kasey a long look as he handed the knife back. "So, you're a pilot then?" At Kasey's nod, he continued. "Good. Hmm, you under contract yet? It seems I need more than I had anticipated."

"Yes sir, two standard years' public routes and system transports. Been flying for as long as I have been able." Kasey replied in what he hoped was a relaxed but professional response as his pulse picked up in rhythm.

For a company's plans to change so close to planet-fall was unlikely at best. Knowing the probe reports showed nothing out of the ordinary that would cause such a change, Kasey took a chance. Giving a slow obvious look over his shoulder, he added, "I suppose the mining guilds are about to be overburdened?"

The foreman's eyes widened and Kasey could see he was right, this man knew the truth of what was going on, but had only just found out himself and was scrambling.

"That's right," he responded with slow intent, casually glanced around for anyone listening, "as word spreads my teams will be bustling to keep up with the demand. The federation keeps its secrets close I suppose. Name's Darnell," he said with a handshake. "Well," pausing, he suddenly got a faraway look in his eyes, "eh, excuse me a minute."

Darnell moved off a few meters and tapped twice on his temple. He was moving his jaw slightly but not making any noise that could be discerned. Kasey had been putting off getting the updated Mimic Interface implants himself, but knew he would have to soon to keep up with others. Besides, they were free and considered part of the basic package everyone onboard received. He was curious how accurately the interface truly mimicked a person's communication, as the name implied. It seemed convenient at least. He had never had the need nor the credits for them back home. Many in his old circles had avoided such devices, and even viewed them more as a restriction than a freedom.

Well if Darnell, who seemed to be in a position that paralleled Kasey's needs, utilized them then he would need to as well. At least for a while, he thought.

Kasey busied himself with the task at hand. Using the hooked side of the knife, he stuck it in the opening and walked around the shuttle, cutting the shell in half. Once parted, he pulled heavily from the back, eventually pulling the top portion off in a great heap of material. Moving to the next shuttle, he slashed at it like Darnell had, and stepped back to watch it expand. He was moving onto his seventh craft when Darnell returned.

"Kasey, right?"

He could only nod in return.

"I see ya have done some time in the Daveri Two system. I have been there myself many turns back—quite a busy place." His eyes unfocused for a minute. "And I see you ran into some trouble…"

Kasey's face reddened darkly, but he managed a quick nod.

"If I read this correctly, you saved a few people that day?"

"Lost a lot more than I saved," he responded a little too harshly before he could catch himself. Hoping the reaction didn't ruin his chance at more information, he said no more.

Pausing for a deep breath, as if making up his mind about something, Darnell replied, "Look boy, it appears a new work order has been issued that I need to handle. I would rather keep it out of the know for now if you understand. And ah, it appears you already know more than you should…" Darnell gave Kasey a hard look.

"I keep my eyes and ears open is all," he stammered in return.

"Well, that could be useful as well, I suppose," an impulsive grin sprouted across the man's face. "If you are willing, I'll buy out your contract, but I need to know now." Seeing the confusion in Kasey's eyes, he expanded. "The Federation suits planned well, they allotted for a lot more public workers than they actually needed, and today I have been given a grant to reallocate several directly into my teams for as long as I deem it necessary."

"How long would that be in your estimation? I don't mind the work, but signing on for more than a year in a new system is…" Kasey left the sentence drop.

"No need to worry there, I can only hold you to the initial contract unless you sign on for more. But if the little I have been told is true, there will be more work than either of us can fill."

"Then you can count me in boss," he said, hardly believing his luck.

"Good, your contract with the Reavestone Mining Company starts today. I will have your prep service hours reallocated to the pool, someone else will need to pick them up. The tasks are well ahead of schedule anyway with all the early-wakers." Whistling for a replacement worker to be assigned the current job, he beckoned Kasey to join him. "Now, let's go see what's in this government bay I have been summoned to."

CHAPTER FIVE

Rows upon rows of huge tubular containers were arrayed before them, each one the size of a small warehouse. Far to the rear of the chamber were truly massive containers, any one of which could easily contain all the warehouse sized containers. They all appeared to Kasey to be deep-space shipping containers. Whatever they contained had not been local to the system they had departed from.

"I guess the secret was more closely guarded than I thought," Darnell whispered, reflecting Kasey's thoughts. "We are assigned to this one here," he directed them toward the nearest container, ignoring the larger ones completely.

Punching in a code on the first tube produced a loud pop followed by a slow rumble. A large portion of the tube's wall scrolled up into itself, air rushing in to fill the void. Lighted panels illuminated the contents, as entry ramps lowered to the bay's floor. The smell of heated plastic washed over them as they ascended the ramp. Before them rested a heavy transport ship unlike any either of them had ever seen.

"I am told she is a *Raven Class Heavy Transport*. We will name her at some point, but for now the navy's designation for this one is RAV-T27."

Kasey nodded, his eyes never leaving the ship.

The raven transport was large, but that was where the resemblance to other transports stopped. Three pairs of multi-purpose lateral thrusters sloped up from the low-placed bridge section to the upper reaches of the ship's stern. The thrusters themselves had a nearly organic look that had Kasey edging closer for a better look. They were designed to be molded into optimal shape and direction based on to the need of the craft, even changing position to some extent.

A blow to his arm drew his attention back to Darnell, who was pointing up at an array of thin tubes below the thruster he had been admiring. Kasey had overlooked the tubes as structural supports of some sort and just shrugged as he waited for an explanation.

"I think, ah yes. That would be a defensive system of some sort. See over there? I saw something like it before on a VIP's ground vehicle during some, uh, negotiations..." The way he spoke did not invite questions.

Emboldened, Kasey took a closer look at the hull. Dispersed evenly over the ship were what appeared to be roundish indentations he had not noticed before. Each hand sized dimple seemed covered with a web-like surface that shimmered in a slightly disturbing way. Both shook their heads, having no guesses as to the purpose.

Instead, Kasey distractedly pointed at several seemingly random placed head-sized, burgundy knobs protruding out nearly a meter from the hull. "What do you suppose all those are?"

Darnell stepped in for a closer look at one of them then shrugged. "Well," he said looking over Kasey's shoulder, "looks like we are about to find out."

Kasey spun around to find a suited woman flanked by

two heavily armed guards.

"Those red knobs," she spoke in a voice that demanded every bit of one's attention, "are your close-range kinetic-impact shield emitters. And before you ask, yes you have the navy version of the EM shields you are used to; they can extend out to nearly a hundred meters from the hull. The KI shield emitters are a newer development that will be explained in detail soon enough, but essentially, they pump out waves of positive electrons around the ship then slam them with bursts of negative electrons as needed. Think of it as directing lightning strikes to obliterate objects trying to hit your ship. As you will learn, it has its own set of limitations, but can save your life."

She walked towards them slowly, stopping when she was within three meters, "The tube arrays you were pointing toward a moment ago, are indeed one part of the craft's point-defense systems as you surmised," She held up her hand to prevent Kasey from asking the question he had begun to blurt out, "again, you will learn all about this system and others soon enough."

She spent a few moments looking the two men up and down, judging them before continuing, "And, those small depressions covering the craft are classified outside of your immediate needs." She nodded at the craft; the dimples, along with several other features of the craft, abruptly disappeared, leaving the hull looking comparable to many other transport vessels. "However, suffice to say they deal directly with the ship's stealth package."

With a quick smile, that relayed no comfort whatsoever, she nodded at the gawking boys, "Let's go aboard, I'll give you a tour. Tomorrow your training will start." She gave Kasey a quick glance, "If you don't already have the mimic interface implants, have them by then. You can't pilot these ships without them. Mr.

MacNamara here can authorize the procedure once he finishes the paperwork on your assignment transfer," She turned staring at Darnell with a raised eyebrow until he nodded in confirmation.

They entered through the ship's aft hanger and he tried to take in every detail of the shiny new craft. Much of it was standard stock as far as transports were concerned. The bays were purpose-configurable, nearly every surface could be moved or removed as needed. But unlike most ships he had flown, this storage bay could be repurposed automatically with a few commands—no manual work required.

What did catch Kasey's attention was that much of the bay's ceiling was covered with what appeared to be inverted pyramid shaped vats. His eyes searched along the pipes leading to the last row of pyramid for clues to what they were.

"Mr. Robinson!"

The sharpness of the woman's voice made Kasey jump back a step.

"I fully realize that you pilots are used to having your heads among the stars, but we are currently inside and without a view of the heavens, so I would appreciate your attention on the here and now." With that, she strode off in front of him at a much-quickened pace.

A slap to the back of his head from a stern looking Darnell got him hustling to catch up, but not before a glance back toward the odd ceiling. He caught his breath. The structures were gone, covered by a seeming flat surface as it they had never been.

What in the verse are we going to be shipping?

* * *

Kasey woke leaning forward in a sitting position. A form fitted mold of his upper body was slowly reforming and sliding back into the wall. The surgery was over. He wondered how much time had passed, and suddenly a clock appeared off to the left of his vision showing nearly an hour had passed since being sedated.

"Guess I should have expected that." he mused, as a plethora of images and words jumbled around on a screen that seemed kilometers away, until he paid it a scant amount of attention. As if on command, the screen zoomed to frontal attention, showing what appeared to be possible interpretations of his questioning thoughts. The disarrayed information changed continually as his focus reformed and fixated on specific topics. Mouthing a few words silently, he redirected and ordered the data further into useable patterns. Within moments, schematics of the mimic interface implants that were now part of him appeared before him, seeming to hover in the air.

I could grow to like this, he thought as he disregarded the schematic, which dissolved into the nether instantly.

It didn't take long after that to understand the other new augments. A distinct thought, 'Messages' for example, brought up a message interface box at the edge of his vision. Paying attention to the box activated it for use. Focusing in front or behind anything had a push and pull effect that naturally allowed the user to swim through information at amazing speeds.

The older system he had witnessed Darnell using functioned similarly, but it required what he thought of as talking to yourself just enough to move your tongue. The words were interpreted instantly, and somehow it knew if and how you wanted to use the formed words for. All in all, it was an impressive system.

Laying down on the bunk, he tried a few dozen

searches for the odd-looking storage chambers he had seen on the new transport ships. An hour later, the best match he had found was a loading module for ground skimmer transports. He was going about this all wrong he realized, this was a new substance they were looking for, not an old one. Still, nothing came to mind or screen.

Getting up, he started pacing in frustration. The new gear allowed him to race through data at an unbelievable speed, yet he had not a single useful find.

What am I missing?

Switching methods, he sought reasons for the location of this Farpoint mission. Other than it being an isolated group of star-systems, there was seemingly nothing of note. On a whim, he considered the other Farpoint destinations. The first thing he noticed was that they all appeared to be in sparse groups of star systems.

That gave him pause. It was odd to begin colonizing a new star cluster in such a sparse section of space. Clusters were meant to grow outward from a starting system, usually in an unbroken stretch of systems under Terrantine Federation control. The Farpoint project's colonization of the Trias system was an exception to normal settlements, which depended heavily on the trade and support from established colonies. As it stood, the longer potential supply lines to systems beyond Trias would limit prospective expansion efforts.

The stream of thoughts brought a plethora of opinions from his mimic interface on the topic, and conspiracies ran a rapid pace throughout the arguments.

The Perseus arm of the Milky Way, where many of the Farpoint ships were generally heading, had many dense groups of star systems compared to the Earth Prime cluster's location in the Orion-Cygnus arm. Yet the Farpoint missions all seemed destined toward the extreme thin areas of stars. Areas that made the original

Earth Prime cluster seem crowded. As many of the threads on the topic noted, it seemed a strange choice for such a huge expedition. One Kasey was disconcerted to have not noticed before.

Officially there was only ever one answer—safety, "The wellbeing of the Farpoint endeavors," they usually began, "is ever foremost in our thoughts when planning…"

Kasey only skimmed the response threads, but generally the idea was that the isolated system groups would be of little interest to other-origin species, yet would provide ample ground to prove out humanity's needs. The remoteness would, they alleged, provide a buffer for the human colonists to create an uncontested foothold in the area. In all cases, they also went on to show that plenty of other systems were indeed close enough to colonize with minimal additional effort.

All good points, Kasey thought. Digging a bit more into arguments, he found no evidence of other species being present anywhere in the Farpoint venture's region, the Cepheus portion of the Perseus galactic arm. *Not that humanity really had any idea what was out here*, he mused. That was part of the excitement. Fifteen thousand light-years was far beyond any known exploration of humanity. If other friendly species had shared their knowledge of the area, it wasn't common knowledge.

Working late into the night, he strove to find meaning or clues that would uncover secrets that would give him an edge in his new life. Keeping his mind occupied was often more important than any finding would ever be. He knew he wouldn't need to thrive to survive here, but survival wasn't the point. The goal was to run away, he reminded himself, to forget.

Unavoidably, his thoughts tracked back to AnnaChi and his loss. She would have loved the intrigue of his new venture. He was sure she would have found the meaning that now eluded him. He drifted off to sleep with her in his thoughts and dreams of a never-ending oblivion.

CHAPTER SIX

Kasey took a moment to admire the raven class vessel before he nodded at a hatch which promptly opened and extended a ramp to the hanger floor. The crafts were highly maneuverable and quicker than anything he had ever flown before. They could shoot into docking or takeoff sequences faster than most ships could begin their power changeover. He could not wait to fly it, but first he needed to pass the certification training.

With another commanding thought, the dark bay lit up brightly before him. His mimic interface tied directly into the ship's AI and played a huge part of the ship's controls. With a thought, he could form any malleable thruster assemblies to his need, activate any system, adjust power flows, even fire weapons if they were set up correctly, nearly anything on the ship could be controlled. The mimic interface was also the ship's access key. It was true that given time, any system could be worked around, but without a lot of effort, it took an authorized mimic interface to fly the ravens.

For Kasey, it all seemed a bit unnecessary, even if it was an amazing craft. It reeked of Terrantine control. The federation imposed their control on everything they touched, forcing restrictions anywhere they could. He found it difficult to imagine living so close to the federation's authority for long. Wondering, once again, if he had made a mistake in thinking the Farpoint colony would be different, yet he shook the thought away. His time was limited today, and he recognized that to have a chance at his goals, he needed this job. For now.

Pushing aside his nerves and doubts, he strode up in into the waiting bay to prepare himself for the evening.

Flight and control training for the raven class transport was intense. It needed to be, or so the instructors continually claimed. The journey, they would quote, was nearing its end, the companies being loaned the crafts needed qualified pilots by that time or the navy would reassign the crafts elsewhere. The mining companies had their own transports, of course, but the ravens would provide advantages beyond a large, low maintenance craft. Finding locations of valuable resources and keeping them secreted was the time-honored key to success on new worlds – something a military-level stealth package would help ensure. That the crafts were also large and fast was icing on the cake.

It all highlighted one fact for Kasey. The navy, and thus the federation, was after something specific in the new system, something they wanted control over.

The stress had set in over the past week of training. His simulator scores dropped each day since the combat instruction had started. The flight review instructors appeared more disappointed at his progress each day as well. It made him want to give up, but that was not his way. Instead, he concentrated on the lessons and getting to know what he hoped would be his ship to command. Telling himself he could worry about giving up after he failed.

Kasey found that walking through the ship after each mornings' class helped to make the evening simulator sessions feel more realistic. While the sims were very convincing, the knowledge that it was not real affected his decisions. Now, he walked the ship daily, imagining he was preparing to truly set sail into unknown dangers – it helped some, and right now he would take any help he could get.

Passing the officers' quarters, he entered the hatchway leading into the bridge then stopped, taking in the overengineered layout. The bridge was far too large for a common transport vessel, even for the navy in Kasey's opinion. Civilian transports simply had no need for more than two or three duty stations, and seldom did more than one station ever actually get used. The raven's eight stations filled the command deck before him. The instructor's explanation had been that the bridge was a modular design used for many types of navy ships, regardless of the intended usage. It was also made clear, that for the intended use of the loaned raven class vessels, only one crewman would be necessary, the pilot. The ship's AI could fill any gaps. Kasey still felt the large bridge was a waste, but he admitted it was sound reasoning for the navy.

Misgivings aside, Kasey delighted in the concept of the design. The entire bridge section was nearly a ship itself, serving as a large escape pod for the crew if needed. Most transport ships had a few small emergency pods, but never an entire bridge section. A well-stocked ready room, a head, and even a tight berthing area were all contained in a sealed area below the bridge's command deck that could be opened in an emergency.

The bridge's helm was the largest station on the bridge, centered directly in front of the command chair. Surrounding them were six additional interchangeable stations set into the port and starboard walls to handle everything from tactical to communications. He could imagine the usefulness of the additional stations in a military operation, but even then, this ship was only a transport – a flying box to take stuff from point A to point B. He smiled. It was overkill, but so long as he wasn't paying the credits, it was good by him.

While nearly every surface within the bridge could double as an interface, the entire forefront of the bridge was a massive hemispheric viewscreen giving a full view of the surrounding space or any other viewpoints required. While some parts of the hull could be made transparent, as most modern ships could, the raven class ship had minimal areas of transparency at best, instead relying on relayed images. Transparent metals were more than sufficient for most spacecraft's needs, however on a warship, as the bridge was designed for, the standards were far higher.

Kasey bit his lip as he left the bridge area. He appreciated the extra protections the raven class transport provided, as well as the amenities, but it was a lot to take in so quickly. He knew there was a lot more to learn about the nature of the job he had blindly signed up for.

Living quarters spread out and up from the bridge across the top of the ship. Yet, where the functions of the ship were all a step above norm, the accommodations were extremely plain, based only on need. It screamed military design. He fondly remembered AnnaChi's vessel—the Cintian—as more of a home than a ship. These federation transports would never be a home to him he resolved, simply a tool.

Kasey decided to skip the mezzanine and cargo bays on this walkthrough, instead cutting down a passageway between a set of crew quarters and a diminutive mess hall. Cycling the airlock at the end of the passage, he entered the portside engineering section. The section was little more than a gap between the inner and outer hulls allowing some access to the thrusters, weapons, and other systems along the outer hulls. An organized-maze of cables and power conduits ran throughout the areas, along with narrow access ramps for maintenance.

Ignoring the upper ramps, he moved swiftly downward to the lowest airlock and cycled through. The engineering deck was Kasey's favorite area of any ship. Much of the deck was cramped with everything that kept the ship alive and moving, but more so, it was a place he could think, dream, or just work on improving how a ship ran. Any ship changed over time, but a good ship was well maintained and continually customized to stay in top performance.

Passing by purifications tanks and lines of air recyclers, he found his way to the maintenance workshop. The shop was a staple for any system-wide ship. Breakdowns happened to every ship, no matter how well they were maintained. Surviving a breakdown on a long run in the dark was never easy, but without a few basic tools, survival was nearly impossible.

Laughing at the open space before him, he realized that not a single ship he had ever served upon had held such a dedicated shop. They had the equipment, but the "shops" were made up of collections of benches, machines and tools spread throughout the ship, crudely wedged into any space they could fit. The raven class ship's shop was a luxury most owners only dreamed of.

Moving on through the deck, he checked each status panel as he went, knowing that they had not changed since yesterday. Having a routine for a ship's upkeep was mostly a habit he had picked up from AnnaChi. She had known every part of her ship, from the smell of the reactor to the dryness of the air pushed out of the oxygen recyclers. Treat a ship like a living thing, she would tell him, it will take care of you and you will know when you need to take care of it.

Many of the pilots simply remote-monitored their

ship from the helm or had the AI oversee the ship's systems for them. With the new mimic interface, raven pilots could monitor everything with merely a thought. It would probably be sufficient for these ships, he admitted to himself. The ships were new, over designed, and would likely not need to fly far beyond the orbit of the planets they would be assigned to. Yet he kept up the habit, even if it was more for the emotional ties to AnnaChi than actual need.

Each day he tried to take a different route through the ship, particularly the engineering deck, which contained more access ports than any other area, even though most were not meant as a standard passage. This day he ended his tour at the system core's room. He didn't enter the core's cleanroom to examine the sixty-four core towers, there was no need. The system was well beyond his abilities to maintain or fix, however the system contained several levels of redundancies and, barring physical damage, there were few ways the cores could be compromised.

After verifying that the room's status panels showed everything to be normal, he checked the room off his list then took a lift to the ship's main bay.

The cargo bay was big, but not quite as large as most heavy transport class ships. Kasey gradually walked to the very center and sat cross-legged on the warm, metallic surface. He needed to prepare for the day's simulations.

Taking a deep breath, he looked up suddenly, remembering the pyramid vats along the ceiling he had noticed on his first visit to the ship. With a smile, he sent a mental command to dismiss the projected illusion of a flat overhead surface. Instantly, rows of the pyramid shapes that he had noted on that first day appeared, tips pointing downward. They were obviously containers of some sort, with pipes and connecting them all, but so far, he had no idea what they were for. All necessary storage for the ship and crew were stored either in the small bays under engineering, or up in the mezzanines, and he knew each one.

He glared at them for a few more seconds before replacing the false overhead projection. He wanted to figure out the mystery, but he had no time for it today. Ever since learning how to control the ship's HWG stealth package, or more officially known as the holographic wave generator, he had little time to explore all its uses on the ship, let alone other mysteries. The standard functions of the stealth package produced either transparent effect or a field of near-pure blackness, or more accurately, a non-reflectivity of most wavelengths impacting the ship. The whole system was coupled with functions to redirect and absorb waves as directed, even wrapping waves completely around the ship as if it wasn't there. All in all, the HWG stealth package could hide a ship from most common scanners short of gravity wave detectors. Yet, Kasey could tell there was far more to the system than he could access, more it was capable of, but the class was given no time to examine the package further, as the class's direction and pace changed dramatically that day.

The day had started out as normal, with the introduction of a new ship system, the new HWG stealth system, but only a few hours later, the KI shielding systems was presented as well; a kinetic impact array that literally blasted near-ship objects to vapor in an energy release larger than some lightning strikes found around gas giants. The two secretive and advanced systems each came with a virtual ton of data, and only Kasey's excitement at finally learning the new technology kept him from noticing the other changes in the training program that day.

It was only when they were dismissed that he noted

that over half the usual trainee pilots were missing from the room. He had later learned that they had all been dismissed from the program before the beginning of the day's lesson. A subtle reminder that the job was not guaranteed, but it did not end there. That night's simulator sessions were distinctly combat related and had continued to be ever since.

He had been scrambling to keep up ever since.

He knew the stress would have been far worse if he had time to worry about it, but with twice the systems to learn, he didn't have that luxury unless he planned to fail. He had known failure in his life, and he was not afraid of it, he was only afraid of not trying. The hectic days had a bittersweet silver lining – he was nearly too busy to dwell on AnnaChi's memory, allowing for some small measure of peace.

Many of the other pilots were not so eager to be thrown into combat training for a simple transport job. Having grown up outside federation-controlled space, Kasey had heard plenty of stories of small but deadly conflicts, pirate attacks and even all-out wars being fought amongst new colonies, particularly when the colonists didn't have a strong military like the federation supporting them. However, it was apparently not a concern the Terrantine Federation citizens were accustomed to dealing with, at least not publicly. Yet, the Farpoint project was different – there was no backup from any government out here. So, Kasey was glad to learn the new skills, he just hoped he wouldn't need to use them.

He ran the past week's simulations through his head, trying to puzzle the correct actions he should have taken in each. Trying to see if there had been a solution at all, or if they were all designed to have him fail. Envisioning many actions that he could have taken, other options he could have used, yet none seemed to ensure positive outcomes as far as he could tell. Without access to the simulator programs there was no real way to know.

A full standard hour passed before Kasey stood and made his way out of the ship, heading to the simulator training area.

* * *

The third simulated mission of the night started without a break as Kasey shifted in the seat and shook his head vigorously to push away the exhaustion that was edging in. So far, the tests had been particularly trying, forcing him to use every bit of concentration he could to keep the ship in one piece while navigating planetary sized debris fields, one-sided firefights, and endless assortments of complex docking procedures. He was tired, but knew he had to continue onward.

Struggling to determine what new trial would be thrown at him, he scanned the screens for clues. A trio of raven transports were linked with his own, in a maneuverer akin to those he had routinely flown back in Daveri Two. Nothing seemed out of place; the passageways were clear and quiet, and his bays were full of undisturbed crates. Kicking off an automated system scan, he switched his attention to outside the ship just as an external sensor started blinking for attention. He knew the game was about to start.

Before the sensors could identify the cause of the ping, an unknown object impacted the center ship, tearing it open. A full load of cargo spewed out filling his starboard viewscreen. Activating the emergency delink sequence, the hatch connecting him to the doomed ship shot away with enough force to shake the bridge, leaving Kasey fighting to stabilize his own trajectory. No sooner did he begin edging the ship away when collision alerts showed multiple hits rupturing the remaining ship from their trio. He was already spinning up the KI shields while moving his own vessel around the edge of the wreckage filling the area, but they were slow to build a useful charge. His EM shielding was nearly useless as well, for the moment. The linked ships had been sharing the EM field generation which had been blown to hell when the ships were torn apart by whenever had impacted them. It was building slowly, but the remains of the other ships were still within range and constantly impacting the weak shield.

The seconds passed slowly as he pushed the ship past the leading edge of debris and began pulling away from the rapidly expanding field. He was just starting to feel safe, to feel like he had successfully passed the scenario, when he spotted two deadly looking ships coming around the port-side of the field, bearing down on him.

His stomach clenched as he realized the encounter was only beginning. Dread washed over him, he knew there was no winning this. His mind felt foggy with indecision as he spun the ship to try and keep the wreckage between him and the attackers, but they were already firing some rapid-fire weapon that was burning directly through his shields and hull.

Almost without thinking Kasey ignored his weapon systems and ejected a full fuel pod toward them. He watched in shock as it slowly cracked open in the debris field, releasing fuel in an explosive burst of liquids that quickly encompassed the enemy ships and wreckage alike.

He had no idea how long he sat at the helm watching. Even when the ships finally drifted out of the fuel cloud and assaulted his own transport, he did nothing but watch the dissipating fuel. Remembering. He watched long after his ship was destroyed, just staring. The simulator shut down, leaving nothing but the images in his memory of AnnaChi's last moments.

Darnell's voice eventually broke through.

"Boy, arc yc there?" Rough hands shook him back to reality. "Kasey…"

"Yea. I'm here," he managed, "Sorry. I, uh…"

"No need. The tech showed me what happened, and I put it together." Kasey could smell traces of some strong alcohol on Darnell's breath as he drew closer. "I understand son. But you need to realize something very important." He paused, "You will never get over her."

Kasey's eyes widened in anger.

"That's right," Darnell continued when he saw Kasey's expression. "Be angry! Anger is the only way you will survive. Use that anger to get what ya need accomplished, use it as fuel. Anger like this will never let you down if you keep it properly directed." His thick finger drove the point home as it prodded Kasey in the head like a mallet. "Like it or not, you will continue on, and you will be my pilot."

The man slowly leaned back and stood before going on. "Besides, the tech said you were the first he had seen to survive that sim. Well, almost survive. He said if you had used your bloody weapons at all you would have won. That's a mark for you that I can count on above the by-the-book learning that the rest of these jockeys know how to replicate. I'll take that bet any day."

"A bet?"

"Yea son, a game of chance. That's what life is most days. The others use their heads, and that's all fine and good, but you have instinct and that's worth immeasurably more."

Nodding, Kasey stared at the console as he rolled the words over in his head.

"Now pull yourself together and meet me in my quarters in twenty minutes. We have things to discuss."

* * *

The door slid open as Kasey approached. Feeling more nervous than he was prepared to admit, Kasey casually strode in only to find the room empty. Unlike his own single-room accommodations, Darnell's spread into several other compartments. It was not opulent by any means, but it promptly reminded Kasey that he had obtained the absolute lowest cost passage that had been available.

It appeared that Darnell was in the midst of several research projects, mostly centered around the new system they were bound for. The walls were filled with various filtered images from the probe data showing planets, moons and even a few blurry land swaths. A desk in the far corner was filled with schedules that Kasey assumed were search patterns across one of the major landmasses, but what caught his attention was a stack of paper notebooks stacked to one side. Paper was rare for the simple matter that it was inconvenient, and nonpermanent. He could not imagine a time where such things were commonly used, only to be lost or destroyed by the simplest of mistakes. So much data must have been lost in those early years of humanity – it was nearly unthinkable.

Before he could give it more thought, Darnell burst in from a kitchen area with bottles clanking.

"Have a beer and rake your eyes over this rock," he pointed an image of a green-blue planet hovering directly above the desk.

"Our destination?" Kasey raised a brow.

"Yup, that there is Lithose. A place where our fortunes are to be made or lost."

"I don't have much to lose boss. A fortune huh?"

"Damn right. Come grab a seat, I have some food coming soon. I hope you're not picky." He didn't wait for an answer as he led the way into a small lounge.

Kasey slumped into a deep-cushioned sofa as Darnell continued talking about his plans to get ahead of the other mining operations. The raven, he was proclaiming, would be key in confusing the competition and keep the Reavestone's own prospecting a secret. But Kasey stopped paying attention, his mind was still back in the simulator and the harsh from words Darnell.

Realizing he was angry, not just depressed or sad, but irrationally angry, was a surprise. Sure, he thought, he had been plenty angry after the actual attack and had wanted to hunt down the people responsible at first. Yet, by the time he had made port and reported the incident, all he had wanted was to run away from it all. But the anger Darnell had exposed in him was something different. It was not anger towards the attackers, instead he was angered at something he could not define. The situation, the human condition, he was not sure, and that was the crux of the problem. He was angry with nothing substantial to blame.

The room had grown quiet. Looking up, he was surprised to find Darnell smiling at him as if he had just won a contest.

"So boy, have you figured it out then?"

"I... What?" Kasey stammered back.

"You're angry still, right?"

Kasey just nodded.

"So, what are you angry at?" he demanded suddenly.

"I don't know," he answered more sharply than he intended. "There is nothing I can really be angry at still, but dammit I am."

The miner bellowed a laugh, "that's close enough."

Kasey felt bewildered, not really understanding.

"Look," Darnell continued in a more somber tone, "like it or not, the universe is trying to kill us all, and eventually it will. She's a real bitch, but the only way to fight back is to survive any way you can. Stand up and keep going as hard as you can. Keep that anger directed at the verse and you will be ready for anything thrown your way."

"I am not really sure…"

"Yea, yea, I know. A bit too metaphorical for ya? Well, it doesn't matter if you believe it or not. Point is, if you want to survive then you need to get pissed off at whatever circumstances you find yourself struggling against—then kick its ass."

"And you really think being mad is the way to live?"

"No. But it's a way to survive, at least for those who know this type of anger. This kind of bottled up rage. You know it already; you don't have a choice about that. You may as well direct that fury into something useful before the despair kills ya."

"Like in the sim…"

"That's right, same as the simulation," Darnell's tone became deadly serious. "Never, ever, let that shit happen again."

Kasey could only nod as Darnell left the room to answer the door chime. When he returned, with food and more beer, Darnell's normal demeanor had returned as well.

Before he started talking again, Kasey's ears began ringing. "You hear that?"

"Hear what? Ship noises? Does that sometimes…"

The ringing had begun to fade, so Kasey just shrugged it off.

"Alright then, we have other business to discuss. That ship. Give me a rundown of what we can expect above the norm. I need to work it into our planning."

The evening wore on, but the questions did not seem

to stop. It was late when Kasey made his way back to his own cabin, but he had not gotten far when his ears suddenly popped. Kasey sighed and wondered just what information the man was truly after. Knowing that Darnell had access to as much information about the ship that he did, likely a lot more, only bewildered Kasey more. The mine boss had been searching for something else in the answers, he realized. *But what?*

Stumbling slightly, he realized he was more intoxicated than he realized. By the time he entered his cabin, he had put the mystery down to the prattling of drunk men.

CHAPTER SEVEN

Kasey's simulated mission success rate improved moderately over the next several days. While he wasn't sure the advice Darnell had given was something he could believe in, it certainly helped achieve a few positive results. He quit trying so hard to solve the simulated issues using what the instructors had taught. He felt they were holding him back from success. Certainly, the skills and tools were useful, and he was happy to make use of them when it made sense. He always considered the lessons when he had time to plan in the sims, but he was no longer going to fail trying to use them. There were no such rules in real-life, and that was supposedly what he was training for. Instead, he began solving issues as if they truly were real, solving them in his own way.

He worried he had pushed it too far a few days later. The day's flight review session was joined by a second officer who began questioning a long list of decisions Kasey had made in the past day's simulations. As Kasey responded to each, the man went on to the next questions, without comment and without opinion. Before long, Kasey had had enough.

"I see here," the officer asserted, "that you ignored

the PDAM array's program, taking control of the targeting yourself?"

Kasey controlled his desire to yell at the man as he considered the question. The ship's PDAM, or point defense antimatter, array was similar to the laser based equivalent normally used by high-end civilian ships, but far more destructive. Antimatter is extremely dangerous to use, and difficult to store, even in micro amounts. Mainly used as an explosive, when interacting with normal matter, it annihilates the equivalent amount of matter, releasing sum-total energy of both. A nearly perfect destructive force, but usually impracticable.

From the moment the fraction of a microgram of antimatter leaves the accelerator tube, it begins to break down. Space is far from empty, and every particle the antimatter packet encounters causes tiny explosions, breaking the packet apart and pushing it off course. Over a great distance, the packet is rendered ineffective and inaccurate. However, as a short-range defensive weapon, it excelled. At least when it successfully hit the intended ordnance.

"The PDAM program attempts to guess the missile's evasive programming, then attempts to strike it with the antimatter packets. This is fine for a laser-based system, but the antimatter packets are much slower than the lightspeed beams. This makes the PDAM's guesses more complex, and thus less accurate. It needs to guess several steps ahead of the missile."

The man cocked an eyebrow, looking slightly up from the list he was holding, but didn't interrupt.

Emboldened, Kasey went on. "There is a better way, at least for the situation I was in today. I set my ship on an arcing trajectory with fixed course adjustments sweeping back and forth. This forced the missiles to predictability course-correct after going tangential from my adjustments. The PDAM's program did not appear to take advantage of this, so I took manual control of the system and laid down a screen of fire directly into the missile's path, where I knew my course would coerce the missile to be. It took a few tries, but it worked well ahead of the missile impacting my EM shields."

The eyes dropped back to the screen, going to the next question. His mouth started to move, forming the next question on the list, but Kasey interrupted with more force than he intended.

"You understand that this system would be a lot more useful if it was tied into the ship's flight plans, Right? A simple AI could work out the trajectory ahead of time and be ready with options. If we are required to use only the taught methods in the sims, it would help if the scenarios actually required them." Kasey felt a rush of angry heat surge into his face as he tried to calm down.

The officer smiled at the outburst. "Tomorrow's lesson will introduce several options for the PDAM system, including a few that will assist with the maneuvers you successfully employed."

Instead of continuing with the list of questions, he stood to leave the room, pausing at the hatchway. "The lessons introduce the tools you may need to protect our assets and our interests. The simulations are to prove that you can *actually* do that. Understand the tools but defeat the simulations. By any means necessary."

The officer's encouraging words unlocked his last doubt. He no longer held back for fear of offending the instructors by his actions in the simulators. No longer feared his own inclinations would lose what could be the perfect job for his ambitions.

Before he knew it, his scores improved to an above-average rating. He wanted to feel a sense of accomplishment, but the accomplishment felt bittersweet. The interacting with the federation personnel felt as if he was betraying his parents. Telling himself they were only a means to an end helped, but not much. When the order came to report the Reavestone Mining offices he was relieved.

* * *

Arriving at the meeting, he was taken aback by the complete lack of formality. The Reavestone offices were exactly what one would expect from a corporation, and while there were several formally attired employees walking around, the members of the meeting were anything but. A dozen men and woman were haphazardly relaxing throughout the room, which was more lounge than a conference room. The crew's garments had clearly seen better days.

These were workers who had clearly been at the job longer than Kasey had been alive. Trying to blend in, Kasey plastered a frown on his face and found a place out of the way to wait.

"Hey Darnie! You order a present for me?"

The voice belonged to rough looking woman covered in tattoos, up to and including the top of her shaved head. With exaggerated effort, she started to get off her perch, eyes never leaving Kasey.

"Ease off Sariyn!" Darnell's voice cut through the room before he went back to his own conversation.

Sariyn found something else to hold her interest and moved to a nearby table. Few others had even bothered to look in his direction.

Shaking off the feeling of being out of place, he ignored the rest of the crew. Finding a nice spot on the wall to admire, he waited for the meeting to begin.

Without preamble, the room light flashed to a brighter setting as the doors to the room closed and sealed. Half the occupants were out of their seats in an instant.

Darnell's laughter boomed as he made his way forward.

"Glad to see a few of ya are awake still."

"What's the deal Darnell? Heard there's been a change in plans. Care to fill us in?" It was hard to make out who spoke, but most seemed to agree with the comments. It was clear most of this crew only recently came out of stasis.

"That is exactly why we are here. Obviously. Now would you like to find out by asking questions, or would you rather I simply told ya what is to come?"

With a few grunts of agreement, the room settled.

"First off, I expect you all to introduce yourselves to our assigned pilot, Mr. Robinson," he said, winking in Kasey's direction. "Kasey will be flying your asses around so you all can dig in mud to your heart's content."

Leaning forward, Kasey gave a quick wave, hoping to just as quickly be forgotten about.

"Now if . "

"Cute," the voice of Sariyn interrupted, probably for her own amusement.

"Anyway," Darnell persisted, "we do indeed have a different assignment. A new mineral is supposedly found here on these rocks we volunteered for. In eight days, we *will* be the first team to find it!"

With some respect, Kasey noted that no face in the room doubted his claim. The confidence the crew had was reassuring, but apparently Darnell thought they needed kicked down a few notches.

"It's really too bad I am stuck with you lot on this." The miners stirred in agitation. "But!" Darnell nearly shouted, "I think we will do just fine, if you all can manage to pay attention for the next few minutes."

Kasey repressed a laugh. Cleary Darnell knew how to handle this particular group. The man was a bit of an enigma over the brief time he had known him. He was either self-assured or anxious, but never in-between.

"Apparently," he continued, once sure he had everyone's full attention, "the federation's science consortium have decided our galaxy just wasn't put together correctly. They've done the math and it didn't add up. I am told they have used their formulas on the Andromeda galaxy and others, and so far, as of thirty years ago, the equation works, but not for our own Milky Way."

"So what, boss, I mean, what's all this mean to us?" A skinny red-haired guy interjected.

"It means nothing to us alone, however, they recently found a solution…"

"If recent is thirty years ago," someone took the opportunity to throw out. Darnell just waited for the laughter to flitter out, but a few caught his unimpressed look and realigned their attention back to him.

"As I was saying, they recently found out why we are so unique. Something they refer to as an exotic seam cut through the galaxy while it was forming. This small seam was made up of something they referred to as negative matter."

A few in the room had apparently heard the term before and started whispering, though what about, Kasey couldn't tell. He had heard the term before but had no idea what it really meant. Finally, after allowing the murmurs to play out, Darnell resumed.

"Right. The material, um negative matter, is basically antigravity, or so I understand. They don't know what it will look like, since it can exist as any other material— except it will rise instead of fall. In theory."

"Negative matter is not antigravity Darnie," Sariyn lowered her voice in wonder. "Not at all. But under some theories it can have an effect that may *seem* like it is. The mass is negative, meaning a rock of the stuff would weigh *less* than nothing. Hell, if it existed, most of it would have drifted away from planets, not towards them. I mean, depending how the system was formed, the negative matter could have been trapped from floating away just like gold is trapped from sinking to a planet's core I suppose. It's a big universe and all that, anything is possible…"

"Bah, we are all on a fool's errand," a voice shouted. "These uh, what did you call them? N-mats? They don't exist. That theory has been proven time and again to be impossible."

Sariyn stood, clearing her throat loudly, "No. *Some* of the theories have been disproven, and some have been proved and disproved several times over, usually because they were replicating a negative mass *effect*, not a true negative mass. There are twelve, no, thirteen current models for negative matter I believe, maybe a handful of those allow for an antigravity type of effect. Several of those *theories* require negative force as well, which unless Darnie is explaining it wrong, is not what we are looking at here. But a couple theories don't require it and still work… I'll need to dig into them. Still, if this anomaly can be measured on a galactic scale, then one of them must be at least partially correct."

Darnell nodded slowly, then shrugged, "Look, this information is not coming from the company, it was vetted by the federation. It could be true, it could be propaganda, or something else altogether. Regardless, we still need raw resources for this colony, so if any of ya want to be on a normal team, you are welcome to transfer. But I can tell you one thing I *am* sure of – the federation believes we will find something that was worth funding the Abscond being built and sent out here. You all know this beast of a ship wasn't the only one built for the Farpoint projects, we are just one of many. The question is, will we be the one to succeed?"

The room erupted with questions. Kasey, as stunned as anyone, had his own, but kept them to himself. None of the queries could really be answered yet anyway, just guessed at.

Darnell strode slowly through the room and waved everyone to silence. Ordering a beer from the wall unit, he quickly took a long swallow, then made his way back to the front. All eyes were on him now.

"Yea," he intoned, "we *are* going to make some history together. No, I don't know how this will all work. No one knows. But *we* are going to figure it out, same as we always do. Now, they believe particles of the stuff will be locked in with other materials. So, we will be prospecting harder and faster than we ever have, to find a good pocket of these n-mats before other teams in the colony do. Ah, right… We are calling them n-mats for now… Stupid name, I know, but get used to it. I am sure some goon will soon give it an official name if we find some."

"If, sir?"

"Yes, *if* it is here, we will find it. No doubt there. But to be honest, this whole thing is one big damn guess, they could be wrong. Even if they are right, they still don't know where the seam came from to begin with. So, yea, we are betting a lot on all this." Taking another long drink, he found a seat. "Look, this is the job and we are going to do it as best we can. You all signed on for this trip and part of that, if you bothered to read it, was a detailed non-disclosure agreement. So, you need to keep all this to yourselves!"

Darnell waited, meeting everyone's eyes and receiving a nod from each. "Now. I will explain the details of how we are going to go about this, and then we will take a look at the new ship we will be camping in for as long as it takes to get this job done. Is everyone with me?" he shouted, spilling his drink as he raised it violently into the air.

Shouts of agreement filled the room and Kasey joined the enthusiasm.

Kasey had found the new information fascinating for many reasons, none of which had to do with any actual science. When it came down to it, nothing had really changed for him. This new substance would become the next luxury fad until something else came along. None of it mattered to him. This knowledge was the key to wealth, and he was in the perfect place to learn how to use it. Wealth enough to buy the freedom his parents had always dreamed of but never found.

CHAPTER EIGHT

Entering the fairway to the local common area, Kasey's senses were assaulted by a mixture of smells and sounds. People were suddenly everywhere, and actual cooking was taking place at makeshift food stands. A major awakening must have taken place for so many people to be gathering.

His thoughts were soon distracted by a garlic aroma wafting from a newly partitioned area. Pasta and pizza, the wall screens advertised. Food choices always seemed to revert to the styles of old Earth Prime before new fads overtook them again, and colonization foods were no exception.

While waiting for his food, he realized he now had a major problem with his plans to exploit the knowledge of the exotic matter. He had no way to detect the stuff on his own. All the information they were given claimed the negatively massed matter would likely be found in miniscule amounts, detectable only through highly specialized methods that no one really knew would work. From what little he had heard, the expensive scanners and survey equipment he had installed on the bard would be useless for detecting negative matter. There would be none of the *upwards falling dirt* he had overheard crewmen complaining about. Then again, if it was easy, it wouldn't be worth the fuss.

The Reavestone crew, he knew, had spent the last several days installing and learning to use the new mission module the navy had delivered to their raven class ships the morning after the meeting. The large lab module now filled a sizeable portion of the bay.

A conglomeration of soil analysis equipment made up one main appliance. He understood that the automated laboratory would run nearly any material sample through hundreds of experiments, analyzing everything from magnetic fields to specific mass to gravitational anomalies. There were over forty different mass spectrometers alone, or so he had heard Sariyn rave about. He almost felt bad for her team; keeping the lab clean and solutions filled would be a full-time job, let alone analyzing the massive amounts of data.

Kasey's main task in the installation project was reforming the bay into useable formations to act as the crew's science center. Sariyn would be heading up the research team, along with three others, all of which had changed their opinions on the layout several times. He didn't mind. Sariyn and the others working with the lab knew more than anyone on the crew what it would take to detect n-mats in the samples the others would dig up. If there was any way for Kasey to prospect for the strange material on his own, he would learn it from them.

The pizza arrived, pulling his attention from the problem. He couldn't identify the grayish meat-like substance he found topping it, but there was a nice spicy taste to it. Attempting to enjoy the food, he listened to the excited din of a journey nearing its end.

It wasn't long before music and drinking started, which was Kasey's cue to leave. Never one to appreciate crowds, he finished his meal and left the rising clamor for the quiet of his own quarters. Besides, he had enough to keep his mind occupied.

A group nearly knocked him over as they excitedly entered the commons. Kasey had to control his anger as they slapped his back and apologized before moving into the room. He pushed the rage away and was glad for the empty hall. Shocked at his own sudden anger, he took a deep breath. Such a small thing setting him off made little sense, but he realized his stress was building. He was way out of his norm on this adventure, and it all was out of his control.

Abruptly he was reminded of what Darnell had said in the simulators. Anger could be directed; anger could be a tool. Fine.

I have been through too much to get here, I am not going to fail now.

He felt the anger burning again at the thought of failure, felt it building. He wanted to scream, but instead took a deep breath and forced a smile on his face and embraced it. He felt a clarity wash over his thoughts, organizing them, tuning them as he sifted through what little he was aware of about the n-mats so far. Before he knew it, he entered his room with a concept of how to accomplish his ambition.

All he required was that Darnell's crew find the n-mats first and learn the best ways to detect them. The lab team had been vocal that the large, highly complex laboratory would not be required once the n-mats were found. They had even set up a few simple scanners of their own to use beforehand to eliminate the need of running the large lab process if a more simplistic method could identify the n-mats from raw samples. With Kasey's ship access, he would be able to access and watch enough to know what testing worked and what failed. After that, he just needed to be lucky enough to understand one or more of the successful test methods –

and then be able to afford the equipment, or at least have access to it.

There were still a lot of points to fail on. The crew may not find the n-mats, the equipment may be too expensive or complex, the n-mats could be easily found everywhere, even the system and planets could be inhospitable forcing the Abscond to redirect to some fallback system. Anything was possible, Kasey knew that. But the n-mats were the best plan he had for now, as long as that was feasible, he would make it happen if he could. If not, he was still in a better position to locate and capitalize on other valuable resources the colony would need, using his bard scouting vehicle and the scanning equipment and every bit of information he was able to obtain from the crew.

The thoughts gave him direction and the energy he needed to continue. For the first time, he felt excited for the Abscond to be reaching the Trias system soon, and the planet-fall soon after that.

* * *

Cursing under his breath, Kasey rushed onto the observation deck just seconds before the space-warping bubble burst in a brilliant blue lightshow. The display lasted for many minutes as the remaining energies cascaded into bright ribbons of plasma that were being channeled towards and eventually absorbed back into the ship's massive star drive.

The Abscond maneuvered, causing the viewscape to shift violently, bringing a bright yellow-dwarf star into the center of the view. A deep-red nebula filled the edges of the western view, sparkling with brilliant blue stars. To the east, a large portion of the Milky Way galaxy could be seen as it wrapped around the stern of the ship. For many, the view alone made this trip worth it – a new perspective of the galaxy, unseen before by human eyes.

The nebula was soon forgotten as information slowly began displaying across the viewport's dome, labeling the yellow dwarf star as Trias. The colony's new home. The Trias system's sun was slightly smaller than that of Earth Prime's Sol but had a significantly higher absolute magnitude.

One after the other, from Trias outwards, planets were slowly highlighted and labeled. As each name appeared, a closeup image of the planet appeared above the crowd until all twelve planets rotated overhead in an orderly line. A moment later, hundreds of moons burst into existence and began to orbit the planets.

The room's silence ended as the fourth planet, Lithose, expanded in size and detail to fill a large section of the overhead area. It was the first of the three habitable bodies in the new system. Lithose was the primary destination of everyone in this portion of the ship, nearly half of the colonists. A clamor of excitement filled the air as plans, hopes and dreams were traded among the passengers.

A superimposed representation of the Abscond appeared to the side and suddenly split into three distinct segments. The great starship would soon split into several segments, each becoming permanent orbiting stations for the habitable planetoids they would be renamed for.

As they watched, the tail-end segment of the Abscond was renamed the Lithose-Abscond station and settled into orbit around Lithose, the group's new home.

There was a brief pause to the talking as the fifth planet, Belrothi, also began to expand, growing slightly larger than Lithose and was given the forward portion of the ship as a station, now named Belrothi-Abscond.

Soon after a large moon named Vethi took its place with the habitable worlds along with the orbiting station Vethi-Abscond. Vethi was a moon of the eighth planet Goligen, a gas giant.

The two planets and one moon made up the, soon to be inhabited, regions of the system. Other worlds would follow once the terraforming got under way, an effort that would take over a decade before hands-on work could begin. Vethi was not precisely habitable. Residents destined for the moon had undergone slight genetic modifications, while in stasis, to allow them to breathe and survive the nitrogen and carbon dioxide rich air. It would take only a few years to convert the atmosphere to normal human standards, until then the population would remain minimal.

The din resumed as the gathering's focus shifted back to Lithose. Kasey considered his new home. It was going to be odd, he decided, to work and live around a single planet for the next several years. He was used to living mostly in the space between a system's planets, only enjoying brief stops on the planets themselves. Both his commitment to the colony and his own plans for success now tied him to this one world for years to come. Perhaps it would be a good thing, he needed to keep his mind occupied and the long journeys in the dark with no place to be alone with dispiriting thoughts.

It would not be long now, he realized. Now that the Abscond had broken from the warp bubble, the ship would start into its slowdown procedure as it closed in on the system. The view would change drastically every day as they drew closer to ship's segments final resting orbit around Lithose.

Kasey turned and walked away suddenly. Embarrassed without really knowing why. He did not feel he belonged with these people who had bought their place in the colony and brought everything they needed to thrive. Somehow, he simply did not feel as prepared as all the relaxed people around him—all of them, it seemed, knew exactly how they would survive and prosper in the new worlds. They had none of the fear the settlers Kasey had known on the worlds his parents had taken him to. These were not people struggling to make a new beginning, they were simply continuing their successful lives on the next new planet. Their plans centered on how to enjoy, not how to survive. Kasey had done little but prepare, yet no definite future stretched before him. He had no home to build nor resources to build one. Nothing more solid than hope lined his pockets.

He had always had issues with long-term planning, the more factors it involved the less he felt able to proceed. Everything, including the task at hand, soon became fuzzy in his mind. Still, it never stopped him from trying. The last seven years of his waking life were the beginning stages of his latest plan, which had only now really begun. He felt the nagging of the overwhelming issues to overcome, and the old worry of failure began to set in again. Shaking the feeling away as best he could, he realized he really had no choice this time. There was no going back, and nowhere to run.

He glanced over his shoulder one last time at the view that lay beyond the crowd, and for the first time really took in the view of his new home. His future. Silent words rang louder to his ears than any bell ever tolled.

"*Now   it   begins   in   earnest.*"

CHAPTER NINE

The last several months were some the busiest she had ever experienced. Running supply transports to Belrothi—the Trias system's fifth planet—from the Belrothi-Abscond station, was an easy jaunt. Yet it seemed tedious and never-ending on this day.

Supplying a new world with everything it would need to thrive was nearly inconceivable, even to the pilots delivering it all. There had already been collisions with several deaths, but even that didn't slow the pace.

When she was awakened from stasis, she expected to finally have the time to think about the monumental step she was taking by going on this escapade. To try and figure out how to retrieve what she had lost, yet no sooner had she begun to get her bearings when she was pulled into a prep team. Less than a week later, the Abscond was entering orbit around the new system and splitting into segments around the various planets and planetoids that made up the Trias system. Then the work really started.

A small black transport darted in front the Cintian, her ship, the only other thing she cared about. Unlike her medium-sized transport ship, the black ship was shiny new, like so many others that had been brought on this journey. The new ship maneuvered into the slot as if made for it, showing the advanced processing its systems must be capable of. The Cintian could not move that fluidly no matter how skilled the pilot.

She reached out and patted the console tenderly. The ship could use an upgrade, but the Cintian was hers, clear and free, and she would never be held to contracts after her colonization-prep service hours were over. More so, the ship felt like home, and most of the time it was.

Easing her own ship out of the dock, she sped after the newer ships lining up. Skillfully she took her place in the long line of others waiting for the go-ahead to enter the descent window. Belrothi's surface awaited them far below. At first, she had enjoyed the waiting almost as much as flying. Waiting in the queue was nearly the only time she had to reflect on her recent mistakes and try to figure out what to do about them. *This whole trip was probably a mistake*, she mused, for what must be the hundredth time today. She had been a fool and she knew it, but there was no turning back now.

It seemed forever ago now, but the real, as well as the emotional, pain was as fresh as if it had just happened. With an involuntarily wince, AnnaChi remembered the searing pain of plasma as it had ripped through both her arm and abdomen.

AnnaChi remembered all that painful experience, until she finally lost consciousness. The raiders had been looking for something in the goods she had been smuggling with the normal cargo; something she was not aware she had even had. The black-market cargo was only a few dozen crates of well-aged wine from the Zief system and some antique artwork made of some local blueish clay. Neither were of any real value, just expensive enough for the smaller resort owners of Daveri One's Beta Moon to find creative ways to skip the middlemen, regardless of import restrictions.

Apparently, they didn't find what they expected and had accused her of having it hidden somewhere. They even ended up nearly killing her. When she regained consciousness three days later, it was all she could do to direct the remaining passengers to get the ship to a port. All the while she was trapped in a barely functioning trauma pod that was the only thing keeping her alive.

The pod was a blessing and a curse. In long distance space travel, a wound like she had taken would have meant death without it. The problem was that it did little more than keep a body alive and medicated. Things like broken bones would heal wrong and frequently needed to be re-broke and set again once port was made. Still, it was better than nothing, but she would have given much to have a newer unit throughout that long trip. She was thankful beyond belief that a passenger had even known how to use the old trauma pod. Had they not, and done so quickly, she would have died.

As it was, she would have had no chance at all if she had not somehow blocked a large portion of the blast with her arm. She remembered the pain all the way down to her fingertips, but later learned that almost nothing had remained from below her elbow. The trauma pod had amputated what was left of it once she was stabilized.

Recovery had taken a long time, and longer still to get used to the new arm and hand. It was silly, she knew, but even though the new arm was grown mostly of her own DNA and attached nearly seamlessly, there was something in its bearing that bothered her. It seemed smaller somehow. Perhaps, she thought, it was just the missing scars and calluses.

Anyone looking would see a few small scars that could be found around her elbow if one looked closely for them. *A fresh start*, she called it, but unplanned; very much a reflection of her life right now.

Her midsection was a completely different story, yet she decided to leave the scars as they were. A reminder of the scars to her being that she could never remove. Yet, she did her best to put it all aside so she could get back to her life and her ship as soon as possible.

She had loved working in the Daveri system, but she no longer had the stomach for it. Her heart had died that awful day as well. Her love had fled, saving many of the passengers, yet abandoning her without the slightest word why, or any concern for what happened to her. Her gut would clench unbidden at the mere thought that maybe he had never cared for her at all. At least that is what she had thought for a long time.

It was strange, she hadn't really known how she felt until she woke without him. She had known he had deep feelings for her, at least she had thought he did. Before.

It was much later, when she was called to present her testimony to the courts which had apprehended one of the raiders, that she learned the truth. His story, given weeks earlier, had seen her shot and apparently dead before he had taken as many passengers as he was able and escaped. He was even considered a hero to the passengers he had saved.

She sat through hours of the testimonies of those who had witnessed the attack, yet even though she had talked to many first-hand from the trauma pod, only then did she start to see the truth of how it must have looked. Doubt slowly washed away, only to be replaced with a nagging emptiness tinged with the panic of never seeing that emptiness filled.

As if waiting to confirm her doubts, a shy looking clerk pulled her aside before she had left the courts.

"Miss, excuse me." The woman's eyes look many times older than her face, common for those of many centuries. It served to catch her attention, "Are you the pilot who was injured, one AnnaChi Acosza?"

AnnaChi had an angry retort ready. She assumed this was someone fishing for information, likely to sell to the media, or lawyers of the raider. Credits were credits to many, but she was in no mood for it.

"Yes, yes, I am, and if you think…" she started, stopping abruptly as she saw moisture circling the woman's eyes.

The woman nodded slowly. "Did he find you, or you him? He had thought you dead you know. It's rare to see someone so completely broken, even here. Oh!"

AnnaChi's face must have betrayed her as the woman realized the truth of the matter. Both now had damp cheeks. Composing herself, the clerk continued. "You need to go after him quickly miss, a person like that won't really live again for a long, long time. Trust me miss, I know. He *needs* to know. He said he was leaving, going far away."

"Thank you, sorry," she finally found her voice as the shock faded, "I didn't really know. Well not till…" she trailed off, not sure how to continue.

"Well, you're a fool dear." Her smile betrayed the words. "But then most of us are."

AnnaChi didn't know how she should respond but was wrapped in a warm hug before she could discern what was happening. She smiled, and it was one of her first real smiles in a long time.

Barely making it back to her ship before breaking down, she let out a great sob the moment the hatch slammed shut. AnnaChi had always been a strong hard woman, one that had not had a real tear in her eyes for over a century, till now. At hearing the truth of what happened to Kasey, something broke the walls she had always kept up, and no force of will she possessed could keep the flow of salty anguish from flowing down the curves of her cheeks.

She had searched for him after that, though he was already long gone from the Daveri system.

With hardly a thought, AnnaChi found herself cashing in all her holdings in the system, loading her ship into the first available star-cruiser, and going after him.

It was a lesson in frustration for her. Kasey had apparently moved through several other systems in haphazard fashion. By the time she had reached the third system, one of the queries she had made finally bore fruit. The Daveri office had received a request from a distant system inquiring on Kasey's work history and broke regs to send the info on to her. That was all she needed to know before she was off on the next star-cruiser.

When she had finally caught up to the system he was in, he had already been accepted and placed into stasis aboard a Farpoint project ship, the Abscond.

Spirit crushed with failure, she stormed into the nearest bar and broke the nose of the first idiot that crossed her. It did nothing to shake the black mood that sat upon her. Soon she settled into a dark corner to stay out of further trouble. Losing control was not a trait of hers that she enjoyed. She had always considered it a weakness, one of many she seemed to be accumulating lately.

As the night wore on, the bar seemed to take on an increasingly unappealing musty odor, though she couldn't bring herself to leave. Several conversations about the Farpoint project and the great ship being prepared for departure kept her attention. Some focused on the negative impact to the resident people of the system, most however, were looking forward to the ship's departure.

For the locals, building the Abscond had been an amazing boon for the local economy for many years. Yet now that it was nearly completed, the work and credits it once generated had all but dried up. Some blamed the Terrantine Federation for spending resources on a project that would not benefit the worlds it left behind. Others claimed the price of passage on the ship was far too steep. As an outsider, she kept her opinions to herself. She was proud of Kasey for joining such an expedition, but angry at him for leaving her behind, even if he had no knowledge that she was still alive.

It was late when three rookie pilots had staggered into a nearby booth. They stunk of brothel, weed, and sweat, making her wrinkle her nose further as they passed. Bragging to each other of the new positions they would have once the Abscond reached the Trias system. They had been promised jobs for a distribution company which would, it seemed, be doing its final sign ups tomorrow.

AnnaChi never even finished her drink. She quickly paid two different serving girls an obscene amount of credits to keep the three drinking for free long into the night. Even if they made their morning appointment, they would not be the least bit fresh.

She had just made the biggest decision of her life, one that would change everything she knew and leave an entire life behind. Strange as it was, she was unable to help the smile that crept onto her face as she left.

* * *

Early that next morning, AnnaChi had shown up hours early for the signing. It had been easy. She had her own ship, well documented experience, and plenty of references. None of which any of the rookies had when they eventually turned up. It had been no contest.

She had spent the following days settling her affairs. Relatives would take over her estates in her name, as well as selling several small apartments she kept around the federation. The contents of which would be stored or sold, with the credits going into an account for her in case she ever returned to the Earth Prime cluster. If possible, the credits would be transferred to the Trias settlement. She knew better than to think she would be back, or if she would ever have access to the funds she left behind, but she wasn't one to count out remote possibilities.

It had all been so long ago.

The colony in the Trias system was fifteen thousand light-years away from Federation space. The trip had taken nearly thirty years of travel in stasis, and communication with the federation was now nonexistent. The shear distance and time of the trip was unfathomable to her. Having been in stasis a few times before on jobs, she had been more than a bit concerned. The longer the stasis, the more disorienting experience waking up was, and more dangerous. And this one had been off the charts.

Still, she had accepted it, and now here she was, helping to build the new Farpoint colony by transporting endless loads of supplies down to the planet Belrothi. Yet, she had still not braved contacting Kasey. Kasey, she hoped, would accept her and share her feelings. She loved him, she knew that now, but they had never confessed their feelings for each other.

She had not really known how she felt until she had realized he was gone. Even then, it was more anger at being abandoned, until she learned the truth of why he left. The acceptance was a shock that was only tempered by the fear that the feelings may not be returned.

She was not the kind of woman that showed anyone her emotions, beyond anger. Still, that didn't mean she had none. Now that she was out of stasis and in the same star system with him again, she began to doubt what she thought she knew.

What if he didn't feel the same? What if she had misread their causal relationship?

When they had first met, she appreciated that he had goals, and had some personal quest to be free from Terrantine Federation rule. She had never really understood his beliefs on the subject. The federation was all she had ever known. She had never thought she wasn't free, yet she accepted his views and knew others who felt the same.

Regardless of his ambitions, during their final months together he had been happy and didn't seem to still have the same push to leave that he once had. She fervently hoped the change had been caused by his feelings for her. Regardless, now, halfway across the galaxy, these subtle fears seemed to rush back into real possibilities. She felt like a schoolgirl with her first crush. Young by federation standards, only into her second century, but certainly not a schoolgirl.

Her turn at the reentry window arrived, bringing her thoughts back to the present. Always thrilled by this part of a trip, she loosened her shoulders with a contented sigh and began yet another dive to the surface with supplies for the colony.

"Cintian, seal all compartments and lockdown non-essential systems for reentry."

"*Confirmed.*"

"Let's have some fun!"

Traveling through space, you didn't notice how fast you were going, not like reentry. Entering a planet's atmosphere was amazingly different than anything else; a scary and exciting peril that few other experiences could match.

The first few pops of aerobraking could be felt as she

slammed into the atmosphere, the world growing larger beneath her. Heat membranes did their job, as she was soon cocooned in flame. In just seconds she was through and falling like a rock toward the surface, just how she liked it. There was really no need to enter so hot, but it was so much more fun.

It was over too soon as she engaged the ship's atmospheric thrust. She thrilled at the sudden feeling of blood being pushed out of her head from the positive g-forces. Her smile faded as the feeling dissipated. The dampeners absorbed nearly all the vertical g-forces as she slowed. At the relatively slow atmospheric speeds, most ships would absorb all the extraneous forces, but AnnaChi preferred to feel the forces when she had the ship to herself. Crew and passengers almost never appreciated the sensation.

Heading east to a farming plantation that awaited the excavating equipment she carried didn't take long. They were anxious to start molding the new lands and, she sensed, a bit anxious to see how well the soil here would perform.

The air smells wonderful here, she mused for the seemingly hundredth time as she stepped into the fresh air. Something in the soil, or one of the grasses found all over this region of Belrothi, were what she guessed was the source. One of many things she would have to explore when she had the time. Finding the path to the main warrens, she went looking for a drink while she waited for the Cintian to be unloaded.

Stopping along the way to watch a young girl painting on a canvas, what looked to be the field checkered with native flowers instead of what was really planted there; the test crops.

"Won't they be crops, instead of flowers?" She smiled.

"Yes," the sweet-voiced child responded, "but

someday we will want to remember how we saw this place, where everything started, where we really started. This is how I want to remember our beginning here."

AnnaChi was taken aback by the maturity in the girl. She had not met many children, few existed in the worlds she had worked on. Few citizens living on high population worlds wanted, or were allowed, to have children. They were there for pleasure or work, little else. In a world where everyone was immortal, sort of anyway, having children could be put off for hundreds of years, or longer. The federation discouraged it as well, as rearing the children slowed down the working class.

Most concentrated on building their fortunes, and then moved to the newer worlds where having offspring was encouraged. Some spent hundreds of years trying to make that leap. AnnaChi had never given it much thought. She had a good bit of credits saved, but her goal was always a newer and bigger ship or upgrades for the ones she had, not children. Now however, after nearly dying and losing so much, she saw children as a possibility in her future. She was growing soft, she decided.

She nodded at the child with an understanding smile that she didn't really feel. Moving on, she reached the common area and found what had to be a bar and frowned. The merchant had yet to unpack, everything was still boxed and sealed.

"Sorry miss, it will be another week before I open her up."

She rounded to see a man getting out of a skimmer with a woman. The land skimmer was loaded with buckets of a pink-orange fruit. At her querying glances, he continued. "A native fruit, sour on the outside but sweet in the middle. Here, take one with you," he said with an encouraging smile, as he gave her a practiced once-over. "Pilot eh? Well, come back in a few months and maybe I'll have some wine, whiskey, or other brews for you to transport from this." His smile was infectious.

She was caught off guard at the friendliness of the man, "I may do just that, um ...?"

"Francis, or Mad Fran once you get to know me. This is Flair, my wife for many ages, and hopefully many more." Flair gave her a silent quick wink and moved to unload the skimmer.

"AnnaChi, Captain of the Cintian, and I am at your pleasure," she managed, in a well-practiced manner she had used for decades to gain new business. "I have my own craft, and would be happy to run some transports for you—but I may take trade over credits if your brewing is any good." Lifting one of the fruits that looked healthy she inhaled and smiled. "Not bad. If it tastes as good as it smells," she said, giving the fruit a nod, "I think I will be back to find out how you do; even if you don't require my services."

He smiled at that then tapped his temple several times frowning. Flair laughed and dismissed his frustration. "I logged her ID for you dear," she pointed at her own head, "we must teach you how to use that thing sooner than later!" Turning to AnnaChi, "why don't you give us a hand storing the rest of these, and I will send you off with a basket full."

Nodding eagerly, she spent the next hour moving and sorting the fruit. They called it Toyasow. The fruit was tasty indeed, as both the sour and sweet of the produce were easy on the tongue. She couldn't wait to see what interesting brews it would make. She would definitely be back, she decided.

After sharing a meal and a few beers, she made her way back to the ship. She had several trips yet to make today. This small town in the making was in stark contrast to the normal systems she has worked in. It would be a nice world to live on for a while, even if she was   cut   off   from   the   rest   of   humanity.

CHAPTER TEN

Kasey enjoyed his days working for Darnell on Lithose. Every day was a new adventure; several actually, he thought pleasantly. New mountains to climb or new rivers to follow, depending on the whims of the crew. He found it hard to tell what reasons some areas were searched, but he was learning. Sometimes Darnell would explain his reasoning to the crew, but not always. Kasey picked up what he was able and kept what notes he could.

Time and again he chastised himself for not spending time to really study the art that was prospecting. Researching the latest in prospecting technology had been more exciting and entertaining. But now he realized it could all be useless without knowing where to use all that equipment. It was a tough lesson, and one there was no time to correct now.

The one grain of hope was that no one, not even Darnell, knew Kasey was planning to stake some claims of his own in the mineral game. Though he would not be able to directly use Reavestone's data, he felt he could pick up enough to mimic the findings in other similar areas. Maybe even areas that Reavestone would someday be interested in, but had passed over on these initial trips.

He knew other companies were watching the Reavestone crew's every move, when they could at least. They did the same in return. Darnell had even shown him a massive collection of route maps of the other mining ships they had tracked so far. It was telling. He had been running a tracking program using the ships sensors on every trip, charting the movements of any ships they passed. When in dock, they tagged any ship they saw that even looked like a survey vessel. Before long, the route maps showed where the other companies were charting. Other Reavestone crews pooled their data and met regularly to discuss what it all meant.

Several of the other companies had government supplied raven transports as well, which made the tracking much more difficult. Darnell had him use the stealth systems liberally as they traveled to new zones to survey. They created hot paths, or areas they routinely traveled toward but never actually went to, just to throw off the others watching their movements. It was all a necessary competition Kasey had never known existed on the new worlds he had seen colonized, yet looking back it was always there if he had known enough to look for it. It was evident the new ships completely changed the game.

The stealthy raven transports were amazing to fly, at least at first. He had never flown anything so advanced. His control over the ship was nearly complete. Hands working the controls as thoughts commanded every system to work just the way he needed them to. After a while he realized it had lost the pleasure. It was certainly a powerful feeling to control so much at once, it was interesting, but it had lost its fascination. Perhaps, Kasey thought, it was too easy.

Kasey longed for a ship of his own. A ship he could call home, as the Cintian had been to AnnaChi. He wished he had known what had happened to that old ship. She had loved it more than anything, and he now understood why. She had worked for every repair, every upgrade to that ship. She had kept it alive and flying, and with it herself. It was fitting that she had died on it, he believed she would have wanted it that way.

* * *

The mining crew had placed several claim markers over areas in the region they had settled in for the night. It was a good area, but as yet they had not found a single particle of the fabled n-mats. No other reports of the negative matter had shown up by any team or company on either planet, at least as far as they could tell. No one on the team had given up yet, and there were plenty of other resources that the colony sorely needed.

The surveys were usually a two-week stint, with Kasey running supplies between the teams and helping with aerial mapping surveys. This one had been stretched out nearly double, in hopes that a discovery would be made soon. With so much on the line, now wasn't the time to take a break. As the work became more monotonous, the off hours each day became more robust.

The last few nights the weather was nearly perfect, and the crews started spending the early evenings around large bonfires. The stories told were endless in both volume and depth, and some were simply unbelievable.

Since AnnaChi's death, Kasey had avoided most gatherings, something he had always been uncomfortable with anyway. But being far out here, in lands never touched by humans, he found some measure of peace—even when surrounded by a dozen ruddy miners.

This evening a crisp chill edged the wind as the makeshift camp started sprouting up and the last of the day's equipment was stored. The two small moons appeared and slowly drifted toward the forest-shrouded horizon as Kasey watched. The few responsibilities Kasey had were long over.

Slowly the work finished as the miners drifted in. As usual at the end of the long workday, talk started about how the workdays would be once things settled into a normal pace. The days here were longer than the Earth Prime standard used throughout the federation, at nearly thirty-five Earth-hours. Lithose was the smaller of the two inhabitable planets but rotated just a bit slower.

The opinions were split three ways, with minds changing nearly every night for one reason or another. Some wanted longer nights, while others wanted to split the day into two shifts. Kasey however, preferred the third option of working three very long workdays, with four days to rest in-between. As a pilot, he didn't always work normal hours like the miners would, but he had his own pursuits to think about. Having the time to follow up on them between work days would be a blessing.

It was a moot point for now, everyone in the mining survey crews worked whenever they could until mines were founded and claimed. As always, they were painfully aware that they were not the only teams hunting for the first n-mats deposit to claim, and the search took focus away from searching out the actual materials the colony needed.

The requests for building and fabrication materials were already mounting. Only a few small foundries had been set up so far between the two planets. Kasey was told this was expected, but not understood by many. Setting up plants before truly worthwhile mines could be located would result in too many costly operations, when one large one would suffice and be more efficient. With a finite number of available workmen, having too many small operations was a recipe for failure. They were in this system for the long game, there was no room for failure.

The area they were currently mapping was rich in a few minor metals, promising zinc deposits, and some decent traces of nickel as well. The water sources in the area were optimal, with plenty of available lumber nearby, so if a sizable vein was found the location would go on the short list.

None of the cores they had drilled so far had any trace of n-mats as far as the lab could detect. Some were starting to worry that n-mats were just a fable some management-type cooked up to boost morale. Kasey quite enjoyed watching Sariyn quash any such comments, usually with insults of threats of violence. The interesting thing was, it was not her rude remarks that convinced the miner, just that she was defending the existence of the n-mats was enough. They respected her knowledge enough to take her word for it.

Kasey knew it was more than only Sariyn's gut belief. Eavesdropping on the lab was becoming second-nature to Kasey, the raven made it too easy. It took less than a thought over his mimic interface to access visuals, sound or any other sensor throughout the ship. The only real exception was the crew quarters, the head and the interior room of the self-contained lab itself. Thankfully, more happened out of the lab than inside. While he understood very little of what was said, he knew she and the other techs had started their research by attempting to prove the Trias star system was as normal as any other. He also knew they had found much the same as the Federation scientists had. The star system was wrong.

The most stressful days around the lab followed their realization. None of the other miners went anywhere near the lab techs, not even Darnell if he could help it. The techs were angry, determined and frankly dangerous to be around. Their world had been cracked wide open and they needed to do what they did best—argue about it. The only set of theories that even seemed to satisfy their irritated demeanor was the possibility of a hidden alien megastructures, but that only lasted a day before lack of any other evidence from the considerable system scanning made it unlikely, if not completely ruled out.

Eventually, all agreed, the negative matter was here somewhere. Finding it first would be a historic moment for them. One that would ensure the future of the company that did.

Desperate to begin his own pursuits, Kasey poured over maps of areas they had searched so far. Worrying that his own plans to locate and claim lands with rich mining resources may be harder than he had anticipated. He reminded himself again and again that companies like this one were only looking for the huge scores of resources, and usually only the ones essential for the colony's initial survival, except for the n-mats of course. They were critical to the company itself, and so overruled the colony's need, to an extent anyway. Still, once the initial push had passed, there would be a flood of treasure hunters with plans mirroring his own. Again, Kasey took some comfort knowing his own service was among the few that would both end early, and give him first-hand knowledge of several operation's research thus far. Even with the apparent edge, these thoughts haunted him daily.

His reverie was broken by an excited shout that rang out from Darnell, waving workers to him. A meeting request appeared suddenly on his mimic interface as he started toward the others, but no information was given. Those that had not heard the initial summons were now heading to the meet as well. Just as they started to gather around, another message came in. This message was addressed only to him—he was being recalled to Lithose-Abscond for reassignment. Something was up.

He found out part of it right away as the foreman gave the group the news. A large thorium deposit had been located in one of the southern regions, so the crew was being diverted to start a mine right away. Thorium was the go-to power source for smaller equipment, a source in the new system was desperately needed before many of the factories could even think about coming online. Breaking ground on this thorium mine would solidify contracts for years to come.

The news left Kasey without a job on the crew. The raven transport he currently piloted was basically a loan from the federation, and they were only to be used for n-mats related work. Still, he worked for Reavestone and the summons was likely more work. He made his way back to the transport, lost in thought. The crew would be moving their gear off to standard transports arriving in the morning, and soon after that he would be on his way to the Lithose-Abscond to find out what new plans were in store for him.

* * *

"You about ready to launch?" Darnell's voice boomed with confidence behind him. Kasey had spent most of the morning packing his meager belongings and making sure to offload everything that had been stored in the bays that would be needed by the crew and normal transports that would depart in the morning.

"Just about," he turned, with a list of questions to see if Darnell knew what the plans were for him, but they turned to confusion as the man stood there holding his own belongs. Behind him sat a skiff piled with a seemingly random collection of supplies they had been using to collect samples for testing. It seemed Kasey wasn't the only one being reassigned.

"Coming along for the ride boss?" He asked lightly.

"Well I can't very well let you have all the fun now, can I?"

Dropping his packs, he nodded towards the open bay doors. "Besides, I have seen thorium mines before. Not much to see."

Kasey eyed the gear the skiff carried. "Planning on a side trip?"

"You always were the astute one," a new voice pierced the air as Sariyn strolled up the ramp.

"Kasey, close her up and prepare to dust off." Darnell beckoned Sariyn over to the skiff. "You get this netted and lashed down, we are not hanging around for farewells."

Kasey had the ship purring before he entered the bridge, Darnell trailing close behind.

"So, we heading back to the office or is the new assignment starting early?"

Darnell pulled up a contoured map of the showing all the prospected areas the company had searched so far. Kasey knew it well, having his own version listing areas he planned to scout on his own once he was able.

"Your new assignment has been, um, delayed. I am sure you will receive the orders soon enough. But this," he said as he highlighted a section of the screen, "is where I want to go."

An image spun down into a small valley between two foothills, in an area named the Thorn Back ranges. The small range was the remains of an ancient and worn mountain that still boasted heights up to three thousand meters above sea levels. The foothills were littered with the sharp looking crags that resembled its name. Kasey had flown over the area many times running wide scans of lands further out in the plains at Darnell's request. Now he wondered if the plains had been the true target of those scans.

"So, that's where the stuff is hiding huh? Good idea sending the others off." Keeping a purposely blank expression on his face, Kasey walked off toward the bridge to start the final launch preparations.

He could almost feel Darnell glaring at him for a few moments before following. "We'll see. But for now, take us in another direction, then put this bucket in stealth mode and let's see what we can find."

"You got it. But, why haven't we tried this place before?"

"Company directs, and I follow. Reavestone may not be a large corporation here, but back in the cluster it's one of the bigger boys in the sandbox. Big company mentality is seldom in line with us field workers. This area makes sense to me, but they don't see it, and they issue the credits, so who am I to argue."

"So why now?"

"Same old same old; better to ask forgiveness than permission. This is still company work, but between jobs, so I have some leeway, and if I am right the company only gains. If I am wrong, there is not much loss and maybe they notice some of our dedication, but don't count on that. Besides, there's a large bonus for the crew who finds this stuff first and I am not wasting a chance to secure that."

Kasey just nodded at that, not having heard of the bonus. While not surprising, it was an opportunity he could not afford to miss. Every credit he had or could obtain equaled more time he would be able to rent a shuttle for his own prospecting. Whatever Darnell had planned, Kasey now planned to do his best to help make it work.

While searching for a good landing site, Darnell confided he had been running numbers on the hills along the old mountain for the past few weeks. This valley's numbers didn't quite add up. While that could mean normal gas or oil deposits, Darnell didn't think so. The crags just didn't feel right to him.

"Set us down there!" He pointed excitedly to a tiny clearing with a wall-like cropping that shaded the whole area. Kasey approved of the landing site, not that many others were available in the area. Large twisty trees filled the open areas between the dark up-shoots of rocks that topped every hill. The craft could easily plow down a swath of the trees while landing without a scratch, but that usually made for a dangerous place to wander around in.

Having no ground vehicles, Kasey landed as close as he could to the first testing area Darnell pointed out. For a moment, he wished he had his modified Bard with them, but it was still packed up in cargo bay 748. He smiled, thankful that no one except himself even knew of its existence, or his plans for it.

They wasted no time lugging rock-picks and shovels to the nearest boulders and started chipping away at anything interesting, bringing buckets of various material back to the ship's lab for Sariyn to process. The day wore on as they made their way further and further up towards the jutting rockface that effectively formed a wall that would end their local explorations. Twice, Sariyn reported a possible hit, but more samples from the same material showed nothing, so they marked the spot and moved on.

When they finally approached the rock wall, Kasey was taken aback. What he had thought to be ivy climbing the rockface turned out to be bright-green crystal deposits covering larger seams of clear crystal. Overpowering his desire to touch the gemstone, he turned to ask Darnell if it was safe, but found the man angrily glaring at the crystals.

"Uh, is this bad somehow boss?"

"I'm a fool, if that is what you mean."

Kasey's smile faded. He had no doubt that Darnell knew his minerals, knew what he was looking at and knew that somehow it was the reason the scanner readings had led him to this mountain range. Apparently, it also meant that the n-mats were not here. He could think of nothing to say, except for the obvious.

"Why?"

Darnell pulled the small shovel from his pack and slammed the spaded end into the seam with enough force to send several sizable chunks of crystal flying. Dropping the shovel, he retrieved the largest chunk and held it out for Kasey to take.

"That green formation is pyromorphite, the rest is just basic quartz. The pyromorphite present here means we are likely looking at a lot of lead ore, possibly enough to account for the scan discrepancies. Also, likely why the company didn't send us here already."

"I see. Not what we are looking for then, but it looks, well… I mean, is it worth anything?"

"Worth? No, not to Reavestone, unless the colony finds itself in desperate need of lead, but I believe sufficient quantity has already been located elsewhere. Otherwise, if you're short on credits you may be able to sell enough of these to collectors or knickknack artists to feed yourself for a while."

Kasey examined the crystal he held with wonder for a long moment, until he noticed Darnell looking at him with concern. Clearing his throat, he placed the crystal gently to the side and turned back to the crystal-lined wall of stone.

"Well then," he proclaimed, ignoring Darnell's look, "we had better finish this job and get samples back to

Sariyn, just to be sure."

"Fine, fine, lets get to it," A smile grew on Darnell's face that Kasey could not miss, "you collect samples from the rockface itself, and check that darker outcropping for anything interesting, and I'll collect some worthwhile samples from the pyromorphite here. It appears to have formed in several different formation types, so ill be sure to gather plenty."

"Thank…"

"Get to work," Darnell cut him off, "tomorrow we can scan deeper and see if there is anything worth digging up, then this party is over."

* * *

Kasey rubbed the aches that now radiated from his shoulders to his blistering fingertips. It was late, and the half-eaten food was cooling as he watched Sariyn repeatedly exit the lab, mark off another sample from their dwindling array of minerals, only to collect the next tray and reenter the lab. If a geologist had made a glockenspiel clock, he imagined, this would be it. The trays had been painstakingly laid out to her satisfaction as they had brought each bucket in to ensure she had a good sampling of each mineral type.

When she finally retrieved the tray with quartz and pyromorphite samples, he noticed Darnell sit up straighter and draw in a deep breath. Kasey tried not to show he noticed, yet he felt his heart begin beating loud enough to betray him. If Darnell was interested in the results of the crystals, Kasey realized the man believed it was their best chance of finding n-mats from the day's work. Needing to do something with his own nervousness, he mumbled the need for a fresh drink and stood too fast, tripping partially over the chair on his way. He returned, setting the unopened water bottle on the table and stood waiting.

When Sariyn exited the lab, she stopped as she noticed their peaked interest. Kasey could tell she was deciding if a witty remark would be tolerated or not, then gave a disappointed shake of her head instead and gathered the next sample. Darnell slammed the table and walked away. With nothing else to do but wait for the remaining samples to be tested, Kasey slid back into the chain and resumed rubbing his sore muscles.

It was hard for Kasey to be overly disappointed. If the crystals had shown signs of n-mats, he would have lost the three extra buckets of the stuff that Darnell had hand-picked for him, and the credits they would bring him eventually. Yet, he had been, and still was excited as anyone over the possibility of finding n-mats for Reavestone and what it would mean for the crew's percentages if it was worth as much as everyone thought. Sure, the day had been a lot of work, work he wanted to see pay off, but it was also a welcome change from watching the mining crews or hauling equipment around the sites for them. He always tried to keep busy and interested in their work, but most of the time he was just waiting around for the next delivery. Today had been a welcome change.

Three more trays went into the lab before Darnell returned and threw himself back into a chair. Sariyn came out soon after and stopped in front of the sample table reading something on it, then grabbed a fresh tray and went over to the buckets of material the samples had been pulled from and filled the tray.

Kasey and Darnell were out of their chairs, intercepting her before she could go back into the lab. Before they could question her, she wheeled on them.

"Where did these samples come from?"

Darnell looked but shrugged and looked at Kasey. Picking up a piece, Kasey examined the flaking rock.

"This is from that outcropping that goes up towards the rock wall, it's mostly flat layered pieces like this."

She snatched it back with a smirk, replacing it onto the tray before rubbing a hand across her shaved head. "Well, you lucky son of a bitch!"

Without another word, she was back through the lab door, leaving them both standing and staring at the closed door.

After a few minutes of waiting and another few of Darnell pounding on the door for an explanation that was only returned in curses that made Kasey blush, they went over to the bucket and examined the rocks themselves. It was a useless effort, they were rocks. Pure and simple, as far as either of them could tell.

When she finally emerged again, they were both waiting with arms crossed in front of them.

Laughing at them both, and shrugged and held up a tablet showing graphs and numbers, "Eureka?"

They looked at each other for several long minutes, exhaustion and pain forgotten.

Darnell shook himself free and started giving orders.

"Break out the hammer-drill Sariyn, we can take a few cores as well as larger samples for corporate. Kasey, grab the seismic scanner, it's the yellow backpack. We will get a bigger one in here, but that should tell if we are looking at the proverbial tip of the iceberg."

"Well it's definitely not the same as the exposed bedrock we see in the mountain samples you brought back," Sariyn interjected, "but flyover scans show similar materials dotting the higher ridges of the Thorn Back."

"What percentage of n-mats are we looking at?"

"Not much, the samples are holding around one point six one thousandth."

"Really? Huh," he paused and seemed to consider the number. "Interesting. Well, unless this runs deep, we'll need several operations running if we want to pull useful amounts."

"Right you are Darnie, shall we place a claim marker?"

"Yup, I'll drop it myself. Let's grab some stims, there won't be any sleep tonight. I want this in the office before business opening tomorrow. What's that give us?"

"About four hours," Kasey chimed in, glad to have some part in the conversation.

"It's doable. Sariyn, help us hoof the equipment up there and then you get back here and run the remaining samples we have here, but make sure you save time enough to run at least one of the cores we pull. What else?"

"Light. The raven can direct a good bit to light up the hill, but it won't be enough. We will have a lot of shadows even if I dial up the brightness. The emergency closet has light-strips we can affix to our clothing and gear, unless you want to break out some balloon lights?"

"Nope, we are on a timeline, the light-strips will work for what we need, and I have a headlamp too, but just one. Let's get this done people!"

CHAPTER ELEVEN

Returning to Lithose-Abscond, they requisitioned a small freight skiff in the docking bay and headed straight to the Reavestone offices, with the n-mats in tow. The first stop were the company's testing labs to drop off the samples. They found the labs empty. Kasey noted the concerned look on Sariyn's face as she opened doors looking for anyone at all.

As they started back out the doors to find someone that could help, they were surprised by a small crowd of stone-faced government suits walking in, the Reavestone board members in tow. None looked particularly happy with the government's presence.

Mr. Cedrick, the chairman came forward, pointing at the samples on the cart, "So, we found it then?" He continued without waiting for an answer, "I understand the source area was appropriately claimed?"

Kasey nodded dumbly with the others, baffled that the discovery was common knowledge among those present. No one should have known, no one had been told. Sharing a look, they realized the only logical explanation was the government raven transport ship itself. The ship's system must have automatically relayed all the data directly back to the government.

They had all been duped. The federation had planned to control the n-mats in every way from the beginning. It made a sick sort of sense looking back at all the support they had been given, but it was apparent that most in the room were as shocked as he was.

A suited man Kasey did not recognize spoke suddenly from the back of the group, interrupting whatever Cedrick was about to say, "Excellent work Mr. Darnell." As he moved forward, he stated dryly, "We appreciate your resourcefulness in this effort. You have, once again, served your federation well."

At the comment, Kasey sensed Darnell stiffen, something about the comment apparently striking a sharp nerve. A sudden indrawn breath revealed something more. *Perhaps Darnell knows the speaker*, thought Kasey.

The man briefly looked back at the others and shook his head slightly, "However, this discovery must remain secret for the foreseeable future. These men will take custody of your samples, and your silence is mandated under oath by the federation." Slowly he peered into the eyes of everyone present until a nod of acceptance was garnered. "If, and when, the existence of negative matter becomes public knowledge, the oath will be lifted and credit for the discovery will, of course, be granted to Reavestone Mining company."

Darnell just stood there, staring into empty space. There was nothing worth saying, and nothing anyone could do to change the situation.

"Pilot Kasey Robinson, it seems your assistance was crucial in this effort as well. I understand that you are relatively new to the Terrantine Federation, however you are also mandated to secrecy and you are required to sign oath documents before leaving this room. We thank you for your continued assistance." Clearing his throat and stepping back, he waved Cedrick to continue with his previous conversation.

Stammering a bit, the chairman eventually spit out, "Planning sessions will begin tomorrow morning. Darnell, you will remain the lead of the team we will put together for this effort. We can discuss what that means tomorrow as well."

About half the group left at that point. Darnell gave Kasey the briefest nod before regaining his stoic demeanor and leaving, and Sariyn was right behind him. The next several hours for Kasey however, were filled with personal inquirers from the various government men, and paperwork.

* * *

The next few months flew by at astronomical speeds for Kasey. Several small, but fully operational, n-mats mines across the planet were soon producing enough to keep him and a handful of other Reavestone pilots busy transporting the refined material. Everything went to a few mine bases that had built special storage areas for the material. Most assumed that all the n-mats would eventually go to the navy, as they were the only client that knew the stuff existed. It was a bitter controversy for the few who knew, but as long as the credits were good, no one took the risk of complaining. This was exactly the kind of control his parents had always fought against.

No one seemed to know what the federation wanted with the n-mats, but the most popular assumptions were that they were sending small ships filled with it heading back to the federation, or were preparing the Abscond for a return trip. From that point, the conspiracies ranged anywhere from military use, to using it to trade for advanced alien technologies.

He did not see Darnell often over that time. The last time they talked, Darnell had been asking questions about which officers were checking in on the cargo deliveries. He seemed curious about the ships or material transfers. Strangely, most questions were about topics he already should know the answers to. Kasey simply put it all down to more theories and speculation on what the n-mats were being used for. He could not care less. To him, it was simply a means to his future.

His future hopes cluttered his mind as he made his way across cargo bay 748 to his own container. The bay was nearly empty now that most the cargo had been moved to the surface. His would remain here for now. Being the engine segment, many assumed it would eventually make a return trip. If, or when that time came, he would need to decide to stay or go. A decision that, he believed, was totally dependent on his next few months here.

For now, he planned to leave Reavestone after his contract ended, which was not long from now. Once he did, he still planned to test for n-mats when he could, but it was no longer his main goal. It was now clear that the government would ruin his livelihood if he found any, and he was not so certain it was the best goal for himself.

The realization that the government was more controlling than ever here, even this far from the federation, forced away the idea that he would be able to find freedom. Maybe, he thought, it would still work out the way he had envisioned, but that would be many, many years away. Perhaps when the colony started pushing further out from this system.

Shaking off his disgust of the situation, he came to the realization that this was a good thing for him. The decision not to look for n-mats on his own solved a crucial issue—he had never found a way to test for it. With the deposits around the mountain being nearly identical, there was little reason for the lab to be used at all. No reason for techs to even be aboard, let alone discuss other testing techniques. Even searching for other sources of n-mats had stopped, as far as he was aware, and until there was a reason to actively test material again, he would not be learning anything new.

He knew the existing scanning equipment on the Bard would find worthwhile minerals. Minerals which he hoped would bring enough wealth to either keep him separated from the federation's clutches or find a way to return to the regions of Earth Prime clusters not yet under federation control. He would always find another option if this failed, that was one of the luxuries of staying young forever after all. Finding a way without being controlled was another thing altogether.

Today though, he had an appointment in his quarters aboard the Lithose-Abscond station. That was the price of immortality—a single appointment a year. The catch was always the cost, a cost that was paid in allegiance to the Terrantine Federation. It was one he still hoped to find a way out of someday.

When he entered his room, the wall was already folded out into a medical table with several arc shaped sensors and other devices all around. With an audible sigh, he undressed and positioned himself onto the soft rubbery table. As soon as the sensors detected that he was ready, the bedding softened dramatically, sinking his body about half way down. Pressure could be felt at several spots as jets delivered medications. The light panels around the room darkened, and just seconds later, it seemed, he woke up. The bed firmed as the lights slowly brightened. The procedure was over, and nearly three hours had passed in a blink.

He made his way to a seat and drank some water

from the bottle he had set out before the ordeal. Turning, he casually noticed the table was now gone, only the wall remained. A message flashed on his mimic interface from the doctor who oversaw the procedure from the medical bay. Everything went well, and his next procedure could be scheduled at a planet-side medical center of his choice in about one year.

Another year over. One-hundred and one non-stasis years old, and still so much to learn, he thought to himself. At least he looked and felt as if he was still in his twenties, even his mind felt young and ready to learn. If it was not for all the memories, he wouldn't know the difference. Where would he be in another hundred years? Wondering didn't help much, as he well knew. Even short-term plans could, and most likely would, change a thousand times over before the next decade passed by.

Kasey did, however, have designs on the next few days and he was eager to get started. Now that he had some time off, he planned to use it well. Using the few credits he had, he secured usage of a small transport for the next three days. He had arranged to have his Bard, still sealed in its container, moved to the docking bay this morning. Filling a pack with food and a few meager supplies, he left to catch a tram-pod to the awaiting transport.

CHAPTER TWELVE

The Bard scout vehicle, small as it was, filled nearly a quarter of the cargo bay on the small transport he was renting for the day. The ship was old, had outdated controls, and most importantly was cheap to rent which suited Kasey's needs perfectly. Storing his gear and checking prelaunch procedures, he whistled an old ditty as he worked. It didn't take long before he was humming down into the upper atmosphere of Lithose.

He had been scanning maps long before the n-mats discovery, and even prior to the Lithose-Abscond crew's planet-fall, but that was all old data now. Instead, he brought up the map of unclaimed lands and picked the ones least occupied to start searching. He made special efforts to avoid areas he knew the Reavestone Mining company had previously scanned. There was no doubt that the government was watching all the company's activity very closely now.

He settled the small transport on top a hillock covered with patches of turquoise-shaded bushes. The landing was rough. He wanted to blame the old ship, but realized it was more about how spoiled he had been in the newer, raven class ships which could practically landed themselves. The view from the hill was amazing towards the south, with tall mountains far in the distance and sporadic pools of water dotting the lands between. So many colors painted the landscape, pulling the eyes to examine each.

Kasey suddenly felt a pang of guilt. This world, and every other in the Trias system, was soon to be overrun with humans. This system would, in time, become the nexus of an ever-growing number of systems in this region. There would not be a meter of untouched land left, the beauty would be gone. For now, though, it was a magnificent sight.

With the Bard loaded with supplies, he wheeled out onto the soft turf, then proceeded to spend much more time than planned to get used to how it handled. The jump jets were archaic compared to anything Kasey had encountered as a pilot, although he understood these were standard designs. He had completely ignored the training simulator, which he now realized was a mistake.

Aptly named, when the craft jumped, the thrusters gave a kick that stayed with you until you landed, and the sound it made was awesome. It literally sang through the air on a worthy, if unchanging, tune.

The first time he had a chance to really use the jets, the valley he was exploring ended in a tight gully which appeared to have a plateau higher up. There was no obvious path that the Bard could take to reach it; exactly the kind of scenario the machine was built to overcome. Setting the initial jump to maximum hover, he tightened his open helmet and immediately executed the procedure. Nearly swallowing his tongue as the craft sprang upwards, he was slammed deep into the springy seat as his ears were filled with an army of violins slowly drawling out a long G note.

Once it leveled off into a high hover, he was glad no one was around to see the panicked expression that he was sure he wore. His screens now displayed a quickly shrinking map of possible landing sites the Bard still had time to land on during this jump, and several were marked as optimal sites. Choosing one further up the hill, it took him to it in the most efficient means possible, which to his estimation was a lot more like falling then flying. Tilting slightly away at the last moment, it landed and gently rocked forward as it touched ground.

Kasey sat there for many moments as his heart calmed. He was a skilled and experienced pilot of many crafts, but this small ground vehicle had made him feel like a novice again. Laughing out loud, he stomped his feet with joy. Damn, but he felt young! With a sigh, he realized it was time to get moving and check out the area.

Before he could get a look around, a flash of bright orange crossed his vision. One of the meter-tall native birds landed on a boulder nearby and chirped impatiently at his vehicle, as if expecting a response. The rusty orange creature did not budge when Kasey opened the craft's translucent panel for a better look. It appeared just as curious as Kasey felt.

It leapt and glided to a closer rock, tilting its nearly saurian head back and forth as it inspected him. What he had thought were only feathers now appeared to be a nearly even mixture of scales and feathers with a good amount of fur covering the areas where they overlapped. The wing's ridges along with other sensitive areas, including a strip from the creature's head all the way down the spine to its tail, appeared to have leathery scales as protective covering. One wing's ridge was mostly missing, perhaps torn off in a fight. He didn't remember hearing of any predators in this area, but that didn't mean they did not exist.

Unlike most avians he had seen, this one had four powerful looking legs ending in vicious claws that seemed to take turns flexing as he watched. All four, as well as the tail and long neck, were covered in scales that matched the orange color of the feathers perfectly.

"Hey there tough guy," Kasey said, more to calm his own nerves than in a greeting.

The creature clicked once, then edged closer, scrutinizing the vehicle with each step. Every so often it cast a penetrating glance toward Kasey, issuing a whistle or chirp as if giving its opinion of the machine.

Fully knowing it was not recommended to feed the native life until the agricultural teams could evaluate everything, he tossed a corner of his ration bar to the animal. The morsel had barely cleared the Bard's frame when it was snatched out of the air in an orange flash.

"Enjoy my lunch, orange one. Have I passed your inspection?" he asked, as it swallowed the piece whole.

Giving a low whistle, it paused to look back at Kasey again. He could almost feel the swirling blue eyes of the creature questioning him.

Closer now, he noticed that the wide, beak-like upper lip came to a wicked tip that curled inward. What raised his eyebrows though were the sets of deadly canines behind it. Perhaps *this* was the predator of the region, he thought.

The penetrating look ended with a final chirp, then it took off suddenly, snatching a bug out of the air, before swooping away faster than he would have thought possible for such a large creature. He watched as it flew towards the ridge where he himself was heading, losing sight of it against the reddening sky.

"Sunset?" he muttered to himself at the strange color of the sky.

The time popped up, showing it was only a bit after noon for the planet. "What the hell?" Before he got a handle on what he was seeing, a bright flashing message started to rapidly flash across his upper vision.

ATTENTION—UNKNOWN ATMOSPHERIC CATASTROPHIC EVENT IN PROGRESS—REMAIN CALM AND SEEK IMMEDIATE SHELTER

It was then that he saw the ribbons of flame streaking from the heavens. A brilliant flash winked twice, hearkening a steady increase of flaming trails. Something was hitting the atmosphere, and hard.

There were thousands of cameras and sensors that anyone could access inside and outside the Abscond, but Kasey was unable to connect to any of them. In fact, he could not connect to any nodes from the orbital ship at all.

Quickly pulling up the Bard's jump interface and noting it was fully recharged, he selected a destination in the direction of his transport. He barely noticed the jump this time, even though he faced away from the destination for most if the jump. Micro thrusters spun him around to face forward and he concentrated on finding a quick path back to the hillock his small transport was on.

He used the jump jets twice again to save time, the sky turning from red to nearly black. The moment he reached the transport, a thunderous boom echoed across the nearby valleys as a great fireball shuttered out of the blackness and brightened the landscape as if it was a small sun.

He knew of only one thing that large in orbit; the Lithose-Abscond station, with its massive antimatter generator and engines. They were built to withstand nearly anything, but smashing into a planet was not a contingency that could really be planned for. If the containment chambers were to be breached… He was unable to finish the thought, no comparisons came to mind. It was beyond any scope he could imagine.

He had the transport lifting off before the loading bay was even sealed, and headed for the deepest valley he thought he could get to before the great star-cruiser's engines impacted the planet. Once there, he headed for the largest lake he could find and dove the transport down into the depths, slamming into the thick muddy bottom. Once settled, he activated every safety system the old ship had and strapped a rebreather over the opening of the helmet he still wore, just in case.

Then everything went black.

CHAPTER THIRTEEN

The Cintian shot out of the Belrothi-Abscond station's bay at breakneck speed. She knew it would earn her severe fines when she returned, but she didn't care. The station's docking bays had been closed for nearly two weeks since the attacks. The current bay had contained two multi-system star-cruisers that were destroyed along with several other nearby ships.

AnnaChi, along with dozens of other ship captains, had maintained a constant protest against the guards who had kept all "unauthorized" personnel out of the bay for the first week. They were only allowed back into the bay after agreeing to assist in the remaining cleanup effort and to check their own ships, now that the initial investigation was over.

Soon after, the reports started trickling in about the loss of contact with Lithose and the Lithose-Abscond station. Speculation ran rapid until survivor transmissions began to come in with waves of the awful news. It was plain to everyone that the government had been heavily filtering information at first, but that did not last.

News finally broke that the Lithose-Abscond's station had somehow been destroyed along with most of the planet Lithose. The latest reports told that the massive engine that had brought the great ship across the galaxy had crashed into the planet. Lithose itself was now a doomed, or possibly already dead, planet, and there was little hope to be had for its survival. It didn't take long for full blown fear and hysteria to be everywhere. Distrust or grief was on every face. AnnaChi however, was plain angry.

Her anger was not directed at the apparent terrorists, but at herself. She had always prided herself on being fearless, yet she realized her fear had controlled her actions over the past months. She knew where Kasey was and could have contacted him at any time, but deep down she was afraid he would reject her. It gave her reason to delay. Excuses were easy as she truly did have commitments with the settlement of Belrothi and the company she had signed up with. But she realized she could have found a way.

What if he had known she survived, but had already moved on? she would ask herself, knowing it was an excuse. Worse yet, she had thought he may see her as weak. The embarrassment of her acting like some spoiled youngster, running after imagined love, was enough to make her want to take a one-way trip out the nearest airlock.

The anger she felt now was because she realized she had been wrong to fear, and now he may have been killed without ever knowing she had lived, or even how she felt about him. If he was dead now, she knew she would never forgive herself.

The moment the bay was deemed open for departures, she wasted no time in setting Cintian on a course toward Lithose at max speeds. A fleet of automated assistance pods had been launched days ahead of her that would be blasting transmissions as they locked on and docked with any incoming crafts. She hoped word of Kasey's whereabouts could be found quickly if he had survived, though there was little chance of the pods encountering many of the survivor's crafts; there simply were not enough.

AnnaChi weaved through the pod's transmissions like a maze. Intercepting any crafts with unknowns or dead aboard so that she could to give herself peace of mind one way or another. So far, she had found nothing of Kasey's situation.

CHAPTER FOURTEEN

Kasey woke to darkness and pain.

The safety harness bit into him as the craft listed far to port and seemed to hang there. He gripped tightly onto the armrest to ease the pressure the straps were placing on his injuries and tried to get his bearings. He breathed a sigh of relief when the ship slowly began tilting back towards an upright position but started to panic when that movement increased rapidly until the ship was leaning nearly forty-five degrees to starboard. It did not stop there, but the momentum slowed considerably as pain erupted from apparent injuries along his right side. It was a slow and agonizing wait for the ship to begin shifting back again towards the port. A fishing boat in a hurricane would have been a treat in comparison.

He didn't need light to know he was covered in bruises from the safety harness. The ship was about to roll towards opposite side again as it had been since he had woken enough to notice. Gritting his teeth, he cried out in pain as his body slipped from one side of the chair to the other. The straps had worked loose from the constant motion, yet he was glad they had not broken completely free in the explosion's shockwave of destruction that must have been enough force to push the lake around the way it was. He didn't want to imagine what would have happened to the ship if he had been on land. Surviving that would not have been a question.

With the ship listing dangerously to port again, he reached out through his agony and switched on the docking stabilizers. Instantly, the movement settled enough that he was no longer in danger of being slowly thrashed to death. Finding another working system, the lighting panels winked on quicker than his eyes could adjust. He was surprised to find little noticeable bridge damage.

It took a few more uncomfortable moments before he could reset and activate the main stabilizing thrusters and inertia dampeners. The movement finally stopped, at least per the sensor readings. To him, everything still moved in a swimming motion he could not shake. Ignoring the room, he was finally able to unstrap himself from the helm. One step away and he found himself on his knees vomiting. Having no time to properly recover, he stumbled to the engineering consoles and quickly checked the systems.

It appeared that most systems had survived. The few critical circuits not responding were listed as *regenerating*. That gave him pause. It was a wonder the ancient ship even had self-repairing circuitry. It was an old, mostly standard, technology, but he had seen several ships without them over the years. It would be astonishing if the connections fully repaired themselves, but he hoped it would be enough to get him to safety.

His best guess was that the damaged systems would be back online in a few hours at most, unless they were too damaged. He wasn't sure he would have that long, but it would have to do. The communications were down as well, but he wasn't too concerned, with the interference the blast must have caused it was not surprising.

With no idea where or how far away the impact had been, his options would be limited. Once out of the lake, he needed to get as far from the impact site as possible and stay out of the radiation spikes he assumed would be everywhere. Flying low and keeping out of the direct line of site of the impact may help, but he honestly was not sure how much. The sensors did not show any critical radiation issues in his current location, but he knew that could quickly change once he exited the lake and this valley.

A warning alert drew his attention, the lake temperature was rapidly rising. The blast had caused a cascade of geological events. He shook the last of the dizziness away and frowned. Whatever the cause of the temperature change, he understood that he needed to move quickly.

The thrusters fired, lifting the old transport out of the lake, and into a black-snow calmness that was horrifying to behold. Radiation was high and climbing, but he was safe for the moment. Below, the screens showed the lake swirling as if it was a glass of wine in the lake bed. Devastation was evident everywhere as far as he could see.

The sky was unnaturally dark even beyond the snow-like ash, but most disturbing was the appearance of bright lava pools beginning to dot the land. No tree still stood on the hills, and many of the fallen trees and other plants were aflame. A major upheaval of volcanic activity was taking place. A chain reaction that would assuredly cause the entire planet to suffer in time.

Setting a flight plan that would keep him low to the ground, he set off in the opposite direction from the crash. At least, as best as he could determine. He hoped the lower altitudes would be safer from the radiation that had permeated the atmosphere, but there was no way to know how much fallout he would be flying through. If he was lucky, he would reach a safe distance without being exposed to lethal levels of radiation. Fumbling, he quieted the rad sensors that had started screeching the moment he rose out of the protective water. The hull would protect him for a while, he hoped.

Unable to concentrate clearly, he had no idea how long or far he traveled before escaping the radiated area. His mimic interface was not connecting to any network hubs, even though the communication circuits showed normal. There should have been several satellites well away from the blast. He set a looping distress signal to send, hopping a relay or satellite could be reached eventually. With nothing he could do about it, he continued onward in hopes of picking up a signal somewhere.

Eventually the sky began to lighten as he moved from the ash covered region, yet before he could enjoy that small comfort, a dark column appeared on the horizon directly in front of him. Slowing for a better look, his gut wrenched at the devastation he saw. The settlement had been a small one, maybe a few thousand people, yet no structure now remained standing.

Spotting a small group of people huddled around a group of skimmers, he adjusted course. Once spotted, they started waving wildly and he had no choice but to try to help. He knew, even if they didn't, that they wouldn't survive long once the growing ash cloud reached them with the radiation.

He landed close by and they immediately gathered around with questions on their faces, many were wounded. He opened the bridge's upper hatch and climbed out, placing himself far above the crowd below. He gave them no answers but could plainly see they were loading the skimmers with all the supplies they could scrounge. He didn't know where they planned to go and didn't care. This rock was done for, and by their faces they knew it, but they also knew they needed to do something.

There wasn't much hc could say as they quieted and looked at him expectantly, "This world is dead." The words came much more sternly then he intended. "The black clouds you see are highly radiated and coming this way. Soon, nothing will survive here. We need to make for Belrothi," pointing to the skimmers he continued, "load all the food and supplies you can in the aft bay, we may need several weeks' worth."

It seemed all of them began to argue and shout questions toward him. He knew he should be overwhelmed by it all, knew he should be angry, but none of it mattered to him now. With resolve, he turned his back on them. Turning instead to watch as the black clouds slowly grew. The talking soon slowed to a whisper, followed by a deadening silence.

When he turned back to them, he saw nothing but tears of defeat. "We leave here in ten minutes." He could see they understood the words were final as he headed back down the hatchway to prepare.

He quickly sealed the Bard back in the crate and locked it. He didn't have much else, but what he did have was quickly locked into the small pilot's quarters near the bridge. Placing a small plasma pistol in his jacket pocket, he made his way to the loading hatch. The refugees didn't look like trouble, but he would never take that chance again. Not since losing AnnaChi.

When he opened the hatch, eleven people, no twelve, he corrected as he saw a small baby held close by a mother, were busy moving the skimmers near the hatch to be loaded.

The ship had three small rooms, as well as an extra head down on the cargo deck. Most walls could be folded out as tables or beds as needed, but they were in disrepair. Storage racks and seats could also fold out of the floor as needed. It wouldn't be comfortable and had never been meant for extended space travel for so many, but it would do. It would have to do.

Other than the pilot bunk, the bridge deck had one room that could be set up as private quarters if needed. He hesitated more than he would admit before offering it to the mother and child. He would rather remain alone and sealed off from the others in the bridge deck area. Children however, were unique in his experience, and he felt they should be protected. He hadn't seen many kids on Lithose, but he knew most every family that came on the Farpoint colony planned to have children. Most would have several. He wasn't about to risk what may be the last surviving child on Lithose for anything.

The cargo bay, as well as every other open floor space, was packed before Kasey closed the loading hatch. There was a lot more stuff than they needed, but he wasn't going to tell the group that. They had brought their entire lives and families halfway across the galaxy, only to have it utterly destroyed. Besides, it wasn't a lot of mass, the ship was rated to haul far more. Who was he to tell them the little they had saved was mostly common and replaceable items of no worth? Let them hold onto what they could.

The dark clouds had moved noticeably closer and all were anxious to be gone, yet dreaded to leave their dead loved ones. He tried not to notice when he heard talk of how many had died or been left under the rubble. The black snow, the ash, would bury them all.

Continuing the previous flight path, he found only one other survivor with an overturned skimmer nearby. He had a broken leg, but the group managed to get him aboard quickly. Before long they were over the southernmost ocean, and he felt it safe enough to try for orbit. With all systems now showing stable, there was no reason to delay. He only hoped the old ship would hold together.

As everyone found a place to strap in, he warned them all about the damage the transport had taken from the initial blast. No one said a word, simply followed his directions or sat, unable to do more than stare off, obviously in shock. Checking the comm one last time, he found nothing again. With a shrug, he increased thrust and headed for orbit.

He laughed as he broke through the planet's magnetosphere, and the thrusters successful transitioned out of atmospheric mode. Apart from some truly huge magnetic waves rolling around, which he had done his best to avoid, the ruins of Lithose quickly became a small dot in the distance. All the systems seemed to check out except for comms and some redundant sensors. That surprised him a bit with all the trauma the craft had absorbed, but he was not one to question such good luck. Slowly he relaxed and set the ship's trajectory for a path that would take them towards Belrothi. He would need to refine it later into the nearly three-week journey, but it would do for now. The trajectory showed clear for days of travel, so he locked it down and limped toward the pilot's quarters in search of a nap, only to be intercepted by the mother. She introduced herself as Yaran and insisted he allow her to examine his wounds and to apply pain easements. Kasey didn't have the energy to refuse, and was asleep before she finished.

CHAPTER FIFTEEN

Having not intercepted any new messages in nearly a day, AnnaChi's hopes faltered. It appeared that most survivors who could leave the planet had already passed her, and well on their way to Belrothi.

She drifted toward the dead planet for another week before the planet came into view. The view was shockingly beautiful and terrifying, as deep black and gray swirls rolled through the once clear atmosphere. Switching spectrums showed half the main landmass aglow with heat. The world had been cracked open like an egg. Nothing moved.

Fresh tears rolled down her cheeks unnoticed as she searched repeatedly for the signature of Kasey's, mimic interface but nothing was showing.

Hope kindled briefly, as small pockets of life signs began to appear alongside rescue pod's beacons scattered along the planet's southern hemisphere. One by one she eliminated each finding. Spending hours doing her best to communicate with the survivors through the stormy atmosphere and searching every active transmission source for some sign of Kasey in the area, she again found nothing. She was glad the survivors would be taken care of, if they could be. The pods would soon launch the survivors into a retrieval orbit where the recue ships that deployed them were waiting. She wished them luck, but for now, she needed to move on with her search.

After staying in orbit for days, she slowly came to realize that he may truly be gone. It was even possible he had been onboard the Lithose-Abscond during the attack, he could have been anywhere for that matter. She knew he was assigned to a mining crew and hoped they were working planet-side when the disaster struck. All reports she had intercepted were from ground-based craft. It didn't take any additional details to know that none aboard the Lithose segment of the Abscond had survived. The saboteurs had been efficient in their work.

Eventually a wave of rescue ships came through, with fresh list of survivor's names. She gave up soon after, knowing there was now nowhere left to search. The pods had long finished finding the survivors planet-side, and habitations had been set up until arrangements could be made for their evacuation. She checked all the reports and findings one last time, before setting a course back to Belrothi. It was over.

She watched as the planet began to fade from view. Frustrated, she smashed her favorite mug against the Cintian's hull and turned to find something else to destroy. As if sparked by her actions, a small blip appeared at the far edge of her screens and then disappeared. She stopped, and it felt as if the entire universe stopped with her. The blip abruptly appeared again, this time staying on the board.

A ship, based on the reading, coming from an area of space that showed only emptiness. Moving so slow that it would take weeks to even reach Lithose. Why any craft would be there, or on such a slow heading was beyond her. Perhaps it was damaged.

Altering course to intercept the blip, her heart gave a

single erratic thump that caught her off guard. Her subconscious sped ahead of her own thoughts. She searched for any sign or signal to identify the craft, but found none that gave up any clues.

CHAPTER SIXTEEN

The jolt shocked the slumbering group into a semi-wakeful state. The meds had been necessary to obtain the partial sleep-like coma that allowed them to ration the remaining air. Kasey's eyes leapt to the environmental station display but it still showed in the green, if barely. He was deciding if he could trust the readings the failing system was reporting, when another jolt shook the ship. Meteorite?

No, I know that sound!

Calling up another screen showed the bay's docking clamps being activated manually, from the outside. Another system failure or are we being boarded? Almost casually he flipped the controls to pressurize the bay hoping the system could handle the added load.

The old transport had been undergoing a cascade of system failures since escaping the doomed planet. While most systems appeared to be running efficiently based on the system checks, in reality they had been catastrophically failing for some time. He assumed the system cores were failing somehow, but had no way to tell for sure.

When the main thrusters blew apart with no warning, they lost any chance of making it to Belrothi.

Communications were dead and showed to be missing completely. He could only guess that the external comm array was somehow torn off when the thruster exploded. Their only chance now was to head back to Lithose's orbit and hope rescue would arrive in time. They realized later that the thruster explosion had changed their trajectory far off from either planet.

Kasey had rigged the small maneuvering thrusters to give an almost continuous, if small, thrust. It would eventually reverse their course and get them back to Lithose, but it would be slow going.

Currently most of the refugees were crammed into the small room he had originally given to the mother and child. Yaran and the baby girl now occupied the pilot's quarters with Kasey.

The child was too young to be put under the sleeping meds, and the room she now occupied with her mother was the best chance she had to survive. They had sealed off the common areas and cargo bay to conserve air and energy by allowing the bay's recyclers to be shut down, in case they were needed later. They hoped the last bit of life in the ship would not be affected by the issues plaguing the rest of it, but there was little they could do regardless.

Slowly, Kasey moved to the desk chair, entering a quick code while doing so. A panel sprung open revealing several adrenaline sprays. Holding one to his neck he waited for the expected energy just as another jolt shook the craft, causing him to drop the spray. Two more jolts caused him to clench his teeth as he retrieved and used the adrenaline to negate his sleepy state.

He had not gone under the same partial coma as the others. Someone needed to be more alert in case additional issues arose. Instead he had used some simple sleeping meds to reduce the strain on the ships failing systems.

Taking up a rebreather just in case, he noted it was the same one he had used during his escape from Lithose. Belting on the pistol that was now never far from his side, he stood and moved to the hatchway. Stopping only to check in on Yaran and the baby, both apparently awakened from a nap by the noise. Yaran shot him a worried look as she prepared a bottle for the babe, Cerine. He tried to return with a comforting smile but was sure it came off more like a grimace.

"We hopefully have some company. The bay is pressurizing now if you need anything from there but take a portable scanner and test the air as you go."

He was soon down in the cargo bay and could hear a steady thumping coming from the docking hatch. None of the external cameras seemed to be working in this area, nor was the old ship built with transparent-capable metals like newer ships were. As he examined the hatch, the pressure indicator switched from red to green. Picking up a hammer, he gave the hatch two solid knocks and was immediately answered by three in return. Swallowing hard, he checked the pressure gauge a final time then released the seal, allowing the hatch to spiral open as he stood back as the cool fresh air from the attached ship flowed into the bay.

The dark helmeted figure stepped through, dropping a large wrench with a clang, drawing his attention. Something was familiar, but too out of place for him to grasp. A gasp escaped him as he realized he knew the ship entryway behind the figure. Knew its marred walls, knew the scratches adorning the hatchway itself. It couldn't exist here. He had left it, and her, fifteen thousand light-years away. Lost with the happiest years of his life.

Certain now it wasn't real, he shook his head and tried to clear the hallucination away or wake up. Dreaming. Asleep and still waiting for rescue.

Yet the dream before him didn't melt away. The figure staggered back, seemingly as shocked as he was. Gloved hands physically shook as they removed the helmet, revealing jet-black hair pulled back into a curly mane and large green eyes staring at him in concern. A woman only his dreams had been able to conjure.

Tears ran freely down AnnaChi's cheeks as the helmet crashed to the floor. Kasey's mouth opened but no sound escaped. The floor seemed to drop far away as reality spun from his grasp. Just as suddenly, the floor flew back toward him too fast.

Before he realized it, AnnaChi was cradling him gently, laying his head in her lap. The wetness of her tears brought him slowly back to full consciousness, and he could hear her sweet voice repeating his name over and over like a sweet lullaby.

Kasey's hands visibly shook as he forced off the vertigo and pulled softly away from AnnaChi's loving embrace. "Am I dreaming? The air recyclers..." his voice cracked as she shook her head, anticipating the question, "I'm not..."

"No, you're not dead either my sweet. Although by the looks of this ship you were close. What in the verse were you doing so far out in the black, and what happened to this wreck?"

"I uh … wait," he stammered, "you survived! No, I saw you die!"

Before she could respond, he pulled her arm closer with a confused look. "Your arm, it… What happened?"

Before she could start to answer, AnnaChi suddenly got the most terrified look on her face. Yaran had come down carrying the now sleeping child, to make sure all was well.

The heartbeats it took for Kasey to realize that AnnaChi thought the child was his seemed an eternity. It took much longer to explain. The laughter they all shared broke the remaining walls of confusion and before they knew it, it was as if they had never been parted.

It took a long while to explain all that had happened to each other over the past year, as well as the series of seemingly incredible chances that found them together again.

Half a day later the old, and nearly dead vessel was fully secured to the Cintian. Her craft taking over the failing systems of the old ship, and they set course for Belrothi.

CHAPTER SEVENTEEN

The journey to Belrothi was unsettlingly sad for most of the passengers. Even when the news of the government relief packages was announced, few did more than nod with the acceptance of their defeat. It did not help matters that, on the same day, news of several other attacks started appearing.

The attackers had targeted the expedition's smaller assorted star-cruisers, which would have been used to explore and expand the colony to the local stars. As the only ships capable of traveling to other star systems, and even the huge galaxy-class engine from the Lithose-Abscond station now gone as well, the colony was now effectively imprisoned within the Trias system. Only a single habitable world and one partially habitable moon remained to humanity in this sector of space.

The advent of star drives had taken humanity to a new level overnight. The event was looked upon as the true birth of humans into the galaxy. Until that moment in time, the Earth Prime cluster consisted of only a handful of viable planets, some of which took years of travel to reach and was, quite often, a one-way trip.

Yet, within a decade of the first star drive being developed, there were ten times as many inhabited worlds. The newly minted star-cruisers soon made routine circuits to each. Populations exploded as old restrictions were thrown away, causing a boom for nearly every industry as needs skyrocketed. The worlds became a true federation, and soon everything changed and changed again, as everything does.

The far larger, galaxy-class star-cruisers like the Abscond were new to the federation. With a speed nearly three times the maximum of the smaller star-cruisers but a cost hundreds of times higher, it was not likely to be built for mainstream in the foreseeable future.

Without star-cruisers, a system would quickly outgrow itself, both in population and its demand on resources. While there was no immediate need to expand, the entire purpose of being in the region of space was colonizing and exploring. It was why so many had risked everything to be on the flight instead of joining a colonization effort closer to the Earth Prime clusters.

Now however, with all such ships and factories either destroyed or rendered inoperable, the expedition faced just such a future. The loss of that ability tore at the hearts of nearly everyone on the expedition.

Conspiracy theorists and news agencies alike raved over terroristic agendas from several possible sources. Chief among them were the Patternists.

The Patternist are a cult-like group, sworn to save humanity from an end seemingly dictated by the galactic histories that had been unearthed as humans spread from system to system.

It was evident, as soon as other worlds started to be colonized, that humans were not the first species to inhabit the galaxy. Humans had known they were not the only species around, but the others they had met could hardly be considered civilizations.

Conversely, many of the ancient races they had uncovered traces of appeared advanced in ways humanity may never be, but some were not all that different. These were the aliens that, in the past, humanity feared were out there. The ones they had always worried would see humans as little more than small insects to be stepped upon without concern.

Yet these ancient and powerful races had somehow disappeared, utterly vanished. No reasons or clues were left behind, nor signs of wars or other catastrophes to explain their vanishing. Nothing marked their passing except the emptiness left in their place.

It was a Pattern. The Pattern. It was found again and again, as far older civilizations were found. Never was there any sign of how they had inexplicably ended.

For humans, the Pattern was now a universal fear of an unescapable future. There is no stopping the need to grow, to advance in the same ways. They will continue down the same path as those before have. There is no choice for a species such as humans. It is their fundamental nature.

Some tried to consider the Pattern a blessing. Had any of the ancient powers survived, humanity would never have had a chance to flourish, or possibly even exist at all. Many more chose simply to ignore that the Pattern even existed, though there is no denying the evidence.

Humans are vain, vastly so. Even knowing the truth, they like to believe that the Pattern is simply not something that applies to humanity. They believe they are special or deserving of their existence. As a whole, they won't stop, indeed they have picked up speed; even the Farpoint project was born with the intent to hasten humanity's proliferation across the universe. They have no choice but to believe a chance exists, for there is nothing else they can do.

The Patternists personified this universal design, and strove to defeat it as if it were a cancer of old science. Humanity's wanderlust was a sickness for them to quash. The group had found countless ways to try and stop expansion of humanity, and to an extent it had slowed it, but not by much. Their order had taken on a nearly religious appeal over the last century, blending into every level of society.

A large expedition such as Farpoint would not have been ignored.

* * *

The passengers of the Cintian debated daily over the many theories and implications of the Patternist movement within the Trias system. It was pointless, but still they tried to keep their minds on topics other than personal losses.

Kasey and AnnaChi hardly noticed any of it. The two pilots spent most of their time rediscovering the relationship they had lost. Their happiness only made life worse for the others, but the two didn't care. What they had gained again overwhelmed their sensibilities for a time.

Few passengers had moved their bunks to the Cintian at first, preferring to stay with their meager possessions aboard the derelict craft that had saved them. Yet before long, all the passengers were forced to move the belongings onto the Cintian anyway. Per the latest comm from Belrothi, the damaged ship would not be allowed to use a docking port when they reached the Belrothi-Abscond station. Until the ship was stabilized, it was considered derelict, and a danger to the station. The external docking ports were cheap to dock at as opposed to the docking bays AnnaChi normally stored her Cintian in. Bays, however, were generally for ships that consistently brought in credits to pay the fees or those actively being repaired for owners who could afford it. Without credits and a plan for repairs, if the refugees wished to keep what they had brought, it needed to be aboard the Cintian.

What to do with the wreck of a ship was another matter. If it came to it, AnnaChi decided she would have to use the Cintian to place the ship in a docking bay, but it would quickly become a serious drain on credits for the ship to sit there.

AnnaChi's honest opinion was that the ship, what was left of it, should be scrapped. Kasey disagreed, insisting he could repair the ship as his own over time, and for far cheaper than he could ever afford his own ship. She wasn't so sure, yet knowing just how much he had always desired to have a ship of his own it wasn't a point she would argue far with him. Besides, the old vessel had saved Kasey's life. That was worth everything in her mind.

Even now she found it hard to believe the reality of all that transpired since they were separated. She was not the same girl she had once been. Kasey had changed too, drastically, and she loved him all the more for it. The shock of seeing her again had been far greater to Kasey than she had ever hoped or imagined. Had she known the pain he was carrying around due to her presumed death, she would have gotten over her adolescent fear and told him straight off.

One good thing came of it all; she now knew without reservation that he loved her, completely.

Kasey had been happy to move his belongings to AnnaChi's quarters on the Cintian when she asked. There was no need for a captain on what was now just a large, empty storage crate.

While the Cintian was small compared to most transports, it was at least twice the size of the broken ship Kasey was hoping to claim. Her ship had gone through several overhauls before she had acquired it and had been used for many different purposes since then. Still, it was her favorite ship, and the largest that she had ever owned. Quite attached to it, she knew she would trade it in for a larger or newer ship someday, but that was business, and she wasn't rushing to that end anytime soon.

There were four smaller suites aboard, besides her own. A seldom used engineer's quarters mirrored her own directly aft and port of the bridge. Her starboard chambers were outfitted as a home, whereas the engineer's reeked of utility. The ships current configuration had little need of an actual engineer, at least not if the pilot was as experienced as AnnaChi.

Her own lodgings began with an antechamber, which also served as a meeting room at times. It was small, and lately very messy. The main chambers were split over two open levels and had all the necessities of a home, if little more. The lower level opened into a private workout room directly below the bridge. On the main level, a second entryway led directly into the bridge, which was only slightly less disarrayed than her quarters.

Between the two quarters stood the main entryway to the bridge. Leading away from the three hatches, a sloping corridor led to the mezzanine areas which overlooked the main storage bays it surrounded.

At either end and furthest aft, were the final set of living quarters. These two rooms were used exclusively for passengers when she had any, and crew members in the infrequent cases she took any on. Yaran and her baby now occupied the starboard suite, while the remaining passengers used the other for gatherings and group meals, but most slept in the storage bays among their belongings.

AnnaChi and Kasey took their time clearing out the engineer's quarters for Kasey to use now that he was essentially homeless. The task was more for something to do than any actual need, as there would be room on the Belrothi-Abscond if needed. It was currently filled with everything one would expect of someone who had quickly packed all their belongings for a move across the galaxy. Having planned to relocate her effects to an on-world apartment, she never bothered to organize the bulk of her belongings.

Belrothi however, was not to be her planned home. She always assumed she would eventually make the move to Lithose and be closer to Kasey. Everything in the interim had remained as she had originally packed it.

Now that relocating to Lithose was no longer possible, they simply moved everything they could to one of the small storage alcoves in the central hall. They were secure recesses she usually used for passenger effects on long trips. Until they returned to Belrothi and found a place to permanently stay, that was secure enough.

Nearly finished cleaning out the chamber, they both paused at a familiar crate that had been shoved into the tight curvature of the room's far corner. It was one of the crates of Zief wine she had been smuggling during the attack.

"After all they put you through, they didn't even take all the cargo they came for?"

"I have never been sure what they came for, but I don't think they were after wine. They smashed most of it in their search," her face soured at the thought. "It was quite a mess once I was finally able to get back on board. Maybe they found what they were looking for, but what you see is all that remained. The merchant never came after them, so I stowed it to sell later."

The faraway look in her eyes did little to comfort Kasey's anger at the situation. Stepping forward he took up one of the bottles.

"Not much reward for your losses, but I believe you and I deserve a sample or two, if it survived the journey." At her nod, he cracked the seal as she located a couple glasses.

Neither were frequent wine drinkers, but they found the deep, copper wine was surprisingly delicious. They agreed it had aged well over the last thirty years, a unique attribute of the Zief system's wine that it aged extremely slowly, some up to three hundred years, before it was deemed ready by the dark color it obtained.

As he went to refill the cups, he noticed the bottle seemed heavier than it should have been. Emptying the remaining liquid into the glasses, he held the bottle up to the brightest panel, but the glass was such a deep red that it let little light through.

Ignoring AnnaChi's looks, he had one of the ships panels increase lighting until he could make out a spherical object attached to the base of the bottle. Peering down the neck showed little else of the object.

Curious, she moved beside him, "What is it?"

"Did any of the broken bottles have glass balls inside like this?" He handed bottle to her.

"Uh, no I don't think so. It feels heavy, I would have noticed a bunch of heavy glass balls when I was cleaning all that up."

The bottle sat there long enough for them to finish a second bottle, which contained no sphere. Scanning the remaining bottles showed no spheres as well.

Inspired by the failed scans, Kasey all but ran to get a scanning array from his Bard. The results were nearly the same, but weighing the bottle showed enough of a difference to prove this was the only bottle with a sphere inside.

"Well I don't want to risk breaking it but I have to know if this is what they were after. I'll get a plasma knife."

She wasn't gone long, but Kasey was backing away and shaking his head when she returned. "I don't think you will need that after all," he spoke, wonderment in his voice.

Before their eyes the bottle was slowly dissolving into a glassy puddle, leaving behind a clear crystal sphere. There was little distinguishing about the orb save the lack of uniqueness. It was perfect to the point of being extremely mundane. The only noticeable characteristic was that light seemed to distort at strange vectors, and not at all in a way that was expected.

"A cheap show trick perhaps? I've seen similar tricks, but why..." She was still fuming at such a reminder of the attack, but he could tell she was getting weary of messing with the object.

"Who knows... wait!" Was all he could respond before she had snatched it up to get a better look.

"Oh. It's warm!" Placing a finger gently on the now solidified puddle that had once been a wine bottle, she shook her head slightly. "Much warmer than the melted glass, and the wine wasn't this warm when we drank it either."

"I didn't really notice."

"Well you are not supposed to gulp it, ya heathen."

"Here, let me see." She dropped it casually into his palm without a word.

"The heat will be detectable. Take a look," she said, as she activated a display showing the thermal-sensor's readings of the room.

The screen showed a constant temperature from all over the orb, but other than the heat, no other signals or radiation were evident.

She yawned and slipped skillfully into his arms, effectively blocking his view of both the sphere, still in his hand, and readings on the screen. "A mystery for another day perhaps?" Her kiss was sweet with wine, and the crystal orb was dropped onto a cushion and forgotten in a fog of lust.

CHAPTER EIGHTEEN

By the next day, AnnaChi had dismissed the orb as a toy that had nothing to do with anything but wine snobs. It was, she persisted, simply a door prize for the wealthy, and none of their concern.

She knew that Kasey was not convinced, but nothing they had tried had given any indications that the orb even existed, beyond the mild heat it gave off. She purposely put the useless, if slightly mysterious, object out of her thoughts and concentrated on repairing the old ship. If Kasey needed this ship to feel complete then, by damn, she would do her best to see it through.

Thankfully, even though they were several days out from Belrothi, the paperwork to transfer ownership of the now 'abandoned' craft into Kasey's name had already come back approved in the latest data comm. Apparently, apart from government owned ships, the same grants were given to all those escaping the dead world. Certainly, most of the old owners were no longer around to complain.

The ship, however, was in severely bad shape. Replacing the missing thrusters would be difficult, if not impossible, in the near future. As no scrapyards existed yet in the Trias system, there were not many alternatives for them to choose from. Having a new set of thrusters built would be far out of both their budgets and would take a long time. She could tell Kasey did not want to let it bother him, acting as if something would come along eventually. She knew better.

Still. She resolved to do everything she could in the meantime, with whatever resources she could scrounge, to help get his ship fly-worthy again.

"Lodestar," Kasey mumbled as he unloaded another box of parts he had been salvaging from the damaged systems around the ship.

AnnaChi looked up, "What's that now?" Attempting to force damaged system nodes together into a single working unit was not going well for her.

"The Lodestar. A good name for her."

"She's a load of something dear," she said, waving away a curl of smoke from her latest effort. "Hold on. Her? This bucket is a she?"

"Of course, I couldn't trust a male ship to take care of me."

"You mean like after it's thruster took a hike and the systems all fried up? You realize how close you all were to being space-sicles, right?" Knowing she had him on that point she tried to rein in her smile, but he was still grinning at her with that slight sideways tilt of his head that she adored.

"You mean," he replied without looking away from her, "when she held together for as long as she possibly could, given her condition?"

Dammit. His gaze never faltered as he waited for her response. Finally, unable to argue the point, she broke the stare-down and peered back into the node's casing before responding.

"She will make you a fine ship someday. I just hope my Cintian approves."

"Competition?"

"Only for me, dear." She smiled. "Only for me."

As Kasey continued to rebuild one system after another, AnnaChi continued assessing the damaged system nodes around the ship. She knew the nodes were critical if the ship was ever going to fly again; they were the nervous system of the ship. Some nodes were salvageable, but quite a few would still need to be completely rebuilt or replaced. They were one of many systems that they couldn't simply fabricate parts for themselves, but they would be available relatively cheap once they reached the Belrothi-Abscond.

The main core banks were another issue altogether. The banks should have been replaced long ago, several looked to have melted down mere weeks before Kasey had borrowed the ship. Presently, only two of the twelve cores were functioning at all, but they wouldn't continue to function for long. Thankfully, the Cintian had taken over the core's functions before they quit too. Regardless, once they reached the planet, something would need to be done to allow the ship to exist on its own when not docked.

The cores themselves could be replaced, but few would be available in the colony, and fewer still would be compatible with the old and outdated systems. Even the Cintian's twenty-four cores were incompatible, and she wasn't even close to a new ship. The only real solution they could see was to update the whole system; not a cost-effective venture.

AnnaChi was less than optimistic, "You know, we may need to think about other options for this," she said, trying to breach the subject over a lunch Yaran and the other passengers had prepared for them.

"What other options do we have?" Kasey responded a bit more sharply than AnnaChi expected. Apparently, he had been expecting this.

"Well, we could dry-dock Lodestar in a semi-permanent orbit until we can raise funds, or…"

"Or?"

"Or, ah, you could use the credits from selling this ship to start saving for a newer, working one."

"No."

"Just no? This still puts you far closer then you ever were before toward getting your own ship."

"Look, I get it. This isn't much of a ship, but I like it and I think it is worth hanging on to." He pushed his meal aside, "I need to get back to the aft recyclers."

She watched him go in silence. She understood his need now. The conversation had proved it as far as she was concerned. He was emotionally attached to this old boat after all the extreme events he had so quickly been through with it. On top of all that, this is the first real ship he ever owned. She knew that feeling all too well, and it was one she knew he would not easily replace. She sighed, maybe there would be a way to make it work.

Her thoughts turned back to the problem at hand. If the system nodes and core systems were in bad shape, the sensor arrays were practically nonexistent. Like the cores, many sensors had sorely needed replacement for quite some time, but between surviving antimatter-induced shockwaves and the thrusters exploding, there was far too much damage for the few working arrays to compensate for. The diagnostics should have detected the insufficiency long before breaking atmosphere, and it seemed Kasey had given the systems plenty of time to self-repair if they could. As it was, the corrupted cores were returning limited data analysis instead of true system-wide reports, which showed most systems to be working instead of failing.

She sat back in wonder, amazed that the ship had survived the launch into orbit, but she dared not tell Kasey that. Had the systems not failed when they had, he would have been stuck on the planet, or at the bottom of a dangerously sloshing lake. The idea of taking a ship in this state into orbit gave her shudders If the true state of the ship's systems had been available, he would have been forced to seek shelter on the planet or find passage on another ship. Then again, the craft would have been grounded for repairs long before Kasey had rented it. For it to have survived through everything it had that day, and then fail in the quiet black was uncanny. Yet everything had impossibly worked out, improbably worked out she corrected herself. She couldn't help shaking her head in disbelief at the nearly perfect disaster, or at the realization that without her finding them they would have all died painfully slow.

Even so, replacing nearly all the destroyed external sensors would need to be a priority on the growing list of necessary repairs. This, she realized, was at least a problem she could do something about. The last time she had updated the Cintian's arrays, she had kept many of the old sensor pods as backups in case of problems. Having planned to rebuild as many pods as she could, using parts from the more damaged pods, but had never gotten around to it. Which meant, her beloved could start his repairs straight away. More importantly, working sensors would allow the ship to be safely marooned in an orbit until it could be made safe for docking to the Belrothi-Abscond station.

Soon, a small skimmer was loaded with all the pyramid shaped array pods she could find in the Cintian's workshop. The area was more of a collection of unused recesses along the generator chambers than an actual shop. After testing to determine the remaining functionality of each, they loaded the sensor pods into the maintenance bay. Taking turns running the external maintenance arms to install the sensors was necessary. Without complete focus, the pods or ship could be further damaged.

The work was not usually such a delicate job, but it had become quickly obvious that the arm itself was also in need of repairs. Not able to determine if the arm had been damaged in the latest events, or if it simply was left in as much disrepair as the rest of the ship, they carried on.

By the time they were in optical range of Belrothi, all the external arrays were installed, with sensor output rerouted through a temporary control system they had borrowed from the Bard. The scouting vehicle's brains had never been meant to fly a ship, not even close, but they were more than up the job of keeping the old ship stable and in orbit. It would control the Lodestar's maneuvering thrusters and the few other systems they had working so far, allowing the old ship to maintain orbit and avoid potential impacts.

Lodestar's life support would be a more manual effort. The Cintian would control it for now, but once in orbit someone would have to check in on it every couple of days to keep it set correctly. Checking the assortment of readouts, which they had setup around the ship to warn of any problems, would be a tiresome task, but worth it. Air quality on a ship could kill a crew faster than most anything, and usually without anyone noticing before it was too late. They tested the hacked together system as well as they could, but soon it would be put to the test.

The sight of the planet and their new home was a welcome one for all aboard, bringing a mixture of tears and joy from many of the survivors.

* * *

Belrothi rolled along beneath the Belrothi-Abscond in a lavender haze; accented with motes of clouds embellishing the atmosphere. Far above the atmosphere, a littering of ship signatures floated in free orbit nearly obscured the slim coil of the Belrothi-Abscond station on the Cintian's screens.

The unlikely scene bespoke of the uneasy tones the colonists now felt. Once details of the initial attacks had spread, the fear of another attack quickly forced most independently owned ships to extremes, protecting their livelihood and families as they could. The pilots that were able, took their ships out of harm's way, even if it meant living without the comforts of the federation's resources.

Soon after entering sensor range of the Belrothi-Abscond, a pair of enforcement cruisers moved to intercept them.

CHAPTER NINETEEN

Kasey was apprehensive as the craft approached, but AnnaChi waved him off.

"I know what you feel, but they are only here to help." He knew she was ignoring his glaring look as she slowed the Cintian to the course and heading the patrol captain's transmission indicated.

Before long, the rhythmic clatter of a ship docking to the portside hatch of the Cintian was punctuated by the soft crying of Cerine, Yaran softly trying to calm her.

AnnaChi opened the lock for the lead ship and stood back. The portal opened to show six lightly armored troopers flanking an officer attired in the green uniform of Abscond's security forces.

"Permission to come aboard Captain AnnaChi Acosza."

"Granted, and just AnnaChi will do." They all watched as a small, but heavily armed, troop marched onto the deck, seeming to absorb every detail of each passenger. "How can we help?"

"Due to recent incidents, we are required to run full inspections of every ship entering the sector. Are you willing to submit to a search and some inquiries?" It wasn't really a question.

"Of course," she replied, "The starboard docking hatch back there leads to the Lodestar, which is currently inoperable, but managed to save the thirteen people in this bay. Systems are currently running on a provisional system, so keep an eye on your environmental as you wonder around."

"The Lodestar, it is also your ship?"

"Registered owner is now Captain Kasey Robinson," indicating him with a nod, "as your records should have shown."

"Captain Kasey Robinson," the officer turned to face Kasey, "do we also have permission to search the Lodestar as well?"

"Would it matter if I said no?"

Several of the security guards bristled at the question, expecting trouble.

The officer in charge removed the visor section of his helmet to allow his face to be seen. "Look, we have a job to do, the same as everyone, and I can understand and accept the attitude in these troubling times. You are right, it does not matter what answer you give me, we will do our job regardless. I am asking for your permission out of respect."

Kasey felt taken aback at the humanness of the response. This was his first real encounter with Federation law, and a lifetime of ominous expectation had not prepared him adequately for the friendly-faced and easy manners of the man.

"You have my permission to search the Lodestar. If you wouldn't mind showing her the same respect, I believe she has more than earned it." Kasey stepped to the side, leaving a clear path between the officer and the hatch leading to the Lodestar.

Satisfied, the officer turned back to AnnaChi who was badly hiding an amused expression at the exchange. Gesturing down the long hall leading to the bridge, she said, "The Cintian's bridge is straight on, and main quarters as well. Secondary quarters are above your head. Bar is open, help yourself."

"Any crew or passengers not in this compartment?"

"Nope, just what you see."

"Weapons?"

"Several." She made no move, but held his gaze.

The man gave her a steady look and finally nodded. With a wave, one set of troopers headed into the Lodestar, and another pair toward the Cintian's bridge to start their inspection.

"We have also been ordered to interview everyone," he raised his voice to address everyone in the room, "Invasive response sensors will be used. Does anyone here object to their usage?"

The use of such devices was normally a gross violation of privacy, but not a sole survivor opposed its usage now. No one questioned such things after escaping Armageddon.

Kasey's interrogation was last, and took far longer than the others. Being both a newer citizen of the Terrantine Federation and harboring strong reservations against it in the first place had tripped several of the sensor's flags, requiring deeper scanning. Finally, after finding nothing outright malicious or relating to the sabotage or attacks, they released him as well.

As they finished, the officer let out a satisfied sigh, and packed and handed the gear off to his men, who were now much more relaxed.

AnnaChi joined them, "Everyone check out?"

"Yes Captain." He looked at the others around the bay, "And I am glad for it. You may as well know; the news is already leaking out anyway. Central command apprehended a woman a few days ago; she is known to be among the Patternist cult." He spit out the words as if they had burned his tongue. "She claimed the disaster to be humanity's fault. That the hands of the Patternists were simply a tool. She ranted about saving us all..." The man's disgust was evident, "they have officially declared responsibility for the attacks that have killed so many."

The room was stunned at the pronouncement. Not usually a terrorist group, the Patternists mainly found other ways to get their points across without loss of life. Not so this time, and countless souls had paid for it, an entire world had perished. Maybe it was the isolation, or perhaps it was the scale of humanity's leap that drove their insanity to new levels. No one in the room had the answers. Whatever the cause, the cult would never be deemed harmless again.

After the officers departed, a grim satisfaction settled on the passengers now that they had a direction for their anger. A cause for the overwhelming sadness they all felt. The nets weren't publicly acknowledging news yet, but as the officers were being free with the information, it soon would be. Even with the minutes' delay in transmission this far out, everyone on board was eager to contact other survivors who had made it to Belrothi and share what little they knew.

It wasn't long before the latest stories were being told around the ship of the sacrifice and bravery of the survivors. Their own story would be added to the tales on and around Belrothi. Still, many aboard remained grievously affected by the confirmation of friends lost. One heartening bit of news told of a few star-cruiser's factory owners, vowing to band together to rebuild regardless of adversity. Even the thinnest bit of hope shone brightly when all else was falling apart.

Kasey stayed away from most of them as he went about his work. He knew he should be feeling the same way, yet somehow the bond the others felt had never come to him. He felt like an outsider who was never really part of the Lithose inhabitants, as if he had just been a visitor to the world. The only person he could even call a friend was Darnell, and even that was more of a work friendship than a personal one. He could now list Yaran as a friend, but again, it was simply not the same kinship that one could observe between any of the other passengers.

Feelings for AnnaChi welled up to dispel his unease. With her at his side, he knew he would never feel so separate again. With her, he knew he belonged. Entering the bridge, her smile was waiting for him. Together they made the final preparations for parking the Lodestar in orbit and making port, as the small dot that was Belrothi grew exponentially in their view.

* * *

A small moon was just cresting Belrothi as the Cintian closed in on the Belrothi-Abscond station. The Lodestar now became a distant speck in the high orbit they had set it. It wasn't long before they were landing in a sparsely occupied bay. The Cintian settled gently as AnnaChi preformed a full inspection before locking it down.

The survivors were eager to leave the ship behind. Still, every single one was grateful enough of the rescue to seek Kasey out for a final farewell embrace before departing. They had divided their belongings and salvaged goods days before. They loaded all they owned onto small skiffs, and they started off to make new lives.

Kasey was surprised to find he was jealous. He had lost nearly all his personal belongings as well, much of which was all he had of his parents. It wasn't a lot, but it had been his. Yet he found that there was something intangible the other survivors seemed to have, something he lacked. He shrugged it off, as a welcome cry sounded from the last of his travelers.

Yaran and Cerine were last to leave.

AnnaChi helped gather all the baby's things and packed them with the small pile of items the others had decided she should have. It wasn't much, but it was more than any of the passengers now owned. Kasey walked her down the ramp and said his goodbye.

Not far from the open hatchway, an entourage of friends and support volunteers were waiting to help with whatever she needed. The mother's grip on his supporting arm tightened like a vise as she took in the small crowd waiting for her. She leaned heavily against him. He realized she would have collapsed had she had the luxury to do so. Taking a deep breath, she straightened for only a moment before she turned to embrace Kasey fully, her wet tears honoring his cheek. He had never felt appreciated in such a raw form before.

Watching her go until the gathering had disbursed, AnnaChi slipped into his arms. Seeing the baby and mother off to safety was a fitting conclusion to their tragic journey.

Gathering up their own gear, he took a long look around the Cintian's bays. They were a dreadful mess, but more so, they were empty. They felt entirely too big, now that no one occupied the spaces.

AnnaChi had already ordered a cleanup detail, which Kasey saw was already waiting to do their job as he exited the ship. AnnaChi practically skipped down the gangway with a small pack over her shoulder, her cheerful attitude was infectious. He could not remember a time she looked more vibrant.

"Ready to see my digs, sailor?"

Unable to retain his dour mindset, he nearly laughed, "Lead on my spacey lil dove."

Her living quarters were slightly larger than Kasey's had been. Yet, where his had been sparse and relatively organized, AnnaChi kept a disarray of belongings and goods scattered about, seemingly haphazardly. But a careful eye could note a system among the chaos. Kasey did not take long to recognize the routine his love had always used, knowing it reflected her character in many ways.

Her pack was unceremoniously dropped in the entryway and kicked to the side. Pockets were emptied, and clothing removed as she moved across the cabin to the kitchenette without really stopping. The beauty of her routine enabled her to do the same in reverse and be ready to leave in moments. Her method was something she claimed to have picked up from some brief stint aboard a military vessel, keeping peace on the outer boarders of the federation. Brief was an understatement in Kasey's mind, fourteen years of her life had been in the navy.

Their respite didn't last long. AnnaChi was called into a meeting for the work group she had abandoned to go in search of Kasey. She was not concerned, what could they do but dock pay or fire her? Both cases were fine by her; there was always work for an experienced pilot.

Kasey was summoned soon after for another security interview. It was quickly apparent to him that very few had witnessed the disaster on Lithose. Only a handful, himself included, had lived to share it. More importantly, they hoped his ship had important logs of the encounter.

Before long, he boarded the small shuttle, along with a collection of interested parties, that quickly took them out to the Lodestar to duplicate the databanks for analysis. In the end, they took not only copies of every shred of data in the old system, but also every one of the old sensors he and AnnaChi had worked so hard to tear out and replace.

At first, he was upset to see them go, having planned to tear them down for parts. However, once he learned he was to be compensated at replacement cost, he was more than happy with the deal.

Returning to the Belrothi-Abscond once again, he headed for the tram-pod system to head back to AnnaChi's apartment. Before he could reach the tram, a beefy hand thumped him on the chest, stopping him cold.

"Now hey there, watch where you are going friend, or you may miss noticing me at all."

"Darnell! Thank the verse, but I wasn't able to contact you. I had thought... um, I thought you gone..."

The big man gave a wolfish smile that seemed to falter almost as soon as it appeared. "Seems my head isn't as thick as I had thought. I woke up here in a medical bay to find I had missed..." He let his thoughts drift off, offering no more explanation.

Finding a quiet spot in the local common area, they talked at length on all that had transpired. The brawny miner was elated to hear of AnnaChi's impossible return and rescue. Having known of Kasey's past, he knew how the loss had affected him. Even to Kasey's ears, talking about all that had happened and the unlikely rescue by AnnaChi seemed unbelievable. Darnell drank it in, asking more questions than Kasey had answers for.

"Another piece of good news," Darnell suddenly looked up after a long pause in the conversation, "Sariyn made it off that rock with some of her family. Says she is out of the mining game for a while, any work at all apparently. Her family is well off, and she is hunkering down with them until this whole Patternist issue blows over. Her words, not mine. In any case, it's a wonder any of us survived." Eventually talk turned to the

Lodestar and the conversation seemed to start anew.

Then for no reason he could discern, Darnell's face fell back into a faraway frown.

"Everything ok Darnell?"

"Eh? Yea. Got lost there for a moment."

"I understand, it's a lot…"

"No, not that. I won't get over the loss of so many friends, but I will be fine. Been through it before." The last was barely audible. Clearing his throat, Darnell moved closer. "Something with the n-mats just isn't right. I think there was…" He paused as other passengers moved through.

"You think the attacks were about the n-mats?" Kasey prodded.

"No, no, I don't." The frown was back and so was the silence.

"Uh, boss, what is it?"

"Nothing. And none of that boss shit. The Reavestone is gone now. They will find us jobs here, don't you doubt it. No n-mats here yet, but I bet they call us soon for that effort."

"But…"

"Really, it's nothing to worry about." He stood as if to leave.

"Ok. But if you need me, let me know."

"I am fine, but do me a favor? Keep those eyes and ears open."

"For what?"

"I need to go," he said moving away. "See ya around."

Kasey was left wondering what was truly bothering his friend. He had not been the same since the n-mats discovery. Knowing Darnell's motivation had never really seemed to be fame or fortune, the complex mood of his friend confounded him. Darnell had not spoken too much about his past, perhaps something had caught up with him.

* * *

AnnaChi was waiting with a smile when he returned.

"They didn't fire you then?"

She ignored him, demanding a kiss instead.

Finally, she relented. "They were more worried that I would quit than upset at my unscheduled leave. Increased my wage to stay on under contract for at least another forty days."

"Why the need? This Abscond segment should be unloaded by now."

"Actually, there is quite a bit left to move. The planet surveys are still not finished, and many don't want to claim until they know all the possibilities and weather patterns. Many of the larger factories are not even set up yet, something about material supply chains not being ready for them. Gibberish really. It's wealthy people and companies looking for an edge." Scoffing at the idea, she picked up her flight jacket.

"So, what will you be running?"

"Hah, everything apparently. Half the fleet was made up of independent pilots like myself. Most of them have gone reclusive after the attacks, not wanting to have their ships and homes near other possible targets. They left ample work, but a lack of ships. The company ship's pilots are stuck, but they don't own ships to lose either."

"Guess I won't find work there then?"

"Nope, I did ask though. Some shifts may open up, but for now there is nothing."

"Oh," he said, noticing for the first time that she was dressed back in fresh flight gear, "flying out already?"

"They have been a bit overwhelmed lately so I have a

delivery tonight," she smiled at his disappointed look, knowing he was looking forward to a meal that wasn't standard ship slop. "But don't worry dear, I already have dinner plans lined up for us at my favorite tavern planet-side. And I, um," she paused uncomfortably, "I have some friends for you to meet as well," she added, a little too casually.

His outlook brightened perceptibly, "Sounds good, if we get there quick, I'm starving you know... Wait, friends?" In all the time he had known her, she had never used the tone he had just heard when mentioning friends. It was a rare occasion that she even made, let alone kept, friends for long.

"Yes... Anyway," she ignored his further queries, "the Cintian is already being loaded; if you are ready, we can leave now. And don't worry, you will soon be stuffed to bursting."

Kasey thought he detected the slightest hint of a blush before she pulled him out the door and back toward the Cintian.

CHAPTER TWENTY

After three drop-offs and some low passes over a few of AnnaChi's favorite landscapes, they landed in a newly cleared field outside a bustling little town. A slight trickle of rain fell, even as the setting sun shone brightly above the horizon. Kasey sucked in the amazingly fresh air, noting some slight flavor hinting at the edges of his tongue.

The small skimmer AnnaChi kept aboard had seen better days, but it suited her needs well enough. Loading in, they set off into the growing settlement.

While all the buildings were new, most were built of a drab material common for new settlements. The material was some of the very few nano-created items the federation allowed. Several industries are allowed, under controlled conditions, to make such basic materials in close systems that literally grow the material in vats of nanite infused goo. Even though these types of nano-bugs were single purposed, making only the one product when exposed to the necessary elements, the robots are still destroyed the moment they left the growing labs.

Centuries prior, in what had been a much smaller federation, a ban on a wide class of nano machines was installed, effectively ending the nano-age of humanity. There was little choice after a badly programmed batch of nanites, that were intended to turn landfills into useful materials ended up destroying homes across several thousands of kilometers, killing many trapped inside. Unfortunately, banning something on a wide scale that that makes people tons of credits almost never ends well. Uncontrolled use of nanites persisted in secret, allowing thousands to die in small accidents each year without much notice. There were no longer civilization-wide research collaborations to learn from, no training for those who were interested in the technology, and no guidelines or conventions on safe usage. The ban only left a single inevitable conclusion.

When it finally came, the disaster nearly ended humanity.

Dozens of systems had been colonized and dozens more had been planned to follow as the first star-cruisers began to speed humanity's progress through the cluster. The first world to die was, at first, determined to be caused by a late-stage terraforming accident that converted a high-oxygen air mix to enough carbon dioxide to kill the colonists. When two more entire systems of new colony worlds went quiet shortly after, the panic began to seep in. But it was only after a well-established world of over one hundred million souls was lost that all traffic in the federation was forcefully stopped to halt the spread of the human engineered plague. It was eventually determined that an airborne nanite that was meant to provide perfect air for the colony went drastically wrong. The nanites were unknowingly shipped to other worlds via supply crates containing the airborne nanites and released when they were unpacked.

The government, of course, had never given up their own nano-research and used their knowledge to develop a strain of nanite-killing nanites. Introducing a single-minded, self-replicating nanite which efficiently sought out and destroyed all others. The nanite-killing nanites were now everywhere and on everything in and out of Federation control. The moment any ship or probe entered the atmosphere of a new planet, these security nanites would begin to cover the planet completely and forever. Always waiting to do their duty.

It wasn't completely the end of nanites. Sealed environments could be created where nanites could be used to produce products humanity needed. These were generally registered and controlled where possible, although full regulation was still impossible. Another exception were some specialized devices that created nanites that lasted a few seconds before being destroyed, usually in controlled medical environments. Accidents could still happen, and did, but the technology was no longer a large-scale threat to humanity.

The town center was fast approaching, and the materials being used for construction materials changed to more of a local flair. One cafe sported hundreds of apparently authentic woods from across the federation, each one carved or built to reflect the culture from which it came. Another seemed to be built entirely from a substance that flowed like water and sent colorful ripples across every aspect of the structure with every movement the occupants made.

Leaving the skimmer in a communal lot, AnnaChi dove through the crowds heading toward an ancient Earth Prime style saloon. Like many businesses in the area, it was many times larger than it needed to be.

The Sarsaparilla Saloon stood out, but not for its size alone. The simplistic design was a beacon of comfort among the mainstream establishments. Mad Fran, the jovial proprietor, intercepted AnnaChi with a bear-hug the moment they entered, hustling them into a private room. It wasn't long before Fran's family, along with several workers, surrounded them to hear what stories had kept her away for so many weeks.

Kasey was genuinely surprised by the close relationships AnnaChi had developed in the last year. Seldom had his partner found friends, or even gotten along with most people. Yet here, across the galaxy, she was the center of attention for an entire group and seemed to be enjoying every second of it. Even on the journey to Belrothi with a ship full of survivors, she had not befriended a single soul, except perhaps Yaran.

It dawned on him just how utterly alone she had been since the incident that tore them apart. There weren't many who would have taken up with the feisty pilot back on Daveri Two. As far as he knew he had been her only friend. More than a little aware himself of how painful the life could be without supporting friends or family, he was elated she had found such warm companionship.

Moving away slightly to give AnnaChi's friends more space, he looked upon the scene in wonderment. For a second, the din swelled from the outer room, breaking his gaze as another worker rushed in. The moment slowed as he felt AnnaChi's attention grab at him. The look conveyed a discomfort with being the center of attention, but she welcomed it all the same. The scene embarrassed her in a way he had not witnessed before. Time quickened as her attentions were pulled back to the questions assaulting her from all directions.

The spell broken, he was glad to find that with the latest newcomer had come a generous tray of appetizers for everyone to share, even the workers. Kasey could not remember a more delicious assortment of foods, yet soon after the conversations slowed, he found himself growing hungry again.

Seeming to anticipate the need, Mad Fran took their

order himself and waved everyone from the room to allow a peaceful dinner for the reunited couple. AnnaChi rested her head onto Kasey's shoulder, content for the first time in ages.

* * *

Many hours later they emerged refreshed from a small apartment AnnaChi kept close to the saloon. Kasey was glad to see she kept up her old quirk of keeping private quarters wherever she seemed to find herself for any amount of time. It wouldn't surprise him if she had several more tucked away in other towns around Belrothi that were similarly small, yet functional. He had always found it strange since there was ample space on her own ship. But he had to admit, they were more than convenient.

They started back to the saloon to take what promised to be a delicious tour of the brewery Fran had set up. Where Mad Fran had earned the Mad prefix was unknown, but even his wife treated him like a crazed scientist when he was busy creating new concoctions. The local fruit, toyasow, had quickly become the primary component for the bulk of his creations. Kasey had sampled more than a few before departing the saloon earlier, and found fault in none.

Before they got far, a great din pulled their attention toward the main square. Small crowds were gathering around several large screens displaying some sort of news report that they couldn't make out. Kasey took off running toward it with AnnaChi close behind—the idea of going through another catastrophic event forefront in his mind. As they grew closer the crowd's anger could be seen on their red faces.

Another attack was made on the low gravity construction rigs orbiting the moon Vethi, one of several moons orbiting the large gas planet Goligen and the only naturally habitable moon in the Trias system. Although the attack was unsuccessful, several lives were lost in the attempt. The rigs were to be primarily used for building large ships like star-cruisers, but had not yet become fully operational. It was a clear statement that the Patternists were not satisfied to simply delay expansion. They wanted to ensure it stopped completely.

Even as they watched the live feed, one of the station's splayed tendrils, which attached to the massive atmospheric lift reaching all the way to the moon's surface, shattered without a sound. Every tendril was thousands of meters long, each with a dedicated lift. Three others drifted, shattered and twisted in curly deaths. If enough had been severed, the weight would eventually snap the remaining tethers and send the main cable swirling down to the moon Vethi below.

The reporters were quick to announce that the latest breakage was an expected one, which had been due to the damage. Still, it was a close call; the destruction that would have been caused by the falling lift cable would have been unfathomable before the loss of Lithose. Now thoughts, words, and blatant anger radiated from the crowd.

Wandering slowly away from the angry crowd, they found themselves at the brewery without really knowing how they got there. Fran showed up minutes later with fire in his eyes about the news, but wouldn't allow AnnaChi to put off their tour, saying he needed a distraction, and time in the barrels always fit the bill.

The next day they found AnnaChi's ship stuffed to bursting with deliveries for the saloon, and they spent the better part of the morning making drops and picking up new deliveries across the planet. They made it back to the saloon for a late lunch and to pick up a final load to fill orders aboard the Belrothi-Abscond.

CHAPTER TWENTY-ONE

Kasey found himself spending his free time working on the Lodestar rather than scouting the planet for mineral claims. He knew he was procrastinating, but didn't want to spend time away from AnnaChi so soon after finding her again. Besides, the Bard's control system was still being used to keep the Lodestar in a stable orbit.

It was with high hopes that he could get AnnaChi to go along on expeditions with him, but the company she was running shipments for had a sizable backlog requiring her attention. In the free time she did have, she helped with the repairs and would usually be around for a lift back to the Belrothi-Abscond for the night.

Appearing in the hatchway hours later than was usual, she could not hide a smile as he shot her a querying look.

"Hey what's up; lot of runs today?" Offering and receiving a casual kiss, he moved back to the torn apart console.

"You will want to more than kiss me, once you hear my news. Unless you would rather wait?"

"Wait? Wait for what?" He looked up. She had his full attention now.

"It seems several transports were destroyed beyond repair when the bays were hit. I caught wind that one of the wrecks was being moved to a repair bay for scraps, so I talked to the owner. I convinced him that he would benefit more by selling me some parts now, before a middleman was involved. He was happy to take my offer over the scrap price, so…"

"Did any of the sensors or…" she bade him to be quiet, before he started rambling through the long list of needs he had.

"Yes, a few survived and I have them on board the Cintian, but what you should really start thanking me for are the barely damaged thrusters that will be arriving…"

She never finished her sentence as he swept her into his arms faster than she realized he could move, and he went on to show her exactly how much he appreciated her in every way.

As they lay in contentment, the familiar sound of a ship docking roused them. "Uh, when did you say the new thrusters would be arriving, my dove?"

"Hmm, you mean the transport quads that you are somehow going to push this over-rated storage crate around with? Right about now I think…" She laughed as he rushed for his clothes.

"Quads? The Lodestar can't run quads." He said, nearly tripping over himself as he pulled on the second boot.

"I am sure you will figure something out. The thorium inverter may help…"

"The Lodestar doesn't even have a thorium reactor!"

"Well, there are two thorium boosters in the Cintian's cargo bay you could use for extra power, if that helps. You may need to extend the hull out bit to fit it all, but it will be the fastest transport anyone has ever seen. Actually, you really should expand the hull for more cargo too while the scrap is cheap." Her laughter grew at the overwhelmed man as he rushed around looking for his shirt.

"My god woman…" was all he managed to mutter before running out to meet the hauler.

* * *

The hours wore into early morning on the planet surface far below, as the thrusters were finally lashed securely against the hull.

It would take weeks or longer to install them on the Lodestar, which was never designed for quad thrusters of their size. He saw no way to make them work on the hull as the ship currently existed, but with a few modifications he knew they could make it work.

The fuzzy edge of exhaustion slowly crept into Kasey's vision, but he wanted none of it yet. Pushing the design thoughts aside he headed to the Cintian, only to find the bay littered with more salvaged goods than she had let on. He felt truly amazed, she had always been frugal, but this was an exceptional haul.

In the center of the bay stood a cluttered collection of forty-eight small core cylinders that would have made up a processing system as was usual in many of the larger ships. The system would have more than enough processing power to run every system on both ships at once and not slow down. It would be overkill for a small transport like the Lodestar. Shaking his head to clear his thoughts, he began to pace around the gear. He knew he couldn't afford such a system, even at scrap prices.

He realized he must have been ranting out loud as, from an unnoticed lounge chair, AnnaChi's sleepy voice answered his thoughts. "They are not for you. My Cintian needs an upgrade."

"That's a lot of processing, for even the Cintian."

"Well, I have plans for her dear. Anyway," she interrupted herself with a long yawn, "you can have her old ones for Lodestar…"

She was asleep again before he could even thank her.

Stifling a yawn himself, he finally realized he needed some rest as well. An end of his efforts was finally in sight, he would soon have a ship of his own and finally be truly free. He wanted to get started, yet he pulled himself away. Gathering AnnaChi into his arms, he went to find a bed.

* * *

Upgrading a ship's core was not a menial task for even the most experienced pilot. It was expected that off-world pilots be capable to maintain critical systems of their craft. A life could be ended in open space far too quickly by simple problems. Still, even with her experience, it took AnnaChi the better part of a week of research to admit it was beyond her abilities.

Settling on the cheapest contractor they could find was their only choice. Most of their funds were gone with the latest purchases. AnnaChi had reached deeper into her rainy-day emergency credits than she would admit. The work quality was not exactly top notch, but it was solid. Regardless, neither was satisfied until they had run every battery of tests and diagnostics they could to weed out potential issues. Every one of which AnnaChi was proud to be able to fix without additional help. It all worked out in the end with the Cintian only out of commission for a couple days.

A week later the Cintian's old system was running on the Lodestar. With the corrupted cores replaced, they were finally able to disconnect the temporary control system that had been keeping the Lodestar in a safe orbit. Soon the old ship was back to life. The Lodestar now controlled its own orbit and life support with an ease it had never known.

There was still a lot to do before the ship would be able to do more than satellite Belrothi.

Kasey soon started running shipments using the Cintian during AnnaChi's downtime. He initially thought she was teasing him when she offered to let him use her ship.

As far as he knew, she had never allowed anyone to fly her ship without her aboard. The only time he as aware of someone captaining the Cintian, without her oversight, was when she was shot and nearly bled to death in the Daveri Two system. That she could so willingly allow him to borrow it meant she had either changed more than he had thought, or their relationship had evolved more than he had imagined.

Glad to be working to cover some expenses, he accepted it without question. She had given so much to be with him. It was her apartments he was living in when not working on the Lodestar. Her credits paying for the system cores she really hadn't needed. Her life that had been on hold and forever changed. It was a debt he wasn't sure he would ever be able to repay.

Now he was using her ship, for just a few days' worth of work a week. Someday, he vowed, he would make sure her sacrifices were worth the efforts.

His thoughts turned toward the Bard, still stored in the Lodestar's cargo bay. As soon as the transport was fly-worthy, he would start scouting for land on Belrothi. Finding a few minutes each night to study the planet, he was sure there was enough free land on this large planet for many generations of humans to explore.

He lamented the loss of all his research back on

Lithose, or more accurately, the usefulness of it. He knew such details of Lithose and its unique landforms and areas he was planning to explore. Everything was wasted now. He could only hope his experiences there would help him here.

From the colony perspective, finding the needed resources for the colony was now more critical than ever. Without the resources and workforce of Lithose, there was serious doubt that this Federation outpost would be sustainable in the long-term. He felt sure the remaining mining and processing companies would be scrambling to compensate quickly.

Each of the two main worlds would have previously been expected to produce at least half the materials needed for the colony to get started. Now Belrothi and the small partially habitable moon, Vethi, that orbited the gas giant Goligen, were the only sources of new materials.

Kasey was sure the negative matter searches would be put on hold for years to come while the system compensated. He had no idea if n-mats had even been found on Belrothi, but if not, he was one of the few that knew something about how to find it. A part of him hoped knowledge of his involvement was lost with the main Lithose-Abscond station; he had no wish to be forced back into government service.

Life became routine over the months it took for the Lodestar to be flight worthy again. The thruster array's design and installation were a larger job than either of them ever imagined. The thorium boosters could provide the extra power needed, but controlling all the new equipment was beyond the old ship's systems.

The bridge was now a mishmash of controls needed to handle the new and old systems. Where the old system still had control of stabilizers, sensors, and many other aspects of the ship, the new controls handled the main flight systems as well as all power distribution and shielding. The ship was truly now a hybrid of systems. It would be a work in progress to update everything to the newer system, but for now a usable ship was complete.

From the outside, the ship looked nothing like it once had. The hull now bulged out significantly where each thruster had been attached. The cargo bay now extended to the rear of the ship twice as far as it previously had. While still nowhere near the capacity of the Cintian, the Lodestar was now the faster ship, at least on paper.

Finally, after a taxing range of tests on the Lodestar, they took both ships to Belrothi to celebrate at Mad Fran's saloon. Fran asked almost immediately to see the Lodestar, and after several skeptical looks at the hodgepodge makeup, he offered Kasey a steady delivery job for the town that would fill the better half of his weeks.

A glance at AnnaChi's expression was all he needed to see. She had known the offer was coming long ago. He took the job without another thought.

CHAPTER TWENTY-TWO

The Bard touched down on the cliffside, followed by a whoop of delight. It was AnnaChi's first jump in the small craft, and Kasey had no doubts she would be itching to drive the Bard herself after the experience. Although first, they needed to make the top ridge and set up camp for the night.

The sight from the cliff was awe-inspiring. Far below in the valley basin he could make out the Lodestar, a small speck of metal glinting in the setting sunlight at the edge of a rocky clearing. The basin was a hodgepodge of prairies and groves of thin trees as a web-like network of streams flowed southward through the basin from the surrounding hills. It was all surrounded by a crescent of tall green mountains, starting low with rolling hills and climbing steeply up several ridges covered with thick trees. The top ridgeline where the bard now perched was steep, nearly vertical in places, and rocky before it flattened out again at the top. He couldn't tell for sure if the ring was caused by a meteorite crater or natural formations, perhaps both. In any case, it was an amazing view from about any point.

The varied terrain was the main reason Kasey had placed this area near the top of the list of hopefuls. A thousand kilometers of amazing land nearly surrounded by a ring of protective mountains could do more than just provide the materials for the colony mining operations, it could be a home. He rather hoped to find something of worth in the area just as an excuse to make a home on one of the lower ridges. Maybe even raise a family if AnnaChi was willing.

Kasey sighed as he took ore samples from the layers of sediments showing in the rocky ridge before moving on. He knew better than to have too high of hopes for finding a wealth here. So far, he had surveyed several similar locations that had little in the way of needed materials for the colony, but if he could locate just one large vein of the right ore, it could produce a decent windfall. His thoughts fell back to the search for n-mats with Darnell and the mining crew. Holding up a chunky bit of ore, he wondered if it held a form of the exotic material locked within. Lowering his hand slowly, he dropped the sample into the container and took in the view of the hillside view instead. He would never know if any of the samples contained n-mats in them, he had no way to test for the troublesome material even if he had wanted to.

The ring of hills had a line of hot springs in the southern end which he had spent the last expedition mapping, but little was of value. Most signs pointed to the northern side having little of value as well. The vegetation was different than the southern area in a lot of ways, but nothing stood out that he hadn't seen elsewhere.

If it hadn't been such a stunning view he would have moved on much sooner, but as it was, he needed to be sure before giving up on it. A huge bonus to him was that AnnaChi was finally along on a trip that afforded such an amazing view. He had high hopes that she would enjoy it enough to come along more often.

Once the scans of their immediate site were finished, they readied the Bard to move on. The next jump excited AnnaChi no less than the first one, making him even happier to have convinced her to come along. Six more jumps placed them near the summit, with only an hour left before dusk.

Leaving AnnaChi to take in the breathtaking views of the expansive valleys below, he set about preparing the camp area he had chosen. Finding a large grassy mound that gave some protection from the wind, he unloaded the gear.

The shelter practically set itself up as it puffed out like a silk sheet caught it the wind, before crystallizing into a wavy structure. A few minor adjustments and it was ready.

He was still setting up a fire pit when AnnaChi dumped an armful of fallen branches, causing him to jump back in surprise.

"Looked like you might need some help," she teased, "there is plenty of good firewood in the grove across the hill and I love a big campfire. Mind if I take the Bard over for a load?"

"I hadn't realized you'd ever camped with a real fire before."

"Actually, I have had more than my fair share. Although it has been longer than I care to admit."

Her faraway expression gave no impression of wanting to talk about her past further.

"Well," glancing at the quickly setting sun, "I think we will make better time working together, besides there isn't much else left to do here."

"And…"

"Yes, you can drive."

* * *

Morning came and went before they emerged from the comfortable tent.

The night before had gone by quickly for the couple. Kasey had brought several campfire-worthy foods along, but had little idea of just how to cook them. AnnaChi eventually suggested using long sharpened sticks, and before long half a dozen sticks circled the pit with various meats. Burning more than they ate, they enjoyed every bite. AnnaChi had located a perfect spot between the fire and hill for them to recline and take in the night sky, which had slowly developed ribbons of a deep green aurora highlighting the red nebula in the lower night sky. It was perfection. Neither wanted it to end as they talked and loved long into the night.

Kasey yawned often while he fixed them breakfast. Soon regaining his energy, he began the daily routine of sorting through the data reports from the previous day's excursions.

One scan stood out immediately, showing the beginnings of an immense cavern system that spread deep into the mountainside, many branches of which showed large enough for the bard to fit comfortably.

He brought up the topographic maps he had collected from his own fly-overs, as well as the initial survey scans from the Belrothi-Abscond's probes when they first entered the Trias system. It seemed there were several potential cavern openings in the area, some of which may have been lava tubes in the far distant past. Marking ones that could be large enough for the Bard to enter, he moved on to the other findings.

The land in the basin near where he had landed the Lodestar seemed high in copper ore, showing some small deposits of natural-copper formations that could be easily be mined, unlike the copper ore. It was a good start, and if more seams could be found it could be profitable, considering the only other copper mine he knew of was back on Lithose, and now lost. His interest grew as a second, smaller vein of natural copper appeared in the data and more ore as well. It still was not a large find, but it showed a lot of potential and the two areas were far enough apart to show there was a good-sized portion of the valley that could be mined.

He smiled to himself. This, by far, was turning out to be his best trip to date. Showing AnnaChi the findings, she picked up the excitement, although she had to do the math herself to believe just how profitable the enterprise could be.

After breaking down the campsite, AnnaChi took over driving the Bard for the reminder of the trip using every excuse she could to use the jump jets. Kasey used the freedom to concentrate more on the incoming scan data, directing AnnaChi to spots of interest for more in-depth scans.

None of the scanning data showed any decent findings on the mountainside. So, they took the bard on a roundabout path that would allow them to scan the larger outcroppings and cavern entrances as they made their way back down to the basin where the Lodestar waited.

Soon after entering the basin, they started up a particularly high mound, the sensors buzzed a warning and Kasey had her stop the Bard. He had several alarms set to go off when certain materials were detected in quantity, but this was the first time an alarm had ever actually sounded.

A large natural copper deposit lay directly beneath the mound. Some formations seemed to be larger than the Bard itself. Without looking up, he directed AnnaChi to finish climbing the hill. The sky was growing dark with heavy clouds, but they never noticed.

Their luck continued. As breathtaking as the views

were, they now only had eyes for the similarly shaped mounds leading off into the distance, all comparable to the hillock they currently sat upon. One by one, all the hills were scouted that rainy evening. All of them appeared to contain large deposits of natural copper.

It was a full-on downpour as they made their way back to the Lodestar. Soaked before they thought to seal the Bard's openings, it was a long and wet trip, yet both were smiling the entire way.

They spent the night there in the loading bay listening to heavy rain and thunder boom throughout the basin, watching from the open hatchway. They didn't speak for many hours, but they knew that this valley was now their future.

The echoing rumbles of thunder were an odd welcome home, nonetheless it felt accepting to them.

* * *

They returned to the valley every chance they could over the following weeks to map out the largest copper deposits and surrounding areas. Planning the best uses of their combined claim-marker beacons was a monumental task. Kasey was proud that AnnaChi thought highly enough of his plans to throw in her beacons as well, even though she claimed she had no real need of the markers she was entitled to.

He knew the caverns intrigued her and as the basin was mostly mapped out, he made a point of starting their latest trip with an excursion to map out the larger caverns, yet thus far, no indication of any worthwhile materials had been found within them. Still, they continued exploring any cave areas the Bard would fit into that appeared safe. Most were formed from lava tubes, although many smaller side caves split off from the main channels, most of which were far too small for the bard to travel.

It was still early as they explored the last of the cave networks and they were surprised at how large it was. At nearly two kilometers below ground-level they were startled to find a sharp rise in the ambient temperature, accompanied by a mustiness sharper than any they had run across so far. Spurred by the possibility of another hot spring, they hastened the Bard down the network of caves to see what treasures lay beyond. Another hour passed when the bard's environmental systems started showing dangerous contaminants in the air, forcing them to seal the bard tight and rely on recycled air.

Stopping the bard at a steep drop-off, Kasey shook his head. "I am not sure we should continue, we are not really equipped for this. I never expected the bard to fit so far down into these systems, let alone kilometers."

"And you think we should turn around now?" She asked calmly.

"I think it would be the safe thing to do. The sensors are less than accurate down here and I really don't know enough about them to understand why. The sandstone layer we are currently in appears stable enough, but the readings fluctuate more than I would like. Not to mention the air outside the bard is getting worse the deeper we go, and we're about to descend another hundred meters."

AnnaChi laughed, "the danger is half the fun, besides do you really want to turn back without seeing what is causing all this?"

"Well, no. But we may not find out if it gets too tight for the bard anyway."

"If that is the case, I am sure my wanderlust will be sated until we can gather proper caving gear."

"Deal, but keep a close eye on the scanners okay?"

"You sure you don't want me to drive?" She pleaded.

Ignoring the remark, he took a breath and started the bard down the steep incline using the jump-jet's stabilizers to stay on track.

Hours later, their search ended in an enormous crimson cavern littered with hot and violently bubbling pools of steaming waters as far as they could see. Scans showed a heavy amount of cinnabar and mercury throughout the cavern, but little else.

The many formations that covered the cavern shimmered with a medley of colors whenever their lights hit, creating a kaleidoscope effect.

High above the nearby pools were oddly flat surfaces tinged in a reddish hue. Steam curled over the flat areas like a wave, obscuring their view.

"Is the mercury worth much?" AnnaChi asked as Kasey was pouring over the scanner readings.

"Hmm, yes and no. It is listed as a priority material, but the price point drops off too quickly to be worthwhile." His eyes creased as he flipped through the colony requirements. "Ah, I see. It is needed, but not in great quantities. So, this is worth a good bit in the short-term, but very little compared to the copper."

AnnaChi pulled two rebreathers from a small equipment locker and handed one to Kasey. "I know its noxious, but I want to take a look."

Stepping from the bard, AnnaChi instinctively picked up a broken piece of stalactite and tossed it at the ceiling area. Neither expected it to splash into the strange surface, only to fall back out several yards away, leaving the once flat surface rippling like an inverted pool.

Kasey slowly walked around a steaming spring to pick up the stalactite and stopped short, instead motioning AnnaChi to follow.

"What do you make of that?" As he spoke, they watched the silvery liquid that now covered the piece pool into tiny silver balls before dripping upward to join the mass of native mercury and cinnabar dust pooling above.

"I think maybe you should bring me along more often, if only for a good luck charm. Is that the magical stuff you were hoping not to find?"

"Yes, I mean no... It's not magical, just improbable. I think it is why the Farpoint project was really dreamed up. But I don't know why it is so important." He tapped the tossed stalactite with his boot, releasing more mercury to drip up to the pool above. "The n-mats must have been brought up from deep in the planet's crust by the hot spring, only to be trapped in this cavern."

"It's amazing!"

It was an amazing find, he had to admit. While he still hated the idea of having any part of dealing with the stuff, and the government that would try to control it, it was hard not to be excited. Particularly when these pools could be mined with a simple pump. His thoughts quavered between happiness and rage, as he weighed the pros and cons of what he now needed to deal with.

All he could think to say was, "It's toxic."

She could see his frustration building but could not resist prodding it along. "And..."

"And, I really don't want the government suits overseeing my every move or even taking control of my entire business. Sorry, I mean our business!" A swift kick launched the piece of stalactite into a hot pool across the chamber.

"Well then, let's not let them! The copper deposits are more than we need. No reason for anyone to even know about this until the copper is gone, and maybe not even then."

"That's a lot of potential credits to walk away from. There is an entire lake of the stuff up there!" He pointed at the scanner's screens, shocked by what he was seeing.

"There is... The density... It's several times that of the refined n-mats we had mined so far on Lithose, maybe more. And this is pure, and in this volume... Do you know what this could be worth?"

"To me? It's worth nothing." Her warm smile was convincing enough to relax his frustration.

He nodded dumbly at her and stared at the silvery red ripples that still crisscrossed the pools above their heads.

"Come on then," she smiled, "let's get out of here."

The heat was exhausting, but before leaving the sweltering cavern they took a small sample of both perplexing elements.

Dusk was already falling as they breached the opening, making for a somber ending to the remarkable trip.

They flew to Fran's saloon using a roundabout method he had been using since finding the copper deposits. The Cintian was already parked and loaded for a day of transports on the morrow. The Lodestar would be loaded at first light for Kasey's deliveries as well.

Landing near the newly built town warehouse, they simply sat for a long time wondering what to do next with their findings. They owned enough markers to cover the copper deposits completely, with a modest claim left over. The mountain, however, was quite a bit outside their ability to claim. Even the few colonists that were selling off their claim markers were doing so at prices well above any they could afford.

Examining the site map the Bard's scans had created of the copper deposits, they looked for some way to skim off the less profitable areas. Still, they came up with far less markers than they needed for the area. They knew it would be a huge risk to only claim a portion of the areas they wanted. There was no doubt that as soon as they announced the land was up for mining lease for the massive natural copper deposits, the surrounding areas would be filled with other prospectors who would quickly claim the land.

Other's claims would not make for a very pleasant place for a home. A real house. Something for them both to share and something they had spent much of the trip to the saloon dreaming up ideas for.

Worse, they realized, some larger companies could swoop in and claim all the surrounding lands. Which the mountain with the n-mats cavern would likely be part of. When the floating mercury was found, even his copper mines could be shut down or appropriated completely by the government. They needed another option.

Eventually they hashed out a semblance of an idea. They could start a business overseeing the mining rights of the copper, but only if they first had a third partner to provide the additional markers. They ran the number against the extra share and still showed many years' worth of hefty profits. With a suitable business partner, they would have just enough claim markers left over to claim the mountain on their own, without it being part of the business. Ostensibly to build a home on one of the lower ridges overseeing the amazing landscapes.

The two were suddenly struck by how alone they both were in this system, the only real friends either of them had were Darnell and Fran.

Darnell would have made an excellent mining partner, but the n-mats were not something they wanted anyone to know about just yet, and with his knowledge of the subject it would be only a matter of time before Darnell would figure out what they were up to. They wanted someone who wouldn't ask too many questions about their other activities in the area.

Mad Fran would fit the bill, and they both trusted him fully. AnnaChi sent Fran a quick message that they would like a private room for dinner, and if he could join them for a talk they would appreciate it.

"We will need a name for this business ya know," AnnaChi prodded as they made their way out of the ship bay.

"Something simple is fine by me." Kasey replied, "got any ideas?"

"Simple huh? Like Kasey's Copper Mines? Or Belrothi Copper?"

"Ha, perfect! Belrothi Copper it is, simple."

* * *

Fran surprisingly didn't need much convincing, but he had a few conditions. He wanted everything written up, properly signed and legal. All of which he wanted to be performed in the saloon, along with all company meetings going forward. He wanted only a thirty percent share of all profits on the land, as well as one huge chunk of the natural copper formation of his choice for display in the saloon.

It was a better deal than either had hoped for. He spent hours with them talking over business points they had never considered. More than that, while he played at using his place as a condition, it truly gave them a real base of operations.

The next day, after their deliveries, they took Fran for an extensive look at the claim. The deal was then signed over a small feast back at the saloon and founding of Belrothi Copper was completed.

Things moved quickly after that. The claim markers were placed and officially accepted soon after. Fran took it upon himself to spread the word through several channels the couple had no idea he had access to. Through it all, the three friends became closer than ever, even if most of their chats now revolved around the budding business.

Even with Kasey contacting the few miners he had worked with that survived the calamity to spread the word, the first two weeks were deadly. Then, without warning, they were overrun with offers from nearly every agency with mining connections, as well as even more offers to buy the land outright at obscene credit amounts.

Kasey would have taken nearly any of the offers if Mad Fran didn't supply the voice of reason and years of apparent knowledge. He persuaded them to wait weeks before even responding to the offers, and then only a brief acknowledging message of interest. It wasn't long before a second, and then a third, round of offers flooded in.

In the end, they accepted three offers and only for specific sections of land chosen specifically for the lower content of copper deposits. The small amounts would be cleared out within a season, and by that time they would each have secretly scanned the adjoining lands that were greatly more profitable. Fran promised the strategy would increase their profits every season and help ensure a high price in the market.

Fran's shrewd negotiating turned what would have been a modest income into what either of them would have considered a small fortune. Since the natural copper deposits could be mined so easily, the credits started rolling in before they even knew what to do with them all.

Soon, they had the entire area guarded with a multitude of security sensors. Some were obvious deterrents to trespassers, others were simple decoys, and even more were passive in nature. AnnaChi designed the entire system with layers of protection for their claim. She assured Kasey and Fran that nothing would enter their properties unmonitored.

Their home, which they made no secret of building at the summit, was not included in the security design. However, AnnaChi put together a completely different set of layered-security for their home and personal lands.

They had all the cavern entrances caved-in and secretly monitored, except one. Upon the largest entrance, they built a small retreat lodge overlooking a nearby pond which they had greatly enlarged. A mountain stream was even diverted to create a waterfall on the grounds feeding into the pond, completing the picturesque scene. But the lodge was simply a distraction. It did not so much hide the cave entrance as give a reason for their activity in the area. It allowed for the construction of a secret entrance into the caverns, complete with skimmers and equipment in case they ever needed to extract the n-mats.

For the foreseeable future, they planned to keep the cavern and the discovery well hidden. Once the copper mine was depleted, they would worry about what to do with the n-mats, if anything.

CHAPTER TWENTY-THREE

In the time since the Lithose's destruction, Darnell had not fared well. The stasis pod that had kept him alive had repaired his body, but it could not prepare his mind for the shock that awaited him when he was awakened. Everything and everyone he had worked with was gone, and he was now half a system away from the planet. It was hard to believe what he was being told, only once he verified the records himself did he accept the reality of it. The loss of his crew hit him hard. The Reavestone company no longer existed anywhere but on paper, unless one were to travel half a galaxy to find the parent company.

At first, he had no problem finding a job in Belrothi's mining industry. Several offers of employment had come the same day he woke. Keeping a job, however, was an entirely different matter.

One by one he found a way to lose every job, and worse, word had gotten around that he was unstable. The current company which had taken him on would only place him in low-end positions. Jobs where he would not be in anyone's way.

Today started like most others had lately. He took a small skimmer far out into the bay of what would someday make a decent port town or vacation spot. Mapping heavy metal content of the bay was not the kind of menial job Darnell was used to, however he had to admit that the isolated quiet was deeply peaceful, even for his troubled mind. Occasionally he could even manage to put aside the burning questions that plagued him night and day.

But not this day. The memories now rolled over and over, demanding to be studied yet again for clues. Darnell knew he was not well, yet he could no longer help himself. Could not keep from being drawn into events that only he apparently could see. Things that he felt were leading the colony into more dangerous peril.

Since first joining the Farpoint project, Darnell felt that something was off, he had seen it, even then. The truth seemed to swirl around him just out of reach, nearly driving him mad. His mental state grew worse as he observed more and more peculiar happenings surrounding the n-mat mining.

The players in the conspiracy were varied, but several he recognized from days he had thought long gone. These people were not simply ambitious politicians looking to rule a new area of space. These were high-up leads involved in classified military-driven scientific operations. A true esoteric government circle of science advisors that were, as far as he knew, of an unnamed government organization.

He had gotten too close now, he recognized that, but it was far too late. Many years prior, Darnell had found himself leading one of many small strike forces against an old enemy of humanity. An alien race known as the Cassian. They were widely regarded as the galaxy's tricksters, deceiving groups of humans into various conflicts. Many knew them to be much more, and much worse. The Cassian had taken their deadly games to new levels on the fringe worlds of a small secondary star cluster several hundred light-years from the Earth Prime cluster.

Eventually their actions forced the federation to take a stand, which ejected Cassians from the cluster completely. Along with the military force, several government scientists were sent along with experimental weapons. One of which appallingly left an entire system in danger of collapsing into its own star, leaving millions of dead in its wake. Soon after, the group abruptly disappeared from the mission, recalled to Earth Prime, apparently. The near catastrophe was blamed on the Cassian. Darnell's forces were directly involved, and they all knew the truth of it. Darnell questioned a lot about the war itself at that point and left it all behind as soon as he was able.

Now, however, at least three of that same group of scientists were directly involved with the n-mat collection efforts. One of them, Dr. Holt, had even made a point to address Darnell after finding the n-mats. There was no doubt they knew exactly who he was and what he knew about them.

Perhaps it made sense that they were involved, this was indeed a unique discovery. Maybe, but he wasn't so sure. After waking from the injuries and realizing the extent of what had happened on Lithose, reliving those last weeks over and over in his mind, one thought rolled continuously through every memory.

They had known that something was going to happen that day.

Weeks prior to the attack, he noticed that a planet-side warehouse had suddenly been emptied of the n-mats Reavestone had been mining and refining. The n-mats were somehow being quietly shuttled up to a restricted hanger aboard the Lithose-Abscond. Following the trend, he watched as the same happened to other warehouses in short order. Real or unfounded, the feeling that something grave was happening ate away at him at a heightened pace every time a Patternist cult issue made the news.

Darnell had started finding more reasons to be at the Reavestone company offices aboard the Lithose-Abscond. He needed to know, even if it meant risking his position with the company. He did what he could to keep track of the scientists who were apparently obtaining the stuff. It wasn't easy, and it took time. He didn't learn much except the location of the hanger bay where the n-mats were being stored.

The hanger bay was familiar to him. It was the same bay where the government's raven class heavy transports had once been stored. In that bay had also been the immense cargo containers. He had often wondered what they contained, but none were ever opened or even mentioned during his training. After the Lithose-Abscond station had entered the system, the ravens assigned to Reavestone were quickly moved to company-run bays.

Knowing it was too dangerous to try to gain entry to the area, Darnell faked a string of personnel inquiries around missing company equipment. The result was pressure upon him to find and dismiss the employee responsible. The directive to root out the thief provided more than enough reasoning to gain access to several monitoring stations around Reavestone's headquarters, including ones near the bay storing the n-mats.

Before long, while superficially reviewing personnel movements, he saw what he thought he needed to see.

There were no direct surveillance feeds of the hanger itself, but there were in several of the hatchways leading into it. More people were involved than he had thought. Several aliens were present as well.

The Grays did not surprise him, they were always interested in new explorations. It was expected that one or two would be aboard, but the relationship was still curious enough to follow-up on. Of more drastic concern was that another race, known as the Sargani, were also involved.

The Sargani were not exactly a trusted race by humanity, yet they were not considered hostile either. The distrust was mainly derived from their disturbing ability to pick up human thoughts, or theta-reading, the sight of them was enough to set any human on edge.

Theta rhythms were most vulnerable while a person was relaxing, or more precisely, when daydreaming. To the average human, the reading of any thoughts without consent, particularity while in a peaceful state, was considered an appalling act. Worse, it was a common perception that the Sargani considered humanity as pawns in their own games and had never hid this fact. As with anything, there were exceptions, and like humans, not all Sargani were the same. Still, if they were involved, it wouldn't be easily accepted by the general public.

Those in the private sector, at least those who dealt with military contracts, would have a different opinion. Darnell was aware of various research projects that the Sargani were directly involved in throughout the federation. Undoubtedly, there were many more that he was not. The species was perspicacious in their understanding of physics and mathematics, but most importantly, they perceived scientific concepts differently than humans could. Having the Sargani on a project usually meant that even a failed project would expose new potentials to be explored.

Dismissing the aliens and their ways, Darnell considered the one thing that was fact, the one thing that he knew was part of the puzzle. The enormous deep space containers.

The containers were a mystery. They were far too big

for any normal craft used in the Trias system, and too small for star-cruiser class ships. If not a ship, then what? Perhaps a machine of some sort, or an orbital station, or a weapon. The possibilities trailed through his thoughts, but nothing fit. The problem now was that the containers were no longer in the bay.

The monitoring systems showed various angles into the bay when visitors came and went. He could see quite a few new sets of equipment, mostly labs running the same kinds of testing Reavestone had performed, but on a greater scale. More importantly, he could see what was not in the hanger any longer. That the containers were moved from the Lithose-Abscond station was not the perplexing issue. It was where they had gone that concerned him most.

Days of searching records showed nothing anywhere in the Trias system that fit the scale. There were no gravitational waves recorded of any star-cruisers leaving the system to take them elsewhere. *So, what had happened to them?* he wondered once again, without any answers.

After the Lithose event, the sudden loss of so many friends and co-workers only served to increase his maddened state. At times, he lost control and anger got the best of him. Soon it became clear to him that a larger conspiracy was in play. The Patternists were not only involved, but had apparently infiltrated the colony on a massive scale.

Yet, instead of driving him further into irrationality, it served to ground him, if only a bit. The Patternists usually had reason and intelligence to their plans. It was evident they wanted to stop this expansion attempt, which meant they were not part of whatever government ploy was behind the Farpoint projects at all.

The skimmer swayed a bit as a breeze kicked up for a few moments. Yawning as the breeze pulled him out of the reverie, he abruptly realized something he had missed before.

These Patternists had gone far beyond their typical actions. They were never an overly violent movement before. Something had changed. Everyone had assumed it was the distance, or the remoteness of the expedition. Darnell realized he had bought into the same reasoning. No, he now realized this was something else. This was action born of fear. They weren't worried about the eventual expansion of humanity along the portended Pattern. They were terrified of something more imminent. Something special. Something new.

The negative material. They feared what the n-mats could, or would, do. They knew what Darnell was looking for. They would be seeking information from a different direction, but they would be looking for anything or anyone related to the n-mats program. They would be looking for Darnell.

Darnell knew more about the substance than any other non-government person still alive, including how to find it. He was a target now, or would soon be. Even so, eventually someone else would discover the n-mats. Even if he disappeared today, the threat to the colony would not be gone.

He believed that somehow, everything—the cult, the aliens, the missing deep space containers, the n-mats, maybe even the Pattern itself—was all now connected. He envisioned himself on a precipice with all of humanity, yet no one except himself could see the edge before them. The view before him mirrored his grim vision.

The acres of sea rippled as he moved about his work, lost in his thoughts. Several large schools of odd small fish flitted noisily on a patch of the surface so close he was tempted to grab at them. Yet the moment he turned in their direction, even slightly, the entire mass disappeared, gone beneath the waves as if they had never been.

"Great... intelligent feeder fish will be the next decade's controversy," he sighed with a small smile that quickly sunk away, "if we survive that long."

He turned back toward the skimmer's controls and immediately wished he could disappear like the fish just had.

Before him, hovering at a slightly pretentious height, hung the silvery crescent shape of a Sargani scout ship.

CHAPTER TWENTY-FOUR

The pod-styled craft slowly settled into the black atmosphere, then plummeted into the thick atmosphere. A second craft followed the progress from a safe distance with AnnaChi at the helm.

"You still with me love?"

"Y …I can h…r but a…t of inter…" and then there was dead silence from Kasey's pod.

"Come back safe!" she all but shouted into the comm but received no answer.

It was expected, but deeply unsettling. They had run several tests with smaller unmanned probes with success, but now with Kasey inside it was another level of risk. Even if he ran into trouble there was little anyone could do. The descent was not sanctioned and, as far as they were aware, no one knew they were even in orbit of the blasted remains of Lithose.

Ever since they had successfully opened the copper mines, Kasey had been talking incessantly about searching out other locations and expanding their business into mining of their claimed properties. It was a good idea in principle, particularly since the destruction of Lithose had left a vacuum in the colony resource needs.

Any new colony required access to vast amounts of available resources to be successful, usually importing what they could not produce locally in the new systems. The closest settled system to the Trias system was fifteen thousand light-years away, a ninety-year journey for a normal star-cruiser, therefore there was no way the colony could import materials they lacked. The Trias system's colonization plan had included a resource infrastructure that required both Lithose and Belrothi as the major contributors. Losing access to Lithose's resources placed the colony in a grim situation for the foreseeable future. The colony would survive but thriving would be difficult. It had already forced the price of many materials to be tripled due to the shortage. Placing most mining operations in a position to make a fortune.

AnnaChi was happy to go along with it all, besides, she thought the prospecting trips alone had been an amazing amount of fun. However, while they now had a healthy and steady income, it was nowhere near the credits they would need to start such an enterprise. Not to mention their two small transport ships alone were not even large enough to transport all the equipment that would be needed from site to site.

They had discussed converting the Cintian into a materials and crew transport, and the Lodestar could airlift some of the larger equipment around as needed. Still, it would be far and away from the necessary requirements they needed if they were to make a worthwhile profit. They knew they really needed a dedicated transport to the operation, and that was beyond what they would be able to afford for some time.

The equipment itself was another problem altogether. Even low-end equipment for a small crew would run more than all Kasey and AnnaChi currently owned. Even if they could afford it, the new machinery simply would not be available fast enough.

There had been no plans for the Trias system colony to build heavy equipment factories within the first decade or so. They only had the machinery the colonists had brought with them, and half of it was lost on Lithose. A few companies had begun restructuring factories to fill the gaps, but it would be years until equipment was affordable for smaller companies.

The idea was nearly killed by the reality of basic economics. Prices wouldn't come down until the demand was lowered, and when that happened the venture would not be as profitable. Kasey nearly gave up. AnnaChi, being more attracted to the adventure than the credits it would bring, persisted that it would still be worthwhile enough to give it a try, someday.

Several times she brought up selling the n-mats, but any time she did, he lost interest in the whole project. The chance of losing freedom was simply not worth the gain in his book. Eventually she gave in. He was right about one thing, as there was still no indication of any mining companies dealing in the exotic material, the government would be trying to track the sellers down no matter how careful they were about it.

Kasey had eventually dreamed up a plan to get the equipment they needed. Lithose, he claimed on several occasions, had everything they needed – and it was all free for the taking. They just needed to get to it. The planet would be nearly impossible to reach for many decades. The atmosphere was filled with several dense layers of ash, iron, and a blend of other dangerous particles all stewed together in a ceaseless and deadly electrical storm.

Which meant no ships could safely pass into low orbit to make planet-fall. Even if they could somehow survive the landing, it would be nearly impossible to make it back to orbit through the storm. Communication would be nearly impossible as well, which meant that anyone insane enough to try was on their own, and not likely to survive long.

This did not discourage Kasey. He insisted he could develop a safe plan, but AnnaChi would hear no more on the subject or any other idea that would risk them losing each other again. He was being foolish she had decided, there was risk that was exciting and risk that would get you killed. This was the later of the two and she could not understand why he did not see it himself.

It was many weeks before she finally allowed him to show her his ideas. She only half listened as he began to explain, having already prepared a mental list of reasons why his plan would fail before he began talking. Halfway through his explanation she realized she was wrong and told him to start over from the beginning. An hour later, she had to admit his plan could work, and would be at least moderately safe. But they would need to test it extensively before making the attempt. An attempt that would only have one shot to work.

Now she watched the swirling black madness through which Kasey's pod had disappeared and hopped she had made the correct choice. It was all up to him now.

* * *

Kasey held his breath in anticipation after losing contact with AnnaChi. He was honestly surprised she had gone along with the plan. There was no way for a powered ship to pass through the atmosphere without sustaining catastrophic damage. However, using the n-mats as reverse ballasts to control his decent to the dead planet, he believed he would have a chance. His craft was little more than a spare escape pod from the Cintian, welded to a mass of large storage containers. They had filled it with water tanks, rocks and whatever heavy scraps they could find, all counterbalanced with tanks of n-mats. After that, it was all up to luck to both find the equipment he had come for, as well as what he would need to escape the planet again.

The plunge into the chaotic storm that filled the planet's atmosphere became an uncontrollable tumble. He resisted the urge to engage the stabilizers as nausea set in. It was a terrifying experience; beyond anything he had ever imagined.

Seconds ticked by, but no lessoning of the storm appeared as their studies had shown. Something had gone wrong, he should have been through the tempest by now, but it continued. Fighting queasiness, he concentrated on the altimeter. He was rising and falling, again and again. Unlike the test pods, this craft was somehow experiencing lift.

Two choices stood before him. Reduce weight and rise out of the storm and try again later, or add weight and sink down through the storm. If he went up, AnnaChi would likely forbid another attempt. It would be game over. A boom shook the makeshift craft before he could finish the thought. He needed to decide quickly, or it would be over for sure.

"Down we go!" he declared.

Releasing one n-mat ballast, and then another, he started to fall. A moment later he was spun at high speed and started to rise again as another boom struck, causing his ears to ring more than they already were. Releasing another ballast, he finally sank below the atmospheric storm and realized his mistake.

"No, no, no. Too fast!" He screamed as he kicked out three normal ballasts in succession, and then a fourth.

He was still too low and had no idea where the storm had moved him. Envisioning that at any second he would slam into a mountain side, panic quickly set in. He needed a safety buffer. Kicking off a fifth ballast, he said a quick prayer as he started up the navigation system, hoping it had survived the storm. Unable to wait, he watched the altimeter as his fall slowed down ever so gradually.

When the sensors finally came back to show he would not crash, he was beyond relieved. Checking the radiation levels bolstered his confidence. It was hard to tell how much radiation would remain, but the estimates were much higher than the reading now showed. He knew his luck could have easily gone the other direction. Pulling a series of levers, the canopy burst open, revealing only sickly blackness beyond and a wave of frigid stale air.

With a stomach-dropping lurch moments later, he realized he had begun to rise again. He had known it was coming and released an n-mats ballast and soon the craft settled into a stable elevation.

Noticing the system had not yet established a location, he released several brightly glowing bulbs on long tethers to light the pitch-dark planet below and flipped on the pod's spotlights, yet only the barest glimmer of land could be seen below. Releasing a smaller carefully weighted n-mats ballast, he eventually descended far enough see landforms on the world below.

The view was heartbreaking.

A bleak blanket of thick, ash-covered hills made up the landscape. Nothing moved as far as he could see, and the sensors were nearly still. Distant flashes of light lit patches of the cloudy sky above as the steady rolling thunder kept his awareness peaked.

Gaining a semblance of bearings, he tested the pod's control jets, thankfully all fired successfully. Setting a course for magnetic north he exhaled a great sigh while waiting for a more accurate location from the sensors.

When they finally refined the estimated location, it was shocking just how far the high winds had pushed him off course.

Adjusting course, he was again thankful for the small thrusters they had installed on the drop craft. Without the small controlling jets, he would have had a long dangerous bard ride back to the large thorium mine, Hammer Wrest, he had targeted for this trip. Assuming the bard had even survived the drop through the storm. He pushed the thought off, it was a worry for after landfall.

He had been to this particular mine several times, yet the landscape had changed drastically. He felt he should recognize the hills and valleys as he grew closer, but the wastelands below looked nothing like the memories he held.

Looking forward to seeing the Hammer Wrest base, he began daydreaming of the wealth of equipment that awaited him there. The mine had been the largest in the system, he knew the gear would be top rated and mostly new. Reavestone had even set up a small shipyard at the location for their standard company ships, the bulk of which had not yet been in use. Kasey was betting on a few still being there under maintenance or repair, hopefully in working order.

Spending several hours keeping the craft on course, he finally located the region where the mine would be in the distance and adjusted his course. Heart thumping, he watched the horizon of the dusty hilltop ahead getting closer and closer.

Once over the hill, he couldn't believe the sight before him.

Slumping back into the hard seat in defeat, he took in the sight of the immense crater where the base had once sat. It was a worst-case scenario—some explosion had devastated the mining outpost; the shipyard was simply gone. It would be worthless to even attempt a landing there now.

Mulling over his next move, he released a small n-mats balloon with a message for AnnaChi. The rumbling storms above would blow the small balloon far off course. He hoped the data he had sent back during the descent would help give her enough coordinates to intercept the message.

There were not many choices before him. He had planned to use one of the ships here to gather equipment and fly to the nearest n-mats mine. The storage vats there would have more than enough to lift the ship through the atmospheric storms with ease.

With no transports, or any other ship remaining in the destroyed mine, he would need to find one elsewhere. The mine Darnell and he had founded was the closest location he knew of and the winds were taking the craft that way anyway, but the mine was unlikely to have ships remaining on location. Surely, any that had been there would have been used to escape, but there was only one way to know.

Once on course he nearly changed his mind. The Thorn Back mine was not a good location for this venture. Not only was the mine unlikely to have any ships at the location, the atmospheric storms above it were some of the worst currently raging. He tried not to imagine how he would land his current craft in the craggy mountains if he was unable to find a clear area.

Growling in frustration, he knew that there was no other choice now. The other n-mats mine was too far for his current craft to get to safely and few were likely to have the n-mats storage that he needed. If he couldn't land at Thorn Back, he would have to find another craft in the surrounding areas to use before attempting another location. Or give up.

"I'm all in now," he murmured to the planet below,

knowing that if he could find what he needed in the Thorn Back base then the risk would be worth it. Yet, it all meant the danger he was placing himself in was far more than he had planned for. He was almost glad AnnaChi was not with him, if not for the danger, then for the *I told you so*.

Darnell was forefront in Kasey's thoughts as he watched the devastated lands roll by below. He felt bad about not including his friend in this venture. Sadly, it was clear Darnell was under a lot of strain and his reactions could be unpredictable in so sensitive an undertaking. If plans worked out, he hoped to eventually bring the experienced miner aboard. For now, he and AnnaChi would go it alone.

The trip was slow going. As he checked over the remaining water, food, and other meager supplies for the third time, the Thorn Back's ranges appeared in the distance before him. It was the most welcome site on the planet so far, being that it was finally a place that he recognized. He could almost picture Darnell shouting out where to set the ship down.

Checking his instruments, the air currents were driving him forward faster than he had realized, almost as if the mountains were drawing him in. Shifting the small thrusters to fight the air currents only helped mildly. He felt a wave a panic wash over him as he realized he had a quick choice to make. He could either attempt to land in the foothills and hope that the bard had both survived and could get him to the mining base somewhere along the mountain range before he ran out of supplies, or go safely over the mountains and find a settlement to make a new plan.

The currents suddenly picked up, swaying the pod awkwardly.

"Dammit!"

Taking a deep breath, he unlatched a few small n-mats ballasts and kicked them free one by one, losing altitude faster each time. The wind lessened as he got lower, but he was committed to a landing now since attempting to regain elevation would have a good chance of crashing into the craggy mountainside. Adjusting the thrusters, he moved the pod towards a lone open field that looked to have most of the ash blown away, and nearly burned out the thrusters keeping the pod on course against the wind.

The ground slammed into the craft, whipping Kasey against the seat's restraints as the sound of twisting metal filled the air. He gripped the seat tighter, watching everything loose in the small cabin flying by as a second impact sent the pod into a spin. He lost all sense of direction as the craft bounced and skidded across the dead world. Fighting the centrifugal forces, he reached out and cut power to the thrusters. The tumbling effect eased off as the craft slowly lurched to a stop.

Taking several deep breaths to relax his nerves, he removed the bulky flight helmet and donned a portable rebreather. Checking the radiation levels while waiting for the eddies of ash to settle, put a smile on his face. The rads were higher than the earlier readings, but not nearly as much as he had expected, and plenty low enough to survive, even for extended periods. As the last of the ash billowed past the porthole, he pushed open the hatchway and stepped out onto the narrow ledge.

The inhospitable surroundings were marred by a jagged wound that cut through the thick layers of matted ash, reaching into the soil below and ending at his small pod. The tether of lights he had deployed lay far in the distance, strung across the landscape, having snagged on something and broken away before touchdown. Climbing down the four meters to the ground, he checked the large water tanks for leaks as he went until finally surveying the damage to the main container. The landing skids were completely torn off and the base was dented and scored, but he was far more concerned with the survival of the container's contents.

Wrenching the latches loose, he opened the container and lowered the ramp before directing the lights inside. The bard had shifted and broken two strapdowns, but the scouting vehicle appeared intact. When its thorium reactor came online, he breathed a relieved sigh. Looking up at the two reinforced tanks above the bard that contained his main n-mats supply, he took the time to thoroughly inspect them for any leaks. Happily, none were found.

Pounding several long spikes into the cold ground, he secured the pod into place. Loading all the survival gear from the capsule onto the bard, he took one last reading from the sensors. The scans were all over the place. Between the ash and radiation, he felt lucky to get anything. However, if what he was seeing was correct, his current position was nearly forty kilometers from the mining base. A long trip, but a feasible one.

Sealing the pod and container, he boarded the bard and started the long trek towards the mining base he had helped make possible.

* * *

Two energy bars and three liters of water. Kasey stared at the remains of his supplies for several minutes then looked back towards Thorn Back Mountains. Over the last two days he had been repeatedly convinced of the local landscape's familiarly. Believing himself to be close to the mine base he had once flown to and from countless times, only to be proven wrong again and again. Feeling a tingling running down his arm, he tore his gaze away to realize he was bleeding again. Changing a tire while knee-deep in slimy ash was quite possibly outside of his skill set, he decided. Taking a deep breath, he dug out the aid kit and reapplied more sealant to the wound, swearing he would replace the cheap and inadequate medical kit as soon as he made it back to Belrothi.

Feeling less confident as the minutes went by, he continued to look back and forth between the energy bars and the mountain as he contemplated his situation. He knew he had already traveled beyond the range his supplies allowed. Turning around now meant he would make it back to the pod hungry and thirsty and, if the winds were calm enough, he could use the n-mats to return to low orbit where AnnaChi could retrieve him. Or, he could press forward in the search.

A fresh crack of thunder made him jump, interrupting his thoughts. Accessing his mimic's interface, he instructed it to cancel out the thunder sounds. It didn't completely work, but the thunder was now muted enough that he could ignore it. With a satisfied sigh, he looked around and nodded to himself.

"Just a little further," the words were barely a whisper.

Punching the jump jets, the craft screamed upwards, then hovered at a little over a thirty meters in the air before arcing forward to spot not far from where he had jumped from. The terrain was hard to read under the blanket of ash, and even the bright beaming lights of the bard showed more shadows than useful features. Rocks and fallen trees were hidden everywhere just under the surface and had caused him several harmless wrecks. Telling himself the path back would be faster with the trail he was leaving, he pushed onward, continuing even after the first energy bar was long gone.

The bard slowly climbed a large sloping hill as he

reached for the second bar, but let It slip through his fingers as a bulky shape formed near the crest. The n-mats mine seemed to grow out of the ground as he reached the summit.

Blurry eyed and hungry, he plowed forward through the ash and up onto a covered portico designating the main visitor's entrance. Using a small crowbar, he pried his way through the locked doors. Tapping a light-strip he had affixed to his ship-suit illuminated the entryway. Ignoring the offices, he worked his way deeper into base until he reached a junction with a double set of glass, soundproof doors. Beyond, he knew, were the miner's domains. Instead of entering, he approached a nondescript side door next to the junction and tried the handle. Finding it locked, he used the crowbar to let himself in.

The electrical room appeared as lifeless as the rest of the building, but for a small red light slowly blinking on a central wall panel. The building was powered down, but the thorium generator was still operable and ready to bring it back to life. Pressing the reset button, he stood back and waited until nearly all the panels in the room lit up. Tapping his light-strip again to turn it off, he strode out into the hallway and waited for the wave of heated air he hoped would soon arrive.

The air, when it came, was thin and musty, but at that moment he didn't care. Removing the rebreather mask, he stood there just breathing until a yawn overtook him. He was hungry, but sleep won the battle as he turned and headed off to the crew quarters to find an empty bunk.

CHAPTER TWENTY-FIVE

Only a few hours had past when Kasey woke in a panic.

Bolting out of the bunk-room, he was several strides down the hall when he stopped in confusion. He had no idea what had unnerved him, it had already faded. A dream perhaps, he reasoned. Shaking it off along with the last vestiges of sleep, his eyes were drawn to the small commissary at the end of the hallway. Fresh clothing, a shower and food were all Kasey thought about for the next hour.

Disappointed the building's air was still musty, he searched out a relatively clean set of coveralls, a heavy jacket and a fresh rebreather before heading to the warehouse exit. Switching on the external building lights, he stepped out into the ash covered main tarmac.

Cold wind buffeted him in waves as he walked across the empty tarmac towards the long-term parking area. His hopes dwindled as he caught the first glimpse of the raised landing pads, all empty. Casting his gaze downward to avoid the all-encompassing truth just a bit longer, he trudged around the final edge of the building. Closing his eyes tightly, he took a deep breath before looking up and opening them.

Emptiness met his visage, but Kasey's eyes abruptly locked onto a dark mound of ash at the far end of the yard. Heart beating loudly, he hastened towards the mound. A single ship had remained! Numerous reasons a ship would have been left behind caused him to stumble, but he did not slow his pace.

It was larger than he had originally assumed. While completely covered in ash, he began to make out the shapes and features as he drew closer and caught his breath. The silhouette formed into a contour he knew well. A raven class heavy transport!

"Yes!" He shouted into his mask.

The raven may not have been the most exciting ship to fly, but it was more than what he required to pull off his task.

Almost subconsciously, he sent the mental command for the ship to open a loading bay. When nothing happened, he sent several other commands without receiving a single response. The ship was dead.

Baffled, he retrieved a loading skimmer from the warehouse and used its magnetic fields to try and clear some of the layers of ash from topside. Hours passed before he finished, but with no sun above he barely noticed time passing until the topside of the craft was relatively cleared.

Setting the skimmer to magnetically dock atop the ship, he climbed out and located the bridge's entry port. Still unresponsive, he punched in the emergency code, knowing it should automatically open the cycle hatch unless an internal alarm canceled the code within a few minutes. He waited. With relief, the lock indicator blazed to life, but he still could not connect to the ship's AI. With a heave, he opened the hatch and dropped into the tube, interior lighting flickering on encouragingly.

Cycling into the bridge area, he looked around and was dismayed at the mess. His irritation at the previous pilot collapsed as he realized they must have died or been injured to have left the ship behind. Only a few pilots, like himself, had been granted access to the systems required to fly the Raven class transports.

Studying the engineering controls for several long moments, he finally nodding to himself and sealed the hatch again. The system's AI had gone into a long-term shutdown mode, that explained the lack of response. Thankfully the AI was now answering, and before long the ship was waking up and fresh air filled the bridge.

The AI was practically in its default state. The previous pilot had barely touched the configuration, let alone anything more complex.

He wished he had someone to complain to about all the programming and fine-tuning he would need to go through to get this ship into a state as efficient as his original Raven had been. Not for the first time, he wished for a true AI that could understand a pilot's needs beyond the logical basics, but they simply didn't exist, even though many agreed it was possible.

Advanced AI research, particularly any development path that could lead to a superintelligence, had been banned at nearly the same time that nano machines had been. While the nanite tragedy had had little to do with artificial intelligence, society's misunderstandings of the facts and general fear of *any* such reoccurrences had forced the federation to impose strict rules on all AI development. Instead of relying purely on regulations to control the research, the government went directly after every company who sold or developed system cores. The hardwiring of cores themselves were redesigned to identify and shut down any processes resembling high level machine learning.

Kasey shrugged to himself. There was nothing for it but to configure the system to his preferences from scratch. It would take weeks or months before he had it right, but, for now, a basic setup would do to get him off the planet.

Fully connected with the ship, Kasey took a quick walkthrough while running system checks over his mimic interface.

The air in the main bay was sour, not just stale like the bridge had been. Grabbing a rebreather mask, he took a lift down to engineering and cycled into the deck. He gagged on the stench, even after the mask was in place. He knew the smell. Knew that the environmental scrubbers had failed before they came into his sight. Every spacer worth his salt knew it. Out in the black, a scrubber failure can kill a crew quickly if it wasn't caught.

He groaned as he took in the sight of the hardened black muck covering the area around the primary environmental system. The buildup had caused at least one seal to burst, and with no one to maintain it, the algae and mold had taken over until they starved.

Moving past the mess, he opened a panel to check the small backup system. It was still running but would need a clean-out soon as well. Starting a checklist, he added maintenance tasks for the other three small environmental backups positioned around the ship as well. He shook his head in disappointment, he should have noticed that the bridge's backup system was running instead of letting in the fresh air when he came aboard. A lot could go wrong very quickly, and there was no one on the entire planet to rescue him. Taking a deep breath to steady his nerves, he opened the maintenance closet, gathered some cleaning supplies, and got to work.

By the time his stomach began growling in hunger, he had the main system cleaned out and replaced the engorged filters with fresh ones. Trudging to the shop to gather what he needed to replace the broken seal, he found himself smiling. He was irritated at the dirty work, but happy as well. Remembering what an instructor long ago had told him; a ship is not really yours until you need to get your hands dirty and fix it. Well, he thought, this ship was well ahead of the curve in that respect.

Finished and satisfied that the remaining maintenance could wait, he munched on some tasteless energy bars while figuring out how he was going to dig the ship out of the ash. Under normal circumstances, the ship would be placed in a hanger outfitted to pressure wash a ship fully and automatically, but there was no such luxury here. Grabbing a fresh rebreather, he exited the ship through the same hatch he had entered. Stopping only a moment to take in the grey, dead landscape, he took the loading skimmer back down to the warehouse for supplies.

Lugging a ton of hoses and pumps across the tarmac, even with the help of a skimmer, was more work than Kasey was used to. Taking a break, he looked up into the black sky watching the barely discernible clouds race across his vision. Every so often, a silent flash would light up a tiny area far above. The heavens appeared at war with itself. Shaking the image away, he reminded himself that AnnaChi was above that storm and waiting for him. The thought energized him as he hefted the hose and dragged it to the next junction.

Pulling the buckles tight, he hovered the skimmer at the top edge of the ship before turning the waterjets on. The craft pitched wildly from the force of water surge. Kasey yelped in panic as he instinctively increased power to the port fields, balancing the small craft. Fully recovered, he directed the skimmer back in towards the raven, putting the water jets to work. Rivers of filth soon flowed down the ship.

The raven class heavy transport was a large ship, as far as transport ships went. The size was something

Kasey had not fully appreciated before attempting to sluice it off with a few oversized garden hoses strapped to a small utility wagon. Once the bulk was washed away, he started over at the top again paying attention to fully clean everything critical. When he came to one of the three communications arrays, he paused for a long while.

Appropriating one of the government's raven class ships was problematic at best. Knowing from personal experience that the government suits monitored the activity of their ships closely, and would know the ship still existed soon after making safe orbit above the storm. These were not attentions he wanted.

While any ships or supplies that survived the flight from the dead world legally belonged to whoever currently possessed them, government assets had been exempt. Everything left on the planet had also been considered a loss, and so theoretically fell under normal scavenger laws. Still, he didn't plan on taking any chances of losing his hard earnings on some technicality. Nor, he knew all too well, did the government follow their own laws.

He spent most of the next day removing the communication arrays and system completely to ensure the craft could not be monitored. Rigging a new antenna array was simple enough, but he could not locate the necessary replacement instrumentation in the base supplies. About to give up and get back to the business of looting, he realized the drop pod's small comm unit could work for short-range if he could recover the craft.

"No time like the present," Kasey mumbled as he started through the preflight checks.

Needing a test flight before loading the ship was critical, and the quick jaunt to retrieve the pod would be more than worth the trip. The pod contained a little over twenty-five metric tons of n-mats aboard, counterweighted just enough to land the craft and make flight adjustments. A bit more than enough for landing, he corrected after recalling the abrasive touchdown. While it would be nowhere near enough to offset the weight of the ship and supplies that he planned to appropriate from the base, the n-mats would go a long way to get him and the ship safely through the deadly storm and into orbit. The base itself should have more than enough to make up the rest.

The test flight and pod retrieval took the rest of his day. The trip had uncovered several issues that he could not ignore as well as a bunch that were added to a list for a full overhaul if, and when, he made it back home with the ship. The maneuvering thrusters were the worst of the problems. They had been sluggish at best, but a few were completely unresponsive. His shoulders slumped as he considered the work he would have before the next liftoff.

Checking the time, he prepared and released an n-mats balloon with updates for AnnaChi. She would not be happy, but she had known delays would be possible. He wished he could talk with her directly, but there was little he could do until the ship as ready and loaded.

After using a large plow to clear the tarmac around the base's maintenance building, he moved the raven into the cleared area. Carefully removing the n-mat tanks from the pod, he strapped them securely in place to the ship's overhead, then dragged the rest of the now-heavy pod out of the ship. He knew that AnnaChi would want to have the escape pod back, the pods were not cheap to replace. He had planned to cut the pod loose from the larger structure, but the raven class transport had several escape pods that were compatible with the Cintian. Not only would she get an upgraded pod, but the Lodestar could be fitted for one too.

Looking around the nearly empty bay, he imagined it

packed full of treasures from the mine base. But he believed he would be lucky to get anywhere close to that. It was a matter of mass. He needed the ship loaded with enough n-mats to get through the atmospheric storm and into low orbit, nearly one thousand kilometers above, and he needed to do it unpowered.

The ship's n-mats reservoir was currently empty but could hold almost enough to offset the mass of the ship, when otherwise empty. With the pod's high-density supply moved over, he now had what he needed to take the ship into low orbit, but little else. He needed to carry far more n-mats to offset the equipment he wanted. Stepping out to the open edge of the bay, he looked across the tarmac to the utility sheds stood. He needed to find more storage.

Plowing a path to the sheds, he searched through the storage until he located enough large water tankers to fill the floor of the raven's bay. One by one, he pumped them full from the base's n-mats storage and carefully brought them to rest against the deck-beams high above before strapping them tightly in place. He hoped it would be enough. The base's remaining storage would barely have enough to fill the ship's built-in reservoir, but he held off filling it until he could fully load the ship to ensure it remained grounded. As it was, the ship was already massing close to the zero range, if it were not for the polymagnetic docking locks, a sharp wind would jostle the ship about.

Checking the base's storage tanks again, Kasey chewed his lip in concern. He had been secretly hoping to find a lot more of the n-mats than he had. It was strange for the base to have been so empty, not that it was his business what Reavestone did with their products. For all he knew, the company had more clandestine storage areas for the rare material or had already sold and transferred them to a client, which could only be the navy. Still, making any return trips could be difficult without a large supply on planet.

He hadn't brought the topic up with AnnaChi, and she had barely approved of this trip as it was. He expected that once she witnessed the magnitude of what he was able to bring back she would agree. The ship alone was worth more than everything they owned combined, and the n-mats could be worth several times that, not that they could openly sell either one. No, he reconsidered, the worth of this trip would be based on what he was able to fit in the ship's bay, and that would still be considerable.

The current venture may have only been for mining supplies, but he saw far more potential in future trips. With enough resources, they could conduct ongoing salvage expeditions and recover much of the colony's riches left behind.

Still, making another trip would all come down to mass again. He either needed to find a store of n-mats on this planet or bring enough expendable mass along to replace with the salvaged goods. The expendable mass would be tricky. Water would be easy, but it would take a lot to make it worthwhile. Sand or stone would be more efficient, but the containers would be forfeit each trip, and heavier resources would be too expensive to use.

Kasey was excited by the idea, but pushed the thoughts aside. It was a business opportunity he needed to discuss with AnnaChi, and one that would need to wait. He now had a mining operation to get started. Once it was up and running, he would give the plan more thought.

With thoughts back on the mining, he walked towards the one storage shed that contained the main item that would make this trip successful. Opening the shed's large doors revealed a massive machine that would fit into any nightmare.

Before him rested what was classified as a medium sized digger-dredge. The diggers were key for any professional mining team. The machines could dig deep into any terrain, separating the useful materials down to a thick concentrate for processing. While this model was highly automated, it still took a team to keep the machine running correctly and supplied.

Looking up, he grimaced at the rows of deadly-looking bucket-teethed drums seemed poised and ready to bear down and rip apart anything in their way. Below, lines of large metallic wheels, all with fist-sized studs, covered the bottom and sides to push the machine along whatever path the miners set it on. He had seen smaller versions in action, both in his own copper fields and on this very mountain, but this one was several times as large. He understood that there were much larger variants but seeing this one up close was impressive.

The whole machine sat on a movable platform, so it could be moved without ripping up unintended surfaces. The platform was another miss on his part. He had not calculated its mass or the need for it before now. He mentally shrugged. It was one more necessary thing he could not control. Climbing into the platform's chair, he guided it across the windy tarmac and into the raven.

It was a tight fit height-wise and he wondered how the larger machines were moved from site to site. The digger-dredge took up nearly a third of the bay and half of his mass allowance. Second-guessing himself, he almost went looking for smaller digger instead. He could fit two, maybe three smaller ones in the same space and mass he guessed, and it would allow for more equipment. Throwing his arms up, he paces around the bay frustrated that a decision was wasting time. Almost without thinking he called up the time and realized he had been up nearly thirty hours. He could not remember the last time he had eaten anything.

With awareness came exhaustion. Sending the command to close the bay he headed to the crew quarters. Decisions could wait until morning.

* * *

Kasey woke dripping in sweat. Something had been chasing him—no, it was a dream. Shaking himself free of the blankets he cleaned up then went back to the bay.

His thoughts the night before had been a jumble, but as he looked over the massive digger, he realized he had made the right decision. The digger would move more dirt then two smaller machines and require less crew. There was only a risk if the ground was bad. He, and now AnnaChi, had a lot to learn about prospecting good land, the copper fields had been pure luck. But with the colony demand for more resources than could be supplied, he believed they could make a profit. In the worst of cases, the digger dredge could be sold. It was worth many times more than the smaller diggers

Something he had heard the miners quote often stuck in his thought as finished locking down the digger; *when in doubt, you need to drill.* With modern scanning equipment, there was not as much need to drill test holes, but he had witnessed a small drill rig being used on nearly every mining site he had spent any time around. Certainly, it would be easier to bring a drilling rig along on prospecting trips to test sites the scanners identified, than it would be to set up a whole operation without being sure of the ground's worth. Once decided, it didn't take long to locate the shed devoted to drilling machines, and to his surprise, a wide range of explosives.

Nearly half the shed was filled with core sample tubes and spare drill heads of different types and sizes. Ignoring the blasting supplies at first, he realized there was several different types of mobile drilling machines before him. After a little research, he took a core drill and smaller hammer drill rig, as well as everything he could identify as belonging to the machines. Even loading a few skids of clear core-sample tubes since they would not mass too much. Before moving on, Kasey took a long look at the blasting equipment. It was tempting, but far out of his skillset to handle the explosives, and he wasn't sure he wanted them on his ship without knowing just how stable they were. A distant rumble of thunder accentuated the decision as he left the shed behind.

Opening the large machine hanger, he was disappointed at what little was left. There was no doubt that much of the company's machinery was left out in the fields when the catastrophe had happened. While no expert, it was easy for Kasey to tell that what remained here was the equipment no team had wanted. All were in lousy condition and he had his doubts if some still worked at all.

Walking up to two well-used excavators that remained in the hanger he assessed the machines. Both were smaller than what he had hoped to find, and both were in questionable working condition. The only saving-grace was that they were both of the same model and had some interchangeable parts. With no other good choices, he took them both, ever-conscious of the mass they would take up. After moving a loader, dozer and a hauler into the ship, he realized there was not enough mass left for another large machine even though he still had the space. He had expected to load several more haulers, but it was a start, and there was a lot of lower mass equipment he needed to gather yet.

Exploring the remnants of the base took more time than he had planned. A good bit of the tools and equipment throughout was gone, apparently taken in a rush during the evacuation. Still, the maintenance buildings proved to be a treasure trove of supplies. Crate after crate of supplies were loaded.

Technically he knew he was rightfully salvaging, but he felt like a pirate as he searched for anything of value. With the mass limitations, he began ignoring heavier items in lieu of lighter, high-cost items that could be traded for credits. With Fran's connections, he trusted that selling or trading the items for what they needed would be feasible.

It was hard to ignore the array of milling machines, lathes and other useful apparatuses around the main shop floor, but the mass was just too great to take any of them. A lot of the shop had still been being set up and only a few project and repairs were in progress. Although the shop could handle a lot more, most of the normal staff had been supplementing the mining teams in locating and setting up operations.

Looking through the rows of crates that lined the walls, one large crate caught his eye. Breaking the seal, he opened the container revealing a small but industrial-grade fabricator. The unit could render most smaller parts, tool and other useful objects if the base materials were available. Looking around he identified crates of various materials and compounds for the fabricator but frowned when he started adding up the mass of it all. It was all too much. Disregarding the materials, he loaded just the fabricator onto the ship, accepting that the base materials could be purchased as needed later, but the machine itself was far beyond what his budget could afford. The raven had a smaller, and simpler, unit on board, but it did not compare to the larger unit's potential.

With little allowance for mass left, he poked around offices, looking for anything of interest, but there was little other than a few rare-looking bottles of scotch that were likely reserved for important clients. It was time to leave, but he found it difficult to go back to the ship knowing it would be the last anyone would walk the building. Passing the base's system core room, he stopped and went inside. It wasn't like a ship's core room at all. On a ship, the cores were protected, instead here there were tablets and boxes everywhere and even a coffee cup on top a core tower.

The scene was nearly an affront to his sensibilities. In space, if a core was damaged people could die, but planet-side; maybe the worst that could happen is a loss of lighting until it was replaced, he assumed. He shrugged and looked over the cores, noticing another difference. Each core had a concise label describing what it stored and controlled, whereas a ship constantly shifted core usage based on need. Two of the cores appeared dedicated to system operations and mapping. Not knowing if they contained useful information or not, he powered the two down and loaded them onto a cart, then made his way to the raven.

Somehow taking the cores made it easier to leave the empty base behind. The base, he realized, likely would not even exist had it not been for Darnel and his discovery of the n-mats in the area. In some respects, he felt he deserved the cores and whatever they contained.

As he exited the building, he was astounded that the winds had stopped blowing for the first time since he had landed. It was fitting to honor all the lost workers and friends who used to work in the mining base. He stopped. Where were they all? He had found no bodies in the base but only a few had made it safely to Belrothi. Something was wrong with what he knew, but there was little he could do until he was airborne.

The last-minute preparation to launch became hours as Kasey pumped the remaining n-mats from the base into the ship's built-in tanks. He then had to dump the majority of his potable water supply as he realized that he had not allowed for the bard's mass. The water was expendable and the Cintian carried plenty to spare, so he dumped all that he could to assist with an expeditious trip through the storm waiting for him in the atmosphere. Every little bit helped.

CHAPTER TWENTY-SIX

Snow had begun to fall as Kasey performed a final check on the external ports atop the ship. Without warning, a strong gust of wind knocked him off balance. Quick-stepping in an attempt to regain balance, he found himself teetering at the ship's edge, waving his arms wildly trying not to fall off. Just before dropping over the side, a weight slammed into his back, sending him sprawling on the hull. A sharp whistle-like chirp pierced the air and was gone before he could see what it had been.

For some time, he only sat, catching his breath as well as his wits. Surprised that any creature had lived for so long on the dead world. It was amazing, but he found he was more astonished that it had apparently just saved his life.

Whatever had saved him was gone, lost in the dark landscape before he could get a look. He had no idea how something could be surviving here, but it was a refreshing feeling to know he wasn't alone.

The more he thought about it, the more he found himself energized from the encounter. Finishing another port, he moved to the next, only to be confronted by a large pale-orange bird that landed before him.

The creature gave a long, drawn-out whistle, which was so near a whine that he felt a pang of guilt.

Kneeling to get a better look through the thickening snow, he was shocked. It was not only the same type of creature he had seen so long ago in the moments before the destruction of this world, but it was quite possibly the very same creature. The same damaged ridge scales on the wing and blue eyes swirled at him. It was, however, much paler and thinner than he remembered. Its beak and talons were worn and heavily chipped from overuse in the harsh environment.

Pulling open his pack he produced some water and a meaty protein bar, offering it to the diminished avian. The meal was gulped down in haste, after which the creature gave him another long penetrating look before flying off. Kasey was thoughtful as he finished his work. He found himself looking over his shoulder every few minutes, expecting the world to be ending once again as it had after his first encounter with the strange creature.

Hours later he was standing before the large opening of the ship's main hanger with a sadness in his eyes. His entire being ached for the lost world. Everyone had thought the world long dead, but it seemed some still struggled for survival here. Looking around, he could not find much real hope that the world would sustain life much longer.

Taking off his rebreather, he tossed it in the ship's bay with abandon and took a deep breath of the cold, stale air of Lithose. He wanted to remember it. Before turning to leave, he gave a long whistle, as close to that of the creature as he could.

The whistle was answered immediately, as if his call was expected. An instant later, the orange creature quickly landed at his feet.

"Do you want to come along my little orange harbinger?" he asked it, feeling more than silly. The feeling, however, was short-lived as the orange creature gave a quick bow-like movement, then gave a piercing call into the air before scurrying past him and into the bay.

Kasey gave a quick laugh then stepped back in surprise. Two smaller versions of the creature zoomed into the bay to join the original with a fretful cooing noise before all three curled up together in a nearby corner. The orange was unmistakably the motherly protector of the smaller avian. One blue, the other green. The pair chirped questioningly at the orange, who gurgled a reassurance that sounded a bit weak and unsure, even to Kasey.

After a few more exchanges, the motherly orange looked directly at Kasey and chirped in a low tone. He was never sure if it was the sound, his own stomach, or if it was just in his head, but he was filled with feelings of hunger. A primal hunger.

Knowing his own emotions were highly on edge, he shrugged off the feeling that the creature could be communicating with him in some strange way. Identifying with the orange and what it had survived on his world was more than enough reason to feel as he was. Still, almost without knowing it, he found himself in search of some preserved meats and more protein bars that he knew would be aboard.

Soon his guests were fed. Kasey did what he could with the bay's configuration system to box off a small corner area to keep them safe. Tossing a few blankets in the enclosure, he hoped it would be suitable for the creatures. Turning to call them over, he was surprised to find all three lined up and waiting to inspect his work. A few clicks and whistles later and they were all settled in.

With no more reason to delay, he released a waiting n-mats balloon to let AnnaChi know his launch plans, then sealed the cargo bay and made ready for takeoff.

Suited up and strapped into the helm, he prepared to release the polymagnetic docking locks but stopped, his thoughts were back on the people who disappeared from the base. If they had not made it to Belrothi, what had happened to them? A quick check of the docking system showed sixteen crafts breaking lock at approximately the same time the day of the disaster, grouped for safety.

Asking the system to compute a basic historical flight plan for the same time period resulted in a handful curved trajectories on his main screen. All pointed south-west before curving over the mountains in a steep ascension.

Nodding to himself, he picked the trajectory he would have chosen then inverted his thrusters to point upwards. With a deep breath, he released the polymagnetic docking locks, immediately sending the n-mats laden craft upwards. Activating the thrusters, he increased power to counteract the n-mats until the ship hovered over the base.

With a last look down at the base, he slowly eased the ship along the trajectory, staying close to the surface. Just as he reached the foothills on the far side of the Thorn Backs, he began picking up anomalies in the terrain below. Descending closer to the largest one showed a debris field of what he assumed had been a basic heavy transport. Checking the computed trajectory showed they would have been nearly twenty kilometers aloft when something had gone wrong. Kasey unsuccessfully tried not to imagine the awful fall they must have experienced.

Mapping the area, he located the remains of all sixteen ships. Very little remained of them. No sign or signal from any escape pods were found, and there was no indication that any had even been launched.

Taking a moment to say his goodbyes, he sealed his pressurized flight suit and helmet. Pulling the helm's straps tight, he sent a silent command to run the script he had prepared. Four of the six thrusters powered down and gimbled one eighty degrees downward while the remaining two midship thrusters took up the slack, keeping the raven hovering. Once in position, the four ignited again and went to full thrust at the same time as the midship thrusters shut down, gimbled downward, then joined the others pushing the raven transport up towards the waiting storm. Speed counted, every millisecond he could shave off his time spent in the storm improved his odds of survival.

Kasey listened to the roar as he watched the single powered monitor showing his ascent. The seconds ticked down as he was pressed further into the well-cushioned helm. Abruptly, the thrusters stopped, and the status screen went dark. All power in the ship was gone, leaving him in a quiet, pitch-dark void. He felt the acceleration boost slipping away quickly as the first crackle of thunder shook the raven. It was up to the n-mats to get him through now. The storm intensified as he felt the ship slow and seemed to stop. He knew he was still ascending but he couldn't shake the feeling that he had miscalculated—that he had brought only enough n-mats to make it up into the storm, but no further. Leaving him trapped in the tempus forever.

Without warning, the ship began tumbling uncontrollably. With no power, he had no control, so he closed his eyes and waited. Time seemed to slow as the sound of the storm began to fade, then abruptly there was nothing but silence. Opening his eyes, he saw only blackness, then without warning a mass of stars rushed by the ports followed again by blackness. The spectacle continued, slowing with each revolution of the spinning craft until it finally settled into drawn-out wobble.

Reaching out, he flipped a newly installed switch allowing a small battery pack to power the incoming comm array. Once it connected to his mimic interface he unstrapped from the helm. Reveling momentary in the weightlessness, he guided himself to a wide port to view the starscape and wait.

Time passed quickly as he watched the planet gradually fall away, his trepidation growing steadily. AnnaChi should have contacted him by now in his estimation. Even if only a couple of the messages he had sent had been intercepted by her, she would have a good idea of when and where he would be emerging. They had discussed this part of the plan in detail many times. While they had not really been expecting to be caught plundering the planet, it had still been a concern worth planning for. The risk of the n-mats being discovered was too big a chance to do otherwise.

All he could think about was what had gone wrong. Ideally, she would have known within a hundred kilometers of where to expect him. Knowing where to look, the Cintian would have no issues detecting whatever ship he brought back, even with him running cold. She should have been sending a directed message to him with updates and instructions. If that didn't work out, then he was to drift for as long as possible while running cold, so he wouldn't be easily detected by anyone who did not know where to look. If two standard days passed, he was to go hot and head for the backup coordinates they had picked out.

Hours went by as he waited for a message, any message. Lithose stopped shrinking when the dark planet was the size of a dinner plate. But his worries grew. Grinding his teeth, he resisted the urge to power up the ship and go into stealth mode to look for her instead. Plans be damned.

He was just about to give up when a message from an unknown source appeared on his mimic interface.

Stay cold. Do not respond unless emergency. Linkup

in D-1 circuit time.

Laughing and delighted, he relaxed. She must have set a buoy with a short-range signal to catch him on his drift. Meaning she was staying away from the area for some reason. He hoped it was nothing too serious. Would they face charges for looting a military ship from a dead planet, he wondered?

He remembered all too well the many small Daveri One moon circuits, or D-1s, he had started out on when he had first started working that system. The D-1 was a twenty-standard hour trip from start to finish, which stopped at all the resort moons to ferry travelers around the vacation spots. Knowing he would see her in about a standard day, he went to check on the cargo, living and otherwise.

Zero-g turned out to be an enjoyable experience for the scaly birds. They had taken to it with an ease that made Kasey jealous. The avian were tremendously skilled in the arena-like atmosphere. Wings, it appeared, were extremely useful in weightless flight. Watching them sail about in apparent merriment passed most of the time waiting for AnnaChi's next contact.

CHAPTER TWENTY-SEVEN

A day passed before another message flitted across his mimic interface.

Safe now. Power up. See you in a moment.

The muffled sounds of a starboard docking bay making contact alerted Kasey that she was already docking.

Starting up systems as quickly as possible, he was happy to finally have his shields under power again. Turning up the localized gravity slowly, so as not to damage or injure anything onboard, he exited the bridge and ran to the dock. Their embrace lasted only a moment before the sharp hissing chirp of the orange caused AnnaChi to jump back in surprise.

"I hope you don't mind, but I picked up a few stowaways." He explained between breaths. The blue and green birds stumbled out to see what all the fuss was about, just in time to emphasize the point. He was glad to see they were none the worse for the return to normal gravity.

She knelt to coax the orange avian forward. "And just who are these pretty creatures?"

"Uh, well I don't really know. I ran into this orange damsel right before the Abscond's engine fell to

Lithose."

"Hmm, I think they are, or were, called Atoss. Not sure why. I've not had much to do while waiting for you, so I read quite a bit on Lithose. The surveyor's notes on the planet were nowhere near completed, but the atoss were noted at the top of the 'to be studied further' list. I think they called them friendly predators."

"Atoss, huh? Well they do seem friendly enough. I have no idea how she could have survived so close to the explosion—I barely did—nor how she found me so far from where I had originally met her. They must be very resistant to radiation."

"How bad was the contamination down there?" AnnaChi interrupted.

"Much lower than we thought, thankfully," He smiled as the orange atoss seemed as taken with AnnaChi has he was. "She saved me yesterday from falling, although it could have just been a coincidence… I think she is quite intelligent," at which the orange gave a gratified chirp, "and well, I couldn't have left them behind."

AnnaChi gave him an understanding squeeze. "Well let's hope it was not for nothing, I saw at least three Cassian orbs scanning the atmosphere…" she let the sentence hang.

It took just a few quickening heartbeats for Kasey to realize the significance, and just as quickly the blood drained from his face.

The Cassian species were not friends of the human worlds. Most viewed them as the galaxy's charlatans, but all knew the horrific atrocities their race had inflicted throughout human history. Hundreds of wars on early Earth Prime had been caused by their mischievous involvements. Entire societies wiped out for their pleasure, usually with them posing as some god-like entity.

Their actions had given humanity a unified cause to fight against; a purpose to come together for. What was once a fractured human race had solidified into a true federation. The Cassian had been routed out of the human controlled star clusters several hundred years ago, never to be allowed to return. Every now and again, a sighting appeared on the distant edges of the federation, and every detection was met with massive resistance in a never-ending galactic cat and mouse game.

For the Cassian to have followed their voyage so far away from the Earth Prime cluster was beyond bad news for the colony. Worse, if the Cassian had seen them, it was a sure bet they would not allow AnnaChi and Kasey to survive long enough to warn the colony.

Kasey came to this conclusion and took off running for the bridge shouting commands to the ship's AI, with AnnaChi hot on his heels. "They didn't see me, if they had they would have attacked me already," she shouted from behind.

He would have responded, but the impact alarm abruptly began to sound. With only a few strides remaining to the bridge, he practicality dove at the weapon system's panel to switch on the point defense arrays. A slight buzzing sound could be heard from all over the ship as the defensive fire homed in on the incoming objects. Panels lit up as several more successive objects were detected arcing towards them from the same origin. Within moments the buzzing stopped as the objects were destroyed.

Kasey didn't stop there; there was no longer a reason to hide. Bringing the ship's defensive systems fully online as quickly as he could, he settled into the helm's cushion and strapped in. Once he had the ship arcing towards the planet's smallest moon, he brought up the ship's accelerator cannon. He was immediately disappointed at the basic setup and took a few moments to program in a defensive firing variant.

The accelerator cannon took a lot of power to run at full capacity and the battery banks could only recharge so fast. Each slug the cannon fired could be positively or negatively charged to eat away at an enemy's shield. The amount of charge, the velocity of the slug leaving the accelerator rails, and the rate of fire could all be independently configured.

Dropping the slug's charge altogether and slowing the rail's velocity down helped him to free up a ton of power. Reallocating most of that power into increasing the cannon's rate of fire. Running a quick simulation, he adjusted the rate back down some to allow a lengthy sustained fire before he would need to stop and allow the batteries to recharge. It would allow him to effectively drop walls of slugs into the path of incoming missiles. He would prefer to reprogram the point defense arrays as well to adjust for the cannon's fire, but now was not the time. A few moments later, he was able to add a couple simple firing variants for attacking as well.

He cursed himself for not taking the time to set up custom routines for the new ship while he was still planet-side. There were far more efficient variants he could program, even using the ship's AI to account for hundreds of factors and adjust settings on the fly. But at least he was in control now. If the Cassian wanted to fight, he could oblige. But he hoped to avoid that if possible.

Quickly launching off two small drones in random directions that would duplicate their own signature, he fired the thrusters to full. No need to make it easy on them.

For now, the space around them seemed clear. Turning, he found AnnaChi pouring over the screens with playful envy.

Without looking up she waved around the bridge. "So… This is no commoner's transport. Just where did you find this lovely ship?"

"You remember the government ships I mentioned we were using for the n-mats?" He didn't wait for her answer. "Well, it was the only ship left at the mine. Actually, nothing was left of the Hammer Wrest base at all, something had leveled the whole area."

He caught her immediate frown at the description, so he plowed on before she could voice her thoughts on the danger he had been in.

"So, I went to the next nearest n-mats mine. I think this ship was only left behind because the pilot was not able to fly. Who knows. But since I have the access to fly these, well, it was very lucky for us."

"Wait. Won't the government be tracking the ship like they did when Darnell and you discovered the n-mats? We may not get to keep it if they…" he stopped her with a mischievous smile.

"I removed all the communication arrays from the ship, the only comm I have is this," he tapped his head to indicate his own mimic interface. "I'm linked into the drop pod's mini array that I rigged in as a temporary replacement, and now the Cintian's."

Her answering look was less than skeptical.

"Yea," he agreed, "we will need to work out some permanent solution if we plan to use this for more than one trip. For now, it is what we have. It would have taken days to get to another base or to find other ships."

Before she could reply, a large blip appeared, representing an orb ship which appeared to be launching more projectiles. Ignoring the attack for a moment, Kasey locked the accelerator cannon onto the orb ship itself and fired until it disappeared off the sensors. The buzzing from the defensive systems he had not noticed starting, ended a few seconds later.

After a few minutes of watching the empty screens, AnnaChi cleared her throat and continued the conversation as if she had not been interrupted by an attack.

"Well, first we will need to get back to the colony in one piece. The Cassian will not stop if they can help it. I really didn't think they had detected me. I guess maybe they were watching during the drop and were just waiting for you to reappear."

Her hands worked over tactical display for a few seconds, "Here, I plotted a new course that may help if they have any friends trying to cut us off. Once we start into this course change," she expanded the trajectory sample, "cut the thrusters and drift, but send another drone off to continue through the course change."

"I see, but I do have several more drones we could use as well."

"Negative," she smiled at him, "if we use more than one, they will follow them all and assume we used drones, but if we use just one then they will hopefully assume it is still us. Hey, didn't you mention these ships had a stealth package?"

"I see. Umm, yes, they do, but the stealth fields wouldn't be able to hide the Cintian, although it would reduce its signature somewhat."

"It will help. You will need to activate it the moment the drone comes online, as well as cutting thrusters. Is that doable?"

"Yes," he responded pointing to his head, "the mimic interface allows for a lot of multitasking. Let's do it. Once we restart our thrusters for the final run, we can put the Cintian's thrusters to use as well if we can match up the frequencies. If they double back to search, they may not account for the additional thrust."

"Okay," she gave him a hard kiss, "I'll go get my baby ready." She happily bounced her way out of the bridge, apparently enjoying every bit of the situation.

CHAPTER TWENTY-EIGHT

Just under a day's travel remained when the first of many distress signals started pouring in.

Within the last few hours, it appeared the Patternists had struck again. A fight to take control of the Belrothi-Abscond station and declaring the colony's independence from the federation had taken place.

It was hard to listen to the reports of a battle hours old, not knowing where it would end and what it meant for the colony. It began with scattered accounts of small skirmishes broadcasting without clear purpose, in many cases with no clear results, but escalated quickly into a full-scale battle. Before long, it was clear that the federation troops had been taken completely unaware. It didn't take long for the battle to turn into a retreat. All that followed were reports of federation forces retreating planet-side.

Rumors ran the net for hours after, but the result was clear. Too many military ships had been taken with the Belrothi-Abscond's seizure, leaving only a trivial force to fight back with. It was unlikely the Belrothi-Abscond could be retaken.

Many speculated that the cult had infiltrated several government and military posts, while others pointed toward groups of the Abscond's workers. It was clear either way that the federation had been overthrown. The Patternists were now fully in charge.

AnnaChi and Kasey scanned the feeds for any mention of the Cassian, but so far, no indication had been made about their possible involvement. AnnaChi had sent several warnings after the Cassian had first attacked. Seemingly these had either been ignored or somehow stopped. She had to admit that it was just as likely that the truth was already known by the government, who then simply chose to cover it up.

It seemed obvious now, to both, that the Patternists movement among the settlers had been greatly exasperated by Cassian influence. This was exactly the kind of historical problems they had been known for. Not that any of it really mattered at this point. Fighting a war wasn't something either wanted any part of.

Kasey was embarrassingly torn on what outcome he wanted. He wanted nothing to do with the federation, but neither did he want Cassian controlled Patternists zealots ruling over his life and livelihood. The Pattern only complicated matters.

The Pattern was a common fact in the federation, and had been proven again and again, to the point that virtually no skeptics existed. The possibility of beating the Pattern was unknown, but was not considered impossible, not that anyone knew how. For that matter, no one knew what the Pattern even was, if it even was a thing or a natural occurrence.

Some theorists, mostly Patternists, claimed that intelligent life was like bees in a yard. No one minds the bees buzzing around until they build a hive. As soon as the hive is noticed by the yard's owners, the hive is destroyed. In the same way, sentient life is tolerated in moderation, but when the life carves out a real slice of the galaxy for themselves, a similar fate could await. Not a future any human would accept, yet not one any had the ability to avoid.

Would being independent of the federation make any difference where the Pattern is concerned? Kasey wondered. Not likely, but being so far away from the Earth Prime cluster, it seemed like a possibility.

All the portents were bad, as far as Kasey was concerned. He just wanted to be left to live his own life, without others controlling or threatening his ability to do so.

By the time they reached the Belrothi atmosphere, all the attacks had subsided. The news streams reported the same stories repeatedly, and the distress calls slowed to a trickle. There was nothing they could do to help, even if they had wanted to. The Belrothi-Abscond was a formidable ship, and with it, the Patternists controlled a superior force of weaponry and ships. Even with the force currently stationed at the Vethi moon colony, Federation forces would be no match for the might of the Belrothi-Abscond's defenses.

Keeping a healthy distance from the Belrothi-Abscond station, they dropped quietly to the planet below, and eventually, home.

The new ship was far too big for the hanger at the main house, but they needed to keep the ship hidden for a while. Instead, Kasey set it down at their getaway lodge directly in front of the cavern entrance. The area was already well shielded from scans and even casual glances, thanks to a dozen holographic projectors providing an illusionary camouflage over the area. The ship just barely fit into the shielded area, but with a few adjustments to the system they had been able to shut the ship down completely, including its own stealth array. The ship needed a full checkup, and AnnaChi insisted it be double checked for any tracking equipment that he may have missed that would allow the government to find it.

Taking a skimmer up to the main house, he was happy to see AnnaChi was only just opening the Cintian's hanger. They had relocated the atoss into the Cintian shortly after linking the ships, as there was currently a lot more open space in the hanger for them.

He was glad to find they had not flown away yet.

The motherly orange atoss was the first to exit the hanger. She circled their home several times before landing in front of AnnaChi and Kasey to warble at them in apparent satisfaction.

"You're welcome Orange," Kasey said awkwardly. The name Orange seemed odd, but Kasey felt strange about naming such a seemingly intelligent creature. However, he had called and referred to the motherly creature as Orange so many times on the trip that the name stuck anyway, and she responded well to it.

AnnaChi had no such hesitation. On their first day, she had named the blue atoss who was usually at her heels, Molly. Molly was female, and seemed to share some bond with AnnaChi after only a few days. AnnaChi named the green as well, Mawk. Mawk was smaller, and shy more often than not.

The couple had gotten to know Orange and the two smaller atoss quite well on the voyage. AnnaChi walked up to her and scratched her scaled back ridge. "You can call Molly and Mawk out. They are in no danger here at our home."

"They are welcome to call it home too if they like." Kasey said, as AnnaChi nodded in agreement. "There is plenty of room for all of us."

A low toned chip in response was all the agreement they needed. Orange chirped again sharply and first the blue, Molly, poked her head out and waddled down the ramp looking about. Mawk, the green, was slower and more cautious. He kept just inside the hatchway until another chirp ordered him out. With a leap, he glided down, narrowly missing Molly's head as he passed.

The trio stayed only long enough to receive a round of ridge scratching before darting away to swoop down into the waiting valley.

"I didn't believe you... Had I blinked, I would have sworn they disappeared."

"Told you they were fast," Kasey squeezed her in a one-armed hug as they watched the valley below, hoping to catch a final glimpse of the creatures. "They will be back. Orange found me half a continent away after a single meeting nearly year ago. I think they will have no problem remembering and finding us here again."

"There is certainly something special about them," she whispered.

"They are the last of their kind now. I just hope humanity doesn't ruin this world for them as well."

The sun sank low toward the horizon before the couple found their way into the mountain home that marked the end of their latest venture.

* * *

They woke to the sound of a shuttle landing in the courtyard. No alarms had sounded, but AnnaChi was already armed before Kasey made it out of bed.

"It's Fran. He is the only one who has the code."

"Check anyway," she scolded. "Always check, codes can be faked."

"Done, and it looks like he brought breakfast."

Before long, they were dressed and rushing out to meet their friend. The shuttle was gone, but had left behind a well-supplied food cart, which Mad Fran was busily unloading onto the garden table.

"Hey, have you been using our place for picnics while we were away?" AnnaChi greeted as she placed a warm kiss on his check.

"Well met, you two. Glad to see you have returned from your salvage mission." Taking a seat, he waved for them to do the same. "So, were there any derelict ships floating around that old planet waiting for you pirates to drag home?"

"Not exactly," Kasey murmured through a mouthful of some kind of bread.

"I see." He turned back to the cart to retrieve a carafe of juice.

Kasey looked at AnnaChi with a questioning look. They had discussed bringing Fran into the new business venture. The barkeep's contacts and resources had been invaluable to them, and he was as true a friend as they had ever known. They planned to wait until they got everything in place before bringing him into the fold, but the time now just seemed right. She nodded her agreement as Fran turned back to the table.

"Um, well," Kasey began, "we didn't actually look for scrap in orbit, but we did visit Lithose."

"I am not following you there young Kasey. What else would be out there worth such a long trip?" His eyes locked onto Kasey as he raised an eyebrow that seemed to question Kasey's sanity.

Kasey lost whatever he had been planning to say and simply blurted out, "I went down to the planet."

Fran was out of his seat in shock, "And they call me Mad! You are a fool to risk your life like that." He moved protectively to AnnaChi's side. "If something had happened to you, do you know what you would have put her through? Again!"

"Stop!" AnnaChi commanded.

No one was sure if she meant the conversation, or the three deadly-looking atoss that were suddenly surrounding the table. Everyone stopped, except for Molly, who hissed from AnnaChi's side.

"My dear Fran," she said sweetly; more to calm the atoss than Fran. "There is something you need to see. Kasey was in less danger than you think."

"AnnaChi?" Kasey asked, a little panicked at giving up this secret.

"We are all-in dear. Fran is as good as family, it's time he knows." She reached down and gave Molly a good scratch until she was calm. "I think breakfast is over. But you three deserve a treat."

Setting a bowl of sausage between them, Mawk and Molly rushed in but stopped at a sharp whistle from Orange. Striding forward to take the largest piece for herself, Orange clicked at the others, who warily followed suit in a nearly polite manner.

"Thank you dear," she addressed Orange with a head rub. "Come on boys. Let's take a ride." Walking off, the men had little choice but to follow.

Fran came last, with a slight smile on his face. Orange swooped silently in front of him, halting him with a strange peering look.

Fran's smile faltered. He nodded at the atoss. "You have nothing to fear from me friend."

Satisfied, Orange dashed back to the meal, leaving Fran with a curious look on his face as he hurried to catch up with Kasey.

Not much was said on the short skimmer ride to the retreat house. Fran had been here many times with the couple and moved toward the pond to enjoy the view, but Kasey called him toward the path leading to the waterfall. Halfway to the fall, they diverted up a rocky hill, devoid of any foliage.

The couple waited for Fran to catch up and then waved him on. As one, they moved forward, and everything changed as the projected camouflaging field was breached.

The strange raven class transport appeared in all its glory.

"Okay," Fran responded to the sight with more curiosity than surprise. "It's a nice ship. Government issue I would guess. Still, I don't see how this would have gotten you through the atmosphere in one piece."

Kasey nodded to the ship and an aft bay door opened; a ramp descending before them, "Come see."

Fran took in the mass of equipment packed into the bay, but Kasey diverted his attention to the pyramid shaped ceiling, and the dozens of barrels that seemed to be strapped to it.

"Odd looking. What's in the barrels?" He asked with little amusement.

"They contain hundreds of metric tons of negative matter."

Fran started to say something but was overcome with a coughing fit. When he finished, he looked at the two, then back to the barrels. "Pardon, swallowed wrong. Negative what now?"

"Negative matter. It's a long story, but suffice to say that it is like any other matter, but somehow has negative mass. Kind of like helium, it floats, but not just in air. It is some kind of antigravity-like effect I suppose."

"I see. Um, metric tons... What kind of this negative matter did you say you have up there?"

"Mostly mercury in the small barrels, but the large storage tanks are a mix of less dense elements..."

AnnaChi cut in, seeing Fran was having a tough time processing it all. "We are sorry we couldn't show you before. You may not understand, but the government wants this controlled. Kasey and a friend discovered some of it on Lithose and they practically took over the entire company."

Kasey stepped forward, "I came here to get away; not

just from my loss," he glanced at AnnaChi, "but from our oppressive federation. I thought we would find more freedom out here so far away from the federation's control."

Fran walked slowly to the bay door and looked out over the valley beyond the pond, "You feel you would lose your home here, and likely the copper mines too?"

There was no need to reply, silence told the tale. The man stood there, seemingly lost in thought for a long while before nodding to himself.

"I see," he finally said, and then took a deep breath and turned back to face Kasey. "As interesting as it is, there doesn't seem to be much use for the stuff, other than maybe saving some fuel by lightening loads. I don't see why it would be so important to them. Although you seemed to put it to good use."

Kasey swallowed his worry, "I agree with you there. I never did see what all the fuss is about."

"Well then," Fran waved at everything around them, "what are we doing with all this lovely equipment you have retrieved? There seems to be a theme to it all."

"Yea, that is something we were hoping to talk with you about. AnnaChi and I would like to try running our own mining crews, with us running the prospecting, logistics end of it directly. Starting out here in the copper fields, but we are hoping to spend more time searching for more resources once we get things running. This ship and the equipment should help us get started."

Fran nodded as they all walked through the maze of machinery. "You know how all this stuff works?"

"No, not much. We would need a good crew and foreman who can deal with the details. But more importantly, we need someone who can take care of the business end and make sure the right people are being hired. We need a business manager to take care of problems while we are away finding the next claim."

AnnaChi chimed in, "We are hoping you would want that job."

Fran bellowed out a laugh, "Don't you two have enough credits rolling in from the copper fields?"

"That was for credits," she laughed, "this is more for fun!"

"Well, and the credits would be nice too," Kasey added.

"Of course, of course…" he replied as he mulled the idea over. "What kind of startup cost are we looking at?"

AnnaChi shrugged and looked to Kasey as he moved to a wall to pull up his inventory lists showing what they had and what they would need.

"I don't have it all worked out yet, but for natural copper mining we are nearly set. We do need a decent smelter for the native copper added onto the dredge, several buildings and processers set up for each site.

"Flair and I can see what the miners are complaining about. Get a feel for the situation so we can hopefully set up correctly the first time. One thing the Sarsaparilla is good for," he smiled wickedly, "is information."

Everyone smiled at that as Kasey continued.

"Lastly, we need to have a plan for land reclamation on the books before we can start anything. There are several outfits who contract out their services for it, but bigger operations have terra-scrapers to take care of the land as they go. They are quite costly, so for now I have added the contractor cost into our downstream balances, over here."

He pulled up another chart showing the worth of equipment in the bay.

"The digger-dredge is nearly new, so its current value here on Belrothi should be respectable. It is more than we need to get started with the copper fields, but it would be nice to have in the long run. However, we could easily sell or trade it for lower end equipment and hopefully for the remaining gear we need…"

"No need," Fran cut in. "We could quickly lease more of the copper claims to make up this difference. While you were gone, we have received unsolicited bids on at least seven of the mid and higher valued plots, all from the current operations down there. I expected some to notice the better ground eventually, but they have been more ambitious than I suspected. Bottom line is that we could have the remaining credits we need in about a month."

"This is why we need you, old man," AnnaChi said playfully. "So, you are on board?"

"Yes, but I need Flair partnered on this one as well. She is better with the books than I am anyway, and she has been getting bored with my saloon, although she hides it well. She wants to hire someone to manage the bulk of it now that business is doing well. I think this will be the excuse she needs to make that happen. Any problems with that?"

They cheerfully agreed and pushed for an even split between the four of them.

"Got a name for this company?" Fran interjected, "Can't very well run it under Belrothi Copper, different shares and more than just copper."

Kasey looked at AnnaChi who just shrugged. "Haven't really given a name any thought, but we can work on that unless you have suggestions?"

Fran laughed, "I thought it would be obvious! You are starting a company with equipment you rescued from a dead, burned out planet of ash. Only one name would suit such a thing…"

They look at each other then back to Fran in confusion.

"Phoenix Mining!"

Once their laughter subsided, they all agreed the name was perfect.

"I think it's time for a drink to celebrate this new enterprise then! I have a few bottles from my latest batch of toyasow wine back at your house, and I need to talk to Flair, best to make sure my boss agrees and all that."

"Use the retreat," AnnaChi responded with a nod toward the pond, "and then meet up back at the house. It's been weeks since my last proper shower, so take your time. I'll send this skimmer back down for you to use after it drops us off."

Kasey was already out the hatch, "I wonder if the atoss left any food. I am hungry again already."

"I highly doubt it. Mawk seems to have an endless appetite."

AnnaChi stopped Fran at the bottom of the ramp and pointed to a darkened panel high up on the craft. "Tell Flair to be careful and keep an ear open. That mark is from a Cassian orb's projectile. Three of the bastards attacked us on our way back."

He made the connection faster than she expected.

"Cassian! Here? Ah, that's why the Patternists are out of control! I knew there had to be more to this conflict..." He shook his head in doubt, "I'll let her know, and she will want to plant the idea among the crowds a bit too. Maybe if someone realizes the source of the troubles they can start to put an end to it. Get things back to normal."

"Wow, okay. That's a great idea. I was going to post it out on the net anonymously when we got back, but we haven't had a chance and we didn't want to do it from here. Then there was all the news about new attacks. None of our transmissions made it to the colony either..." She shook her head, "Enough, we will talk back at the house."

* * *

242

Fran stood watching as the skimmer took the two back to the house. "Unbelievable... Flair, are you there? Yea things may be heating up and those two are in the thick of it again. I don't think the verse is going to leave them alone just yet... Yes, yes, I agree. But first, I have a job you may be interested in."

* * *

Kasey was looking over the copper field surveys when Fran walk in.

"Your damn bird followed me all the way here. Where did that protective beast come from anyway? They weren't here last time, and that was right before you left."

"Not sure they are actually birds, but which one?"

"The bigger one, Orange you called it, I think..."

"Her actually. And, I am glad they stayed around. I didn't think they would after finally getting out of the ship."

"Woah wait, you mean they are from Lithose? I'm not sure that was a good idea. There are some very strict rules about moving wildlife..."

"Honestly, I don't care. If there is still a government left in a year, I'll be sure to let them know."

"But..."

"But nothing, she saved my life down there. Maybe twice if you count the first time, which was over a year ago, and seconds before the fall. I am likely only here due to her. Anyway, they are quite intelligent, and humanity destroyed their world—I wasn't going to abandon them after they somehow survived down there in that hell for so long."

"Fair enough. I'll back you if you need it." He abruptly changed the subject, "So, what are you working on?"

"Looking for a plot to start this project on. Here are the better groups."

"Always keeping the best plots to yourself, eh?"

"Of course, just following your lead. The heavier concentrations are mostly closer to home here, near the mountain. I would rather our teams mine them and leave the grounds how we want them. Not to mention that the atoss won't be happy with strangers in their territory as it is."

"Makes sense. Hmm. What about this area? We have three good plots together here. If we drop a warehouse in the middle..."

"Where? Ah, we could unload the ship there and set up, as soon as we have a warehouse built, and have a semi-permanent base of operations. Once the paperwork and crew are ready, we could start."

Fran was ever thinking about the cost, "If we first mine the area where the three plots join, it should give us the capital we need to run conveyers to the warehouse from each plot."

"We would still need smelters at each site, the natural copper would be too hard on the conveyers."

"We should have the credits by that point." Fran snapped his fingers, "Oh speaking of which. I was thinking about the terra-scraper. Is it something you could get from Lithose?

"You want to send him back to Lithose?" AnnaChi entered with edge in her voice that left no doubt that the men were in trouble.

"Not at all," Fran attempted to sooth the comment over, "I was only curious. Besides, the Lithose seed bank didn't make it back and there are some indigenous fruits that I had planned on using in new drinks…"

"I can't believe you would even be thinking of this. Just a few hours ago you were enraged that he went!"

"I am much more informed now."

Kasey took a shot, "Using the new raven class ship instead of a drop pod would be a lot safer. If we used water to offset the n-mats I would have much better control within the storm."

"No," she retorted, "we just got back and there is no need. We got what we needed." She turned to Fran, "and you can have the seeds created from the digital DNA, which I am sure made it onto the net."

"I suppose I could."

"And the Cassian are still out there in case you boys forgot."

Fran relented, "Speaking of the Cassian, you said you sent a warning transmission to the colony? How far out were you?"

"About ten standard days at top speed. I can show you the logs."

"No need. But there is no easy way they intercepted a signal from that far out. Fran suggested that they may have done something to your ship somehow…"

AnnaChi was out the door and halfway to her ship before the men realized they were supposed to follow.

They were nearly impossible to see until you knew they were there. All over the outer skin of the small ship were tiny, sticky barbs that were emitting a net-like field that dampened and disbursed all outgoing signals. None were found on the raven or the few parts of the drop pod that he returned with. They eventually concluded the barbs had been placed on her ship while she was waiting for Kasey's return.

AnnaChi's cheeks turned red in anger as she realized the Cassian had been waiting for Kasey's return before attacking. They could have taken out the Cintian at any time and she would have been helpless. She knew it had been a possibility, but now it was a fact that burned to the forefront of her mind. She employed several maintenance bots to remove the devices, then vented her rage on the first breakable object she came across.

The men followed her, unwilling to even try to reason with her until she opened a concealed weapons locker in the back of a tool shed that neither of them knew existed.

She wanted to go to war, and now. While she couldn't be convinced to stop, they abated her immediate rashness by agreeing to join her, but insisted she needed a real plan.

The first order of business was to alert the colony of the Cassian involvement. Fran took care of it anonymously using what he said were back channels. There wasn't enough useful data in the ship's logs to show anything except that an attack happened. But many, they hoped, would believe them. Normally that would be enough to bring the federation's might against the foe, but not here and now. The colony was on its own.

AnnaChi felt personally violated and guilty for not knowing she had been used to put Kasey in danger. She insisted on hashing out a plan to launch some sort of counterattack against the sphere wielders. It took a while to convince the guys, but they gave in once she explained her initial plan. Strangely, it was still unclear who would be enforcing the laws and restrictions now that the government was basically overthrown. If AnnaChi had her way, they would need to break several.

CHAPTER TWENTY-NINE

With the assistance of Fran's resourcefulness, the two pilots were in the air with all three ships a few weeks later. The Cintian was heading to the Sarsaparilla to pick up a delivery to take up to Belrothi-Abscond, as per her normal delivery schedule.

Leaving on a different route, the Lodestar, now slaved to the newly christened raven class transport, the Argonaut, rose out of the atmosphere. The larger raven transport carried enough n-mats to offset its own gravity signature as well as the other ship's, but also carried a bay full of water tankers to equal the mass of the smaller ship's mass. Any gravity wave detectors pointed their way would only note the Lodestar's mass. More direct scans other than a closeup inspection wouldn't note the shimmering effect of the Argonaut's HWG Stealth Package wrapping the ship in a stealth field that allowed light and other waves to wrap around it as if it didn't exist.

Kasey's flight plan set him on a trajectory toward a small gas mining platform around the gas giant Goligen. It would take him on a path very near the area they had been while fleeing the Cassian. Reaching the agreed upon area, he detonated a small charge on his thrusters to simulate a major breakdown and sent out a distress beacon, which had been modified to only broadcast away from the colony.

He drifted for a good hour before the expected response came from the Cintian offering rescue. AnnaChi had replaced a few of the barbed devices onto her ship's hull, hoping it would help her ship be identified by the Cassian if they were still monitoring the area.

The Cintian had barely docked with the Lodestar when Kasey informed her of the incoming cloud of identically barbed dampening devices closing in. They were expecting the Cassian tactic, and had been monitoring for the frequencies they gave off.

She joined him on the Argonaut's bridge in time to watch the ship's AI locate the cloud's point of origin. A moment later the AI had located the orb ship's signature as well and began searching for others like it. AnnaChi settled onto the weapon station's cushion and smiled at the busy Kasey, who pointed to the five other sphere ships that were now revealed on the screens. They were closing fast.

He waited for the last possible moment before releasing a charged shockwave that short-circuited a large portion of the cloud of dampening devices. His accelerator cannon began firing low energy shots at the spheres that would do little damage, but hopefully giving the enemy false confidence. In the confusion of his sudden, but weak attack, he hoped they wouldn't notice the targeting lasers he had painting the orb's hulls.

The spheres pressed in closer as they launched a continuous stream of missiles for Kasey's point defenses to destroy. The attacks increased the closer they came, and soon the missiles were getting so close the shockwaves could be felt as each were destroyed.

Just as they began to really worry, new signatures

started to appear on each of the orb's hulls. The attacks started to slow and eventually stopped.

Hours earlier, AnnaChi had deployed nearly a hundred of the heat exchanger rods which Fran had somehow acquired and modified for this operation. Now, the needle-like kinetic projectiles pierced the orbs with ease, but did little damage at first. Slowly, each rod began to glow red, and then white-hot as they bled off massive amounts of energy from the sphere every second.

Escape pods launched from the orbs as Kasey increased power to the accelerator cannon, turning its full potential upon the nearest orb ships. In the end, three ships lay in ruins as the others fled for deep space. It was a small victory, knowing that if so many ships were in this one area, hundreds more could be scattered throughout the system.

"Well, that went well," Kasey smiled over toward AnnaChi.

"Yep," she responded with a smug smile, as she wiggled down low in the station and propped her legs up on the weapons console as if to take a nap.

"I don't mean to interrupt your rest, but we need get moving."

She stifled a yawn and smiled at him.

"Um, we need to move the n-mats to the other ships and jettison some of the water so we can take advantage of some low mass speeds in case they come back for us. This *was* your plan dear."

She opened one eye and muttered, "It *was* my plan, as in past tense. There has been a slight change."

"What?"

A new voice entered the cabin, "We are all set to go. Just need to collect the remains of the orbs to take back and… Uh. Oh, you didn't tell him, did you?"

"Well that wouldn't have been any fun," AnnaChi

giggled.

"Fran? What the hell are you doing here... Flair too? Well welcome aboard and all that, but would someone mind explaining what the hell is going on?"

"I hired us a cheap crew."

"We are not your crew lass!" Fran shot back.

Flair, ever the voice of reason, spoke up, "I will be piloting your Lodestar with the Cintian in tow back to Belrothi, with the remains of the Cassian orbs. Contrary to AnnaChi's claims that we would need the extra speed to outrun any other orbs in the area, we won't. There is a patrol coming in from Vethi, and they are still under Terrantine Federation command. We will intercept their route in about three hours if we leave soon. We will be more than safe," she grinned playfully at the guilty-looking AnnaChi. "All per her plan."

"AnnaChi, dear," Kasey was failing at suppressing a smile, "what are you planning next?"

Giving up the game, she abruptly sat up to explain. "This attack was risky, more so than I would admit even with both you boys trying to tell me so. You all accepted this risk, but I shot you down when you wanted to go back down to Lithose. Flair had to explain it all to me really..."

She looked down in mock remorse, but when no one was buying it, she continued on, "Right, so I felt bad and all, so I decided that since we were going to be out here already... You will notice Lithose's orbit is quite a bit closer now, we are only a week or so out. I figured that if we could put the Cassian on the run, well... We would be clear for a while, right? And with this fancy stealth ship and all, while we would be in the neighborhood, I thought we might as well stop by and do some pirating."

"You want to be a pirate, is that it?" Kasey smiled.

"Well yea! I mean, kind of... Anyway, Flair, do you want to explain what you heard?"

"Don't let her pin this on me, Kasey, this is *her* plan. But yes, lots of Federation military types come through the saloon. They like to drink, and even more so, they like to talk. All they talk about now are ways to take back the Belrothi-Abscond and the like. Several times sailors have mentioned the depot on Lithose, in a way that sounds like it, or something there, would make all the difference in the war. Something they feel will help take back the station."

Fran spoke up, in a solemn voice, "Those boys and girls think they are defeated. They need a win to get them back in the fight. If you can get to the depot and find what they need, it could salvage what is left of this colony."

"So," Kasey complained in a voice that left no doubt, "I am supposed to help a Federation who killed my parents just so they can keep their precious immortality treatments under their dominance?"

Fran, his voice grave, asked, "Would you rather the Patternists kill the rest of us off?"

"No, of course not. But I don't know if I want do this for the federation either."

Fran looked at Flair, and several conversations seemed to take place within the glance, but before they finished AnnaChi spoke again.

"I am with you dear," she placed a hand on his arm to draw him in, "but the Cassian have changed this game. Even with the evidence Fran and Flair will take back, the people can't fight and win as it now stands. This colony may not always be tied to the federation, but we will always be tied to the people here, whatever name we go under. Out here, the federation is just a name, but the colony is more than that. And you have lived alongside enough of these people to know that, even if you haven't admitted it yet. We need to help our people."

It took a while to respond, "Okay. Fine, I can agree

with all that." He looked over at Fran and Flair who had a worried looks on their faces. "And I don't think of any of you as I do the federation. You are right, it's the people who matter here. We can do this, but," a smile settled back on his face, "we are keeping a share of the loot for ourselves."

"Well then, let's not forget the terra-scraper and my seeds too," Fran proclaimed, "I'll have the only Lithose beverages in existence!"

"Okay, so we have enough potential water mass to handle just about anything we could fit in the bay. Any idea what we are going after?"

Flair shrugged. "Not sure on that. It would be something they couldn't easily build or wasn't available here. Antimatter for example, but I don't think that's it."

"Likely something made for fighting an unknown alien force," Fran put in. "Farpoint couldn't have known what would be waiting here when we showed up. Backup plans and all that."

"Do we at least have a location?"

"Better than that, we have a key." Flair proudly presented a small, clear glass ring. "It's a navy command ring coded to several bases on Lithose. When in range of a base, about ten or so kilometers, it is supposed to alert the wearer and should grant access to most areas in the base."

"Uh, where exactly did you get that from, and are you sure it will do all that?" It was AnnaChi's turn to doubt their luck.

"The commander who owned it has a habit of playing with it while drinking with his troops. It was easy to switch with a fake. Unless he lied about it, it only works on Lithose, so he will never know the one he has isn't real."

"That's a significant risk you took to get this Flair, I hope it's worth it."

"Maybe, but it's for their own good. It's not like he can use it anyway."

"Right. So, ten kilometers is still a tough spot to find."

"Well," Fran admitted, "most bases are not public knowledge, and most are hidden as well, but we have a few ideas. Still, you will need to search a bit until you get a hit. Any base should have the location of depot bases. Look for a depot base with the name *Faraday* in it, that should be the one."

"So, wait, Belrothi is bigger and has a higher population than Lithose had, right?" Kasey didn't wait for an answer, "So why don't the bases here have what is needed?"

"Ah, well that is something few understand, but it is rather basic. Credits of course." Fran waited for acceptance of his explanation, but found nothing but confused faces staring back. "Ok... Well in case you didn't notice, nearly all the wealthiest families in the colony chose Lithose as their destination, and not by accident. It was expected that much of Lithose would become a luxury planet within the first twenty to forty years of colonization. Several large and exclusive communities and country clubs were planned before the Abscond was even built. In any case, Lithose was far wealthier than Belrothi. Logic demands that military protection follows the credits, even if it is held by a small portion of the community."

Kasey filed that away to consider when he had time to think.

"Okay, got it," Kasey said as he slipped the ring on, which seemed to resize itself to fit his finger. A connectivity signal blipped in his mimic interface, asking for access, which he accepted. "I assume we are still loaded with all the n-mats? We will need to off-ship a bit to drop through the storms..."

"We have it covered, Captain," AnnaChi mocked. "We are now running ninety metric tons heavy, which are set in three quick-released pods, manual or automatic. We can be gravity-neutral seconds after passing through the storm. I will have the rest worked out before we arrive, but we can run some tests as well." She scoffed, "Personally I wanted to remain gravity-neutral for ten thousand meters and break atmosphere at speed at around twenty-five degrees, but Flair insisted the storm could knock us around too much to predict, and with no power to stabilize…" Catching her breath, she waved the idea away, "but apparently, this is not a *fun* trip."

"All credit to Flair then if we survive this," he replied, with as honest an expression as he could muster.

Before long, several fragments of the destroyed orb crafts were loaded into the Lodestar to use as proof. A warning buoy was deployed to monitor the area, which would send a continuous feed back to the colony. If the buoy was destroyed or removed, they would know.

Eight standard days later, the heavy raven class transport Argonaut entered geosynchronous orbit around Lithose and began the slow, unpowered descent into the turbulent lightning storm that had replaced the once calm atmosphere.

CHAPTER THIRTY

"Holy damn!" AnnaChi shrieked in astonishment over the violent clamor assaulting the craft, "This is amazing... We are supposed to survive this, right?"

The translucent-capable sections of the hull were flickering uncontrollably as waves of electrical fields washed over the ship. Flashes lit the abyss in a relentless succession as balls of plasma shot by.

Kasey swallowed his trepidation and forced himself to breathe through the acrid smells permeating the cabin. The storm was far worse than his last trip, but the excitement he heard in AnnaChi's voice was not something he wanted to kill if he decided to cancel this mission.

"We're tumbling, but not as bad as last time," Kasey lied over the din.

The sickening ride lasted far longer than Kasey had anticipated, then without warning, the flashes stopped, "Release the first pod! I am charging EM shields, and thrusters are coming online now."

"We're inverted!" She exclaimed.

"Drop the second pod, I can flip us when thrusters are up in... Ten seconds. We will need to talk about weight distribution before we do this again."

"Dropped. We are falling faster than I expected."

"Too fast. Starboard thrusters are offline. Damn, we're still too heavy! Compensating with stabilizers... This isn't working." He failed to keep the fear from his voice as the ship plummeted into the dark void, toward the planet below.

"I am ready to drop last pod on your go," AnnaChi stated in a flat voice. He could tell she was disappointed. If he ordered her to dump the remaining water pod, they would rise back through the storm into the relative safety of space, and the mission would be over.

"Hold off. Bringing port thrusters lateral and for orbital burn in a transverse plane."

"Are you sure this craft can?"

"No, but we are about to find out. Hold on!" He nearly blacked out from the pressure but fought through it.

They were now descending at a much slower rate, but it was all he could do to keep the craft from spinning. He stole a glance and realized she was having fun. The realization calmed him.

"Can you take over stabilizers and try keeping the pitch controlled? I should be able to get us some more lift."

"Aye-aye Captain," she returned happily.

"We are leveling out, but he's shaky. Holding thrust. Trying to recycle the starboard thrusters."

"He?"

"Yes, he. I don't care much for flying these types of ships. They are kind of boring. No personality. So yes, it's a he."

"Well, *He* feels plenty personal now," she exclaimed as they dropped a hundred meters suddenly, "Compensating... How are those thrusters coming?"

"Partially recovered. Forward starboard thruster is still offline and not regenerating, but I can fly without it.

Argonaut, can you redirect any power from the damaged thruster to level us out?"

"*Twenty two percent able to be recommitted. Suggest a twelve-degree forward adjustment on midship starboard thruster before reallocating power to starboard midship and aft thrusters.*"

"Approved. Bring power up slowly."

"*Confirmed.*"

"AnnaChi, be ready to deactivate the extra stabilizers, but keep them handy."

"Ready when you are."

"Almost there. And… I have us. Kill the stabilizers."

"Stabilizers returning to standby," turbulence heightened for a moment and then settled.

He relaxed his breathing as he took in all the readings, looking for the next problem. But the board seemed clear except for a higher than normal level of ozone in a few compartments, and dozens of external sensor-pod malfunctions. The sensors fared better than he had expected. A quick search through internal camera feeds showed nothing out of the ordinary to explain the ozone.

"Taking back stabilizer control. Systems appear adequate. We are slowing to standard atmospheric speeds."

AnnaChi sat back and propped her feet up, "You undersold this part of the adventure."

"Wouldn't have been as fun otherwise. Do we know where we are yet?"

"No, but we are over a low landmass with a river. No mountains nearby and sensors are working well. Suggest we drop to two thousand meters for a look."

"Sounds like a plan. We are now at zero-point-two thrust and holding at nine thousand meters. Adjusting stabilizers to push us down to two thousand meters. Deploying flares."

Shapes started to form in the distance as Kasey silently brought up all external lighting and camera views on the upper screens as the hull became translucent where able.

AnnaChi's voice was subdued to a level he had never heard before, "This... I never imagined," she whispered. "That we could cause something like this. It's beyond anything I imagined."

Kasey could only nod, as he once again took in the devastation of the shattered planet.

* * *

Wide beams of light raked the ash covered world below as they sailed silently above. The rivers below that were not frozen over ran edged with black runoff.

"You may not believe it," Kasey broke the silence that had formed, "but this is an improvement on what I saw last time. The blizzard that was starting before I left must have been the first in a while. The ash seems less dense."

"I don't think it will matter until the storms above run their course, and they show no signs of getting better soon."

"We should be approaching the n-mats mine soon. Start scanning the area for a terra-scraper. There should be one out in the fields somewhere, it wasn't in the warehouse."

"Scanning... Do you think more atoss could have survived?"

"I don't know, but it's possible. I imagine Orange's motherly ways was the only reason Mawk and Molly survived. They seem very young. We should have had them analyzed to see just how young."

"They seem to learn fast, but who knows. Damn, I wish I had thought about this, I was too concerned with the trip itself."

"If you wouldn't have kept all of this a secret…"

"Yea, yea," she chided.

"If others were in this area, I expect Orange would have brought them. If I am right, others that survived may not be found here. Hell, I still don't know how she found me, this base is over two thousand kilometers from where I first met her."

"She, and anything else that survived in the north, would have had to leave that area quickly to survive, like you did. But yea, I don't know how that was possible," she admitted. "Oh, I found something. Eastern field, one thousand meters out."

"Whatever it is, it's frozen over. Hmm. Yea that must be it. Let's take a closer look."

"I expected there to be ash blowing everywhere," she commented as the craft settled on the field.

"There was last time, but I think the snow did us a favor. I wonder if the ash was fresher than I thought—I assumed it was from the original disaster."

"We are not on a geological mission dear. Without light, this planet is as good as dead regardless."

"True enough. Deploying one of the crawlers Fran provided to clean that thing off. Let's go suit up and take a look."

"Full of surprises, that man…"

"Yea, makes me wonder what he did before Farpoint and brew-mastery."

"He has at least three hundred years under his belt from what I have gathered so far Kasey dear, maybe a lot more. I am sure he has done just about everything."

They returned to the ship a short time later. The terra-scraper was a disappointment. A fire had gutted the internals completely and most of the satellite bots were gone, lost in the fields.

"What a waste," AnnaChi was disgusted as she tossed a battered planting bot into a corner. "I was hoping for a better start to this trip."

"Don't get too disappointed, my first stop on the last trip turned out to be a crater. Let's head for the southern town, we may get lucky there. Besides, I want to repair the thruster before we turn in tonight."

The sight of the small town did nothing to boost their outlook.

"What did they do here?" AnnaChi wondered out loud.

"I have no idea. I didn't spend much time anywhere but the Reavestone camps. Place was called Sweet Meadow, population around seven hundred."

"Detecting several strange clearways. Roads maybe, but... Ah, racing tracks. Several of various types I would guess. Could have been a fun place."

"Nice," he responded without looking up from the sensor readings, "anything that would be useful for us?"

"Should be plenty of equipment to fix the thruster with, but unless we plan to enter the skimmer races there isn't much... Wait, there is a lodging complex that seems half built."

"And?" He prompted, not understanding the significance.

"Wouldn't they have some form of landscaping units, something similar to terra-scrapers? Maybe some survey bots too."

"They may indeed."

Locating the site's planning office, they landed the Argonaut as close as they could. The ash was finer here, the majority blowing away in wispy sheets from the touchdown. Several utility skimmers, parked haphazardly around, were revealed. A thorough search revealed little of interest left in the vehicles and office.

Taking one of the skimmers, AnnaChi went in search of what she referred to as "more worthy plunder," while Kasey assessed the Argonaut's damage.

Finding a small lift, he scanned the exterior but found nothing. One by one, he opened the hull plates covering the conduit, and was astonished to find a fist sized hole burned directly through the area with no obvious cause. Most of the hull damage would heal itself in time, but a large section of the power feeds was completely gone.

Before long, he had a meter-long section removed. The same channeling sections were universal throughout the military designed ship, and plenty of spares were below deck for repairs. Far more concerning to him was how the damage had occurred.

They had witnessed several bright plasma balls during the descent through the electrical storm. Far above, the chaos still reigned and would for years to come. The only possibility he could determine was that maybe one of the plasma balls had formed inside the outer hull and dissipated an instant later. The damage was both impressive and alarming. The ball could have formed anywhere and could have been catastrophic for the ship or occupants.

New channeling in hand, he exited the craft to find AnnaChi examining the destroyed section.

"This could easily have been a lot worse." Apparently, she had already come to the same conclusion.

Kasey could not tell if she was angry at him or the situation. "I didn't know that," he pointed at the ruined equipment, "was even possible."

"Yea, I know. But we are not doing this again without a better solution. You can only walk through so many minefields before, well, you know…"

"I agree, and we need to go through it again one more time yet."

"Suited up and ungrounded will help."

"Looks like you found a replacement already?"

"The sections are all the same, this is a spare."

"Speaking of spares," she glanced over her shoulder, "I found one of my own."

A dusty but new Bard with a flashy green and blue paint job, rested in place of the skimmer she had left with.

"Worthy plunder?" he asked, impressed.

"Oh yes. I am looking forward to using it on our next prospecting trip," her excitement was infectious, "it will need some scanning enhancements like yours, but it will do, and we can cover twice the ground."

Kasey couldn't help but smile as he moved back to the lift to replace the channel. From the high vantage point, he noticed the new Bard was packed full, "Has your shopping trip turned up anything else useful? A landscaping unit perhaps?" he asked, raising his voice to cover the distance.

"Mostly building supplies we don't really need, and nothing like a terra-scraper that I could identify. Oh, and I kind of cleaned out a small jewelry store…"

That caused him to pause his work. "Jewelry?" He asked, knowing such things usually did not appeal to her.

"Easy credits. The vault was a bit tough to get into…"

"You broke into the vault!"

"Of course, I couldn't think of a reason not to…"

"Ah," he tried to contain his smile as he moved back to his work.

"It was worth it, I think. Likely get enough from it all to buy a new terra-scraper if we need to. Also found a small warehouse with some old vehicles I wouldn't want, and newer ones that are not practical for anything but racing although they had some nice tools that I grabbed. Honestly, it's been a long day," she paused to stretch, "robing ghosts is tiring…"

A wave of thunder rolled through the meadow as he failed to contain his laughter.

"I'll be done here shortly. I am ready to get out of this stale, cold air too."

* * *

"Ready to give up yet?" AnnaChi slid into the tactical station with an exaggerated sigh.

"Getting closer every day, and the list of potential locations is getting smaller."

"Yea, yea. I just miss the stars. At least on Belrothi we can still see them."

He knew what she meant. If he hadn't been focused on getting this ship loaded and space-worthy on the last trip, it would have been maddening.

"Tell you what, lets skip the next search area, and head here instead," he indicated a coastline region to the far west. "A good bit of the thorium we mined went to a factory near there. I believe they made power plants, and the like, for shuttles and smaller transports."

"Okay flyboy, you have piqued my interests."

"I was thinking you may be able to find something useful there for the Cintian. Have any upgrades planned for her?"

"I think I could find a thing or three she could use. I suppose the Lodestar could too, you know. The heat exchangers run far too hot for the thrusters you have on her."

"Well then, let's get to it," he said, adjusting course.

"I, ah, just got a ping," Kasey mumbled as the craft

settled on the platform. "Looks to be from a military base on an island off the coast."

"Hmm," was all she responded.

"But first things first; the base is not going anywhere. Let's go shopping."

"It's plundering honey; shopping is a bit different." She laughed.

"Arr!"

* * *

The walls of the Argonaut's bays were soon stacked with crates of everything from cutting-edge sensor pods to control panels, before hunger forced them to stop. After devouring several helpings of vegetable stew, they were ready to move on.

They could see the military base was in bad shape as they approached the island. A single tower jutted up from rows of muck covered mounds. It slowly became apparent that some form of tsunami had obliterated the island.

"Can we connect to the base's systems with that ring?"

"I am trying," he responded. "It recognizes the command ring but won't process most commands."

"Put it up on the main."

"There you go, not much to see. Name is Atoll-Orion base."

"Hmm, main system is offline. Look for a communication log."

"Ah, here we go. Damn, there is a lot of comm activity from the Lithose-Abscond—doesn't look like they had much more time than I did to escape."

"Go back further, there should be normal checks-ins

from other bases."

"Okay. Yea, there are several here."

"There!" AnnaChi pointed, "Faraday-Canis, should be the one we want. Drill down to see if it has a location."

"Got it. Northern hemisphere, but thankfully on the opposite side of the planet from the Lithose-Abscond's fall."

"Good. Let's get this mission over with."

The Faraday base was hidden in a mountainside obscured by cloud cover. Entering the massive hanger was daunting even knowing it was no longer manned. Rows upon rows of ships-sized bays lined the interior of the mountain. Several bays at the entrance had been crushed, along with ships, in an apparent cave-in that had also destroyed a good portion of the massive the hanger doors in the process. Many of the other bays were still in the process of being dug out and fitted, but no ships remained.

The rows ended at a wide control tower. Kasey accepted the base system's autopilot request and sat back as the ship slid into the last bay, automatically connecting to the waiting fuel leads. Military maintenance bots appeared to clean the ship as they disembarked.

The air in the cavern was the cleanest they had encountered thus far. The eerie quiet was oppressive as they made their way to the entrances below the tower. Doors slid open as Kasey approached. Following the map his mimic interface provided, he led them to a room listed as an armory, but it had been emptied of gear.

AnnaChi recognized the problem, "they took what they were able from the base's armory. We need to find the depot area. It should contain far more than they could transport."

"Down this way."

Backtracking a bit, they found another wide hallway that was littered with carts. Checking every door showed the area to hold food, clothing and other essential supplies, everything but weapons.

"This could be a good place to hole up for a while if things back on Belrothi don't improve soon," he mentioned. "There's enough here to last a very long time, and the radiation is nearly normal in here."

"Would get boring after a while, don't you think?"

"Looks like there are some recreation areas further in, but I see what you mean. Still…"

"Yep agreed, I do like to have options… Uh, ya know, maybe see if you can activate some cleaning bots for after we leave, this place is filthy."

He grinned, her need to have small apartments tucked away throughout places she traveled often had always fascinated him.

"I think we need to head back to the main hanger. If I am reading this right, there should be some large lifts that either lead to storage or hangers."

They walked through the back of the hanger twice before realizing the large open area itself was a giant lift. After spending a few moments at a discrete and dusty control panel, the section began descending with a smattering of warning lights, alarms and great plumes of dust shooting into the air. It was a slow start, however its speed increased dramatically, then just as quickly slowed to a stop in a well-lit cavern.

Gaping halls led off in eight different directions. Several were obviously for additional ship storage. AnnaChi immediately started toward the rows of fighters, still sealed in clear coverings, but she stopped short.

"I am guessing bringing back one or two fighters would not be all that helpful huh?"

"I doubt it. But unless we can find something else…"

"Well, two halls have what appears to be check points. Let's start there."

The first three rooms were empty, but the fourth was loaded with crates. AnnaChi darted through the entryway the instant she realized it was.

"Plasma rifles," she shouted after inspecting the first stack. She pulled a crate out into the middle of the walkway and ran on to the next set.

Kasey barely had time to peer in at the new rifles before her next announcement.

"Impact-laser rifles. Never fired one of these, but…" Another crate was added to the walk way. "Pistols over here, standard plasma based." Out came another crate.

Shaking his head, Kasey went out into to the hallway and returned with a freight skiff to load the crates onto.

"Hey, over here. You will like this!" she called from a few rows back.

A small oblong bot floated in front of her, above its case.

"Is that safe to be messing with?"

"Should be, it's not a weapon exactly. It burrows a small hole through, well, just about anything, and then plants a charge before sealing it back up. Boom. New doorway or whatever, thanks to our new demo bot here. We need a few of these."

"Um, ok. Wait, why exactly?"

"Mining of course. Maybe cut out a nice grotto by the retreat?"

"Okay, sure, but why not use something a bit safer, like the sonic crushers in the unfinished bays up in the hanger?"

"Slow and boring dear," she replied, as she pulled several other cases out. "On our way home, we need to start designing an armory for the house."

"Wait, I thought this was to help the fight?"

"Nope, this is our share of the loot, as per your verbal

contract with Mad Fran. We really don't have a choice here," she stated in the most sarcastic voice she could muster.

"Uh huh. I assume all this is to be stored below decks, safely out of the way too?"

"It's always nice when you see my reasoning dear."

"I am sure it is," he mumbled, "There is plenty of room in the engineering shop, unless you're planning to bring a tank home."

"Now, if you can open the ammo cage over there with that ring of yours, I am betting the next room will have body armor and the like."

After several full skiffs were loaded onto the lift platform, they checked the last of the secured halls. The first thing they noticed were the reinforced walls and vault-like doors.

"I think this is the place, but I don't think they got around to storing whatever it was here yet," AnnaChi complained.

"Well, at least we can bring them some weapons…"

"Actually, I am sure they have all the weapons they need and can likely make more planet-side if they need to."

"Then what do they need?" he asked yet again.

"Perhaps, whatever is in there," she was pointing to the next entryway, which appeared to have been sealed.

As they approached, three turrets appeared from the walls.

Warning. Authorization is required to pass.

Not knowing what else to do, Kasey held up the hand with the command ring. Immediately the turrets disengaged, but it was clear access would not be granted.

Warning. You do not have clearances to pass.

Waving his hand again produced the same answer, and the turrets moved ever so slightly in an additional warning.

Needing no additional prompting, they retreated down the hall.

"Only one thing left to do now," AnnaChi commented.

Kasey had a bad feeling about her tone. Hoping for the best, he offered, "Take what we have and go home?" Knowing that was not at all what she had in mind.

"Silly boy," she had a faraway look as she turned into the empty chamber along the same wall.

He noted casually that sconces for turrets were at this chamber door as well but had not yet been installed. He watched with growing suspicion as she inspected the empty chamber's walls. When she stopped again to stare with a far-off look and two demo bots floated in, his fears were confirmed.

Nearly silent, the bots began boring a series of precisely aligned holes across the wall adjoining the fortified room.

"Uh dear, what do you think the base system will do when we start blasting whole walls apart in secure areas?"

"You should be able to control any base security with that fancy ring."

"Should?" he prompted.

"Right… Maybe we should be a bit prepared?"

"Suggestions?"

Her laugh removed any fear he had as she listed off orders, "Bring the Argonaut down on the main lift and keep him hot. Load up what we have, and keep a bay open for more. I'll gather some portable shield-walls and create a corridor and maybe add some surprises…"

"Done this before?" he asked as they trotted toward the lift.

"Maybe…" she teased then sprinted toward the weapon storage chambers.

* * *

Armed and armored, they crouched outside the chamber with the two demo bots floating before her.

"Ready?"

"Do it."

The blast was a disappointment. No fiery explosion or deafening boom, just a sickening crunch, followed by tumbling bits of wall. The floors shook slightly for a few seconds and then stopped.

"Hmm," was all she remarked before moving into the chamber for a look.

The dust was still settling, but the wall was clearly thicker and more reinforced then they had suspected.

"You two, get to work, and triple charge this time."

Directing the bots to place the charges closer as well, they soon were back in the hall. This time, the blast gave an appreciable report, leaving his ears ringing.

As soon as the dust began to settle, neither the ringing in his ears, nor the gradual shaking of the floors, deterred them from rushing inside to view the carnage. Through the haze stood what appeared to be rows of large killer robots. They edged closer, praying the machines would not start moving.

Kasey relaxed as he realized they were suites, meant to be piloted. Ears still ringing, he waved AnnaChi to join him, and she crept up onto the fallen wall. He could see her saying something, he could not hear over the incessant ringing, but she didn't seem concerned, so he continued into the room.

Forty of the machines stood before them, each housed on a tracked transport platform. They weren't standing, he found as he got close, but were on hands and knees all secured to the platforms. Guessing they would stand at nearly three meters tall, and entirely as deadly as they looked, he could not imagine being on the wrong side of a fight with the beasts.

The platforms also held two additional crates containing weapons and kit for the suit and operator. The whole system appeared ready to deploy to his untrained eyes, but he realized that was a weak assumption and looked around. The room was empty otherwise, no additional supplies, no repair bay, not even a diagnostics station. Simply a storeroom.

He examined the first suit's mobile platform as AnnaChi climbed up on the suit's back and tried to open the hatch. Detaching control pad, he remotely linked up all the platforms to follow, then looked up at AnnaChi who was still trying in vain to get the suit open.

"Ready if you are," he said holding up the pad – realizing as he did that he could hear his own voice and that the ringing he assumed was his ears were in reality the base's alarms.

Waving off any reply she was about to make, he pointed to his ears and shouted, "We are about to have company!"

She stiffened for a moment to listen, then smiled as distant weapon fire began to punctuate the alarm noise. Moving quickly, they went back through the previous room and down the hall to find a squad of hovering defense bots attempting to blast through the shield-wall closest to the hall. He could see the wall steadily weakening and knew he had to do something. Taking a chance, he stepped out and waved his hand with the command ring at them. They paused only a second then continued.

"Stop!" He commanded. "Halt, there is no threat here!" Instantly the laser fire stopped. "Return to post!" The bots shot off in various directions apparently looking for the real enemies.

Hearing more fire ahead he handed the pad to AnnaChi and ran forward and disbanded two more groups of defenders before checking on the ship. Thankfully it had been ignored.

Heading back, he found AnnaChi leading the train of the platforms down the hallway. She waved and gave him a thumbs-up as she led the procession past him. Halfway to the ship, something set off a new alert and the shield-walls nearest them were swarmed with laser fire again.

Kasey attempted to stop them again, but they only stopped for a moment to issue a warning, before the fire resumed.

Warning. You do not have clearance for transfer of NX72 I.C.E. Suits.

AnnaChi soon had the transport platforms moving at top speed, which seemed slow to Kasey. When the shield started to flicker again, he tried to get her attention.

"We need to stop, they are going to break through soon!"

"Look," she pointed at the ceiling above the bots. It was pockmarked with rows of something, then it dawned on him what they were. Looking back at her, he saw she was crouched down with her hands over her ears. He barely had time to do the same before the blasting caps exploded, bringing down sizable chunks of the ceiling on top of the attacking defense bots.

Before he opened his eyes, a message scrolled across his mimic interface.

Get to the ship and ready all point defenses to open fire the moment the bay closes.

Nodding, he ran.

The platforms were just beginning to line up in the bay as he entered. Somewhere behind him laser fire was again assaulting the shield walls. Stopping briefly, he was relieved to see AnnaChi not far behind him as two more explosions sounded in the distance.

Reaching the bridge, he dropped hard onto the helm's cushion and strapped in, screens already lit up with activity. More defensive bots were flooding into the area, and it took all the patience he could muster to not activate the ships defenses.

Don't activate the PD yet! We are loaded but they are still attacking the portable shields. Let them. Don't take off yet—I'll be right there.

Switching on camera views he watched the shield-walls fail just as AnnaChi jumped into her station.

"Just in time. They may not attack the ship unless we move."

"We should go then," he shouted at her, "there are lots more on the way to back them up!"

"More the merrier. Wait for that next group to join the swarm, and then get us out of here," her hands flew over the tactical controls.

"Almost here!"

"Go now! I am activating point defenses now."

Milliseconds after taking off, a large explosion rocked them, nearly pushing the ship into the walls of the lift shaft. He glanced over to see her smiling to herself but still working on something.

"They will be closing on the main hanger if they haven't already…" A cascaded of detonations appeared on the scanners as the craft exited the shaft.

"That should slow them down but go faster if you please."

"Didn't help, the gates are still closing," he gestured to entrance ahead.

"Damn! I don't think this will be a safe-haven for us after all," she said as she slammed her palm on the controls to activate her final surprise.

The blast shook the mountain itself as a ball of flame

filled the cavern behind them. The doors stopped moving but the whole complex was rapidly coming apart around them.

The ship jarred sharply as it was struck by falling boulders. Gritting his teeth, Kasey managed to keep the ship aloft as they sped for the entrance.

A row of bots rose from hidden chambers to block the opening and began firing. The point defense raked across the bots, stopping only a few.

"EM shields are failing! Will the kinetic shields hold?" AnnaChi asked, with the first traces of trepidation lacing her voice.

"They are useless against energy blasts, but the hull should hold up to a few hits, and we are about to find out about the projectiles!"

Accelerating as much as he could without losing control, the Argonaut smashed through the bots, rocketing out the of the hanger with their fiery remains falling away into the mountainside below.

Pouring on the speed in the open air, they shot away to safety as black acrid smoke began billowing from the base.

"Missiles?" Kasey asked as he glanced over the damage reports."

"No, skies are clear."

Sweat was rolling down Kasey's forehead as he locked eyes with AnnaChi. They needed no words to express the relief they both felt. The Argonaut shifted suddenly as a thruster cut out, reminding them of the damage the ship had taken in the escape.

"Find a place to patch him up, and then home?"

"Yes, and then home," she replied without the usual mirth, "I am very much ready to go home now."

CHAPTER THIRTY-ONE

The Argonaut settled into an orbit matching the Cintian's return path from the Belrothi-Abscond station above the planet Belrothi.

The familiar sound of linking up the ships was met with trepidation as they made their way to the hatch. If the Patternists had somehow detected their stealth transitions and set a trap, there would be nothing they could do now but run or fight. They only hoped a friendly face waited behind the hatch.

Flair stepped out of the Cintian's hatch with a wide smile, ignoring the deadly weapons they were fast to point away from her.

"Thought you two had found a home over there."

"Almost," AnnaChi nudged Kasey playfully, "but unfortunately we didn't leave much standing on our way out."

Flair blanched, "Didn't the command ring work?"

Kasey shook his head, "It worked for most of the areas, but not where we needed it. The last room we checked was above the ring's clearance level. So, we, uh…"

"We improvised," AnnaChi chimed in. "Hopefully these will be useful."

As they walked into the cluttered bay, Flair quickened her pace, "Well, you seem to have gotten a lot of… What am I looking at?"

"We were hoping you would know," he admitted. "The system called them, NX72 I.C.E. Suits, I believe. Just big suits of armor I assume. They were under heavy guard, so they must be worth something to the resistance. Not much else was worth taking except some basic weapons."

AnnaChi glared at him from behind Flair, "yea, too bad we couldn't get *any* of those. Running for our lives and all."

"I see," Flair nodded as she inspected the first suit. "Well these will have to do. I had hoped there would have been more at the depot. The sailors really seemed to think it would have made a difference, but this is not a ground fight."

"In another month or so there may have been more, but that base was far from finished. Whatever was supposed to be there was likely still aboard the Lithose-Abscond station when it blew." Kasey suddenly felt defensive and continued tersely, "Where can we drop these off for you?"

"Sorry, I didn't mean you didn't do everything you could. I am just disappointed with fate itself, for leaving this expedition so unprepared." She moved away from the suit's platform and her demeanor changed instantaneously. "I forget that you would have been out of contact with the happenings here. After we dropped the Cassian artifacts in a few towns, the net went ballistic. The people demanded action."

"That's wonderful," AnnaChi began, but stopped at the look from Flair that radiated anything but good news.

"The damn Patternists turned it around on us. They made a show of launching a huge investigation and by morning they had confiscated the artifacts. Within days they had convinced, or forced, the reporters that there was no perceived threat any more. That it had been an isolated incident!" She paused to gather herself. After a few calming breaths she went on, "At the same time they started imposing new rules and limitations on us all which quickly served as a distraction from the real issues. Today they said it was in the colony's best interest to limit reproduction and began issuing child-permits—if you can imagine that."

"In a new colony?" AnnaChi demanded.

Kasey thought he saw her cheeks redden but she stepped out of his view too fast to be sure. Flair was continuing.

"It has ever been the politics of the Patternists to control population, but yes, such a thing is unheard of in a new outpost. Regardless, it is escalating things a bit, and not in the best direction. Best that we get these where they need to go quickly. Fran has had the Sarsaparilla's portion of the warehouse blocked off for the last week. We will wait for nightfall before we make the drop. Keep your stealth active till we are close in, then decouple and act as any normal ship. Got it?"

"Yep, but I am piloting my Cintian. You can keep Kasey out of trouble. I need to go change," AnnaChi made a quick exit, hurrying through the portal to the Cintian and into her personal chambers.

* * *

Time flew by with no improvement to the colony's situation. Kasey tried to ignore the happenings and useless politics. Until the Patternists were overthrown, they would do what they wanted. Trying not to care, he threw himself into their new mining business.

Starting an actual mining company was not a venture Kasey believed they could really succeed at without expert help. Flair and Fran had found a willing crew to get them started, but so far no one seemed to fit the foreman profile.

Knowing that Darnell's experience would fit the bill, he waited till their mine base was properly setup and moved the Argonaut back into hiding before seeking the old miner out. A decision he quickly regretted.

After days of failure to get any responses from his old friend, he decided to pay him a personal visit, but found his quarters to have been unoccupied for quite some time. His last known employer was just as mystified. The company had initially reported that Darnell must have fallen off the craft he was working on and drowned. Yet they had searched the waters for his remains and none were found. It was as if he no longer existed, but the company insisted that he had likely decided he no longer wanted the work and left on his own. It was then that Kasey learned of his friend's many job-related issues since the Lithose incident.

In the few times he had talked to him since the disaster, he never noticed anything more wrong than what was expected from a survivor. To Kasey, Darnell was always an extremely strong-minded man who seemed to know more about every situation than most. Not the kind of person who needed help or even welcomed it if offered. The idea, which was hinted at heavily by those who had dealt with him lately, was that he may have somehow taken his own life. To Kasey, the thought was unfathomable; something was not right.

The sun was high when he entered the Sarsaparilla's main room. Weaving through the crowds he found his way to the more restricted areas, wherein Fran was usually found. A group of unsmiling patrons had the man's attention on a balcony overlooking the main square when Kasey found him. Leaving him to his conversation, he found a cold beverage to wait with, but had barely touched it when Fran appeared.

"Kasey my friend, I didn't expect you here today. Is business or pleasure the dealing for today?"

Kasey slumped further down into the chair, "Neither. Or well, I am not sure. I need some help finding someone and was hoping you may have some ideas on where to start."

"I see. Is this someone a friend of foe?" Fran asked with a comical grin.

"Friend, he is my old boss actually. One Darnell MacNamara. Was planning to see if he would be willing to fill in our foreman position at the mine, a job he is more than qualified for," he said rubbing the back of his neck. "He disappeared off a sea skimmer without a trace and no body was found."

"I see," Fran repeated to himself in thought. "I think Flair may know someone who can assist. Finish that drink and have another, I'll be back shortly."

When he returned, he took Kasey to a private room. Flair was already there speaking with a man on the wall-screen. The man didn't look happy when Kasey and Fran walked in.

"Yes uh, I can do that," he was saying. "Except, I will r-require payment first," he stuttered.

"Sure you do…" replied Flair. "I understand a thousand credits is the usual fee?"

"I-I'm, yes, that will do. What d-did you say the name was?"

Kasey spoke up, "Darnell MacNamara, and I can pay the fee now…"

"Taken care of," Flair interjected, "this is a business expense. A finder's fee for finding our needed foreman, of course."

Kasey swallowed his nerves, "Of course, thank you.

Darnell was last seen…"

"No need," the man held his hand up to stop Kasey. "I have it. The p-per… the man's last mimic interface signal was on the Lohnell B-Bay, about two k-kilometers out. The signal stops suddenly…"

"What does that mean?" Kasey couldn't help the strain in his voice.

"I, yes well, t-the mimic interface doesn't just stop cold like this," he glanced to the others in the room, as if seeking help, but finding none he went on. "This would happen if the interface was d-destroyed in some way, or taken out of range…"

"His company said his water skimmer was still out in the bay and there was no damage to it. They thought he may have drowned…"

"Unlikely," the man suddenly shifted in his seat, and with another look around he began typing furiously. "No," he eventually replied, "there would have been p-panicked signals, but none were recorded. The signal loss was instant. There are records that he was c-calmly thinking directly beforehand. The man c-could have been shot in the, um, or ah, maybe a damping field…"

"Damping field?" Kasey asked.

"Well… Yes. He could have activated a field to st-stop any signals from leaving his mimic interface, but that is not consistent with his thought p-patterns…. Not that we know what he was thinking, but his waves were rather normal for him." The man shrugged, apparently having nothing more to offer.

After a few moments of silence, Flair thanked the man and terminated the call.

Kasey paced across the small room. "I don't think he would have killed himself. He was odd occasionally, but not in that way."

"We will ask around," Fran rested a hand on his shoulder, "if there is more we can do, we will."

"I appreciate that, and your help too Flair."

She did not respond, but had a hand to her ear listening to something. She turned with concern in her voice, "There has been another attack."

"Where?" the men asked in unison.

"Vethi-Abscond base. Wait, no, they were heading to attack the ship-plants near the base. A few of the companies have been trying to lawyer their way into staying in business, even though the Patternists have ordered them to shut down."

"A grave mistake," Fran frowned.

"Perhaps soon," she replied, "but the attackers never made it to the shipyards. Another force intercepted the Patternists group somehow. I can't tell who was involved but it seems like a mix of civilian and military."

"This is a good thing then?" Kasey wondered.

"Hard to tell, it is mostly over, but the information is scattered. The companies will survive a while longer, but if they are smart they will mothball what they have so far and hide it until this all blows over."

"Will it?"

Fran and Flair looked at each other to find the answer. Finally, Fran replied, "It will end, but it may be a while yet. And it may get worse before it gets better. Federation troops seem to be planning something. Maybe those suits you brought back were worth something after all."

"Did they say how?" he asked with sincere curiosity.

"No," he responded slowly, "but I gathered they had some interesting plans for them."

"The Abscond maybe?"

Fran shrugged, "Who knows. They will help in some way, and that is the point, right?"

"I suppose. Well, I better get back. AnnaChi wants to take the Bards out to 'test,'" he formed quotes in the air with his fingers, "the new scanners. I think she just wants to play with her new toy."

They all smiled at that.

* * *

He found AnnaChi near the front of their hanger struggling with some component of her Bard.

"Everything ok there dear? I thought we paid to have the new scanners installed."

As he moved into the hanger he noticed for the first time that the fabricator was churning away at something with several apparent earlier prototypes strewn about.

"There!" A loud pop heralded her success. "Yes, everything is great, but I am glad you are here. I have another one nearly ready for yours, and this new arm is not as strong as the old one yet. I need to adjust my exercise routines."

"I uh, sure," he watched as she pulled a mean looking plasma rifle from its case and slid it into the new green holster that matched up with the bard's design. "I love the way you think, but is that a bit much?"

"Nope. I would prefer a turret, but this will do for now. I have more planned, so get used to it." She moved to embrace him warmly.

"I am all for upgrades dear," he laughed, "I almost wish we knew what new toys they have cooked up back in the cluster in the last three decades."

"That would be a trick to find that out. But with enough time, the colony will develop plenty of new tech as well – colony survival nearly always demands invention. Hell, I have a few of my own I wouldn't mind trying out now that we are generating a moderate means to do so."

"I look forward to seeing them. Everything since the Abscond has definitely changed my perspective on what is possible. Oh, did you hear about the attack at Vethi?"

"Yea, news was released a bit ago," she shook her head in disgust before changing the topic, "Did you find Darnell?"

"No, nothing I can do anything with anyway, I even had some help from our favorite bartenders," he sighed. "But I can fill you in later, I want to clean out the Lodestar's bay before dark."

"Actually, I hope you don't mind, but I cleared our schedule for the next few days. How do you feel about getting away for a few days?"

"Away? What did you have in mind?"

"The winds have been getting colder here, so I was thinking about the heading south for some camping, and we can test the new scanners out while we are there. Maybe explore a bit?"

"Sounds perfect." A series of chirps sounded in the distance. "Are our friends coming along?"

AnnaChi laughed. "I am not sure. As soon as I started packing the ship, Molly showed up to keep me company. But that sounds like Orange."

"They always seem to know, don't they? I wish we would have found more of them to rescue on that last trip. It's a shame they are the last of their kind."

"Yea, but I don't think we can go back there again anytime soon. I went through the Argonaut's logs the other day. There were nearly twenty hull regeneration incidents noted just in the time we spent in the atmosphere. They were much smaller, but matched the signature of the plasma burn damage to the thruster."

He looked alarmed, "That explains the increased ozone I suppose. Anything major?"

"No, the damage is already healed, but I think we were incredibly lucky. If one had penetrated a fuel pod or system core we would have been in serious trouble. Hell, they could have burned through us for that matter."

"Okay, wow. Well it's not like we need to go there for anything, we have so much more here than I have ever had. It was kind of fun though."

"Most of it was," she said, her gaze turning downward. "I underestimated the security that base would have."

"Nonsense, we made it out just fine. What more could we have done?"

"A lot more actually, but I should have just left it alone. It's not the first time I have been too curious for my own good... I get carried away, ya know."

"Well, it all worked out, and from what I hear the suits we brought back will be useful after all. So, in the grand scheme of things it was worth it."

A whistle-chirp from the open hanger announced atoss entering.

"It must be time to get going. The fabricator looks to have finished your Bard's holster. It's black for now – you really need to get some paint on your bard dear. Let's get it fitted and load them onto the Cintian."

CHAPTER THIRTY-TWO

The couple reclined in the darkness of their room, staring through the translucent ceiling at the now starry sky above. Winter on Belrothi had begun with a harsh blizzard laying a thick blanket of snow across much of the northern hemisphere, before calming to the lazy flurries that now fell in the still air.

The past several months had brought a steady onslaught of action from the Patternists' leadership. Even off-world travel had been prohibited weeks earlier. Grumblings had stirred the air everywhere across the planet, but little more could be done than complaining.

Three days ago, the Vethi moon base had again been attacked. There had been no defense mounted this time. Thankfully, most of the inhabitants had been able to flee to Belrothi. The small Vethi-Abscond station that had been stationed there was now little more than a husk of refuse.

During the retreat, several fights had taken place, and one of them had changed the face of the conflict for everyone.

The few defender's ships that could, had drawn the Patternists fighters off, buying the residents time to get away. Not many of the brave pilots had returned. It was surprising then, that the final escaping craft to land safely on Belrothi contained not only one of the hero pilots, but had a fully intact Cassian orb grappled to its underside. It was the only evidence of the Cassian involvement since the debris from AnnaChi's revenge attack.

It seemed the fighter had been chased far from the fray, and took a heavy hit, causing a loss of all power. The Patternists aggressor had left the damaged ship to return to the fight. A Cassian orb had apparently been alerted to finish off the wounded ship.

The fighter had regained power to his ship just as the orb was slowing to launch its attack. The pilot had evidently made a rash decision to use what power he had to ram the orb. The orb pulled away in time to minimize the impact damage, however both hulls were meshed together long enough for the quick-thinking Federation pilot and his crew to lock the orb against their ship. The much smaller Cassian vessel was soon ripped open and disabled.

The reports claimed that the centipede-bodied Cassian died as the orb's life support was destroyed in the ship's takeover. Both the Cassian's body and ship had been brought back to Belrothi for the people to see. The event had overtaken any coverage of the actual battle. The feat took on a nearly legendary status throughout the colony within hours of the landing.

Many had debated the authenticity of the artifacts Fran and Flair had dispersed throughout the colony months earlier, but there was no doubt now. The Cassian body and captured orb were all the proof that anyone still holding onto disbelief needed. The fact that it happened during the Patternists attack corroborated that they were in league with the Cassian.

That colony finally understood the reality of the situation they were in. They learned that they were no longer just being ruled over by a volatile Patternist government, but were being systematically corralled and eradicated by an aggressive alien-controlled force.

Several Patternists had given themselves up soon after, finding out that the actions they had taken against the colony may not have been the sole will of the Patternist movement. Yet it had not been enough dissent to make a true difference; they still had overwhelming control, as long as they controlled the resources of the Belrothi-Abscond station.

The loss of the moon base and shipyards were a huge blow to the colony's future. Yet a major victory had also occurred in the federation forces, winning the hearts of the people they still were struggling to protect. Soldiers who had been shunned were now praised wherever they went.

Now, with nowhere to go and no one to help, few held onto hope of a peaceful future. The net was full of malcontent rants and angry callings for change, yet none carried the weight to do so. While the federation's rebellion against the Pattern-fearing tyrants still existed, they wouldn't make any real moves now. Everyone feared the Cassian would interfere. Many were angered that the federation had not been more prepared, stating they should have known this possibility existed. Others asked why the military protection sent with the mission was so meager.

Kasey had more than a bit of turmoil running his own thoughts. He had always wanted to be free of the Terrantine Federation's rule, as had his parents who had perished for that honorable cause. Now that it appeared his wishes had been granted, he was no longer sure it would ever become a good thing. The Patternists' rule was worse by far with the restrictions and power abuse. Yet even if they were somehow ousted from power, there was no guarantee the next wouldn't be just as bad.

Worse, if a weak government took over there was the very real possibility that the Cassian would find ways to again influence their own agendas.

Even now, most believed war seemed to be the next logical step. Historically, human infighting was exactly what the Cassian wanted. Kasey wanted no part of it, and he knew AnnaChi only stayed out of it for his sake alone. Fran, on the other hand, only claimed to stay out of it all. Kasey knew the saloon's various back rooms had become an epicenter of clandestine activities for the resistance.

Kasey's reveries were broken as a strong wind-gust loosed a cascade of snow from the trees looming above their home, momentarily obstructing their view of the heavens. The glass-like material of the ceiling instantly increased temperature to vaporize the snow into a fine mist that was gone in seconds, leaving the view crystal clear once again. *If only the colony's problems could be so easily banished*, he thought.

He felt AnnaChi's body suddenly stiffen, but he missed whatever had startled her. She was up in an instant, pulling up several outdoor camera views on the walls. The system quickly interpreted her need, bringing up an array of recordings and statistical data.

Kasey felt a slight pang of panic as he realized he was seeing a strange object that had arched across their skyline. The dark shape was so barely perceptible, he wasn't sure how AnnaChi had even spotted it.

"Systems show no indication that the thing exists," she mumbled. "I think it's a ship, but not one from the colonies. Or the Cassian."

"An animal maybe?" He knew he was wrong the moment he said it, the sensors they had could pick up an insect's wings fluttering several kilometers away.

A warning abruptly appeared along with several new displays. The system inferred her interests in the object and was now reporting on another visual anomaly matching the first appearance. They still couldn't determine what the object was, but it seemed to have changed direction and was heading their way.

"Our systems are not picking it up properly. The defenses will be nearly useless," he noted.

"We would be safer in a ship, in case we needed to escape. Or we could hide in the caverns if we could make it to them."

"No. We would never make it. The Cintian is closest, we should head there."

"Fine, I am sending a few maintenance bots toward the Lodestar. Maybe the distraction will buy some time." She was already tossing him a shield belt from a chest by the door and offered a plasma rifle once he caught up.

"Nice how my ship gets to play the decoy again," he noted with a teasing frown.

"Well it certainly wasn't going to be my baby!" Shouldering him away from the doorway she slipped ahead, scouting the way with a practiced ease.

The maintenance bay had a door facing the house. A large skimmer was parked off to the side partially blocking them from view. They waited a handful of heartbeats, listening to the wind for anything out of place. AnnaChi's silent words counted down across Kasey's vision as she crouched.

A moment later, they both took off for the skimmer, using it for cover. The hanger door was only ten meters away now, and nothing but the frigid wind stirred the night. Just as they were about to make last dash, a familiar whistling chirp cut through the air back above the house.

A large orange shape bolted toward them and disappeared. A very human grunt sounded as man and avian shimmered back into being. Mawk and Molly landed on either side of the newcomer, hissing, as

Orange quickly claimed her spot between the man and Kasey.

Darnell sputtered out several curses as he slowly regained his feet with a cautious eye on the predatory creatures.

"Yea, yea! I am not gonna do anything but talk." Holding out his arms to show Orange he wasn't threatening.

Orange ignored him and chirped toward the air behind Darnell.

"Smart birds you have here Kasey." He gave a look over his shoulder and shouted, "Turn the field off, or this will take all day, eh?"

Seconds later, a silvery crescent-shaped ship materialized, hovering just off the ground. Two short Sargani stood at the top of a short ramp, watching the exchange as their yellow medusa-like tentacles waved around their oblong heads in repeating arrangements. Both bipedal creatures were adorned in grey robes that were in stark contrast to the bright orange and yellows of their skin. Neither moved, nor had any weapons showing.

Kasey stepped forward a few steps as AnnaChi remained crouched, aiming down the length of her rifle.

"It's good to see you Darnell?" It was more of a question than a greeting. "I had almost thought you dead. Brought some friends I see?"

"I did at that. Hmm. If you will call off your noble protectors, we have some issues to discuss."

The avian relaxed at the words which surprised Kasey, but they kept their positions. Kasey glanced back at AnnaChi and received a careful nod. It was his call.

Lowering his rifle, he waved Darnell toward the bay door and to the Cintian. Kasey noticed several of their security bots scampering into position to cover the Sargani craft, causing him to smile at AnnaChi's foresight. Once Darnell got close, Mawk took off, gone in a blink. Molly followed him, but only after receiving a thankful nod from AnnaChi. Orange followed the humans into the hanger, eyes never leaving Darnell.

"Nice pets you have…"

"Not pets. They are simply our friends," Kasey explained, stopping just outside the Cintian while AnnaChi unlocked the hatch.

He did his best to stay alert as the causal chat continued. He knew, as most did, that Sargani could essentially read a lax mind. Having them around put any human on edge, but they usually were not dangerous. Kasey felt very surprised to find his old friend in their company. If Darnell trusted them, he must have a good reason.

"So, boss, what's the score out there," thumbing the general direction of the Sargani craft, "this a good or bad deal?"

"Little of both to be honest," he replied shaking his head. "But they are not our enemy, we need them."

"And?"

"Well that's a bit more complicated," he paused to look around, "but, somewhere quiet to talk may be best." It was clear he wasn't referring to the Cintian's loading bay, where which they now stood.

AnnaChi ushered them to her antechamber before heading to the bridge. Orange slipped in and curled up on a chair, eyes still locked on the newcomer. Within moments they felt, as much as heard, the whirring of the Cintian's shields spinning up. AnnaChi was back and pulling the hatch closed before the shield cycle completed.

Opening a panel, she proceeded to engage several switches and waited for a matching set of lights to turn green before returning the waiting gazes.

"That's as quiet as I can make it, so it will have to do.

Now spill." Her tone left no room for questions as she crossed her arms. It was an order in the purest form.

Darnell quickly caught them up with all his observations on the voyage, as well as why the government scientist had singled him out when they had discovered the n-mats on Lithose.

"I knew something was going on, but I had no idea. I thought this mission across the galaxy was a one-way trip. Hell, I came because I wanted to mine my way across all the new systems out here."

Leaning back, he stared at the ceiling for what seemed an eternity. "I understand why the Patternists are working so hard against this colony. We all thought we would have centuries to fill this expanse with human worlds. Lies."

"What do you mean?"

"I was wrong. We were all wrong. Our n-mats, the negative matter, is the key to it all, don't you see?"

"No, I don't see. Key to what?" Kasey felt himself losing patience with his friend.

"Wormholes, or black holes if you like, they all go somewhere. To us, they have always just been tools to drag our star-cruisers around to circumvent lightspeed. Not anymore! They are going to open the universe up and change everything. But where do they go? Well that's one question we may be able to answer now." Clearing his throat he broke from the ramble and looked around. "Uh, got anything to drink?"

"A real storyteller this one is dear, but he is not making sense." AnnaChi turned to Orange, "Keep an eye on him huh?" Orange intensified its gaze, greedy for a wrong move to be made and briefly showing a few razor-like teeth behind a set of sharp canines.

AnnaChi returned, carrying a trio of Mad Fran's dark ales and a small bowl of fresh meat cubes that she placed directly between Orange and Darnell. The closest cube disappeared in a blur leaving behind a bloody smear as Orange gulped it down, leaving the other as she resumed her gazing.

"So," Kasey prodded, "the answer?"

"Ah, um yes," continuing at a slightly slower pace. "You see, the science guys can apparently create a wormhole in a gate that connects to a paired gate far away. Entangled fields or some such crap. It is apparently old news for them, as it was useless in practice. Unstable events, as I understand. Anything sent through was either absorbed or torn apart. Honestly, I got a bit lost around the specifics, but it sounds messy."

"And the n-mats are involved with this somehow?"

"Yes! With enough, they stabilize the portal somehow, I guess. Allows for safe travel through to the other side in an instant…"

"A portal?" Kasey interjected.

"Wait," AnnaChi stopped Darnell's response, "I thought you two had mined tons of n-mats on Lithose. If we can get back and forth to the federation, why are we looing a fight with annoying Patternlsts and Cassian?"

"Because the n-mats were lost with the Lithose-Abscond station, and these portals, or gates, haven't been able to be opened because they don't have the key." He ignored their questioning looks and pushed on. "For now, the gates are useless. The Cassian knew of the plans for the gates somehow and used that knowledge to turn the Patternists into an army to stop our expansion. For all I know, the Patternists may be right and the Pattern may be closer to us than ever, once we open those gates."

Kasey swatted the air in frustration "Maybe. But if you are correct the federation will flood into this, and the surrounding star cluster, the moment they have access, searching out n-mats in every damn system."

"So why hasn't it been turned on yet?" she

demanded.

"Ah, well, it was the attacks." Darnell laughed. "They destroyed our storage of n-mats. But more importantly, when they blew the Lithose-Abscond station, they also destroyed the gate key."

"So, without the key and n-mats we are stuck here, helpless?"

"Yup. Apparently, it is part of why the Sargani are here. They developed the key and helped with the gates from what I understand."

"So, no key means no gate. Can the Sargani make a new key?"

"Yes, they are reverse engineering it based on this gate set. They tell me it will take many years."

Kasey was deep in thought and not sharing, but AnnaChi would have none of it. "So, why are you here? Why bother us with the latest failure of the federation?" Her laugh was harsh. "Surely they don't need our copper."

"Copper... Oh no. They have no interest in your mining, although I am mightily impressed!"

Kasey barely noticed the compliment and pushed on, "What then are they interested in us for?"

"Oh... Well you know there were two keys created, right?" He waited, but getting no reaction, he continued. "The Sargani can sense the keys, something about how they are made..."

"No, we don't know about any keys or gates or any of this," AnnaChi let out a pointed sigh. "Get to your point!"

"They believe you have it."

She was up and pointing the rifle at him in an instant. Orange was poised to strike, following her lead. "Explain. Fast."

"Um... See, I am told it was being moved through the Daveri Two system where it was to be handed over to an agent at some resort or some such place. Patternists attacked the transport ship carrying the key and it had been thought to have been stolen. Apparently, they were going to use it to somehow destroy the gate itself, but no attempt was ever made."

"Wait…"

"I'm sorry, but the Sargani pulled your story from my head before I knew they were even monitoring me. I knew none of this at the time. It is why they abducted me."

"Wait…" she whispered again, covering her face in shaking hands as the rifle dropped to the floor.

He stopped, but when she didn't say more he went on. "They knew the key was on this planet, but not where it was located. They have been spending a lot of time, all their time really, scanning nearly everyone until they found me."

"Shut up Darnell." Kasey was at her side, her head drooped over his shoulder as he embraced her.

Embarrassed, she regained her composure and pushed Kasey away. "Go get the damn party trick and let's be done with this all."

"It's in the ship's vault. But I'm not sure that…"

"We will be just fine here," she said, nodding to Orange.

He took off without another word.

Kasey rushed back in moments later with a small pack in hand and Molly at his side, who immediately took her place at AnnaChi's side.

Tossing the pack to Darnell, he said, "That, I assume, is what you want. Take it and go."

"There is more. I'm sorry… The Sargani and I will get the key to where it needs to go. But Kasey… They uh, they need your ship."

"Why would they want the Lodestar, it's a not even much of a ship?"

"Sorry again my friend, they need your *other* ship. The one you took from Lithose…"

Kasey didn't miss a beat. "Fine. Take it. Whatever. Just tell them to leave us alone."

"You know I need you to fly it… There are only a few other pilots trained on them, and none are available. They don't really want the ship anyway, they just need the n-mats you have in it." He shook his head sadly. "They monitored your creative acquisition of it. They know it's full of n-mats based on the gravity signature."

"Why haven't they come for it before now?"

"It was safe here. The other n-mats were being kept near Vethi. It was the real reason for the attack there, not the star-ship factories, and the n-mats were lost or destroyed. There are very little of the n-mats remaining now. In fact, even with your ship, there is only enough for a small portal to be opened. Just big enough to send the rest to the federation so they can open the return gate and maybe save us all."

"And take control of all us again," Kasey replied, defeat dripping on every word.

"Kasey, my friend, its only control if you let it be. Someday you will learn that. Look, they will let you keep the ship, they won't need it if this works. The n-mats won't be secret for long after the portals are secured, so you'll have plenty of work from it all too if you want it."

Kasey was shaking his head in anger, but AnnaChi laid a hand softly on his shoulder. "Take it dear, they owe us. Let's end all this, then we can make our own future wherever, and however, we want."

Finally, he nodded. "Fine. Let's go finish this."

CHAPTER THIRTY-THREE

AnnaChi set the Cintian down as close to the Sarsaparilla as she could. The message from Flair had been cryptic but simple, Fran needed her there, and now. She had wanted to go with Kasey and fought with him over it. While he wanted her along, he had assured her this trip was just a delivery like any other, and he had an armed and armored stealth ship to protect him. Besides, Fran was a true friend, if he was in trouble, she had to go. Simple logic, but simple was not how it felt to her.

Opening the lower hatch, she was astonished to see both Fran and Flair heading toward her. They were all smiles and waving until they pushed inside and sealed the hatch before she knew what was happening.

"We don't have much time, we need to get back to the mine and quick."

"Why, what's wrong?"

Flair gave AnnaChi's arm a quick squeeze as she slipped by, heading for the bridge, "we will explain in the air, but we need to move."

She turned to Fran who gave her the same look. "She's right, we need to move now, there isn't time. But take off slow, or however you would leave for a delivery."

Giving up, she picked up her pace to catch up to Flair. "Slow? You have never seen me take off before, have you?"

Once they were underway, Flair took over the controls like she owned the ship and waved the others away. AnnaChi bit back her anger only when Fran pulled her away with a fatherly look, which she was not sure suited him very well at all.

"Come on," said Fran, "we need to talk." Before she knew it, he had led her to her own antechamber.

Without bothering to ask, she opened the panel and activated the security filters, then turned to look at Fran with fists clenched at her sides.

"I'm sorry dearie, but I am afraid Kasey may be in more trouble. We need…"

"What do you mean," she cut him off, "and how would you even know where he is?"

"I know more than you think. Although I just found out about you having the missing key, ha! While that's a story I would love to know more of, we have much more pressing matters." He took a seat and motioned for her to do the same. "There are only a few who know about his other ship and where he is currently headed with it, but we believe someone in that chain is working for the Patternists."

She made no move to sit as her face swelled red with anger, "You mean he could be heading into a trap! We need to change course and go after them. I should have been with him!"

"No, not yet. We… You were needed here."

"Why not!" She shouted in a piercing tone that Fran felt more than heard.

"For one thing, if you left now your ship would be attacked the moment you start toward Goligen." He put up a hand before she could interrupt again. "But, we will go and soon. Yes, we *are* going after him, but we are not going alone."

"What do you mean," she asked taking a breath, "who else is coming with us?"

"Everyone," He shrugged. "The resistance, if you will. Anyone who is still able to fly and willing to fight is now mobilizing to head to the gates with us. The Belrothi-Abscond's forces here are minimal at best right now. We have forty Federation marines piloting the I.C.E. suits you retrieved hidden in the Belrothi-Abscond's hangers waiting to cause some serious havoc. They will take control of the Belrothi-Abscond station if possible or disable its ability to monitor our ships at the least."

"How do you even know about where he is heading? But wait, why now?"

"I don't know why or how, but the enemy is sending everything they have in the direction of the gates right now. Gates they are not supposed to know even exist, but they are very informed for reasons we are not yet aware of. We assume because they know the key is heading there. They will try to destroy the gates if they can."

"Why? If you knew all this then why the hell did you let Kasey go?"

"We didn't know they knew anything about this. We only learned of the Patternist fleet's motives after he left. Keeping you behind was only so we could have a secondary…"

The blow nearly knocked Fran from the seat. "Ann…" He took the next slap in silence, then positioned himself to openly accept the punishment. It never came.

Relenting, AnnaChi sat to catch her breath.

"I know you do not understand," he said, calmly ignoring the reddening handprint appearing on his cheek, "but we needed to do this."

"Wa… Fine, but who is *we*?"

"Ah… Well, you see I was sent on this mission as insurance. I was to organize a backup plan. In this case, the resistance. If the negative matter was found here and everything went um, well sideways—which it did, the n-mats still needed to get back to the Earth Prime cluster, no matter what. If none were found, then I would get to retire, for a while anyway. Ha! So much for that…"

"Uh huh, and this resistance you drummed up. Can it stop them?"

"No that's very unlikely, but it's a chance to hold them off long enough. I have gathered about seventy or so armed ships, and supplied simple manual load missile batteries to others that were willing to help, but most are otherwise unarmed. It won't be much. But it's a fleet to protect the gates if we can. At least for a while."

She stood, "So what then, can we save Kasey? I don't care about your damn gates!"

He waved her to a seat again and this time she listened. "If he is quick to unload the n-mats into the transfer tanks, he will be fine. We have some of the remaining military ships out there already to protect him, but not many. They should be able to hold out until our fleet joins them."

"Well why are we going to the mine then? We need to hurry up…"

"We will join the fleet as soon as we can. First we need more n-mats." He held up his hand again. "Yes, I know you have more than what came from Lithose. You'll be happy to know I am the only one who knows that little secret. I have been watching closely since you brought the business of the claim markers to me for the copper mines. Something didn't add up and so I watched. It *is* part of my job you realize? I had a drone follow and scan your caverns before you even had a chance to seal them up."

"But… You could have taken them whenever you wanted," she clasped her hands together to stop them from shaking, "I wish you had and left us alone."

"Hard as it may be to hear, we need to make sure the gates are opened. There is more at stake than this colony. We needed a backup if the shipments from Lithose didn't make it to through the gate. Kasey's ship fit that bill already. But if Kasey's ship is taken, well, we need another backup."

Fran looked at the floor in embarrassment. "I really didn't want you two involved, I had other plans for your n-mats as well. I am sorry, but that is the truth. You didn't want them, and the federation, hell humanity, needs them. But I hoped to wait till it was public knowledge, and then use a fake depot to sell the stuff for you. With our existing delivery patterns in place, no one would be the wiser where it was coming from. We may still be able to…"

"Ha!" Nearly rising to her feet again, she thought better of it and dismissed what he was saying in an incensed wave, "Sorry, but I have had my fill of lies for one day. Get back to what you are planning today."

"I… Okay," he yielded, as his shoulders drooped slightly. "The n-mats you have are extremely dense, which will allow us to easily bring enough to send through the portal if Kasey is unable to send the Lithose n-mats. But we won't have a second chance, so we are bringing all that we can."

Sitting back, she sighed. "Fine, whatever. We don't really want the stuff anyway, we just want to be left alone."

"I know you do dearie, but the universe doesn't think so." He gave her a hard look and seemed satisfied she was really on board. "You should know, the mining crews we put on the west plot are some of my people. We are stopping there first to pick up some specialized equipment we will need. I swear, I only had it in place for an emergency like this."

"Fine. What are we picking up?"

"Pumps and weighted storage containers, of course."

"Of course," she mouthed quietly, not quite to herself, "how convenient for us all."

Making it clear she had no desire to continue the conversation, she disappeared into her private quarters until she was needed.

* * *

As they brought the last of the weighted barrels out of the cavern, the Lodestar landed with textbook precision next to the Cintian.

"Flair I assume?"

"Yes," he declared proudly. "I think she is enjoying being a pilot again. It's been years since she has flown this much."

"I need to talk to Kasey about securing his ship better…"

"Wouldn't have helped," he muttered with a smile.

"And what do we need his ship for?"

"We don't, but I like having contingencies, and I didn't want to risk bringing an unusual ship out here. We are just not sure what all they know and who is being watched. The federation only needs about two of these barrels for now. If we load five on each we double our chances and they still get enough to keep the team happy for a while."

"And here I thought you were some sweet old barkeep."

"Oh, I am that too."

"Right… Go load the Lodestar, I have this."

He was not gone long before a whistle-chirp brought a smile to her face. She turned as Molly landed a few meters behind her. She knelt to greet her friend as Orange and Mawk landed in turn, flanking Molly. Something about Mawk seemed off, but she was too distracted by Molly to decide what it was.

After a few nuzzles the blue atoss began a soft whistle while locking her gaze onto AnnaChi. Without knowing why, AnnaChi knew the creature was questioning her, it somehow knew something had happened. Before she could form an answer, Orange darted forward and chirped demandingly at her and Molly.

AnnaChi nodded sadly to the atoss, "Yes, Kasey is in more danger now. It is why they are here." She looked over her shoulder at the ships being loaded. "I am going to find him and bring him home. Try not to worry, I am sure he is fine."

The scolding from Orange that followed left no doubt that being insincere to an atoss was not a good idea. Molly seemed unaffected by Orange's outburst and continued to nuzzle AnnaChi in sympathy. Once done, Orange whistled sharply at Molly, and the two females trotted over to Mawk, the green male atoss. They both nuzzled him as the three exchanged low whistles of what passed for conversation.

AnnaChi didn't know what to make of it all. The whole exchange was unexpected and unique in her experience with the atoss so far. She promised herself that when they returned she would put more time into researching the amazing creatures.

When the atoss finished, Mawk gave a low-pitched whistle and chirped a few times, and then slowly turned back toward the trees. AnnaChi gasped, noticing what was different with the green atoss. He had a large bulge forming on his abdomen.

"What…" she started but never finished as Molly caught her gaze and chirped at her in a low tone. Instantly, AnnaChi knew the male was carrying a litter of baby atoss. They would soon have many more of these wonderful creatures. It was such a happy feeling she barely realized the feelings were not wholly her own. She put the thoughts aside and forced herself back to the present.

"I am so happy for you all! But, I am sorry, I do really need to go and find Kasey. We will be back as soon as we can."

The two female atoss dismissed the sentiment and were in the air in an instant, swooping past her, landing in the Cintian's open bay.

"Or," she laughed, "you could just come along I suppose."

CHAPTER THIRTY-FOUR

The Belrothi-Abscond station came into view as they joined the throng of ships surrounding it. The battle for the under-staffed segment of the galaxy class star-cruiser had been fought and won in the time it took for AnnaChi to make orbit. Small flights of commandeered ships were leaving the Belrothi-Abscond's bays and forming up with the fleet as she watched and waited for the next heading.

Nearly a hundred ships had gathered now. It was a structured mass, AnnaChi noted, as she slipped through the outer reaches of the fleet where the most heavily armed and armored ships were stationed.

The next layer was peppered with well-armed civilian ships, most of which had been built purely for speed and opulence, not combat. The closer to the core she went, the more ragtag the crafts became. There were many of similar mass and design as the Cintian, some had been armed with the simple looking missile batteries Fran had mentioned. They did not inspire confidence to her eyes.

The interior was clearly support ships of various types, at the center of which was a small knot of large transports docked together. Noticing the Lodestar's overlarge thrusters already docked to a makeshift maintenance platform the transports were attached to, she couldn't help but wonder how Kasey was faring.

She was not able to ponder long as her comm started flashing urgently. Swatting at it, she scowled for the message. *Prepare for docking. That ship is scheduled for an upgrade.*

That ship is my Cintian, and if you so much as scratch her, you will wish you never laid eyes on her. Got it?

Yes ma'am, not a scratch. Follow the way-points to docking, and you are welcome to assist if you have the experience.

* * *

Both the Cintian and Lodestar soon had launchers installed, as well as some basic reactive shielding units. The following days were filled with mock maneuvers as they traveled toward the mysterious gates. AnnaChi felt she performed more than adequately, but she took no joy from it. While she didn't care to be taking orders again, she knew it was necessary if she was to save Kasey. After that, all bets were off.

Most of the exercises entailed lighter ships launching quick attack runs before retreating. The heavier ships would mop up afterward and provide cover for rearming and positioning. AnnaChi knew all too well from past experiences that there would be a lot of losses on both sides from such attacks.

Fran docked with her when they were in the final hours of approach.

"Are you ready for this?" he asked, after seating himself across from her.

"Well sure, as much as anyone can be. But I don't know how well any of it will work. The enemy won't act how we want them to, you know."

"Oh," he looked at the floor for several moments before meeting her gaze again. "I don't think it will work at all. I expect it will fail actually."

"What? Then what's the point of all this? Why waste lives if we are going to lose?"

"The attack plans may fail, but I am not convinced we will lose. The attack is just a diversion. You *do* realize that, don't you?" Not waiting for a response, he went on. "We won't be in the first attack in any case."

AnnaChi leaned forward slowly, "So, where exactly will we be?"

"From the old light that we have picked up so far, we are going to be cutting this operation close. There is no sign of Kasey yet, which is good I believe, but they must be tracking him or the key somehow."

She just gave him a hard look instead of commenting, for fear her voice would betray her calm.

"In a few hours, I am going to split the fleet in two.

Same plan but we will come in on two vectors, so two battle fronts. Before we start our deceleration, we are going to speed up quite a bit and each ship will differ from the others. Then we will spread both groups out randomly over a few thousand kilometers. The time dilations will increase enough that our two ship's position changes won't be noticed until too late."

"Ok, so again, where are we going to be?"

Furrowing his brow at her terse response, he worked the display until she began to understand, "See on these edges? We will each be at the furthest points out from the fleets. Then we will curve in to the top and bottom the opening the two fleets will leave here. Our two ships will be late to the battle and off target of the main fleets. By that time, the light from the fleets trajectory will have already reached the enemy's forces, who should split to take on each of those groups."

She spun the view for a better look. "So, we will arrive about the same time as our heavier ships do. Which I guess means we hope the enemy will have their hands full?"

"Right. We should come out here and here, about fifty seconds after the medium ships have arrived. It should allow us to have a clear shot to the gates."

"Yea. Let's hope so," she frowned, "and if we don't?"

Fran sighed, "well, then we would need to follow the battle patterns and find our hole. If no way presents itself, we fall back with the light ships. They should present the least threat, so shouldn't attract too much attention until they reload. At least I hope. "

"Do we have any idea what we are actually up against?"

"Hard to say, we know they have fifty-eight cruisers and nearly twenty scout ships. That was the Belrothi-Abscond's remaining complement when they took it."

"What about the raven class ships like the one Kasey has? I assume there were some aboard."

"Several, yes, however as far as I know there are no pilots with the training to fly them in their forces. They may have stripped or converted some of them for normal use, but I doubt they had the time yet."

"How about the Cassian forces? And will the Sargani help?"

"Ha! The Sargani have only one ship, and they are with Kasey, but I don't know how much assistance they would be." A somber look filled his visage. "The Cassian are a big unknown here. We know there are at least thirty of them out there, but we need to assume there are many more. They have always been difficult to detect at range, so there could be any number out there."

"Wonderful... Should I even ask about Grays?"

"Sadly, the few we had with us were lost with the main Lithose-Abscond station at Lithose, not that they would be much help anyway. We are really on our own out here until we get the gates opened."

There wasn't much else to say as he left. Little was left that she could do but check and recheck her systems. She took one last walkthrough of the cargo bay to check on the n-mats containers and the pod that would take them through the gate, if required.

As she returned to the bridge the orders came to reposition the fleet. She made the adjustments to the flight plan and tried to convince herself that everything would go as planned and Kasey would be waiting at the gate unharmed.

The Cintian would be the last ship to move into the new position. It was comforting to know her light would be the last to reach the enemy and hoped they would have a lot more to worry about by the time she appeared on their scopes. Had the situation been different she would have felt guilty for having an edge in the coming fight. She knew she would later, but she did her best to disassociate emotions as best she could for now. Long ago, as a soldier, she had been able to turn off her feelings with ease, but that was a lifetime ago and far across the galaxy. It was hard for her to admit, even to herself, that she was no longer that same person she was then.

CHAPTER THIRTY-FIVE

An eternity passed as she dropped from relativistic speeds and locked into a semi-orbit of the unnamed moon that harbored the gates. Before she could even gage her position, an electromagnetic shockwave washed over the ship as proximity alerts sounded.

A minefield was slowly outlined on the display as the Cintian's scanners detected them. Quick wits saved her as she decelerated to a stop while maneuvering around what mines she could. The new reactive shielding modules stopped most damage from two other mines, but she knew each unit was good for just one save. The systems showed no major damage and it appeared the upper edge of the mine field was a short distance above her current position. Plotting a careful course to escape the field was easy but took far longer than she liked.

Before she was out, the light from the rest of the arriving fleet had reached her sensors and was mapped out before her. More than a quarter of the fleet had been destroyed or disabled by the minefields so far. Several enemy cruisers, which had apparently been laying mines, were now incapacitated by the sheer force of the arriving fleet. They were fortunate the Patternists had not been able to lay more mines than they had.

As she took stock of the battlefield, a sinking feeling began to grow in her stomach. It was a losing battle. The fleet they had brought had dropped to nearly half strength by the time she repositioned around the last mine.

Regardless of the losses, the mass of federation ships were still creeping deliberately toward the two gates. All their planning was now forfeit she realized. She plotted a course to try and take advantage of what gaps she could find, knowing there was now a very slim chance of making it to the gates and Kasey without being noticed.

Near the gates, she could detect a few clusters of federation ships taking advantage of the confusion to attack where they could, but it was apparent they wouldn't leave the gates undefended to help the fleet's losing battle.

"Cintian, how large are the circular structures?"

"Approximately twelve hundred meters diameter at maximum detected structure. The inner orifice is…"

"Thanks," she cut it off, "too much info as usual."

Her course would take her toward the gate on her port side. Struggling to keep her nerve, she searched the screens for Kasey's ship. If he had made it to the gates, he would be among the defenders there and likely under stealth. Finding nothing at first, she breathed a sigh of relief but immediately caught her breath. The wider scans searching the open space between the battle and the gates had locked onto a signal.

Screaming in frustration as the Argonaut's transponder was identified along with the fragments of several other ships. Molly was instantly pressed against her leg, offering support and giving AnnaChi the willpower she needed to press on.

Adjusting course, she headed for the wreckage instead of the gate.

Before she had closed a tenth of the distance, a

proximity alert sounded, followed by her point defenses destroying an inbound object. Two Cassian orbs had appeared, seemingly out of nowhere, to harass her.

Launching a missile at each orb, she accelerated as best she could. Adjusting course again to intersect with one of the groups of gate defenders, she hoped they would be able to assist if she could make it close enough. The fleet was closer, but it would mean slowing down, which was no longer an option.

Her missiles were shot down before impacting the orbs, which responded in kind with their own sets of warheads. She flung the accelerator to maximum and launched her only drone to help draw off the attack.

Choosing the nearest of the two orbs, she launched another salvo of missiles at it. She had a second to smile as the orb was destroyed before the Cassian's missiles came into range of her defenses. Spinning the Cintian to place one of the remaining shield units in line with the incoming warheads resulted in an appalling boom.

Only one of the Cassian projectiles made it through, but it knocked her main thruster and the Cintian's own EM shields offline. She needed more time before she would be in range of the defender's help, but sent them a narrow beam distress signal anyway. Launching an array of her own non-lethal civilian counter measures designed to blind an attacker, she watched in satisfaction as the orb darted past.

Without warning, the outgoing gate jumped to life. Lines of cobalt power surged across the fields inside it, causing her gravity wave alarms to squawk excitedly. A disturbing blackness sucked up the arcs of current and soon nothing could be seen but the gate's ring and a quaking blackness inside it that hurt her eyes.

From one of the ship groups, a massive ring was launched to the middle of the active gate. Once it reached the center, it stopped and hung there as if suspended. It was hard to tell what changed as the ring fell into place, but she decided it was far less disturbing to look at now. Glancing to the area outside of the new ring she found her thoughts confirmed. Looking anywhere except inside the center ring hurt the eyes and gave her a vertigo sensation. This, she decided, must be the n-mats stabilizing ring that would allow the wormhole to be traveled. The key must have been delivered, but she knew that without the additional n-mats to stabilize the entire event horizon, nothing bigger than an escape pod could be sent through to the federation.

A blast brought her back to the more pressing concern of the remaining orb. It was gaining on her, making it harder for her counter measures to have any effect. She needed to deal with it, but missiles were offline and the Cintian's small guns were more for defense than offense.

She checked the main thruster status and found it would be regenerated enough to use in about twenty seconds. Nodding to herself as a plan formed she smiled viciously. Using maneuvering thrusters, she set the Cintian into a slow spin and waited as the orb grew closer. The main thruster came online only a moment before she pushed it to full power, forcing the Cintian to arc out of the spin on a collision course for the orb ship.

"Molly!" She called out, hoping the atoss would understand, "get Orange and yourself into the escape pod, now!"

While Cassian orbs were more maneuverable than most ships, it was still accelerating and far too close to significantly change course away from the inbound Cintian. There was no way for it to avoid the collision.

AnnaChi waited as long as she could before deploying the landing sleds and pulling away slightly. The impact tore one of the sleds completely away from her ship, jarring her more violently than any of the attacks had so far. Ignoring the pain, she waved the alarms silent and closed off the lower recesses of her ship. Several breach warnings were in the area, but she had no time to deal with them individually.

Bringing the Cintian back under control took more effort than she would have liked. Maneuvering thrusters were reacting sluggishly at best. The hit must have done a lot more damage than she had thought. Pulling the ship back on course, she checked the status of the orb following her.

Something protruded out a rupture on its hull, but she couldn't tell if it was her landing gear or not. More satisfying to her was the thick cloud of yellow gas spilling out of the opening. The orb didn't look disabled, but she was satisfied that it was drifting off her route. Smiling, she sent more power to the main thruster to increase her lead.

Her grin faltered after only a few minutes of silence as two more ships appeared on an intercept course. Not a heartbeat later, another set of ships appeared seeming out of nowhere an opposing vector. None were registering as friendly ships. The enemy maneuver would pinch her in-between the two sets of ships, with little room to escape.

"Damn!" They were already too close to avoid.

Tightening the harness, she prepared make the best of it. She knew she couldn't out-maneuver four ships, no matter how bad the pilots were.

The leading ships launched four large missiles. *Apparently surrender isn't an option*, she thought, as she searched for a way out.

"Cintian, you were a good ship… Activate escape pod one, ready to launch on my mark." Positioning the ship to launch in the general direction of the gate, she watched the missiles close the distance. As they neared the halfway mark they burst into smaller projectiles that spread out like mines.

"These guys aren't kidding around..." Scrambling out of the helm and dashing toward the escape pod, she was glad to see the atoss inside it watching her every move. At the last moment she glanced back to the screen and witnessed a scene that made her pause before entering the small hatch.

The smaller missiles, all sixteen of them, powered up and shot in the direction of the other ships instead of her. Running back to the helm controls, she spun the view before slipping back into the cushion and strapping in. Before the missiles impacted, the ships had closed within gun range of each other and shields lit up as thousands of pellets burst against them.

When the first missiles hit, the shields were nearly burned out on the ships. Although nearly half of the missiles were cut down before striking, neither ship survived the impacts.

Waving at the new comm request, she wonder if they would be asking for surrender or not. The ships were not part the fleet they had brought here, she had them all marked and tracked by the Cintian. *These vessels had to have already been in the area*, she thought, as a voice cut in.

"Captain AnnaChi, we have been instructed to escort you in."

"Under who's orders?"

"Admiral Maddock Francis, commander of the Terrantine Federation forces within the Trias system."

"Admiral... You mean Mad Fran?"

"Uh, Yes ma'am. His ship is derelict in a mine field and cargo is irretrievable at this time. However, the Admiral and Commander Flair are aboard a shuttle and en route to the departure gate area now."

"I see." She took a long moment to review the data on the ships.

"Your ships don't look to have seen much combat. Is the battle going well?"

"No ma'am, we have not engaged yet. We are poised to do so only when the field conditions are met."

"And what conditions are they?" She nearly yelled, "People are dying out there man!"

"I understand ma'am. I am very sorry about that, but we have very clear orders."

"And they are?"

"All auxiliary forces are to remain under active stealth packages until the primary shipment is sent through to the federation. You carry that shipment; we just need to get it to the gates. Ma'am, the moment that happens we will engage the forces out there."

AnnaChi calmed as they talked, she understood the situation, although she didn't like it. The battle would be worthless if the gate wasn't activated.

"The gate, is it active?"

Yes ma'am, the key was delivered by a Sargani ship. The departure gate is ready to take the delivery."

"Ok what's our new heading, uh Captain?"

"It's Commander Knoc, ma'am. Sending you a flight plan linkup, but stay on the Scryer's tail. We will link up with group three and then head for the gate departure zone."

"Thank you, Commander."

She waved off the comm link and looked down toward Molly who had joined her, cooing the whole time.

"Perhaps I should have left you on the planet, this is far too dangerous." A sharp rebuking whistle was all she received in response.

Without warning, Orange shot forward and started making excited noises. Molly soon joined her, until they both settled down and positioned themselves on either side of AnnaChi.

"You two are weird," AnnaChi shook her head at the odd display, "but you are both going right back to the pod if things heat up again."

Reaching the ships guarding the gate was bittersweet, she had become a target for every enemy ship in the area. While most were a long way off, they still launched dozens of missiles her way. The gate defenders formed a wall around the Cintian and destroyed nearly every warhead that was thrown, intercepting the others with their own ships and shields when their point defenses failed.

It seemed to her that time slowed, as she watched the shell of chaos around her. She was impressed with the federation cruisers doing everything they could to protect her. Some had already been lost, but she only detected a few pods being launched. She did her best to put emotions in check and concentrated on the small portal ahead of her at the center of the looming gate.

When the moment came, she lined up and deployed the n-mats pod into the ring as she had been instructed. She and all the other ships followed it until it blinked out of existence, into the dark event horizon and beyond.

CHAPTER THIRTY-SIX

Kasey woke as pain lanced across the back of his head before fading to a dull ache. Stinging lights flashed by and assaulted his vision, but it was the first indication that he was moving. Blurred forms of uniformed men and woman were milling around as the movement stopped. Unable to make out what was being said, he tried to ask what was happening to him, but nothing came out. Trying to grab for a passing figure caused panic to set in as he realized he did not feel or sense his body moving at all. A man noticed his struggle and stooped down to a few centimeters from Kasey's face.

"You're going to be fine. Just rest for now," the man said. "Oh, and sir, welcome aboard the Endeavour."

Everything shifted abruptly, as he found himself being hoisted into an overly sterile-smelling trauma pod. A small pressure on the side of his neck caught him off guard, then reality slipped away.

* * *

When he woke again there was no longer anyone in

the room, but his vision was back to normal. He realized he was on a ship as he took in the size and barely noticeable arc of the main beam cutting through the room. A very big ship. Trying to remember something about the people who had brought him to the machine did not help. The ordeal was mostly a blur, except for a name. He was on a ship named Endeavour.

The table he was on shifted slowly, allowing him to sit up. As his weight shifted, he noticed some aches, but nothing seemed broken. The left side of his face was banged up and that eye didn't want to focus, but it didn't cause him much pain.

Had he been attacked? he wondered. Something had impacted the Argonaut, maybe several somethings. Then there was just darkness and waking up on this ship.

The nearby wall screens flashed at him several times, indicating he was cleared to get up. Moving was slow and painful, but eventually he located some clothing. Finding the garments marked with Terrantine Federation crests stopped him, and the clothing dropped back into the container. Knowing it was only clothing did little to calm his turmoil. Unconsciously rubbing his temple, he paced back toward the table he had woke upon.

Silently he raged, glad his parents were not around to see him being forced to put on the very symbol of the federation they had fought against. Here he was, running their errands and giving the federation his own property. He found himself back at the clothing containers. Slowly he picked up the uniform as he realized there would never be a way to escape the federation.

He shrugged. It all would mean nothing if he could not get out of whatever situation he was now in. For all he knew, he could now be aboard a Patternist ship who simply had better things to do then replace old Federation uniforms.

Attired, he moved to the entryway. "Fine. Let's get

this over with."

Waving the hatch open, he was only mildly surprised to see a pair of waiting guards regarding him expectantly. Officers, by the look of the uniforms.

"Sir," the nearest intoned, "if you are feeling up to it, the Admiral would like to see you." He didn't wait for an answer as he turned to lead the way.

"Admiral huh? Well I guess we shouldn't keep the *Admiral* waiting." Kasey fell into a quick pace to keep up as the other guard trailed behind.

It was evident the ship, the Endeavour, was a cruiser design, and a big one at that. Kasey stumbled and leaned against a wall to catch his breath, using the excuse to look around. He had trained on several cruisers over the years, although none had been even a quarter the size of this vessel.

This wasn't a normal ship, he realized. Walking down a wide causeway, he knew the end of which would normally be the bridge. Yet, for the size of the ship, it was shorter than it should have been. Manned stations enveloped each entrance leading from the causeway, conceivably for security. From the markings, the nearest duty station guarded a control center for a cloaking system far beyond the rudimentary HWG stealth packages the Argonaut. A stealthed, or cloaked he corrected himself, ship this size would be an impressive feat.

Passing a duty station with a medical symbol over it, the guard halted as if waiting. Without any warning Kasey could detect, the hatch to the medical station opened and several young nurses hurried out and headed back the way Kasey had come from. A quick glance beyond the portal showed rows of tables and trauma pods curving around out of sight. Many of which were occupied.

The ship was overly organized and professional. The

manner of everyone he passed alluded to a single purposed objective. All of them appeared committed to a cause, and even though he had never served in the military directly, he knew this was not normal behavior. Something big was happening.

As they passed through the main hatch that should have led to the bridge, they instead emerged into a massive communication and control room. Dozens of analysts were frantically pouring over holographic tables and screens that filled the room from top to bottom. It was loud and chaotic, contrasting with the other areas of the ship he had seen.

More disturbing were the contents of the screens. There was a full-fledged war going on. He stopped and stared. Hundreds of ships seemed to dance over several different regions. The swirling masses would leap at each other every so often, as if the ships were all part of large creatures swatting at each other.

Other screens showed the two colossal gateways. There were a few ships around them as well, but before he got a good look, the lead officer urged him along, obviously in a rush.

A large portal opened, showing the actual bridge this time. He was instantly aware of the change in manner the crew had here. Even the officers that escorted him positioned themselves in perfect attention, awaiting orders.

Several stations were arrayed around the room, and were quietly being worked over. A great oblong holographic table was positioned in the center with several important looking people crowded around it.

"Sixty seconds sir!" A woman from a nearby station called.

"Aye. Put her up on the main." A familiar voice replied as the main screen changed, displaying one of the massive gates.

The view made Kasey feel dizzy until he looked at the center, which seemed to have a ring floating within it.

"Kasey. Get up here, you will want to see this," the voice intoned again.

Kasey moved forward without realizing it. His reality seemed to split apart. He knew the man, but didn't recognize him. The man shouldn't be here. Couldn't be here.

"Fran? What…"

"No time boy," the Admiral grabbed Kasey's shoulder and spun him back toward the screen, focused at a ring of ships that were taking fire to shield a ship he knew all too well.

The Cintian, Kasey's mind screamed.

"She's in range sir!" The woman who had spoken earlier shouted. "Sir, she has launched it!"

"Good girl." Admiral Maddock Francis spoke quietly into the screen.

"Fran!" Kasey pleaded, terrified for AnnaChi's safety.

"She will be fine Kasey," he smiled as he smacked him hard on the back. A small pod flew out from the Cintian's belly toward the small ring in the center of the gate. All the ships continued course toward the gate, including the Cintian, closing in tight around the pod.

"Your girl is saving us all and making history right now. Let's give her some respect huh?"

It was hard to tell if he spoke to just him or the whole room, but instantly everyone snapped to attention as they watched the procession toward the portal. Kasey could do little but watch the ship of the girl he loved as it slowed to a stop the moment the ejected pod was swallowed up into the nothingness of the gate.

"Well, that is going to change things a bit around here soon. Interesting days are coming, my boy."

Spinning, Fran pointed to a station whose occupant waited expectantly. "Sergeant! Activate the auxiliaries."

"Yes sir!" The man responded with relish.

"I want every ship that is able protecting the reentry gate as soon as possible. Exit gate is minor priority from now on, we no longer need it." The room of people moved in a wave of action.

"What of the Endeavour sir?"

"Keep her cloaked and head to the reentry gate. Drop the cloak only if we need the speed to catch incoming. We will remain the last little surprise for any ships that get through."

"Yes sir!"

"Fran, explain! Please!"

"Kasey, I am truly sorry for subterfuge, but there is no time for that now."

"But AnnaChi… Can we get her aboard? The Cintian looks less than whole, she may be hurt, and you need those ships to defend the other gate, if I understand the situation."

"Sorry, we can't do that." He shook his head sadly. "However, I do owe you a ship since there isn't much left of your Argonaut, and I intend to repay that debt right now. Head to the hanger C, there is a raven transport, the Altair, waiting for you. Same model as the one you had, and it needs a pilot. Drift out under stealth until you are clear of us. Stay under stealth if you can," he smiled mischievously. "I actually owe you two ships now, but we can talk about that later."

Before Kasey could form a response, a new voice rang out with a hint of panic.

"Contacts! Far side and below reentry gate."

"How many?"

"We can't tell yet, but it appears to be a massive swarm of Cassian. There are hundreds sir…"

"Damn. Can we get into position while under the

cloak?"

"It will be close sir."

"Make it happen. I want to be well inside that swarm when we drop the cloak. Place Torus-Alpha on notice and recall Beta for the fallback."

"You really are *mad*, Fran…"

"Kasey my friend, the Endeavour is my very last backup plan. It needs to count. But you boy, you're going to need to run. Now. Go save AnnaChi!"

He ran. An officer sprinted at his heels shouting directions as they went.

CHAPTER THIRTY-SEVEN

The Endeavour's docking hanger was only large enough for four normal sized ships along the hemispherical landing pad. At either end sat small militarized shuttles, or maybe small fighters. They wouldn't hold more than a few occupants, but they currently had ground crews unloading some odd barrel shaped supply crates from the ships.

The center of the hanger drew his attention. A large freighter, identical to Kasey's recently destroyed Argonaut, filled the area. Sending a mental signal to the ship, a hatch appeared and slid open, welcoming him, as a ramp extended to the deck.

"Resupply ship?" he asked the officer as they trotted to a stop.

"Yes sir. I suppose we either won't need the Altair after this battle, and we should be able to requisition a new one if we succeed. Either way, the Admiral insisted Altair now belonged solely to you the moment he came aboard to take command." The man nodded and stepped back hurriedly.

"Uh, thank you. He has only been in command recently then?"

The officer swallowed. "Of this ship, yes. But he has

been in command of our auxiliary fleet long before the Abscond entered the Trias system."

Kasey shook his head as he ascended Altair's ramp, but he paused at the opening, only briefly noting the absence of the lab module his previous raven class transport, the Argonaut, had been issued. Fear and worry had been pooling in his gut, but now it stopped him from boarding the new ship.

"Sir? If I may ask…" Kasey turned to regard the young officer again. "Will you be joining the fight? The Admiral… he wasn't sure if you would."

There it was, Kasey realized. He had been asking himself that very question since Fran had offered the ship. He nodded before he really knew the answer. "Yes, I will fight. I will because my friend needs me to; but not for what he fights for."

The man nodded quickly. "Yes sir, I understand. He is who we all fight for."

Kasey nodded absently at the odd remark as the officer jogged away. Then he too hastened toward his new ship's bridge. AnnaChi needed him.

The ship rose off the platform before he was even seated, anticipating his needs. Waving up the HWG stealth package controls, he nodded at the instructions and the ship melted away into a black smudge across the hanger.

"You are clear to disembark at minimum acceleration." The aft wall slid open to space.

Nudging the ship forward, he angled toward the opening and let it drift out through the shield and in the blackness of space.

He was still getting his bearing as the ship again predicted his needs and locked on to the Cintian. The cruisers around AnnaChi's ship were moving off toward the reentry gate, a few winked away as their stealth systems kicked in.

Two cruisers stayed near the Cintian as it tried and failed to get back up to speed. Kasey hailed the nearest ship and explained his need. When he finally came close enough, the ship disappeared in the same moment Kasey dropped his own stealth. The other ship followed suit and was gone a moment later.

Breathing a sigh, he hailed the Cintian. "If you would be so kind as to set that tattered ship adrift and prepare to disembark, we have somewhere to be."

Only silence greeted him, but the main docking light lit green as he closed the gap. The skies around the gate looked clear of threats, so he left the ship to finish docking itself, and leaped out of the cabin see if she needed help.

The hatches had scarcely opened as AnnaChi shot through to tackle him hard onto the floor as an orange streak shot by. "Tattered ship! I'll have you know my Cintian had bested two Cassian orb ships before completing the mission you failed!" She kissed him on the nose as he lay catching his breath. "She just needs a breather after that last round..."

Their embrace ended too quickly, but Kasey knew they had to move. "Well welcome aboard the Altair, but we need to go, there is an entire fleet of Cassian closing on the gate and Fran needs our help."

"Good, you smell like a hospital by the way, wait, you want to join this fight?" She cocked her head to the side while getting to her feet. "Are you sure you are ok? You seem a bit banged up... Wait, you said Fran? Mr. Admiral is ok then?"

"Hah! Yes, he is fine, and apparently in charge cleaning up this catastrophe. And yea, I am surprised about wanting to join the fight too. I don't want to fight for the federation, but..."

"You'll fight for Fran, the damned Admiral?" she shouted over her shoulder as she led an impromptu race for the ship's bridge.

"Yea, there is something about that son of a… Wait, he said something about owing me two ships. What do you know about that?"

"Umm…" she teased, sprinting ahead.

He caught up as they reached the bridge's hatch and was surprised to find Molly and Orange had appropriated an aft station as their own. Orange gave a quick whistle and nod as greeting, apparently understanding the situation.

"Brought some stowaways?"

"I didn't really have a choice," she returned.

"Where is Mawk?"

"Oh, he uh, he is either pregnant or carrying a clutch of young. I am not sure, but it seems more atoss will be joining our little valley soon."

"Amazing…"

He checked the scans as he slipped into the helm. "So, what was that you were telling me back there?" He nodded back toward the gangway.

"Was I telling you something?"

"I am positive you were. Something about my ship." They disengaged the coupled ships and leaped away from the Cintian. The view shimmered slightly as stealth covered the hull, then he turned his full attention on AnnaChi.

"Oh, well… Ah, you see Flair and Fran brought the Lodestar with a second load of n-mats from the cavern," she ignored his look of honest shock. "From what I understand, your Lodestar, or whatever's left of it, is somewhere out there in a mine field." She smiled sweetly at him as she waved toward a general area of space.

It was a long while before he spoke. The Lodestar had always been more than just his ship. It represented everything he had always striven to achieve. It had represented his survival and his freedom.

"Well, okay then."

"That's it! That's all you have to say?"

"I don't know, it just doesn't seem as important now."

Watching him with pride, she seated herself in the tactical station and pulled up the screens. "There are a lot of ships out there…"

"Ours or theirs?"

"Mostly theirs. Want to grant me weapon access? I don't seem to have the control I had in the Argonaut."

Several minutes passed as he rebuilt the command access to the ship's key areas to include her. She wouldn't be able to fly it without some training, but it was now as much her ship as it was his.

"Done. You have primary weapon control and secondary control of countermeasures in case I am otherwise engaged."

"Ok, assuming tactical as well. We will reach the reentry gate area in twenty-three minutes, which is not much time to work out a plan," she complained.

"Pull up a comm list and see if you can locate a ship named Endeavour."

"Okay, I have it. It's offline."

"That's fine, just keep an eye on it. It's Fran's, I mean, the Admiral's flagship. They rescued me out of whatever was left on my last one of these," he said indicating the ship. "I think it has been quietly monitoring the whole Trias system since the Abscond arrived here."

"Do they have a plan?"

"Well, if there is a plan that will get us all out of this, they would have it. He has quite an operation going on in that ship."

"Any idea where in that mess he would be?"

"Ha, well, he seemed to be planning to attack the orb

swarm directly. He has a big, well-supplied ship, but I am not sure it would last long by itself."

"He must have some plan. He seems to have a knack for planning ahead."

The reentry gate crept ever larger in their view as they shared all the happenings and revelations that had occurred since Darnell had come for the key. Emotions had run high, and the day was long from over. They knew their friend's lives were on the line. Knew they were together once again, and anything was now possible.

CHAPTER THIRTY-EIGHT

Kasey was glad for the ship's stealth package as they approached the engagement area. The aches and pains he had sustained were nearly gone now, yet as they approached the battle, anxieties seemed to replace them. Looking over the enlarged scenes of individual battles that dotted their displays, he suppressed a grimace.

AnnaChi suddenly looked back and backhanded him in the chest with enough force that he was sure left a row of knuckle-sized bruises.

"Get in the game sweetie, it's time to go to work. Most of the fleet is spread out nearly as far as we are, but there is no doubt that all of them will be converging on that gate."

"Okay," he replied a little too quickly and high pitched for his own liking. "What do we have to work with?"

The screens changed to a series of course changes. "First, we need to get in close enough to help. There shouldn't be any mine fields in this region, but if there are any surprises, we should be able to avoid them by following corridors of space we have record of safe travel through. This course will get us near the gate where this ship can do the most good."

AnnaChi 's attention to the tactical command was a relief for Kasey. The protocol scripts he had developed while training on the raven transports were now out of his reach. He had rebuilt many for the Argonaut, but they too were now lost, and there was no time to develop new ones. The ship's basic controls would suffice, but tactical control had been more of an art form that needed to adapt for each ship and purpose.

Rubbing his now sore chest, he maneuvered into the new flight path and then settled in to watch the updates that flickered across the screen. He was amazed as she raced through the libraries of controls with apparent ease, enhancing the current buildout left by the previous pilot to her liking. Within minutes, each friendly ship was marked with a glowing white dot. Each dot expanded into a zoomed view of the ship it represented the moment he paid any attention to it, as well as showing any available information. Known Patternists ships appeared as a sickly green color, and their Cassian cohort orbs were red.

Kasey flinched as a ding heralded a new white dot appearing.

"Well that works, but I'll make it a bit more subtle" AnnaChi remarked without looking up, "what ship is it?"

"The Jate-Markay. Looks like she surprised a few Cassian orbs that were making a strafing run on the gate."

She glanced up at the comment and gestured at the screen to zoom in on the gate. "They did some damage, but it seems negligible. I wonder how much that monstrosity can take."

"Looks like we may find out."

Another group was attempting the same maneuver. This group was too slow and were intercepted by a band of motley ships AnnaChi recognized as part of the fleet

Fran and she had traveled here with.

The both cheered for the successful defense, but Kasey noted the sagging of AnnaChi's shoulders afterwards.

"Our forces are outnumbered three to one. We won't be able to hold them back for long." She concentrated over her station a moment. "Let's get into a steep vector approaching the gate here," she sent the course adjustment over to his station, "like this."

"I see it. That should give us a better chance to disrupt an attack, but what about..."

A startling number of dings unexpectedly announced the appearance of a small gathering of ships centered on the Cassian swarm that was now entering the outer edge of the battle.

"It's the Endeavour, and seven cruisers." AnnaChi stated as she superimposed the unfolding battle over the display. "Damn, that is one huge ship!"

The flagship tore through the swarm, charging against the tide of Cassian. Unleashing an awesome quantity of ordnances, they cut through the scores of orbs before the Cassian could react. The ships didn't stop until they nearly reached the far edge of the swarm, by which time a hoard of the orbs had begun to reverse direction in pursuit. In well-rehearsed precision, the federation ships came together into a tight line as they hooked around the edge of the swarm, facing back toward the gate.

Destruction reigned over the swathe of enemies as the Endeavour's company made its approach back to the front of the orb mass and headed toward the gates once again. They were being hit hard as the Cassian recovered from the shock and confusion. Nearly half now followed the Endeavour, chipping away at the group's shielding as the other orbs recovered and joined the chase.

It was clear Fran was increasing speed to outrun the

chasing armada, and failing. Kasey and AnnaChi could only watch the scene unfold as more and more orbs closed in. They gasped, standing to watch as the Endeavour stopped running and turned to fight a seemingly hopeless battle. The smaller cruisers turned a moment later to join their leader, but they would be little help too.

Hope gleamed for a moment as the leading edges of the swarm blossomed into a torus shaped cascade of destruction. The Endeavour was crowned in devastation as it spewed death into the center of the circular minefield it had drawn the orbs into. The cruisers added their fire a moment later, helping to obliterate the pinnacle of the swarm. A minute later, another handful of raven transports appeared within the minefield and opened fire on any orb still intact within their range.

The encroaching swarm slowed and began firing projectiles toward the Endeavour, then just as quickly, stopped and began retreating. Kasey and AnnaChi realized why an instant later, as their screen's edge erupted with scores of friendly ship's missiles angling toward the swarm. They pounded into the fray haphazardly but effectively. The Cassian wave was broken. As one, the swarm pulled back to gather their strength.

Kasey shouted with relief, but AnnaChi had already started taking stock of the full battlefield. Her frowning expression showed her to be underwhelmed. Ships still fought a battle of attrition throughout the sector. Fran and the Endeavour had stopped the gate from being attacked for now, but it wouldn't last long.

AnnaChi faced Kasey and shook her head as she gave her assessment. "We will be able to help, but it won't make a difference unless Fran has more of those ships up his sleeve. Or some other trick."

"That ship was Fran's last backup plan, or so he had

claimed. From now on, all we have is what we see."

An incoming comm chimed, interrupted their contemplations.

"It's Fran, or the Admiral; he is rallying all capable ships to the gate," her look was thoughtful as she read the message.

Withdraw routes followed the message, bringing the forces together in strength before making a break towards the gate's protectors. A schedule was also included that would allow the rallying ships to intercept with planned patrols when possible.

AnnaChi looked up in admiration. "This is a bit of impressive planning. Just how many people were on that ship?"

Kasey chuckled at that. "A lot. The comm room alone had at least thirty analysts monitoring the entire system. That is one well-organized ship, I have never seen anything like it. Not that I would know much about federation ship standards."

"Well, it better be, and they better know what they are doing. Looks like we have been ordered into one of the patrols. Sending you the headings now." She spared him a quick smile. "The show's over, time to get into the fight."

CHAPTER THIRTY-NINE

The battle had raged for endless hours, draining Kasey of strength as they patrolled the last of the zones assigned to them. Twice in the last hour they had uncovered pairs of orb ships attempting to slip through the battle lines. None had escaped so far.

The Cassian ships were difficult to detect at a distance, but at close-range they were like any other ship. Fran's patrols had placed the few stealth capable ships that were left into the largest voids, as the remaining federation fleet ships withdrew at the speed of the slowest ships. The sphere of protectors surrounding the gate grew ever smaller, so too did the opening for orbs to slip through.

"Distress beacon," AnnaChi beckoned, "dead ahead. Adjust five down and hold as I get a bearing."

"Time till we reach weapon range?"

"Ten for guns, missiles are ready now, but they would be useless." A grainy image appeared on the screen of four bulky ships dancing around one another angrily. "Three are ours, but that one looks to be an Patternist controlled federation cruiser," she pointed angrily.

"They don't look to be faring well against that beast.

Do we have the time to get close at stealth speeds?" As he spoke, one of the smaller ships lost control and spun off, out of control. The cruiser was winning; would win given time.

"Not a chance." Concentrating a moment on her screens before shrugging in defeat, she continued "I'm not sure we would make a difference here… Wait! Their lower aft shielding is showing fluctuations. If we can get in close, we may be able to take advantage of that."

"I'll send command our location and make these friendlies aware of our plan—as soon as you figure out what plan that is."

"See if you can have that damaged ship steadied and vacated of crew. If so, then get the others to lure the Patternists toward it. We will use it as a shield."

"On it," he confirmed, as he began composing messages.

"Transition twenty to port please. Launching a drone on delayed ignition," AnnaChi called out.

"The crippled ship is abandoning as planned, but they are attempting to get their shields online first and sending us control codes. They believe their stabilizer thrusters will be regenerated in three, but not much else."

"Good enough, I am syncing the codes now. Sending you coordinates for our friends out there. If they can get that ship anywhere close to them, it will help."

Just before they reached the damaged ship's shadow, a burst of stray fire strafed across their port side thrusters. A gap in the stealth field appeared for less than a second, but that was all it took for the enemy cruiser to notice them.

The cruiser ignored the smaller ships and placed all its attention upon Kasey and AnnaChi. Their vicinity was soon alight with a host of small weapon's fire and signal pulses designed to locate them again.

"We need to drop out of stealth so we can put in

some speed!" Kasey shouted.

"Dropping stealth on a three count, and pumping EM shield to max. As soon as you make the wreck's shadow, use it to close on that cruiser with all haste... Stealth dropping now!"

Kasey bore down on the Patternists cruiser. "Thrusters at full, I need forty seconds. We're taking heavy fire!"

"Adjusting EM shields. Keep the port toward him, I'll... Incoming missiles!"

"I can handle them," he replied, with a confidence he didn't feel as the familiar buzz of the defensive systems came online. "Stay with the shields. Do we have control of that wreck's stabilizers yet?"

"Working on it... Yes, I should be able to buy you a few seconds with them. Doesn't look like they got the shields back before they punched out though."

"He is adjusting to our maneuver, and I am seeing another set of missiles. Oh, they are targeting the wreck!"

"I am detecting a light EM shield spinning up on that ship—Damn, some of them are still aboard!"

"Entering shadow in two seconds... Missiles impacting. I see two pods, but they don't look like a clean launch. What can you see?"

AnnaChi sighed in frustration. "The shields on that wreck are down again, but they deflected most of the damage. The escape pods are both running silent, although I am not sure if that is by design or not."

"Our other ships are holding back, but they are asking for orders. I can stay in this shadow for maybe a minute, but the cruiser is ripping it apart and is closing the distance to get to us."

"Have them start an attack run on his lower starboard thruster the moment we come out of the shadow. If we manage to pull off this attack, there is a good chance that area could be weakened as well."

He responded after a moment, "They are ready."

"Good. I need you to slow down a bit and activate the stealth array on my mark. Then change our heading to this vector. Ready?"

"It will only be a partial stealth; Altair took a lot of hits to the port side. But we are ready."

"It will do. And… Now!"

Deploying another drone as Kasey adjusted course, AnnaChi activated it to mimic their ships previous path the moment the stealth system was online.

"At this range, that won't fool him."

"He should already be distracted by the drone we dropped off earlier—it is spinning up now. This one will come out of the shadow and for a moment he will think it is us. We won't know until we exit, but if he reacts to them at all, he should be positioned on a vector that that may give us an advantage."

"I'll take your word for it dear. We are at ten seconds…"

"Spin us around. We only want to expose our lower starboard side until we are in close."

"Exiting!"

"Drop stealth and get me in there, fast and close!" she shouted as her weapons began to fire.

"He's turning. We are taking only light fire so far."

"Perfect," she pushed a new flight plan onto the main screen. "He will come at us much harder once he realizes the position he is in. Do you see it?"

"No… Wait, he is stuck on that trajectory now, isn't he?"

"Right, unless he decides to run from us, he can't roll over to maneuver. That would only make him more vulnerable, but he would likely escape if he tried. I am betting he will trust in his shields to survive our pass."

Kasey could not hide a wicked grin, "Five seconds

till transition. Incoming missiles—I'm on them."

"Hold on spin until the missiles are destroyed! We need to save our top armor."

"Got them both! Transitioning now," he added as he pitched the ship over to face the enemy head on. "All main guns should now have clear shot shots. Missiles?"

"Not yet," she acknowledged, "once we are under him the chance of them making it to that ship will be greatly increased. Just a bit more, and... Now!"

Only one missile made it through to impact, but fluctuations in the cruiser's shield panel increased dramatically.

"Another set?" He winced as incoming fire started to increase again.

"No, we only have time for one more, so I am keeping them on snap launch."

"His shields are spotting, we are getting through... He's noticed and is starting to turn for a run!"

"Launching!" AnnaChi growled, as she concentrated on making every shot count.

Before the cruiser could turn the damaged shield away, the panel evaporated. Hull plating shredded into dust under AnnaChi's continuous fire. Then her missiles streaked into the hole.

Silence flowed over them as all weapons ceased to fire.

"It's coming apart!" Kasey cried as he pushed the thrusters to maximum.

The debris shockwave rocked them more than either liked. Three large chunks of the ship spiraled away, the cruiser's only remains.

Shrill atoss whistles of excitement filled the bridge, mirroring their own exhilaration.

"Not too bad for a transport ship I suppose," AnnaChi commented. "Why don't you like these ships again?"

"Uh, well they are not usually this exciting…"

"Right, hmm. Well let's make sure our ships can make the staging area. Looks like they are heading to retrieve the escape pods now."

Kasey had no doubt that this day's encounters would have had a drastically different outcome had it not been for AnnaChi's clever strategies. The way she adapted to battle so easily was surprising to him. Soon, he promised himself, he would pry more into her past, once this was over. She had been a soldier once, he knew, but she had always changed the subject as soon as any details were asked for.

His musings ended as AnnaChi relayed the latest comm message.

"Woah, all ships are being called to one of the three main staging areas. Any ship not able to get there should withdraw from engagements if possible. A few secondary areas have been plotted as well."

"Why? What's going on, and I thought there were five staging areas around the gate?"

"There *were* five. While we were messing with that last cruiser there was a major push against the gate. All the defenses suffered losses. The remnants reformed to the three that are left."

"That doesn't sound good at all."

"It doesn't look good either," she responded. "They are assuming another attack will hit soon. I don't think this fleet can withstand another attack like what they just faced."

Kasey set a course to the closest staging area without comment. "Are Altair's stealth emitters back online yet?"

"Not a chance. It will be hours before we can even attempt to activate them again. Even if it comes online then, it will only be a partial effect. We completely lost several emitters; we will need an overhaul to get it working fully again."

"We do this the hard way then."

Kasey took a moment and watched his love work on some new plan and smiled. She was beautiful in her element. He knew she was a far better pilot than he was, but this was altogether different. She was really enjoying this horrible situation they had been thrown into.

Feeling his gaze, she peered up to see what was wrong. His smile threw her off briefly, then she realized nothing was amiss. Her visage softened as she gazed back. She smiled too, her whole body seeming to relax before she turned back to her work.

The interlude seemed to organize her thoughts. "Maybe it's time to put the gate to use in this battle. If we lose, the gate will be destroyed anyway, right?"

"I'm not following. This gate doesn't do anything except allow a pairing with the gate it's bonded to back in the federation. How can we use it?"

She grinned roguishly. "The gate has mass, a lot of mass. If our ships are close enough to it, the attackers won't be able to get clean locks on our ships."

"But the gate will take damage, isn't that what we are trying to avoid?"

"Yes, but it can still take a lot of damage and survive, at least I assume it can. We should be able to pick what hits we can absorb or shoot down. If we use it right, our ships will survive longer. The longer we survive the longer the gate does."

"Interesting, but it's all a bit beyond me." He gave her a shrug. "Send your reasoning to the Endeavour. I am betting Fran's people know exactly how much punishment that gate can take."

CHAPTER FORTY

The gate remained dormant as Kasey and AnnaChi joined the fleet surrounding the immense ring. The Admiral had improved on AnnaChi's plan. Two ragtag rings of ships weaved around the gate in opposing directions. Heavier ships were spread throughout to provide support where needed. Few of the military vessels retained any useful stealth ability, but here and there Kasey noted a ship or two disappearing and reappearing as systems were repaired and tested.

The Patternists and their cohorts had pulled their own ships back as well, effectively halting the battle momentarily. The gate's defenders watched intently as the Cassian orb swarm, what was left of it, flittered protectively around the edge of the Patternist fleet. Sharp debates flowed among comm channels, attempting to deduce if the Cassian were corralling the Patternists to do their bidding, or if they simply encouraged the willing traitors to humanity.

"Eat," AnnaChi commanded as she rushed by. "It may be our last chance for a while. We need to keep our energy up, and booster stims will only go so far."

"I will, as soon as I finish replacing this last emitter from the KI shields." Kasey's hands moved through the cabin air as he directed the maintenance bots outside the ship. "The EM shields did very little once we got up close to that cruiser, the kinetics are the only reason this boat is still in one piece."

She tossed an energy bar at his chest, "I doubt we will get that close again. We are packed in to densely now, but I will feel better having the extra shielding."

"Did the supply drone drop off anything useful?" He bit into the bar, ignoring the looks Orange was giving him, "maybe some food before Orange devours the rest of our supplies?"

"I think we have enough for her," she laughed, "but mainly a rack of missiles, standard fire-n-forgets. Junk really. I have them set up in the close-range queue, but they won't last long. We have eight more class twos left as well, which will likely be used and controlled by fleet."

"Anything defensive?"

She sighed, "Only some low-tech countermeasures. Some chaff wire spools, which we definitely needed, but this stuff is unlikely to make much of a difference. They must be melting down anything they can scavenge for the extruders. There are a few simple drones as well, class ones, so don't expect much there either."

"Better than nothing I suppose."

"Not much better."

Her dry tone left little hope in Kasey's mind how she believed this battle would end. "I guess we will just be acting as a shield for the incoming?"

"Likely, but who knows. Plans only last until..." Alerts began flashing across the ship's consoles. "Multiple blue-shifts detected. Looks like we will find out soon enough."

Kasey watched apprehensively as the edges of the enemy fleet slowly came into view range. Ship after ship was identified as Patternist controlled vessels until, ever so slowly, orb crafts began to emerge at the back edges of the fleet. The positioning left little doubt who was truly in control.

"We've been ordered to launch the first salvo in forty," she remarked bitterly. They exchanged glances as the missiles were queued.

Feeling a loss of something deep within himself, he realized what launching the next missiles would mean. The lives they would take would be innocent humans now being forcibly controlled by the true enemy. He had killed in this war, but it was somehow different now. The Patternists had seemed to have a choice then, now however, they were being used as a shield for the Cassian.

"We don't have a choice, do we?"

AnnaChi shook her head regretfully. "No, we are forced into this action by the Cassian, just as the foolish Patternists now are."

A soft blue light began blinking on AnnaChi's console as he watched her, indicating it was time, but she was ignoring it. Swallowing his fear, he tried to don a brace face.

"Go ahead, lets finish this," he said, watching her react instantly to his request, sending the deadly missiles sailing into the blackness.

"We have new flight vectors coming in from command," she announced, "sending them over now. Our targets for next launch are changing as well."

"Is Fran trying to confuse us or them?"

"It's a good move, he's forcing them be reactive. A reactive force is usually a losing force. It won't last, since we will need to react to protect the gate. Nothing will change that."

Feeling frustrated, Kasey tried to get his mind back to their current situation, "Have they launched at us yet?"

"Nothing showing yet, but relative time is still behind

a bit. They could have fired up to a minute ago, the light we are seeing is still a bit old."

"Of course, wonderful," he murmured, but quickly perked up. "Good timing on our course change then."

"It is nice to know you can be taught dear."

Blips silently appeared across the main screen indicating weapon fire.

"Any idea if we have been targeted, or are they too far behind the relativity curve?"

He appreciated the sweet smile of her response before concentrating on the task.

"System is working it out faster than I would have expected with the unknown variables. It is far more powerful than.... Oh, we have an answer. We have two heading our way with a thirty second gap."

"That shouldn't be much of an issue."

"No, but I assume the attack waves will get more compressed as we close the distance between fleets." She frowned.

Kasey let her comment sink at in as he watched new incoming missiles appear on the screen. "How many more do we have?"

Her response was nearly instantaneous, "Three, at a fifteen second spread."

"Well that will be a lot more interesting... Same origin ship?"

"Yes, I haven't identified the ship type yet."

"If they can launch three at a time, we may be outclassed a bit."

"Don't worry, I bet their next launch will not be at us." She gestured toward the main screen. "They have closer vessels to target now. If they have any leadership, or brains at all, they will change targets."

He watched in silence as the layers of ordnances filled the battlefield display in great ribbons from both fleets. Occasional blips appeared as missiles came into range of the cruiser's long range defenses and were destroyed. Not long after, he found himself too busy directing the ship's own defenses to pay attention to the larger battle.

"The orbs are dropping further behind the ranks of Patternists," AnnaChi noted in a lull. "Without the orb's firepower, their leading ships are going to take massive losses."

"I don't get it, why would they weaken their own fleet?"

"Control would be my guess, but impossible to know just yet. The Patternists are human after all, and we never deal well with being controlled for long."

Already committed to the assault, the Patternists had no alternative but continue onward as both fleets launched wave after wave of warheads at each other.

Kasey found the carnage hard to watch. The Patternists were taking a staggering amount of damage. If it had not been for the quality of the federation fleet ships they had assumed control of when taking over the Belrothi-Abscond station, they would have been decimated already.

AnnaChi suddenly straightened in her station catching his attention. "We have a ship closing within gun range in twenty. Take us in closer to the gate, but try to keep him just within my firing range."

"Will do, but I don't have the acceleration to keep the distance for long. Use that window fast."

"Looks to be a commandeered patrol ship, so it should be well armored and fast, but weapons should be about equal to ours. Scans are showing leaks along their lower weapon pod, which could mean the area is damaged. Targeting."

AnnaChi's fire began blistering off the enemy shields with little noticeable effect. The craft returned torrents of fire but remained out of effective range—a consequence of being the chaser at such speeds.

"We are starting to take hits," Kasey yelled, louder than he intended, "EM shields are holding for now, but we are losing kilometers every second."

"Edge to port and down by ten, I need a better angle on it. Make that fifteen."

"Adjusting. Should we launch a…"

"No! Not yet, I am starting to eat through it. Prepare to full reverse and get me a line perpendicular to that section as they pull by."

"They are well armored. Hold on."

Glad for once of the mimic interface linkup these ships required, he pulled up schematics of the patrol ship looking for any vulnerable systems in that area.

"Their secondary thruster port has fuel lines running about a meter above your location. Marking location, make those shots count!"

"I'm through and that gun port is already getting torn apart, break and reverse when ready."

Kasey cut Altair's thrusters and rotated them one-hundred and eighty degrees before reengaging at max thrust. There was a slight sickening feeling as the ship radically slowed. Collision warnings sounded almost immediately, indicating the proximity the other craft was about to obtain. He could almost imagine the other crew scrambling to adjust as the ships pulled abreast of either other.

The firing continued till they were nearly past each other, then without warning the scene changed as the lower side of the patrol ship swelled and seemed to tear itself apart.

The ship survived, but it was now crippled beyond repair. To his surprise, AnnaChi didn't stop firing.

"Anna…"

Ignoring his plea, she walked her gunfire along the bare and unarmored innards of the vessel until it was collapsing in on itself.

Kasey focused himself on taking their ship away from the wreckage. The debris shockwave that overtook them sent a shiver up his spine that he did his best to shake off.

"So, this is war?" He ignored the excited atoss clamor as they celebrated the triumph.

"No one wins in a battlefield like this Kasey dear, you only survive. Or not."

He didn't try to respond for some time, and when he finally opened his mouth, he found no words to say. Instead he put his mind to the task at hand.

"Status?"

She nodded once before starting down a list of updates. "EM shields are rebuilding, no new damage to emitters. One stray missile is inbound but looks to be without guidance—take it out when it reaches range. We have new flight vectors again."

She went on, but Kasey only half listened as the battlefield caught his attention. "What of the Cassian?"

"Um, their numbers are half what they were. Checking with fleet." She highlighted several areas before continuing. "It appears they are stealthed, but fleet is tracking several areas where they believe small swarms to be. They expect the Cassian to take runs at the gate once the Patternists have weakened our forces enough."

"I don't see how we can defend against them, and we are more than a bit thinly spread."

"I agree, but we do have some time before that happens, if fleet location estimates are correct. Maybe they will come up with a plan."

"Hold onto that thought." He zoomed a screen in on a set of ships. "There is a battle going on near where we will pick up the new flight path. Shall we assist?"

"By all means," she laughed.

VINCENT BEK

CHAPTER FORTY-ONE

Kasey pulled his ship out of a steep dive toward the gate, as AnnaChi destroyed the last of the orb missiles he had been evading. The constant fight had been taking a toll on him, and the familiar feel of exhaustion was settling in again, only to be replaced with a stim-induced burst of energy from the flight helmet. The effect was lasting shorter and shorter periods of time, and as he settled the ship back into the protective vector around the gate, he could already feel it wearing off.

The gate had been taking a real pounding. Too many missiles were getting through the weakened lines of protectors. It surprised neither of them when the fleet comm lit up with orders to begin intercepting every warhead possible, using and abandoning ships as needed.

Kasey and AnnaChi had more than their share of the fight thus far. Their EM shields were no longer able to rise above forty-eight percent, and half the cargo bays were open to space. They had managed to eliminate most missiles in their zone so far but were left with nothing but guns and weak shields to fight with.

"Kasey," AnnaChi said without a hint of concern in her voice, "the orb swarms... Fleet scans are showing the swarms are starting their runs now."

He saw them too, but welcomed her voice among the chaos. "I have you with me, there is nothing else I need in this life."

"And I have you."

The next wave came without mercy.

Kasey ignored the flight plans, instead concentrating on keeping above the undamaged areas of the gate to draw fire. Missiles got through to the gate, but only caused minor damage. The ship was another matter.

"EM shields at ten percent. KI shields are offline. Another wave inbound."

Kasey stared at the incoming missiles hopelessly, realizing this was the end. "Prepare to…" He stopped and pushed the ship forward at full acceleration. "Hang on!"

Racing the missiles, he slid the ship under the bulk of a freshly abandoned cruiser and arced down toward the gate. Eleven missiles impacted the dead cruiser in slow succession. The ship erupted in a blinding ball of light that illuminated the gate.

Debris pelted their shields as they escaped the barrage.

"Three made it through, impact in ten!" AnnaChi shouted.

The defenses shrilled unnoticed as Kasey pushed the throttle to full and manually piloted the ship in an arc away from the missiles.

"One down," she called out. "We are not going to…"

The ship rocked with a massive impact, throwing them violently against their restraints.

"EM shields are gone!" AnnaChi exclaimed, as the first real edges of fear crept into her voice. "Stern defense arrays are offline…"

"Port thrusters are offline as well," he replied. "We need some cover."

"The last missile is gone," she sighed in relief, "the debris must have taken it out, but our sensors are spotty at best right now, so I am not positive."

Kasey concentrated on keeping his hands steady as he took the ship around the edge of the gate and into its shadow. The battle faded from their view for only a moment as he came around the other side. The enemy had completed the run and were circling away to ready another assault.

With effort, he released his grip from the controls. Easing back into the helm's cushion he tried to control his breathing as he assessed the battle.

The fleet was shattered. Wreckage floated in every direction. The number of enemies had been reduced slightly, but not enough. There were no longer enough defenders to protect the gate. The next attack would succeed in destroying the gate, and most of the defenders as well.

A priority comm message came in and Kasey cringed as it started, hearing the finality in his friend's voice.

"Fleet, soldiers, friends, Terrans" Fran's voice broke through. "You have done more than anyone should have ever asked of you. We only had a chance, and we have taken that chance as far as we were able. I thank you, each and every one. Perhaps one day the Terrantine Federation will thank you as well…"

AnnaChi used the pause to put an image of the Endeavour up on the main. It was pulling away from the formation, heading for the center of the incoming enemy wave. Two small fighters shot out of the battleship's bay and joined the Endeavour on its final run.

"My last order to you all, is to retreat. The remaining Federation ships will escort you to the entry gate. Use escape pods and small shuttles to enter the center ring. Help will be on the other side, which can assist you once you are through." A handful of heartbeats passed before he continued. "Godspeed, and luck to you all!"

The transmission ended as the Endeavour accelerated toward the enemy lines. The flagship was too tempting of a target. The enemy swarms changed course in droves to eliminate their biggest threat.

Kasey couldn't find the strength to change course. They sat, watching the Endeavour climb ever closer to its end. Buying the fleet time to escape.

"Kasey... We need to go."

Silently pointing to the battlefield as several ships ignored orders and directed their course to support the Endeavour, he started, "Perhaps we should..."

"No. Throwing our lives away won't save anyone. It sucks, but Fran needs to do this; we can't waste his sacrifice."

Kasey took a deep breath and reached forward with sagging shoulders to punch in the new coordinates, when every hair on his body stood up. An instant later, alarms blared while sensors went off the charts; then everything went offline just as quickly. Darkness engulfed the bridge of the now dead ship. Not a single backup system flickered.

"What the hell! Are we hit?" Kasey muttered loudly as a low and questioning whistle from Orange sounded in the dark.

"I don't think so... I can't tell. Everything is down... Wait! Sensors are coming back."

The screen began rippling with interference as systems winked back on. As the screen cleared, activity drew their gaze to the gate's center which was now filled with blackness.

"We have unknown contacts!" AnnaChi's voice was oddly strained.

Ships, large and small, poured out from the blackness. Some curled around the gate's edge in a protective fashion, while more shot out to meet the approaching hoard. They overtook the Endeavour and continued to track down and destroy the Patternist and Cassian vessels completely and without compassion.

The federation was taking no chances. Thousands of ships flowed into the system via the gate, followed by rows of mobile defense platforms and repair bases that were quickly placed around both gates. Maintenance and medical ships followed the platforms, hastening toward ships in need of help as others converged to repair the gate.

Hours went by as Kasey and AnnaChi simply watched the activity, unbelieving that they had somehow survived; somehow succeeded.

They were still watching when a Sargani scout ship materialized above their bow.

"Permission to come aboard?" A familiar voice came through the com. "I could use a ride if you don't mind."

"Can you take the helm dear?" Kasey laughed while switching on the midway docking lights. "I hope you don't mind some company?"

"Not at all. But if you could find some food on the way, I would appreciate it."

He responded with a kiss that lasted till the sounds of docking startled them apart.

CHAPTER FORTY-TWO

Small cargo pods constantly came and went from the sizable repair platform stationed between the two fully active gates. A second set of gates was being installed far above the threesome's table as they watched. A week had stretched by as they waited for repairs to be made to the Cintian and Altair.

Darnell, ever watchful, moved to the window as a new ship was hauled into the repair hanger below. "That your old ship boy? That old one you escaped Lithose in?"

Rushing to look, he took in the tattered remains of his Lodestar being lowered into a bay. "Damn. The bridge took a hard hit, it's completely caved in. How did Fran and Flair survive that?"

"You don't survive a hit like that," AnnaChi whispered over his shoulder, "unless you are not in the bridge at all."

"Why am I not surprised. Let's get a closer look and see what they are planning for her."

Orange and Molly glided from the rafters to land on Kasey and AnnaChi's shoulders. Military space stations, with their tight corridors and grated floors, were not designed with avians in mind.

Darnell spoke up, "If you two don't mind, I'll catch up with you later. I have been asked for yet another debrief on the Sargani."

They all exchanged looks before saying their farewell. Officials were digging for more information about the n-mats.

Darnell stopped a few steps away, "Oh, I nearly forgot! I got a message from the Reavestone's navy representative this morning. The damn navy is in talks with them over the n-mats rights and have officially named Reavestone and our team with the discovery. Although not yet public news, the message made it clear that significant compensation is heading our way. They will also be sending a new crew to Belrothi once the public gates are available."

Kasey coughed and sat up straighter, "That is nice and all, but are you planning to go back to work for Reavestone once all this settles down?"

"I am not really sure honestly, I haven't really adjusted to this new reality yet. May take some time off..."

"I get it. But, I um, well we were actually hoping to talk to you about taking a job with our small new company, Phoenix Mining. You may know a bit about our copper mines already I think, but we had also begun to put together a mining crew before all of this started and could really use your expertise, even if only to get us started. There is a lot more to it that you would need to know. We had wanted to bring you in a while ago, but you were nowhere to be found." Kasey stopped rambling and looked up to Darnell expectantly.

"Huh. Well, I heard you had something going on, but this is a bit of a surprise. Tell ya what, I won't make any decisions until you two are able to show me around and I can see what you have planned. Deal?"

"Deal!"

Darnell nodded and waved as Kasey and AnnaChi made their way to the repair hanger. The hanger was a masterpiece of anarchy to navigate with so much work going on. When they finally found their way to the Lodestar's bay, the damage appeared even more extensive than they thought.

The ship's small bay seemed to be the only undamaged area. AnnaChi kept a deep frown on her face as she took the lead through the ship's hatchway into a very empty bay. "Damn."

Molly and Orange slipped away into the recesses of the craft as the hatchway slammed closed behind them.

"I thought you may want this old ship back, but I am afraid it requires a few repairs first."

They turned to find Fran holding up one hand for silence as he set a small item on the deck that flashed for a moment before making their ears pop.

"That's better," he continued.

AnnaChi was done holding back, "What the hell *Admiral*? There is no way you were on this ship when that happened," she pointed toward the direction of the bridge, "and I thought the cargo was not retrievable. More lies!"

"I understand," he countered slowly, but without any sign of remorse. "You are right of course, but it was necessary to leave it, the minefield was a happenstance. Had you failed, we would have needed the additional n-mats, but you succeeded and all is well for now."

"Another backup plan? That's the story you are going with?" Her anger cooled slightly, "so where are they now?"

Kasey laughed bitterly, "They are on the Endeavour. That's what I saw being uploaded from the small fighters in the landing bay, right?"

Fran looked back and forth between the two and nodded. "That is correct. And I hope you believe me that there was really a good reason for me to be so cautious. Look, all it would have taken is one Patternist informant in my command, and the Lodestar would be dust right now. As it is, the ship can be repaired, and we have a backup supply of n-mats from a ship that was reported as destroyed."

"Fine," AnnaChi relented, "I am glad we all made it. I just don't appreciate being used."

Kasey stepped forward and pointed his boot toward the privacy devices Fran had activated when he entered, "I am guessing command is not aware of the n-mats survival?"

"Ah, yes well, there is more to it of course…"

"There always is with you," AnnaChi added. "If you needed some, we would have gladly made them available to you…"

"Getting a supply off planet now may be difficult for a while. Best to have it safe, but that is a story for another day. But I see your point, it is yet something else I owe you for."

She nodded, without comment, for him to continue.

"The important thing to know at this moment," he continued, "is that there was always a follow-up mission if n-mats were located. It appears we are the first to find any of the exotic material, and so I have learned that the mission will fall to myself." He swallowed hard before continuing. "The Patternists, you see, are not wrong. The powers that be are positive that if humanity continues to expand at the rate we have been, we will fall into the Pattern and be wiped out somehow."

"But then why do all this?" Kasey exclaimed. "We should slow down, not find more ways to expand!"

"That has been tried in the past, several times, and failed. In fact, if you look back at history for the War of Rights, you will see it caused a tenfold increase in colonization and expansion efforts." He shook his head violently. "No! Humanity won't slow down, and we won't be held back, so there is only one other option. It is time you two wake up and understand that."

AnnaChi caught on first, "Wait, you mean to speed it up."

"Right, we need to get ahead of whatever universal curve is in humanity's future."

"How do we know that will work?" asked Kasey. "It could just bring about our end faster."

"Well, honestly we don't know, but doing nothing has never won anything. We plan to win if we can, and it all starts here, with you finding the n-mats."

"They are really that important?"

"They are the key to everything! Technology akin to what the gates can do are what we in the military call force multipliers. We will eventually be able to put our ships in any system that requires them immediately, instead of waiting months. For our expansion efforts, that means we can drop a gate in a new system and the entire Terrantine Federation can work together to colonize it in months. It is how humanity survives this pattern. Everything changes now; all because you found a cave."

"So anywhere you have a portal, you have power."

"That remains to be seen," he remarked a bit cryptically. "Which brings me to my actual reason for this visit. You two seem to find your way into unlikely situations despite your best efforts to stay out of civilization's eye. Finding the n-mats for one…"

"It wasn't just me who found the first n-mats, Darnell had a lot more to do with that than me."

"Perhaps. But I am not sure it is the discovery itself that seems important, it may be that you were part of the equation." He let out a bellowing laugh. "I would write that off as being lucky, but then you were the one to find n-mats again on Belrothi."

"That took a lot of work you know," Kasey defended. "Everything I had went into affording that Bard and scanning array. So, I was a bit motivated, and I knew what to look for."

"Right, of course. It all explains away rather nicely if you keep your eyes closed, yet there is also the situation with the gate key…"

AnnaChi stepped forward, "Just what are you getting at?"

"Put your sour face away, no blame intended. I just want you to understand where my offer is coming from."

"Offer?"

He ignored her. "None of this would have happened if you were not involved. The universe has rules, and every once in a while, history gets pushed along at new angles by a few, usually unwilling, individuals. Nearly any history will show this to be at least somewhat true. I believe you may have whatever it is that forces change along in this verse. That is something our human race needs to survive right now."

"Are you saying we have some sort of destiny?" She scoffed.

"Ha, no. I don't believe in destiny or fate for that matter. No, I am speaking of the grease in the machine that keeps it moving. That's what we need to survive. Humanity has plenty of cogs and gears moving the wheels, but without the grease it will stop working soon enough."

Kasey broke his silence. "Look Fran, you are entitled to your beliefs, but I just want to be left alone. I don't want any part of whatever you are attempting to pull us into. We deserve a break without the federation's influence."

"Open your eyes, the federation is just another cog, Kasey. Look at you, trying to stay out of it and yet you end up fighting a battle for your hated Federation. Even now you are wearing their insignia on your chest. Why haven't you had the base's fabricators make something more fitting for you?"

"I am not sure honestly; it just didn't seem important with everything going on."

"Exactly! Most of what has been going on is the federation's doing. You fought with them and are wearing their uniform. Do you really still feel like being a part of the federation is a bad thing?"

Kasey had to stop himself from shouting yes, but something had changed, "Honestly, I don't really know."

"Well," Fran's voice took on a serious tone, "that really is the best answer I could hope for. Never stop questioning, but sometimes it is beneficial to not completely avoid the things you question."

Kasey took a moment for the words to sink in. "Fine, so what's this offer you mentioned?"

"Well, I want you both to come on a trip with me. I need some of that grease to speed things along, and I am hoping I can count on you to help out."

"A trip where exactly?"

"The *where* is not really an important factor right now, just know that I want you along. I think it is important for you both to be there."

"It's all a bit much to ask right now, Fran," Kasey returned quietly.

Fran nodded in understanding, "Look, your Altair is nearly repaired. Go home. Put your estate in order and give my offer some thought. We have time, and there are many plans to be made before we can leave."

"This is much more of a request than an offer, Fran. But there is something else you are forgetting." It was evident AnnaChi was still on the verge of anger. "These n-mats; you told me you had plans for them that *wouldn't* involve our location being public. Were you serious about that, or was it another necessary untruth?"

"All true intentions of mine. With your permission, I will set things in motion. However, I had expected at least *some* of the other Farpoint colonies to have found n-mats and open their gates by now. Our colony is far behind the anticipated schedule, but we are the only one to succeed so far. I'll do whatever I can to protect you, that I promise – but humanity is at stake…"

"So, what then? The federation will just take it from us anyway?"

"I will make it right if I am able. I hope you both will make the right choices as well, because we need you with us."

Kasey tried to keep his attention on the conversation but was starting to feel exhausted by all of it. He caught AnnaChi's eye and shrugged. "Let's go home. We can talk on all this later." He watched her anger fade away, before turning back to Fran. "I trust you to make the correct decision for the n-mats. Let us know what you need and try to give us a head's up if things don't work out."

He took AnnaChi's hand and headed for the bay door, patting Fran's shoulder in a friendly gesture as he passed.

In near silence, Orange and Molly found their places upon the couple's shoulders again.

"The trip," Fran's tone was subdued, "you *will* give it some thought, won't you?"

"We will. Give Flair our best."

They left the ship without looking back.

The Adventure continues in...

Farpoint Rising

VINCENT BEK

Vincent Bek grew up in the Appalachian Mountains dreaming up stories while making trails through the woodlands. He has since been seduced by science and technology and now spends his days dreaming about where humanity's creativity will someday lead. Vincent has been writing for several decades in both the Fantasy and Science Fiction genres while working in the technology sector to pay the bills. Blessed with an amazing wife and two beautiful children, he is currently living happily in Pennsylvania and loves to hear from his readers.

Vincent Bek can be contacted at:
https://www.VincentBek.com/

Made in the USA
Las Vegas, NV
13 October 2022

57181143R00215